# AN IMPROPER PROPOSAL

# PATRICIA CABOT

St. Martin's Paperbacks

AN IMPROPER PROPOSAL

Copyright © 1999 by Patricia Cabot.

All rights reserved. No part of this book may be used or reproduced in any manner whatsoever without written permission except in the case of brief quotations embodied in critical articles or reviews. For information address St. Martin's Press, 175 Fifth Avenue, New York, NY 10010.

ISBN: 0-312-97190-7

Printed in the United States of America

St. Martin's Paperbacks edition / November 1999

St. Martin's Paperbacks are published by St. Martin's Press, 175 Fifth Avenue, New York, NY 10010.

10 9 8 7 6 5 4 3 2 1

FOR BENJAMIN

Thanks once again to my editor Jennifer Weis, my friend Jennifer Brown, and my agent Laura Langlie. Many thanks also to Joan Druett, author of *Hen Frigates: Wives of Merchant Captains Under Sail*, from which I gathered much of the nautical information used in this book.

# AN
# IMPROPER
# PROPOSAL

# Chapter One

SHROPSHIRE, ENGLAND
JUNE 1830

*D*ammit, Payton," Ross Dixon exploded. "I can't tie the wretched thing. *You* do it."

Payton, at too crucial a stage with her second-eldest brother's cravat even to risk a glance at her eldest, snapped, "Wait your turn."

"*Bleeding* turn." Hudson, holding his chin up, had to look down the slopes of his high cheekbones to see his little sister as she worked on his necktie, and then he only saw the top of her head. "Wait your *bleeding* turn."

"Wait your bleeding turn," Payton said, correcting herself.

The ends of his cravat hanging limply round his neck, Ross turned away from the mirror, outraged. "Damn your eyes, Hud! Stop encouragin' her to swear. You want her to tell the first bloke who asks her to dance tonight to wait his bleeding turn?"

"No one's goin' to ask Payton to dance," Raleigh informed them, from the window seat. His cravat already tied, he'd been banished to the far side of the room by his sister with a dire warning not to stir and unloose it again. He sat in a flood of western sunlight, watching a line of carriages pull up to the front of the house. "She's far too ugly."

"Shut your bleeding mouth, Raleigh," Payton advised him.

Ross ground his teeth. "Payton," he growled. "Stop swearing. You aren't home, and you aren't shipboard. Remember our agreement? You can behave like a hoyden all you want while we're at home or at sea, but in other people's houses you'll conduct yourself like a—"

"You know," Hudson interrupted. "Payton's not *that* ugly, Raleigh. It's just her damned hair." Since he had an eagle's eye view of it, Hudson felt qualified to criticize. "When you were shavin' all our heads this past summer, Ross, why didn't you shave Payton's, too? It might have helped if she'd just got rid of the whole thing, and started over."

"Why did you," Ross countered, irritably, "hire a cook inflicted with lice? If you hadn't hired him on, none of us would have needed to shave our heads, and Georgiana wouldn't be forever needling me to purchase Payton a switch."

"A *switch*?" Payton wrinkled her freckled nose. "What would I want with a *switch*? Wear some other woman's hair on top of mine?" She shuddered. "No, *thank you*. I'm perfectly happy waiting until my own grows out again."

Hudson snorted. "You love havin' your hair cropped short. Admit it. You're a lazy puss, and never liked combin' out those damned Indian braids you used to wear."

Payton turned bright gray eyes up toward him. "Careful," she warned, tightening the cravat teasingly. "I may not have my Indian braids anymore, but I can still sever a throat with ease."

"Bloodthirsty wench, aren't you?" Hudson tugged on one of the short russet-brown curls that Payton had tried—unsuccessfully, she feared—to tuck into a pair of tortoiseshell combs. "You're going to have to learn to curb your tendency toward violence, my girl, or you'll never get yourself a husband."

Payton made a moue of distaste. "I fail to see what I need a husband for, when I already have you three telling me what to do."

"Because eventually," Ross said, "Hud and Raleigh are going to follow my example and take wives, leaving you all alone."

"What do you mean, alone?" Payton glared at him over a bare shoulder. "There's always Papa."

"Georgiana and I are taking care of Papa," Ross informed her. "And neither of us cares to be saddled with my spinster sister, in addition."

"If you would stop being such an ass and give me a ship of my own to command," Payton said coolly, "you wouldn't have to worry about being saddled with a spinster sister, let alone finding me a husband."

Ross looked horrified. "Over my dead body," he declared, "are you ever going to command a Dixon ship."

"And why not? I'm twice the navigator Raleigh is, and he's had his own ship for eight years now." She narrowed her eyes as she glanced in Raleigh's direction. "For all he spent most of those years hopelessly *lost*."

Looking up once again from the window, Raleigh informed her kindly, "I wasn't *lost,* my dear. I was exploring previously uncharted territory. There's a difference."

"You were *lost,* Raleigh. Your cargo rotted while you were floundering about, trying to find your way around the Cape of Good Hope. Only you weren't at the Cape of Good Hope, were you?"

Raleigh waved a hand at her. "Cape Horn, Cape Hope. Those capes all look the same. Is it any wonder I mistook one for the other?"

Payton turned to glare at her eldest brother, who was fussing with his shirt collar in the mirror above the dressing table. "See? You give *him* a command, but not me? At least *I* can tell the continents apart."

"The company," Ross explained to his reflection, as patiently as if he were speaking to a child, "is called Dixon and *Sons* Shipping, Payton." At her sharp inhalation, Ross held up a hand, and said, "And kindly don't start arguing again that we should change the name to Dixon and Sons and *Daughter.* I haven't the slightest intention of becoming the laughingstock of the shipping industry by introducing lady ship captains."

"What's wrong with lady ship captains?" Payton demanded

tartly. "I've commanded your crews often enough, and quite ably, thank you very much, when you three were too drunk to hold the wheel. I don't see why I have to be married off like some kind of half-wit when I have at least as much experience as any of you—"

"I say." Hudson cleared his throat. "Are you going to tie my cravat, Pay, or fight with Ross?" When her hot-eyed glare landed on him, he took a quick step backward. "Never mind. Continue fighting with Ross, by all means."

"Don't worry, Pay," Raleigh drawled from the window seat. "Ross'll have no choice but to make you a lady ship captain in the end. No bloke's ever goin' to ask you to marry him. You're far too ugly."

"She ain't ugly!" Ross exploded, finally turning away from the mirror. "Well, at least, not anymore. Not after I paid damn near a hundred quid for that bleeding dress she's got on."

"Don't forget," Hudson reminded him, "the matching slippers. And the hat and cloak."

"Another hundred pounds." Ross lifted a snifter of brandy he'd placed on top of the dresser, and drained it in a single quick gulp. "And for what, I'd like to know? It's not like there's enough material in that dress to even cover 'er decently."

Payton glanced down at her décolletage. It *was* a bit daring. She didn't have a lot to show, but what was there was on rather prominent display. When she looked up again, she saw that Hudson had followed her gaze.

"Yes, Pay," he said. "I'd noticed you'd gotten a bosom. When did that happen?"

"I don't know." Payton shook her head bewilderedly. "Last summer, I think. Somewhere between New Providence and the Keys."

"I didn't notice you having any breasts when we were in Nassau," Ross declared. The eldest child, it always irked him whenever Payton, the youngest, did anything without asking— such as grow, for instance.

"That's because she wore nothing all summer but that vest

and those dreadful striped trousers." Raleigh, the fop of the family, heaved a delicate shudder. "Remember? Georgiana practically had to peel her out of 'em when we got back to London."

"I wore the trousers," Payton pointed out severely, "because I didn't need everyone looking up my skirts every time I climbed the mizzenpost—"

"Wishful thinking," Hudson observed.

Ignoring him, Payton continued. "And I wore the vest because I hadn't anything to support what was going on beneath my shirt. No thanks to any of *you*."

"Underthings." Ross nodded. "I forgot. Another hundred quid. And for what, I ask you?"

The door to the bedroom opened, and Georgiana Dixon said matter-of-factly, "To get her married, of course." Then, taking in the sight of her husband's loose collar with a sigh, she added, "I don't suppose it would have occurred to any of you that most men employ valets to tie their cravats, not their little sisters."

It was Hudson's turn to shudder. "I don't want some bloke touching me, let alone my *clothes*."

"Really, Georgiana." Ross, Payton had noticed, was not quite as patient with his new wife as he'd been but a few months earlier. After all, *then* he'd only been courting her. Now that they were safely married, and she couldn't very well escape, he made it quite clear that the newfangled ideas she'd brought with her from London were no longer going to be tolerated. "There's something . . . well, *unnatural* about a man helping another man to dress. That's women's work."

Georgiana nodded. She'd grown, Payton observed, quite used to the backward logic frequently employed by the family into which she'd married.

"I see," she said. "And so poor Payton's got to dress all of you before you'll let her see to herself." Tut-tutting, she went to Payton's side, and began to remove her hair combs. "You three ought to be ashamed of yourselves," Georgiana chastised. "For heaven's sake, learn to tie your own cravats. I've noticed Captain Drake can do it. There's no reason any of you can't. You're not feeble."

"Oh, well, *Captain Drake,*" Hudson said, rolling his eyes.

"Captain Drake can do *anything,*" mimicked Raleigh in a high-pitched voice, and although it was not clear who precisely he was mimicking, Payton shot him a warning look. She had a sneaking suspicion he was imitating her, in which case, she'd have to give him a taste of her fist, first chance she got.

"I met the captain just now in the hallway." Using the hair combs, Georgiana began working the tangles from Payton's scandalously short curls. If she applied them at just the right angle, Georgiana had found that she could almost create the illusion that Payton's hair was longer than jaw-length, which, in actual truth, it was not. "And he looked right presentable. A good deal more presentable than *you* looked, Ross, the night before *we* were married."

"Right," Hudson said, with a laugh. "But Ross had, I believe, consumed most of a bottle of rum that night, so it's understandable he mightn't have looked his best—"

"I understand," Georgiana continued, as if Hudson had not interrupted, "that Captain Drake keeps no valet, so I can only assume that *he,* at least, is capable of dressing himself."

"Or Miss Whitby helped him," Raleigh quipped.

Payton was so startled that she jumped, yanking her hair out of Georgiana's reach as she whirled around to face her brother. "She did *not,*" she declared.

But even as she said it, and with all the contempt she could summon, a part of her was wondering whether or not it might be true. Unfortunately, that doubt must have sounded in her voice, since Georgiana said, shooting Raleigh a disapproving look, "Of course not. Miss Whitby did no such thing. Really, Raleigh, why must you provoke your sister so?"

Payton felt her cheeks growing hot, and it was not, she well knew, because the room faced west, and the last rays of the setting sun were slanting straight through the ten-foot-high window casements.

"It doesn't," she said, moving quickly back to within her sister-in-law's reach. "Provoke me, I mean. *I* certainly don't care who dresses Captain Drake. He could have an entire seraglio of women to dress him, for all *I* care."

Georgiana frowned and went back to work with the hair combs. After three months of marriage, Georgiana was already quite used to the risqué talk that passed between her husband and his brothers—and sometimes even their sister—as humor. She could only do her best to discourage such talk by ignoring it, or, like now, taking it calmly.

"Well, whoever dressed him," she said, "it wasn't Miss Whitby. I saw her myself downstairs not half an hour ago. She was with your father. He was showing her the latest addition to his collection."

All four Dixon siblings groaned. Sir Henry Dixon had been a very successful businessman in his day, the founder of Dixon and Sons, a merchant shipping company that had earned him a tidy fortune. But since the death of his beloved wife following Payton's birth, he'd lost a good deal of interest in his business, and had finally turned the entire operation over to his sons. Now Sir Henry spent most of his time reminiscing about his dead wife and collecting pirate memorabilia. The pride of his life was a collection of musket balls he'd purchased in Nassau, musket balls said to have been discharged from pistols belonging to various pirate captains, Blackbeard among them. It was a collection he carried everywhere with him, and would show to anyone who had the bad luck to express the slightest interest in it.

Payton could not help but feel a fierce satisfaction that the odious Miss Whitby should have fallen into her father's trap. Now she'd be spending the better part of an hour listening to Sir Henry drone on about calibers and the chemical composition of lead, something Payton would only wish upon her worst enemy. Miss Whitby being that enemy, she felt quite happy suddenly.

"And what," Payton asked her sister-in-law, with deceptive nonchalance, "is Miss Whitby wearing this evening?"

"Oh, la," Georgiana said. "A frothy blue thing, with pink rosettes. I can't imagine where she got it. It's much too young for her, if you ask me. And with that red hair of hers, pink is *not* the thing." Payton was small for her age, and Georgiana had to lean down to whisper, "*Your* dress is much prettier."

Despite Georgiana's attempt at tact, her husband overheard. "I should certainly hope Payton's is prettier, after what I paid for it," he bellowed.

Payton tugged self-consciously on the puffed sleeves of her white satin evening gown. She longed to tug on the points of her corset, too, which were digging uncomfortably into her thighs, but didn't dare, with her brothers in the room. The ribbing she'd receive if they learned she was wearing one would be merciless, and, knowing them, they'd feel compelled to share the information with every single person they met at dinner. Payton had never worn a corset before, let alone hair combs, earrings, or even perfume. She couldn't help marveling a little at her own transformation. Really, the addition of a sister-in-law to her family had not turned out the detriment Hudson and Raleigh had assured her it would. Sisters-in-law, Payton found, knew all sorts of things, and weren't the least bit reticent about sharing that knowledge.

The information about Miss Whitby's dress, for instance. Payton couldn't have hoped any of her brothers would have been observant enough to deliver *that*. Raleigh might have got the color right, and Hudson might have had something to say about the size and shape of Miss Whitby's breasts, but that would be all. How useful women could be! Having lived the entirety of her life almost exclusively in the company of men, Payton was quite astounded by the discovery.

"So she's full rigged, is she?" Payton frowned at her reflection in the mirror above the bureau. "What's she got on her masthead?"

"By that I suppose you mean how is Miss Whitby wearing her hair." Georgiana shook her head. "Well, I'll tell you. Down."

"Miss Whitby, Miss Whitby," Ross thundered. "Am I to

hear of nothing but Miss Bloody Whitby for the rest of my eternal life? Isn't anyone going to tie my damned cravat?"

Georgiana tucked the last of Payton's curls into the tortoiseshell comb. "Really, Ross," she said mildly. "Must you swear so?"

"Yes, Ross," Payton said, eager to follow her sister-in-law's ladylike example. "Shut your bleeding mouth."

Hudson, who happened to be taking a sip from his own snifter of brandy, sprayed the contents across the room in his amusement over Payton's indignant declaration. A few droplets of the amber stuff landed on the sleeve of Raleigh's new evening coat. He leapt up from the window seat with an oath even more colorful than Payton's, and the two men began instantly to wrestle, while Ross continued to demand loudly that his wife—or his sister, he didn't care *who* did it, as long as it was done—tie his cravat. Georgiana commenced to insisting, for the thousandth time, that the Dixons employ a manservant, while Payton, to get Raleigh back for mimicking her, threw herself upon his back, and reached around his neck to destroy the cravat she'd so carefully tied a half hour before.

Raleigh let out a growl and put up both hands to seize hold of her wrists. Too late, it occurred to Payton that she might have thought first, and acted later, an axiom with which her sister-in-law often admonished her. Wrestling with her brothers in her current state of dress was a bit different from wrestling with them in breeches. As she clung to Raleigh's back with her knees, knowing that he was doing his best to unseat her, the stays of Payton's tight corset dug into her ribs and thighs; the tight lacings restricted her movement more effectively than the most impassioned embrace—not that Payton was at all familiar with embraces, impassioned or otherwise. Small-boned and weighing less than half what her brothers weighed, Payton had always heavily relied upon her flexibility to get her out of whatever torture they thought up for her. The ironlike grip of her corset, however, now made such flexibility impossible.

Her sister-in-law must have realized this, since behind her,

Payton heard Georgiana calling frantically, "Raleigh! Put her down. This isn't amusing. Someone might get hurt. Put her *down*, Raleigh!"

"I'll put her down," Raleigh asserted. "Head first into the privy."

Then, with a diabolical laugh, Raleigh made as if to pitch her over his head and shoulders.

Payton refused to beg. She was a Dixon, after all. Biting, scratching, and begging for mercy were all considered beneath the dignity of the Dixons—as was kicking one's assailant in his privates, something Payton had learned early on in her life was guaranteed to unloose her from any man's hold, but tended to engender in him a most unforgiving rage. She could only hope that Raleigh might realize, from the fact that she hadn't yet escaped, that she was not exactly in her usual top fighting form. Closing her eyes, Payton silently cursed the day she'd allowed her sister-in-law to talk her into wearing a corset, and resigned herself to landing in an ignominious heap on the hard parquet floor beneath her . . .

Until a long, strong arm circled her waist from behind. Oh, good, Payton thought. It's Ross. Thank God *one* of her brothers, anyway, had noticed her predicament, even if it *was* only because his wife was making him.

But when the man who had hold of her waist spoke, Payton realized it wasn't Ross at all.

"How many times do I have to warn you, Raleigh?" Connor Drake inquired in his deep, rumbling voice. "Hands off your baby sister."

"Baby my arse," Raleigh asserted, keeping Payton's wrists locked in iron grips. "*She* attacked *me,* I'll have you know."

"Nevertheless, you'll release her."

"Why should I?" Raleigh sounded peevish. "She—"

"Because," Drake said, "I said so."

Payton couldn't see what Drake did with his free hand, but whatever it was, it caused Raleigh to let out a bark of pain. Suddenly, her wrists were free. The next thing she knew, Payton was being lifted from her brother's back by the strength of the single arm around her waist. An arm that was pressing her closely against the body to which it was attached. A very hard, very large, very masculine body. A body that Payton, over the past few years, had gotten to know very well, indeed—through observation only, unfortunately. To feel that body, now, molded against her—even if it was only for a second or two, and through a good many layers of petticoats and whalebone—made Payton feel as if Raleigh had succeeded in his boast, and that she was reeling from the impact of the floor to her skull.

But it was really only the impact of Connor Drake's body against hers that was causing her head to spin.

"And you," she heard Drake say, his warm breath tickling her ear. "I thought I warned *you* to stick to picking fights you can win, with people your own size."

As soon as her feet touched the parquet, Payton felt Drake withdraw his arm. *No,* she thought, with regret as sharp as an actual physical pain.

But she couldn't, for the life of her, think of any way she could induce him to keep that arm there. Miss Whitby would certainly have swooned, or pulled some other such stunt, to remain in his arms. But Payton had never swooned before in her life, and hadn't the slightest idea how to fake it, either.

So she had no choice but to turn toward her rescuer and say, as tartly as she could, "Thank you for your help, but I can assure you, it was unnecessary. I had the situation entirely under control."

Or at least, that's what she thought she said. When she actually raised her gaze to look Drake in the eye—and she had to tilt her chin up pretty far to do so, since he was so outlandishly tall, taller even than her brothers, and they had been considered giants in some of the distant lands they'd visited—all rational thought fled, and she could only stare.

Leaning casually against one of the bedposts, Drake had folded his arms across his chest, and was looking down at her with a smile playing at the corners of his wide, expressive mouth, his blue eyes very bright. He appeared quite devastating in a new black evening coat that fit his broad shoulders a little too well, in Payton's opinion. In addition to the jacket, there was a new waistcoat of white satin, and a pair of breeches that, when she lowered her gaze to take them in, struck her as being perhaps a little too tight—to the point of being *extremely* distracting to a young lady like herself, who was interested in such things—in the front.

Then again, she seemed to think that about *all* of Captain Drake's trousers; her sister-in-law had assured her that, actually, the captain's pants were of quite a loose cut, and had suggested that perhaps Payton needed to direct her attention elsewhere.

While this was probably very sound advice, Payton had lately found it impossible to follow.

"Is that so?" Drake said with a drawl. "Well, I hope you'll beg my pardon, then. To me, you appeared to be in some distress."

"Nonsense." Payton tossed her head, and realized, to her dismay, that one of her combs had slipped out during the tussle with Raleigh. It was hanging loose, dangling just above a bare shoulder. She lifted a hand to it, and tried to shove it back into place. "I'm perfectly capable of taking care of myself . . ."

Payton's voice trailed off, and not because her brothers were continuing to wrestle loudly behind her, but because Drake's gaze, when she'd raised her hands to adjust her hair comb, had suddenly dipped away from hers and down to the neckline of her gown, which, as Ross had been lamenting a little while earlier, was already quite daring. A quick glance downward revealed that now it was not only daring, but downright obscene: while nothing absolutely *crucial* was showing, a good deal more than was supposed to had escaped from the lace cups of that treacherous corset during her wrestling match with her brothers.

Payton immediately began tucking her breasts back where they belonged. She hadn't much in the way of a bosom—it seemed as if every other woman in the world had a good deal more up front than she did—but what she had was really getting to be quite unmanageable . . . at least to a girl who was used to having nothing there at all.

But her sister-in-law's sharp intake of breath told her perhaps she ought to have left well enough alone—at least while she was in the presence of gentlemen who did not happen to be her blood relations.

"Oh, Captain Drake," Georgiana cried, rushing forward and seizing the captain's arm. "Did we disturb you? Just another Dixon family disagreement, I'm afraid." When the captain's gaze still did not leave the vicinity of Payton's chest, Georgiana gave his arm a tug, pulling him back toward the open door through which he'd managed to stroll so completely unnoticed moments before. This, Payton supposed, was a strategy Georgiana had devised with the hope of distracting the captain long enough to give Payton time to put things to rights beneath her bodice, and she took advantage of it, giving her corset a violent tug.

"They are such *boys,* aren't they, Captain?" Georgiana said, with a tinkly laugh, as they stepped over the prone bodies of her brothers-in-law—who had continued to wrestle with one another long after Payton's rescue, finally falling together to the floor with a mighty crash. "I can't think how you put up with them for so many years. Raleigh, Hudson," she sang. "Our host is here. Do get up."

Raleigh got up first, pulling his waistcoat back into place. "Host," he muttered. "It's only *Drake,* for pity's sake."

Hudson echoed his younger brother's sentiment. "Really, Georgiana," he said, miffed. "You're going to give the fellow airs, calling him a host, like that. Next thing you know, he'll be going around insisting he's a baronet, or something."

"Actually," Drake said, "I *am* a baronet."

Hudson regarded his sister-in-law sourly. "See what you've done," he said.

Georgiana looked pained. "Hudson," she said. "Captain Drake *is* a baronet. Remember, I explained to you in the carriage that he inherited the title when his brother died—"

"Don't believe it," Hudson declared.

"I *won't* believe it," Raleigh insisted. "We don't have to *sir* you now, Drake, do we? Because I for one won't stand for it, not after all we've been through together."

"I don't think," Hudson agreed, thoughtfully, "that I could *sir* a man I've beaten at cards as many times as I've beaten Drake."

Drake gave a low bow. "Gentlemen," he said with mock gravity, "I have full faith that neither of you will allow the change in my social status to tarnish the respect I know you've always harbored for me."

"Kiss my arse, Drake," Hudson suggested, and Raleigh made a rude noise with his lips.

"Oh," Georgiana said, opening her fan and applying it to her burning cheeks with energy. "Dear."

Drake rose from his bow with a smile across his face—one of those smiles that made Payton, even when she wasn't wrestling with her brothers, feel a little breathless.

"It's nice to know," he commented, "that while a good many things may change, some things will always stay the same."

"I say, Drake." Ross fingered his still-open collar. "Georgiana says you tied that knot yourself. Is that true? You've got to show me how to do it, old man. I can't quite seem to get the hang of it."

"The gentlemen are gathering in the billiard room," Drake replied, still smiling. "I'll join you there, and happily give you what cravat-tying advice I can."

"Billiard room," Hudson echoed. "The blighter's got a billiard room. There's something to this baronet stuff, Ral."

"I wager there'll be whisky there," Raleigh said. "There's always whisky in a billiard room."

There was no doorway in the world wide enough to admit all three Dixon brothers when they were on a quest for whisky, and the doorways of Daring Park were no exception. Payton watched with raised eyebrows as her brothers elbowed and jostled one another in their haste to exit the room. It wasn't until they were gone that Drake, his own eyebrows similarly raised, turned to Georgiana and said, as mildly as if nothing unusual at all had occurred since he'd entered the room, "Mrs. Dixon, the ladies are gathering before supper in the drawing room, I believe."

"Oh." Georgiana fanned herself frantically, not having quite recovered from Hudson's suggestion that Connor Drake kiss his posterior. "Thank you, Captain. That's quite—It's very kind of you to stop by, personally, to let us know—"

"It was my pleasure, Mrs. Dixon. I'm delighted to have you all here at Daring Park. I trust you find your rooms comfortable?"

"Oh," Georgiana said. "Very. The house is charming, simply charming."

Georgiana seemed quite anxious to get out from beneath the captain's penetrating gaze. Payton could understand the inclination. She'd been the recipient of that cool, calculating gaze more times than she liked to remember.

"Come along, Payton," Georgiana continued nervously. "We had better get downstairs, before your brothers get themselves into even more trouble . . ."

"I'll be along," Payton said, "in a minute."

Payton realized that she'd suddenly been presented with a golden opportunity. She hoped she'd injected her voice with enough syrupy sweetness that her sister-in-law wouldn't guess she hadn't the slightest intention of following any time soon.

She succeeded. Georgiana disappeared into the hallway, too upset by her new family's bad manners to pay much attention to what that family's youngest member was up to. Which was just as well, since she would hardly have approved of what Payton did next, which was seize the baronet by the arm as he attempted to stand aside, allowing her to pass through the doorway first, and hiss, "Thanks for bloody nothing!"

Drake looked considerably surprised at being thus addressed. He raised his tawny eyebrows again and said, with a little indignation, "I beg your pardon?"

"How am I ever going to convince Ross to give me my

own command if you're forever interfering?" Payton demanded hotly.

"Interfering?" Comprehension finally dawned over the captain's face. "Oh, I see. You mean by my keeping your brother from hurling you over his shoulder, I was interfering?" The corners of his lips curled into a very definite grin. "I'll have to beg your forgiveness, then, Payton. I rather thought I was saving you from a crushing blow to the head. Terribly ignoble of me, I realize now."

Payton refused to be swayed by either the captain's charming manner or devastating good looks. This was excessively difficult just at that moment, since the sun slanting into the room had brought out the highlights in his golden hair. It almost made it look as if there were a halo behind Captain Drake's head, as if he were a saint—or the archangel Gabriel, perhaps—in a stained-glass window. Thankfully, Captain Drake had not been on the lice-infested clipper, and so his fine hair had been spared from Ross's sheers. It hung as long as his shirt collar. Sometimes he wore it tied back in a black ribbon, a style which Payton approved of highly.

Good Lord! What was she doing, standing there, admiring his hair?

Placing her hands on either side of her narrow waist, Payton glared up at him. "It isn't funny," she informed him. "This is my future we're talking about. You know Ross has this ridiculous idea of marrying me off, instead of doing the sensible thing, and letting me have the *Constant*."

"Right," Drake said. He appeared to be attempting to school his features into a suitably serious expression, but was having some trouble. "The *Constant*. The newest and fastest ship in the Dixon fleet. And you think your brother should give you command of it."

"And why not?" Payton tapped a daintily slippered foot. "I'll be nineteen next month. Both Hudson and Raleigh got their own ships on their nineteenth birthdays. Why should I be treated any differently?"

Once again, Drake's cool blue gaze dipped below her neck.

"Well," he said. "Perhaps because you're a—"

"Don't say it." Payton held up a single hand, palm out. "Don't you dare say it."

"Why?" Drake looked genuinely puzzled. "There's nothing wrong with it, you know, Payton. It has its advantages, you know."

"Oh? Name one. And if you mention the word 'motherhood,' I swear I'll start screaming."

Drake hesitated. He either could not think of anything advantageous to being born female, or did not feel that what he had thought up was appropriate to mention in Payton's presence, since he abruptly changed the subject. "Perhaps your brother feels he's already given you your birthday gift. Isn't that one of the new gowns Ross has been complaining about? It's quite lovely."

Payton's jaw dropped incredulously. "*What?* A *gown*? A bloody *gown*? You must be joking. I'm supposed to be satisfied with a new gown when I could have command of a *clipper*?"

"Well," Drake said. "I don't suppose that seems fair to you. But to be honest, Payton, I'm not sure I disagree with Ross about your commanding your own ship. It's one thing when you go to sea with your brothers. After all, then they're there to protect you. But for a young lady to go to sea all by herself, with a crew of men she doesn't know—"

"*Protect* me?" Payton's voice dripped with disgust. "Since when has any of my brothers ever *protected* me? You saw them back there. *Protecting* me was hardly foremost in Raleigh's mind. *Killing* me was more like it. No—" Here she laid her hand upon his arm once more, hoping he wouldn't notice that this very mild gesture was enough to cause the pulse in her throat to leap spasmodically. Still, she didn't feel she had any choice. This might well be her last chance. "Promise you'll help me to convince Ross to give me the *Constant*. Please, Drake. Ross listens to you, you know. Please will you promise to try?"

Determined that this one time, she was going to look him

in the eye and not blink or turn away until he did, Payton raised her gaze to meet his. It never failed to unnerve her, the unnatural blueness of his irises, so like the color of the water off the shoals of the Bahamas. The only difference was that there the water was so clear, she was able to see all the way to the ocean floor. She could not—had never been able to—read what lay behind Drake's clear blue eyes. They might as well have been black as pitch, for all she could see through them.

How he might have answered her, she had no idea, for she could not read his expression, and they were interrupted before he could reply.

"Connor?" The musical voice drifted from the open doorway, quite startling them both. Jerking her hand from Drake's arm, Payton turned, and saw in the hallway a pretty redheaded woman in a pale blue dress trimmed with pink rosettes. Matching rosettes adorned her slippers and hair.

"I thought I heard your voice, Connor," the woman said sweetly. "Good evening, Miss Dixon. I just had the loveliest chat with your father. He showed me the latest addition to his musket-ball collection. He's such a dear man. I quite adore him."

Payton managed a tepid smile. "Oh," she said. "I'm so glad."

To Captain Drake, Miss Whitby said, "Are you coming down, dearest? I understand your grandmother has just arrived, and has been asking for you."

Captain Drake's smile, which he'd seemed to have so much trouble controlling a moment before, had entirely disappeared. Now, instead of bringing out the golden highlights in his hair, the fading sunlight brought into extreme relief the lines in his face, of which, Payton noted, there were a great many more since she'd seen him last. Two particularly deep lines stood out from the corners of his mouth to the tips of his flaring nostrils. He looked, suddenly, like a man much older than his thirtieth year.

"Of course," he said to Miss Whitby. "I'll be down momentarily."

Miss Whitby, however, didn't move. "I do think we ought not to keep your grandmother waiting, my love," she said brightly.

Captain Drake said nothing for a moment. He seemed extremely interested in the pattern on the carpet. Then, suddenly, he looked up, and pinned Payton where she stood with the full intensity of his unbearably bright gaze. "Will you accompany us downstairs, Miss Dixon?" he asked.

Payton, still a little alarmed by the transformation his face had undergone since Miss Whitby's appearance—and completely transfixed, as always, by his stare—could only shake her head. "Um, thank you," she murmured, through lips that had gone quite dry. "But no. I . . . I need a moment."

To her relief, the captain lowered his gaze.

"Very well, then," Drake said, and he offered his arm to the redheaded woman.

"Good evening, Miss Dixon," Miss Whitby said very sweetly. And then the two of them turned to go, and Payton watched as Miss Whitby slipped her gloved fingers into the crook of the captain's arm, and smiled sunnily up at him. "I imagine," she said, "that your grandmother must be very curious to finally meet your fiancée."

"Yes," Payton heard Drake reply. "I imagine that she is."

# Chapter Two

$C$rossing the room after the captain and his fiancée had left it, Payton went to the mirror hanging above the bureau.

The tortoiseshell comb her brothers' horseplay had knocked from her hair dangled behind her ear in a woeful manner. It had probably been there the whole time she'd been talking to Captain Drake. It had most certainly been there while she'd been talking to Miss Whitby.

Sighing, Payton reached up and tried to tuck the comb back into place. But as hard as she tried, she couldn't get it at the same angle as Georgiana had had it. When she was done, the comb ended up sticking out rather comically from the side of her head. Rolling her eyes, she turned away from the mirror in disgust.

Really, Payton thought to herself. Her hair was the *least* of her problems. Even with her freckled and sunburned nose, her small stature and relative lack of bosom, she knew she was not, as Raleigh had so diplomatically put it, *ugly*. If she'd been truly ugly, her brothers would not have been so cavalier as to joke about it. But she also knew perfectly well that she looked nothing like other girls her age. She certainly didn't look a thing like Miss Whitby, with her creamy white skin—not a freckle to be seen—and her waist-length auburn hair. Payton looked nothing like Miss Whitby, and *acted* nothing like her, either.

Take just now, for instance. Never in her life would Payton have been able to say, "Are you coming down, dearest?" to Connor Drake, and keep a straight face. Connor Drake was infinitely more dear to Payton than he would ever be to Miss Whitby—and anyone who said otherwise would get a taste of Payton's knuckles—but she'd have sooner cut out her tongue than actually *call* him dearest. Of course, that might be because, had any of her brothers heard her calling their friend Drake dearest, she'd never have lived to hear the end of it.

But still, Payton didn't think men really *liked* being called dear. It certainly hadn't looked to her as if Drake had much appreciated it. At least, his face, when Miss Whitby had uttered her "dearests" and "my loves," hadn't changed a bit, except maybe to get a little harder and more stern-looking.

Then again, Ross never looked any different when Georgiana called *him* dear. But that was probably because his wife only called him dear when he was doing something of which she disapproved. Payton rather suspected that behind closed doors, Ross and Georgiana were quite different with one another—*definitely* different with one another, since she'd once walked into the parlor unannounced and overheard Ross calling Georgiana his little monkey, a pet name to which Payton would have had definite objections, had anyone—even Captain Drake—ever used it on *her*.

But perhaps, she thought, Captain Drake and Miss Whitby, like Ross and Georgiana, were different with one another when they were alone. Maybe when they were alone, Drake enjoyed being called dearest. And Miss Whitby enjoyed being called his little monkey.

The image of Captain Drake and Miss Whitby alone with one another made Payton feel a little ill, so she hastily put such thoughts out of her head.

Turning back to the mirror, Payton spread her skirt wide and fluttered her eyelids, mimicking, in a stilted little voice that was much more highly pitched than her normal tone, "*I*

*imagine your grandmother must be very curious to finally meet
your fiancée.*"

Rising from the curtsy, she made a violent motion, as if
she were kicking something—or someone. But the sudden
movement caused her corset stays to pinch, and she immediately regretted the action, and put a hand to her hip to rub the
tender spot there. "Bloody hell," she murmured, to make herself feel better.

Judging that the captain and his bride-to-be were well down
the stairs by that time, and that she could, without fear of
running into either of them, descend, Payton did so, looking
about her with interest. She felt a certain curiosity about the
house, which she had never visited before that day. In fact,
though she'd never have admitted it aloud, she'd slept little
the night before, so excited had she been about their impending visit.

And, except for the fact that the master of the house was
marrying a woman whom she couldn't abide, Payton couldn't
say she'd been disappointed. Daring Park was the estate upon
which Drake had been raised, where he'd lived most of his
life before a disagreement with his family about his future had
sent him to London to seek his fortune. The rambling, three-
storied house was over a hundred years old, and filled with
lovely old furniture that Georgiana assured her were all price-
less antiques. This was very different indeed from the Dixon
town house in London, where all the furniture had been bought
new soon after Payton's father had made his first five thousand
pounds. It still looked new, since the Dixons were never at
home for more than a few weeks a year, spending the rest of
their time at sea.

Still, Payton quite liked the look of Daring Park. It was one
of the few places on land where, she fancied, one could safely
walk around barefoot and never fear stepping on something
sharp.

And although she could see no telltale signs of Drake ever
having inhabited it—no initials carved into the balustrade, or
portraits of him hanging in the Great Hall—she could still

picture him tearing about the place as a young boy, tormenting his tutors and making his elder brother, with whom he'd never got on, cry. She liked the place all the better for that.

These were of course completely fabricated imaginings: Drake never spoke much about his childhood, which had apparently been somewhat unhappy. Still, Payton's overactive imagination filled in what she did not know, until she had him leaping about the roofbeams overhead with the same energy he leapt about the rigging on board the *Virago,* the ship he'd been commanding for Dixon and Sons for the past half a decade, and would presumably continue to command for a decade more to come.

Not that Drake needed the job, let alone the salary. His brother's untimely death nearly eight weeks earlier had left him a wealthy man, indeed. In fact, he needed never to go to sea again . . . at least, not in order to earn his keep. Whether he chose to continue sailing was entirely up to him . . .

And the woman he was to marry upon the morrow, of course.

But from what Payton had gathered, Miss Whitby had no great love for the sea. She had once stated, with a sideways glance in Payton's direction that one would have to have been blind to have missed, that she thought salt air was rather hard on the complexion.

But if Payton's complexion had suffered from the years she'd spent accompanying her father, and then her brothers, at sea, evidently Mr. Matthew Hayford failed to notice it. Either he liked a woman with a tan, or he wasn't shallow enough to let such incidentals get in the way of his friendships. Because as Payton reached the landing, she saw that Matthew was waiting for her at the end of the stairs, looking quite different in evening clothes than he did in his first mate's uniform.

"Ahoy, there, Miss Dixon!" he cried, obviously pleased to see her. "The captain said you were on your way. And I must say, it was worth the wait. Don't you look a picture!"

Payton, a little taken aback by this enthusiastic greeting,

glanced around to make certain it was really she to whom it had been addressed. But there was no one on the stairs behind her. Unlikely as it seemed, the admiration on the young man's face appeared to be for *her*. But she'd known Matthew Hayford for years, and he'd never told her she looked like a picture before. Could it be the corset? She glanced down at herself. More likely it was the décolletage. Men were strange creatures, indeed. Perhaps she ought to heed Drake's advice, and think twice about being alone aboard an entire ship of them . . .

Still, Payton greeted Matthew with a sunny smile and an outstretched hand.

"Well met, Mr. Hayford," she said, giving his callused fingers a hearty shake. "When did you arrive?"

"Only just," Matthew said. "Isn't this place posh? Did you see those swans in the lake out back?"

"Oh, that's nothing." Payton pointed to one side of the Great Hall. "Look at those suits of armor. Georgiana says they're *real*. *Real* knights bashed about in them. Drake's ancestors, I suppose. Can you *imagine*?"

Matthew followed her gaze. "Lord," he breathed. "Captain Drake's ancestors were right short, weren't they?"

"They were not," Payton cried defensively. Then, seeing that quite a few of the suits would have fit *her*, she said, "Well, they didn't know anything about proper nutrition back then. You couldn't expect them to grow much."

Matthew turned his admiring gaze back upon her. "Is there anything you *don't* know about, Miss Dixon?"

She gave the appearance of giving this question thoughtful consideration. Really, if she were to be perfectly honest about it, Payton would have to admit that there wasn't much she didn't know. She certainly considered herself better educated than most girls her age. What did *they* know about, except hair arranging and gossip? *She* knew how to bring down a sail during a squall, chart a course using only the position of the sun and stars in the heavens as a guide, and kill, skin, and cook a sea turtle with no other utensils than a knife, a few rocks, and some dried-out seaweed. If she hadn't seen it for herself from the deck of one of her family's ships, then she'd heard about it from Mei-Ling, the Cantonese cook who had accompanied the Dixon children on almost every voyage they'd ever undertaken. It was only since Mei-Ling had returned to her native land to enjoy her well-earned retirement—and Ross had brought Georgiana into the family as a sort of replacement—that Payton had begun to realize how very lacking her education had been on one subject in particular: love and marriage.

What, for instance, would Mei-Ling have made over the fact that, when he could have had any woman in the world, Connor Drake had chosen to marry the odious Miss Whitby? Payton had a feeling Mei-Ling's thoughts on the matter would have been quite illuminating.

But since she wasn't prepared to share with anyone her dissatisfaction over the upcoming nuptials, let alone admit her ignorance in matters that involved the heart and not a compass, Payton simply shrugged her shoulders and said, "No."

She was a little startled when Matthew let out a horse laugh that was so loud, it echoed about the massive chamber. In fact, she had to smack him rather forcefully upon the shoulder to get him to be quiet.

"It wasn't *that* amusing," she said. It was truly baffling to her how men seemed to go right out of their heads whenever there was a hint of bosom showing anywhere. Well, some men, anyway. Connor Drake had, unfortunately, seemed to remain in perfect possession of his wits when her bodice slipped.

"Listen, Miss Dixon," Matthew said, when he'd recovered himself sufficiently to speak again. "I was talking to the captain a minute ago, and what do you think he said?"

Fumbling with her hair combs again, Payton said, "I can honestly say I haven't the slightest idea what the captain said, Mr. Hayford."

"Oh, only that after dinner, there's to be dancing. Real dancing, with an orchestra, not just some bloke playing his accordion."

Payton nodded. "I saw the musicians pulling up out front," she said.

"Well, Miss Dixon, would it be too forward of me to ask that you please save a dance for me? Would you mind?"

Payton nearly stabbed the hair comb directly into her scalp. Turning her astonished gaze toward the young man, she stared at him, her mouth slightly ajar—not an attractive look, she realized, and one Georgiana had warned her to avoid at all costs. She remembered too late, and snapped her lips together like a grouper sampling air for the first time.

Good Lord! A man had just asked her to dance! For the first time in her life—nearly nineteen years of life, to be exact—a man had actually asked her to dance. Payton couldn't believe it. Hudson and Raleigh had been proved wrong in one swift, brilliant stroke!

Struggling to remember what she was supposed to do—Georgiana had warned her this might happen, despite Payton's assurances that she was far too boyish for any man even to consider asking her to dance—Payton chewed on her lower lip. She quite liked Matthew Hayford, a young man who, at twenty years of age, had a promising career ahead of him, and a rather nice head of thick dark hair—he had not been on the clipper with the lice infestation.

Still, it was only as a *friend* that she liked him. He was quite handy with a sail, and played a clever game of whist, a favorite shipboard pastime amongst the officers. She certainly would never hesitate to hire him on as a mate when she finally got her own command. But *dance* with him? That was different.

Still, it *was* only an invitation to dance, after all. He wasn't asking her to *marry* him, for pity's sake. So what was she waiting for?

For *him*, a voice whispered in her head. For *him*.

*Right*, she said to herself. *Well, he is marrying Miss Whitby on the morrow, so you'd better bloody well set your sights elsewhere, missy.*

"Yes, thank you, Mr. Hayford," she said politely. "That would be lovely."

"Oh." Matthew looked a little astonished, but pumped her hand up and down quite emphatically, anyway. "That's champion, Miss Dixon. Just *champion*. Till dinner, then?"

"Till dinner," Payton agreed.

The two young people parted ways, Matthew heading for the billiard room, and Payton for the parlor where the ladies were said to be gathered. She had no trouble finding this room, since she could hear the tinkling of a pianoforte drifting out from behind the solid door, and recognized Miss Whitby's lilting soprano as she sang a rendition of "The Ash Grove." This song was a particular favorite of Miss Whitby's, though Payton couldn't think why, since it had a rather nasty narrative to it, about a young man finding his love lying dead beneath a tree. But then, Payton tended to find love ballads as a whole morbid, and vastly preferred sea chanteys, most especially those with beats that made one want to stamp one's foot very hard upon the quarterdeck.

The parlor, she found, when she opened the door to it, was decorated in only a little less masculine style than the rest of the house, with fawn being the color most primary. Slipping into the room quietly enough to attract no attention—everyone was too engrossed in Miss Whitby's performance to pay any mind to *her*—Payton sat down on the first vacant seat she found, a luxuriously soft, but somewhat worn, leather sofa.

" 'The ash grove, how graceful,' " warbled Miss Whitby.

She had a nice enough voice, Payton supposed, but she had a feeling that's not why Miss Whitby so loved to sing. She loved to sing because she looked so good doing it. Every time she took a breath to swell her song, her bosom rose to startling new and dramatic heights. She made quite a picture there with her blue skirts billowing about her and her bosom puffed up so much that it looked as if any second it might all spill out of the daringly cut gown she wore. Looking down at her own bosom, Payton felt rather depressed. She wondered if Miss Whitby hadn't, by any chance, stuffed handkerchiefs into the cups of her corset to add padding to what was already naturally there.

" 'The dear ones I mourn for, again gather here,' " sang Miss Whitby.

Payton was rather surprised to see Miss Whitby wasting such a fine performance on a lot of women. Surely her time would have been better spent saving her song for after dinner, when the gentlemen would be gathered round. Her bosom would be put to much better use *there*.

Then again, Miss Whitby's bosom had already done its work: it had snared her the finest catch in England. Or at least, that's what Payton supposed had attracted Drake, since it didn't seem to her that the odious Miss Whitby possessed anything *else* that would be of interest to a man.

*The ash grove, how* boring, Payton thought, as she began to look about the room. She recognized quite a few of the women gathered there. There was Georgiana, of course, pretending to look engrossed in Miss Whitby's performance (Georgiana had confided to Payton that she found Miss Whitby's insistence on employing vibrato when she sang in front of company a bit affected). There were the wives and daughters of some of the officers with whom Captain Drake had sailed in the past. In fact, except for the rather grand-looking old woman who was entering the room just then, there wasn't a single person she didn't recognize. Where, Payton wondered, were Miss Whitby's guests? Even if she hadn't any family, surely the bride-to-be had invited *someone* to join her on such a momentous occasion . . .

But not, evidently, the old lady who'd just entered the room. After a casual glance through a pair of lorgnettes at Miss Whitby, the woman moved with decorous intent toward the empty cushion on Payton's couch. It was only after she'd lowered herself onto it—with the help of a handsome cane—and arranged her voluminous skirts around her legs that she leaned over and inquired of Payton in a creaky whisper, her eyes very bright behind the lenses of her spectacles, "Who is that, pray? That creature singing so abominably?"

Payton, who'd been thinking something very much along the same lines, couldn't help bursting out laughing at such an unexpected observation. She clapped a hand over her mouth to keep from interrupting the performance, but even so, Georgiana heard her, and turned in her chair to shoot her a warning look.

The old woman beside Payton, however, seemed to possess not the slightest qualm about conversing during Miss Whitby's musicale.

"Is *that* the one he's marrying tomorrow?" The old lady's hands—which were quite elegant, despite their being flecked with age spots—clutched the handle of an ornately carved ebony cane. "That one singing?"

Payton, recovering herself, nodded. "Yes, ma'am," she whispered. "That's Miss Becky Whitby."

"Whitby?" The old lady flicked the songstress a skeptical glance. "I never heard of anyone called Whitby. Where do her people come from?"

"She hasn't any people, ma'am." Payton had to lean close to the old woman's shoulder in order for her whispered responses to be heard. "Everyone in her family is dead."

"All dead?" The old woman raised her fine silver eyebrows. "How convenient. I expected as much. Well, marry in haste, repent at leisure, I always say. Go on. You seem to know all about it. Where did he meet her?"

Payton *did* know all about it, much to her displeasure. She would have much preferred to have known nothing about the matter at all. It had occurred to her shortly after Ross's wedding that her other brothers, and even their friends, might one day marry, as well. But it had never entered her mind that the next wedding she'd attend would be Connor Drake's. Even thinking about it now caused an uncomfortable knot in her stomach that she was very much afraid might never, ever go away. At least, it hadn't gone away, not even for a few minutes, since she'd first heard about the impending nuptials between Captain Drake and Miss Whitby. She'd even been to see the ship surgeon about it, and he, baffled, had declared the discomfort to have no *physical* cause that he could find. Was it possible there might be an emotional cause?

But Payton had indignantly denied any such possibility, and put it down to a bad batch of oysters she'd consumed in Havana. She would continue to do so too until the day she died.

"We were in London," Payton explained, keeping her voice low enough so that she would not be the recipient of any more disapproving stares from her sister-in-law. "We'd just got back from the West Indies run. Drake had—I mean, *Captain* Drake—had learned upon our docking that his brother had died, and he was supposed to meet some solicitors at an office near Downing Street. Well, no one liked for him to go alone, because it was such a sad thing, even though he hadn't liked his brother much. So we all up-anchored and went with him, and as we were coming out again from the solicitors' offices, we heard some screaming, and saw that there was a great row outside this inn across the street. A woman—Miss Whitby, as it turned out—was being shanghaied by some galley rats, and so of course we went to help her. I boshed a fellow flat on the head with a bagatelle cue—"

"I beg your pardon?" The old woman raised her lorgnette to get a better look at Payton.

"Well, there happened to be a bagatelle table in the inn—"

"Of course," the old lady said. "A bagatelle cue. How stupid of me. Do go on."

"Well, in any case, we managed to drive the galley rats away—well, except for that one Hudson killed—and then we took Miss Whitby inside, because she was fainting. When we'd revived her, she told us the men had stolen her reticule, which contained all the money she had in the world, because she's an orphan and hasn't any family."

The old woman stared down at Payton with an inscrutable expression on her face. Her eyes, behind the lenses of the lorgnette, were a very bright blue, and seemed strangely familiar to Payton, though she couldn't, for the life of her, think why.

"You," the woman said, finally, "must be the Dixon girl, then."

"Payton Dixon, ma'am," Payton said, extending her right hand amiably. "How d'you do?"

"Payton?" the woman echoed. "What kind of name is *that*?"

Used to the question, Payton replied, "The name my father gave me. He called me after Admiral Payton, ma'am. All of my brothers and I are named for seafaring explorers or naval heroes. Ross is named for my father's good friend Captain James Ross, who was killed by hostile natives whilst he was looking for the Northwest Passage, and Hudson for Henry Hudson, who—"

"I ought to have known straight off." The old woman ignored her hand. "You're quite disgracefully tan. Still, the freckles led me to think you were much younger. Are you really eighteen?"

Payton put her hand down. She supposed that, once again, she'd managed to offend someone with her mannish forwardness. Oh, well. She hoped the old lady wasn't anybody important, or Georgiana would skin her alive. "I'll be nineteen next month."

"Extraordinary." The blue eyes raked her. "You don't look a day over twelve."

Payton hadn't taken any offense at the old lady's interrupting her, her reference to her freckles, or her refusal to shake her hand. But to accuse her of not looking a day over twelve—now *that* was just too much.

"I may not be as filled out as *some* people"—Payton cast a baleful glance at Miss Whitby, who was still pounding away at the keyboard—"but I assure you, I'm full grown."

The old woman made a tsk-tsking noise with her tongue. "Well, then, your father hadn't ought to be letting you go about—how did you put it? Boshing people on the head with bagatelle cues. You ought to be concentrating on the kinds of activities girls your age normally pursue."

Payton looked disgusted. "If you mean finding a husband and all of that, you needn't worry. Ross—my eldest brother—

has already informed me that I'm to come out this year, and that I hadn't ought to count on sailing again anytime soon."

The old woman nodded approvingly. "He's perfectly correct."

"Well, I don't think so," Payton grumbled. "I've been at sea for most of my life, and I've turned out all right."

"That," the old woman sniffed, "is a matter of opinion. I've heard about you, Miss Dixon."

Pleased to hear that her seafaring skills were being so widely discussed, Payton inclined her head modestly. "Well," she said. "I *did* once make the West Indies run in under seventeen days, but I admit I had my brother Hudson's help—"

"That's not what I meant. I mean that I understand you possess some rather . . . forward-thinking opinions."

"Oh." Payton nodded. "Well, if you mean that I believe there's no job a man can do that a woman can't do as well or better, then yes, I suppose I do. Ross says I oughtn't get my hopes up, but I fully expect that for my birthday next month, I'll be given a ship of my own to command. I'm hoping for our fastest clipper, the *Constant,* but I suppose I could settle for something a little older, to practice on, you know, until I—"

The old lady gave the floor a sharp rap with her cane. Fortunately Miss Whitby was too absorbed in her performance to notice. Several other guests, however—Georgiana included—looked in the direction of the sofa.

"Young woman." The grande dame eyed Payton severely over the tops of her lorgnette. "Only a person who had spent the whole of her life trapped on a ship with a lot of men would aspire to something like *that.*"

Payton said, "Oh, but I think I'd make a fine captain. I mean, except for the heavy lifting, which I admit, because of the way we're shaped, is harder for women, there really isn't anything men can do that we can't. On top of which, we have the added advantage of being able to give birth—"

Another rap of the cane. This time, the look Georgiana shot in their direction was decidedly alarmed.

"Miss Dixon." The old woman's lips were quivering, and

not, Payton thought, with amusement. "I must say, I think it quite negligent of your family, allowing you to go about discussing such topics. Not to mention boshing people on the head."

"But if I hadn't boshed him on the head," Payton said, "he'd have hurt someone."

"Despite what you might think, Miss Dixon, it isn't at all attractive, this declaring yourself equal to men. Nor do I think it particularly wise of you to go about helping your brothers to capture—what did you call them? Oh, yes. Galley rats."

Payton raised her eyebrows. "And what was I supposed to do, pray, while they were under such insidious attack?"

"You ought to have been fainting, like Miss Whitly."

Payton flashed the old lady an annoyed glance. "It's Whit*by*, and what good does fainting ever do? It only causes everybody else a lot of bother, while they run around looking for smelling salts and things. Besides, if Miss Whitby had had the sense to up-anchor and seize a bagatelle cue, like I did, she might have been able to hang on to her money."

"Yes," the old lady said. "Well. Be that as it may, men prefer women who faint over women who wield bagatelle cues."

"That isn't true," Payton drew breath to insist, but the old woman lifted an imperious finger to silence her.

"It isn't *you* the captain is marrying, is it?" she said pointedly. "It's *her*."

Payton followed the old woman's gaze. Miss Whitby had finished singing about her revolting discovery under the ash grove, and had moved on to describe how her love was doing her wrong, casting her off so discourteously.

Only if she had stabbed Payton in the heart with a whaling hook, then twisted the handle, could that old woman have hurt her more. Because of course she was right. Payton *wasn't* the one the captain was marrying. The captain had probably never considered the Honorable Miss Payton Dixon as a potential wife for a single moment in his life. At least, not seriously. It was Miss Whitby who seemed to be all that he wanted in a bride, and more.

Bloody hell.

Well, she couldn't let it bother her. If Miss Whitby was the woman he wanted, then Payton would do her almighty best to make sure it was Miss Whitby he got. After all, she loved Connor Drake too much to deny him his heart's desire—even if his heart's desire was burning a hole through hers.

Besides, if he was stupid enough to want someone like Miss Whitby, then he bloody well deserved her.

"Well," the old woman said imperiously. "What happened next?"

Having been lost in her thoughts, Payton blinked at her. "What?"

"Don't say 'what,' child. Beg my pardon, then tell me what happened after you and your brothers saved the unfortunate Miss Whitby from her assailants."

"Oh."

Payton couldn't imagine why she was behaving so stupidly. Perhaps it was the heat. The drawing room, like the bedroom Ross and Georgiana had been assigned, faced full west, and had not, perhaps, been the best room in which to gather at that time of day, since the bright rays of the sinking sun were streaming at full strength through the twin sets of French doors that led out to Daring Park's lawns. Fans were moving at no sluggish pace, and even Georgiana, who always appeared cool and collected, was beginning to look a bit wilted.

But the old woman seated beside Payton didn't appear the slightest bit discomfited by the heat, in spite of the fact that she was dressed in a long-sleeved gown of heavy purple velvet. Her silver hair had been coiffed into an elaborate arrangement on top of her head, beneath which her scalp had to be prickling. She did not, however, lift a finger to it, nor did she reach for the black lace fan in her lap.

"Well," she said. "Get on with it."

Payton sighed. This was the part of the story where, she felt, she'd made her crucial mistake. For when the girl they'd rescued had wakened from her faint, she had seemed so help-less and childlike that Payton hadn't had any objection what-soever to her brothers' insistence that they invite her to stay at the town house until her health and financial circumstances improved.

The problem, of course, was that there was nothing at all wrong with Miss Whitby's health: she was really quite re-markably hearty for a woman who claimed to be without fam-ily or income. And, being that she was quite without any skills whatsoever, her financial situation remained exactly the same.

"I see," the old woman said, after Payton had imparted these facts. "And was Captain Drake besotted with her from the beginning? Or did his affection for her seem to come on suddenly?"

Quite suddenly, indeed. In fact, it had been Payton's broth-ers Hudson and Raleigh who had expressed the most interest in their houseguest, squiring her about the city and flirting with her rather outrageously at times. They had even come to blows once or twice over her, although, Payton assured her listener, Hudson and Raleigh came to blows over just about anything, their most vicious fight to date having been over a pair of socks.

"One morning, a fortnight ago," Payton explained to the grande dame, "we were all eating breakfast, and Drake—I mean, Captain Drake—came down—He was staying with us, too, did I mention that? Anyway, he announced that he and Miss Whitby were getting married, and that he'd be honored if we'd all come to Daring Park for the ceremony. He said—he said he knew it was sudden, and that it would shock a lot of people, his marrying so suddenly after his brother's death, but that it couldn't be helped, and he hoped we'd all understand."

Payton did not go on to describe how the piece of scone she'd been swallowing at the time had jammed in her throat, and how her brother Hudson had had to whack her on the back in order to keep her from choking to death on it. And how, despite the embarrassment of having choked so unat-tractively at breakfast, she'd actually been glad she'd done so, since the tears streaming down her face were taken as a side effect of the choking, and not as a consequence of the announcement—which, in fact, was what they were.

Instead, she shrugged. "And that was all."

The old woman's eyes narrowed behind the lorgnette. "And he hadn't shown any signs of marked preference for the lady before that?"

Payton didn't think it was jealousy that made her shake her head and declare, "None."

"How odd," the old lady said. She pursed her lips, then went on to say, "So you're telling me this Miss Whitby has no family and no fortune? Nothing, that is, except for her pretty face and manners?"

Payton shrugged again. "I suppose so." Mentally, she added, *If you call* that *pretty.*

"Stop that shrugging," the old woman said. "It isn't attractive. Do you like her?"

Payton raised her eyebrows. "I beg your pardon?"

"That's better. I asked whether you like her. Miss Whitby. Do you like her?"

Payton looked at Miss Whitby. She had stopped playing. Everyone had begun tapping the sides of their fans in polite appreciation. Payton thought that the only thing they could be appreciative of was that the performance was over, and they could now move freely about the room—perhaps even open the French doors, and go outside for a breath of fresh air. As she watched, Miss Whitby rose and bowed modestly, smiling beatifically at her audience, most of whom could only be strangers to her. Then, collecting her voluminous skirts, she moved away from the pianoforte.

Miss Whitby's lustrous red hair—in which, Payton was certain, lice had never nested—gleamed in the light from the setting sun. Her skin, upon which not a freckle showed, glowed pale as the moon. Payton thought about how she'd opened up her home to this young woman, a poor orphan who'd claimed to know not a soul in London, and to whom she had extended every civility, from lending her gowns—the fronts of which had had to be let out to better accommodate Miss Whitby's more rounded form—to letting her borrow her favorite mare to ride round Hyde Park of a morning.

And she had paid Payton back by stealing away the only thing that she'd ever really wanted.

"Actually," Payton said, "I believe I hate her."

The old woman pursed her lips. "That is unfortunate."

Payton looked at her. "Is it? Why?"

And then a voice that was all too familiar asked, shyly, "I beg your pardon, but aren't you Lady Bisson?"

The old woman beside Payton smiled up at Miss Whitby, who'd come to stand in front of them.

"Indeed," she said coolly. "And you must be the young woman who's marrying my grandson upon the morrow."

Payton blanched. *Bloody hell.*

# Chapter Three

$\mathcal{D}$rake exhaled, aiming a thin stream of blue smoke through the open French doors and at the ball of fire sinking fast to the west.

"I spoke to the gardeners, as you requested, sir."

Gerald McDermott, who'd been butler at Daring Park for only a year, was anxious to please his new employer. He had enjoyed his situation with Sir Richard immensely—particularly as it kept him in proximity to his mother, who cooked for the nearby vicarage—and very much hoped the new baronet would maintain his employment.

It was rumored in the kitchens, of course, that Sir Connor intended to sack all of the servants and shut the house up immediately following tomorrow's wedding ceremony, so that he could return to the sea he loved so much. But McDermott could not give this rumor any credence. Where, were the baronet to do this, would his bride reside? For surely even a man as adventurous and unpredictable as Sir Connor could not expect his wife to risk her health and safety with him on the high seas—not when it was so fraught with pirates and other maritime dangers. The idea was ridiculous.

No, McDermott had faith he would be living at Daring Park—and enjoying his mother's tasty tea cakes—for some time to come. He had met the future Lady Drake, and he did not think her the type of woman to spend any significant amount of time on the wind-driven deck of a boat—even the well-built, highly livable clippers of the Dixon and Sons line.

Referring to the list he held, McDermott continued. "And per your instructions, sir, tomorrow morning the gardeners will fasten bouquets of orange blossoms to the sides of only the first four chapel pews—"

"Did you," Drake interrupted, his eyes on the long shadows stretching across the front lawn, "reassign the rooms of those guests that I mentioned?"

"Certainly, sir." McDermott refused, unlike the others belowstairs, to be intimidated by the cool gaze of his new employer. It was always easier to refuse to be so, however, when, like now, the baronet was not looking in his direction. "According to your specifications. I put Mr. Raybourne and Captain Gainsforth in the east wing—"

"Good." Drake took another long drag on the cheroot he was smoking. "Thank you."

McDermott had inhaled, about to move on to the next point on his list, when his employer uttered the words "thank you." The butler looked up sharply. Sir Richard, as pleasant as he had been to work for, had never once, in the admittedly short time McDermott had been in his employ, thanked him. It was commonly asserted by members of the gentry that *thanking* their staff was unnecessary. After all, they paid them salaries to perform their duties: why thank someone for a service for which one had paid?

The fact that Sir Connor chose to thank his butler now, and for such a small act as rearranging the room assignments for a few of his guests, struck McDermott as gentlemanly to the extreme. He felt a sudden rush of warmth toward his new employer, and was just opening his mouth to say, "Why, sir, it was nothing," when Sir Connor stopped him by saying, tersely, "And that will be all for now, McDermott."

McDermott, taken aback, glanced down at his list. There were still seven or eight items that he needed to go over with the baronet. "Um, sir—" he began.

But Drake cut him off. "I'm certain," he said, in that voice of his that was so deep, it quite frightened the chambermaids, forcing them to go to all manner of lengths to avoid his presence, "that you have duties to attend to elsewhere, Mr. McDermott."

They were uttered quite pleasantly, those words of dismissal, but there was no mistaking the tone underlying them. It was unquestionably a tone of authority, of supreme confidence that the order given would be carried out, and with prompt efficiency. For a moment, McDermott had a glimpse into the reason why the baronet was so successful a ship captain—even the most hard-bitten sailor would hardly dare to disobey an order issued from that grim mouth, in such a commanding voice.

Gulping, McDermott made an awkward bow, nearly dropping his precious list in his haste to scurry from the room.

"Y-yes," he said. "Yes, *sir*."

He could not exit the room fast enough. It seemed to him it might not be such a bad idea to pour himself a taste of the port he was decanting for the gentlemen to consume after dinner. His mother would certainly disapprove, but it wouldn't do for the butler's hands to be shaking as he called his master's guests in to supper. It wouldn't do at all.

Drake, still leaning in the open French doors, looked out at the sloping lawns of his childhood home, perfectly unaware of the state of unease into which he'd thrown his butler. Or, if he was aware of it, he gave no more thought to it than he would a fly at which he'd swatted. He had far more pressing things to think about at the moment. The end of the cheroot he gripped between his teeth glowed as red as the sun setting behind the line of oaks at the edge of his estate, as he stood there wondering how he was going to handle this particular mess.

Connor Drake was used to trouble. It seemed that since the day of his birth, he'd known little else. His mother had died during his complicated delivery, and, having arrived a month too soon, Connor was considered by the midwife not long for this world, either. Ignored by his heartbroken father, who blamed his infant son for killing his wife, Connor's care was relegated to a succession of wet nurses. A weak, unhealthy child, he was an object of near-constant derision by his elder brother, and was despised and ultimately rejected by his father. Small wonder, then, that at the age of seventeen, he'd run away from his unhappy home.

No one had been more surprised than Connor Drake when his pleas to be hired as cabin boy were taken seriously by an amiable ship captain, who caught a glimpse of the iron will in the boy's silver-blue eyes, a will that belied those spindly shoulders and milk-white skin.

Henry Dixon often boasted that he never regretted his decision to hire Connor Drake, especially after that first summer he spent at sea, when he grew six inches and gained untold pounds in hard muscle. The milk-white skin turned brown and hard as coconut shell, and the spindly shoulders filled out until they resembled melons. When Drake returned to Daring Park three years later to attend his father's funeral, no one recognized the tall, powerfully built man who stood in the back of the chapel, radiating strength and good health. It was a shock to everyone when it was revealed he was the whey-faced second son they'd all pitied or scorned.

But rather than remain at the park, as his brother, Richard, whom he was now larger than, had rather timidly suggested, Connor headed back to sea, and remained there for another ten years. He'd missed his brother's funeral—there was no helping that. His death had been so sudden, there'd been no time to send warning of it, like there'd been with their father. Drake was back now, however, and for what was supposed to be a happy occasion . . . a wedding this time, and not a funeral.

So why couldn't he stop wishing he were anywhere—anywhere at all—but here? Why couldn't he look out at the green fields on his country estate and not fancy that the gently blowing grass was actually the rippling waves of the Caribbean? Why couldn't he stop regretting that he was not standing on the foredeck of a fast-moving frigate, but on the parquet floor of a grand, richly furnished dining room?

A dining room that he now owned, and in which he'd received so many lectures on his inferiority to his superior—and now deceased—elder brother.

Maybe that was why.

He recognized the voice that croaked at him from the doorway behind him, even though he hadn't heard it in a decade.

"Well," his grandmother said. "You've certainly made a mess of things *this* time."

Drake didn't turn around. There was no need to. He knew what he'd see. A silver-haired replica of how his mother would have looked, had delivering him not killed her.

"I could not even begin," Drake said, his lips moving around the cheroot, "to guess your meaning, Grandmama."

"You know precisely what I mean, you black-hearted devil." He heard the tap of her cane on the shiny wood floor as she came closer. "I've just met her."

"Ah." Drake removed the cheroot, and blew out a plume of blue smoke. "And won't she make the perfect wife for a man of my exalted wealth and status?"

"Stop talking nonsense." Lady Bisson stood beside him now. He could smell the all-too familiar scent she wore, rose water, a fragrance that never failed to fill him with foreboding, since his childhood interviews with this esteemed lady had rarely resulted in anything except a verbal lashing. "And put out that nasty cigar. You might have spent most of your life out at sea with a lot of pirates, but that doesn't mean you have the right to act like one. Smoking's a nasty habit, and I'll thank you not to indulge it in my presence."

Drake, unable to restrain a smile, threw the cheroot with all his might in the direction of the fish pond. The two swans swimming there heard it splash, and glided immediately to the area where it had hit. Serve them right, Drake thought perversely, if they found the bloody thing and ate it. He hadn't much affection for swans; he had too many youthful memories of being chased by them, their giant wings flapping, their mouths opened to emit shrieking hisses. They were, he often thought, the most ill-tempered creatures imaginable, and several trips around the world had not given him cause to amend that opinion.

Lady Bisson had her fan out, and was paddling it rapidly in front of her face.

"I'm not going to ask you," she said, her gaze also on the swans, "why you're marrying her. I believe I know the answer to that. I am going to ask you, however, if you hadn't considered there might be a less . . . permanent way to take care of the matter."

"Matter, Grandmama?" For the first time all day—well, except for when he'd been talking to Payton, whose antics invariably put a smile on his lips—he felt amused. The Dowager Lady Bisson was actually stooping to impart some of her worldly wisdom upon him. This ought, he thought, to be interesting.

"We both know what I'm talking about. The Dixon girl told me all about it."

This caused one of Drake's tawny eyebrows to lift. "Did she, now? And what, precisely, did Miss Dixon have to say on the matter?"

"She's in perfect ignorance of the *matter,* thankfully. But that's only because she worships you, and it would never enter her head that her precious Captain Drake would be capable of doing anything less than noble."

Now Drake did look down at his grandmother, straightening his shoulders uncomfortably beneath his well-cut evening coat. "Payton hardly worships me," he said, recalling the many times she had very unworshipfully mocked him to his face.

Lady Bisson waved that remark away impatiently with her fan. "It hadn't occurred to you, I suppose," she went on, as if he hadn't spoken, "that it might be simpler to pay her off, rather than marry her."

Drake felt amusement again. Never in his life had he ever fancied he'd be having this sort of conversation with his oh-so-proper grandmother. "It did indeed occur to me," he said dryly. "My offer was unduly rejected, however. The lady was very much offended at the very idea."

Lady Bisson sniffed. "Then you didn't offer enough. This isn't any time to be stingy. She's a fast piece of baggage, Connor, and sly as a fox. However were you stupid enough not to see through that helpless-maiden charade of hers?"

"Too many months away at sea, I suppose." Drake let out a mockly regretful sigh. "I was a man primed to rescue helpless maidens."

The fan was dropped to hang from a silken cord round a deceptively frail-looking wrist as Lady Bisson raised her lorgnette to her nose to peer up at her grandson's face. "You're teasing me," she said at length. "You aren't taking this a bit seriously. But I assure you, Connor, this is a very serious matter, indeed. Your good name is at stake here. This girl could seriously compromise it."

Drake stopped smiling. "I know it. Why do you think," he growled, "that I'm marrying her?"

"She could compromise it just as easily after the two of you are wed. She seems the sort, to me. You're going to have to keep a very close eye on her."

"That's going to be difficult," Drake observed.

Lady Bisson's eyes, behind the lorgnette, widened. "Oh, no. No, you don't. Connor, you are not leaving that girl with me. I will not spend the rest of my life cleaning up your messes—"

"Don't upset yourself, Grandmama." Drake turned his attention back to the fish pond, where the swans were squabbling over his cigar. "I'm closing up the park, effective immediately after tomorrow's ceremony. I'm installing her in the villa in Nassau. You'll never have to see her again—nor any of the *messes* I may or may not have engendered."

Lady Bisson looked a little alarmed at this speech—and not just by the words, but the bitterness with which they'd been delivered. Her grandson may have been a milksop as a child, but the man he'd grown into was as hard and sarcastic as any she'd known. In fact, she hardly recognized him as her sweet, gentle daughter's own progeny. He was nothing like his brother, Richard, who'd always been a good, if somewhat easily guided, boy.

Her youngest grandchild, however, was not one who followed, but one who led—and seemed not to tolerate anyone who might cause him to divert from a path, once he'd started down it.

"Well," she said hesitantly. "I hardly meant for you to feel it necessary to keep her in the Bahamas, for heaven's sake. I only meant it might be wise to keep her from the neighborhood, not the whole of Europe."

"Thank you for the clarification." He was smiling again, but his gaze held not the slightest bit of warmth.

Lady Bisson could see he'd missed the point. "It's not that I wouldn't welcome grandchildren, Connor," she said quickly. "With the right kind of woman, I mean."

"You're forgetting that the right kind of woman wouldn't have me, Grandmama." Drake slumped back against the door frame, wondering what he could say that would shock this woman enough to make her go away. He had a sinking feeling there wasn't anything he could do that would offend the dowager enough to cause her to stop speaking to him. God only knew, he'd tried. "I'm not exactly what women in your set consider a catch, you know. Certainly, I've a title now, and some wealth, but what good is a husband who won't put in to port, if he can help it? And I'm sure you don't know anyone who'd let their daughter spend the whole of her married life away at sea."

"I most certainly do." Lady Bisson pursed her well-formed lips. "And so do you. What's wrong with the Dixon girl?"

Drake immediately straightened up, appalled. "Good God. You can't be serious."

"I most certainly am." Seeing her grandson's horrified expression, she thumped her cane sharply upon the parquet. "Well? What's wrong with her? She's obviously as enchanted by the sea as you are. And she certainly seems attached to you."

"She's a child," Drake sputtered.

"She tells me she'll be nineteen next month. I'd been married to your grandfather for two years by the time I was nineteen. *And* I'd had your mother."

"That was fifty years ago," Drake said. "Things were different back then."

He hardly knew what he was saying, he was so disturbed by what his grandmother had suggested. Had everyone gone mad overnight? It seemed so. It had been seeming so since his guests had started to arrive. Imagine his complete bewilderment when he'd overheard two old friends, Raybourne and Gainsforth, waxing eloquent on the charms of a certain young lady. He'd supposed it was some nubile county miss who'd gotten them in such a lather. He'd hardly been able to credit it when he'd learned it was *Payton.* Raybourne had always been something of a hound, but to lust after a *child* . . .

Drake had been sure both men had taken leave of their senses, and had gone so far as to arrange to have their rooms changed to the opposite wing of the house from the Dixons', just to be on the safe side.

But then he'd seen for himself that it wasn't a child at all his friends had been discussing: oh, her brothers might treat her like one, but someone in the family—Georgiana, no doubt—had realized she no longer was one, and had decided to start forcing her to dress accordingly. And the truth was, Payton Dixon in a corset was a far different girl from the Payton Dixon Drake was used to, the one in vest and trousers. Payton Dixon in a corset was very definitely not a child. He'd seen the proof himself when he'd come to her rescue after the wrestling match she and her brothers had engaged in earlier that day. What had come dislodged during that battle were most definitely the breasts of a woman—a young woman, maybe; but definitely, most definitely, a woman.

When, he wondered again, as he'd wondered back then, had Payton Dixon gone and grown breasts?

"Things weren't so very different then." His grandmother's creaky voice broke in on his ruminations on Payton Dixon's chest. "Nineteen is a perfectly reasonable age at which to marry. I fail to see why you consider it—or her—too young."

Drake shook his head, trying to clear it. It wasn't right to think of Payton that way. She was, after all, the little sister of his best friends, and a guest in his house. He would protect her from any and all advances, even if it meant he had to ask Raybourne and Gainsforth to sleep in the *dairy*.

"This discussion is pointless," Drake declared, a little more churlishly than he meant to. "I'm marrying Becky Whitby tomorrow morning, and if you'll forgive me, Grandmother, I don't much care what you think about it . . . or her, for that matter. After tomorrow, I can assure you, you'll never see either of us again."

Lady Bisson lowered the lorgnette. "I see," she said, in tones of extreme mortification. "That's the way it is, then?"

Drake looked away. The sun was sinking rapidly in the west. Soon it would be time to gather his guests for dinner. "That's the way it is," he said firmly.

But his grandmother's voice was equally firm. "We shall see about that," she said, and with a haughty toss of her head, she turned, and left the room.

Drake watched her go, the long purple train of her gown trailing behind her with a gentle swishing sound. He couldn't say he loved his grandmother, but he respected her. She was, in many ways, as stubborn as he was.

But she didn't have any idea what she was up against. No idea at all.

And Drake, who had a very good idea, knew fighting it was futile. He gave the fish pond one final glance—the swans had disappeared; hopefully, they'd choked to death on his cigar, the pair of them—then shrugged his shoulders. It was time to get back to his guests.

And his fiancée.

# *Chapter Four*

$O$h, *no*," said the man at Payton's right upon discovering that his seat was beside hers.

"Not *you*," said the man at her left.

Payton hissed, "I *won't*. I *won't* sit between you. It's not *fair*!"

"*You* think it's unfair?" Hudson looked around the dining room furiously. "There's scads of attractive, eligible ladies at this function, and we have to sit by our little *sister*? How do you think *we* feel?"

"I don't know what Drake could have been thinking." Raleigh glared daggers at his host. "There must be some kind of mistake. Quick, let's see if we can trade—"

But chairs were already being pulled out all around them. It was too late to trade places. Besides, Lady Bisson, Drake's grandmother, seated on Hudson's right, had already given them a strange look as her grandson had helped her into her chair. While the look might have been directed solely at Payton, who had already thoroughly embarrassed herself by admitting—albeit unknowingly—to the groom's family that she didn't care for his bride, the two brothers thought it was meant for them, and they quickly took their seats.

The Dixons—at least the younger ones—were, it appeared, stuck with each other.

"Well," Hudson muttered, unfolding his napkin. "*This* is a fine how-d'you-do."

"Really," Raleigh agreed. "Try not to embarrass us this time, Pay."

"*Me?*" Payton scowled at them. "What did *I* ever do?"

"Oh, let me see," Hudson said, feigning thoughtful contemplation. "There was the time you drove the fork into the waiter's hand in Canton."

"He deserved it," Payton asserted. "I saw him try to lift Drake's wallet. Besides, it wasn't a fork, it was a chopstick."

"What about that year you refused to eat anything yellow?"

"Need I remind you that I was eight years old at the time?"

"We were in the West Indies, for pity's sake. *All* the food there was yellow."

"Well, you needn't worry. I shan't embarrass you tonight. I'm sure that's why Drake seated me between you." She couldn't help leveling a bitter glare at their host, who was chatting amiably with his grandmother. "He doesn't trust me not to stab his footmen with my fish fork."

"Right," Raleigh agreed with a smirk. "Any more than he trusts us around those cousins of his, eh, Hud?"

Hudson chuckled lasciviously, and the two men exchanged leers over the top of Payton's head.

Payton rolled her eyes. She didn't blame Drake, she supposed, for forcing her to sit between her brothers, who were such incorrigible bachelors. Especially since so many of his pretty young cousins were in the room. But she wondered if that was really the reason he'd sat her there. More likely, it was because Connor Drake considered her a child, in need of adult supervision, and probably expected her to stand up and throw things during the course of the meal. If there'd been a separate table for his underage guests, Payton had no doubt she'd have found herself seated there.

Well, and why shouldn't he consider her a child? Every time he saw her she was engaged in some kind of buffoonery, like that wrestling match earlier with her brothers. And now she had that embarrassing gaffe with his grandmother to worry about. How was she to have known that the old lady was related to him? Of course, she ought to have guessed by all the questions—not to mention the old woman's piercing gaze, an exact replica of Drake's.

Lord, *of course* he thought her a child! She was forever acting like one. She twisted disgustedly in her chair. Georgiana could put her in all the corsets she wanted: the truth was, no one would *ever* consider Payton an adult woman, with an adult woman's body, and an adult woman's heart.

Payton slumped defeatedly in her seat—or as much as she could slump, with those stays pointing so uncomfortably into her ribs—and turned her attention to the head of the table, where Drake had risen, a glass of champagne in his hand. She sat only a few place settings away from him, since her brothers, as groomsmen, were part of the bridal party. She could see that the harsh lines that had been in his face earlier in the evening were still there. In fact, now that the sun had finally set, and the room was lit by candle flame, those lines were thrown into harsher relief than ever. Whatever was eating away at him, it wasn't getting any better as the evening progressed. Well, it wouldn't, she supposed. Not until tomorrow. Every man was nervous before his wedding day. She remembered that Ross had retched repeatedly the night before his wedding to Georgiana.

But then again, that might have been a result of all the rum.

"If I could have your attention, please," Drake said, in his deep voice, the one that reminded Payton of velvet sky on a summer evening—not unlike this one. The fifty or so people seated at the long dining table quieted, and turned in their seats to look expectantly at their host. He managed a smile, though it wasn't a very convincing one. Payton had seen Drake converse with hostile island natives with more ease.

Well, she supposed, it had to be nerve-wracking: seated on either side of him was his bride-to-be and his grandmother, each woman gazing up at him raptly, Miss Whitby with a tiny smile that, to Payton's admittedly jealous eye, was triumphant, Lady Bisson with a frown that, as far as Payton could tell, was directed more at the footmen behind her grandson, whom she didn't seem to feel were pouring the champagne into the guests' glasses quickly enough.

"I'd like to thank all of you," Drake went on, "for joining me on this very special occasion. I know that some of you have come a very long way, indeed—"

"Aye," Payton's father burst out, unable to contain his good humor. "All the way from London!" He elbowed Georgiana, who had the misfortune to be seated on his right. "All the way from London, right, my dear?"

"Indeed," Drake said solemnly. "Some of you from as far away as London. And Becky—Miss Whitby, I mean"—the bride blushed prettily at this blunder—"and I would like to thank you heartily for coming, and helping us to celebrate what will, I hope, be a very happy day."

"Here, here," Raleigh cried, raising his glass.

"Cheers," Hudson bellowed.

Everyone raised their glasses and tipped them in the direction of the bride and groom. Even Payton toasted them, and then wondered if she was going to burn in hell for uttering a swift and silent prayer as she did so that Miss Whitby might perish in her sleep. Quickly and painlessly, of course.

Was it really so very wicked of her to wish something like that? Yes, she supposed it was. She offered up another prayer, this one asking the Lord's forgiveness.

When she set her glass down, she wasn't the only one who was surprised to see that she'd swallowed the whole of its contents.

"Heave to, Pay," Raleigh cried. "You'll be tipsy before the soup comes."

"She's not the only one," Hudson said, poking her rather hard in the ribs. "Look at Drake."

Their host had swallowed everything in his own glass, as well. Smiling—this time more genuinely—he took his seat again with a shrug.

"Well," he said. "I suppose that means Payton and I will just have to have some more."

His footmen seemed only too happy to oblige. The champagne flowed very freely, indeed. According to the menu, which Payton found beside her plate, tied up with a piece of pink silk ribbon—a pink silk, she noticed, that matched the color of the rosettes in the bride's hair—they were to expect a veritable feast, including lobster tails and lamb cutlets, two of her favorite foods, with a different wine or liqueur for each course.

Still, she could not enjoy the talents of Daring Park's exemplary cook, or share in the high spirits—both literally as well as figuratively—of the rest of the table. She hated herself for this. Why—and when—had she developed this insufferable weakness for Connor Drake? She could not put her finger on the exact date it had occurred, but it was as clear as the bubbles in the champagne that was continuously poured into her glass:

She was in love with this man. And he was marrying someone else.

Not only marrying someone else, but marrying someone else without ever once having cast her, the Honorable Miss Payton Dixon, a second glance!

Oh, he'd shown her a gentlemanly civility once or twice: that summer night she'd been stretched out on the deck of the *Virago,* watching a spectacular display of falling stars. No sooner had she spied one flashing white streak in the sky than there'd been another. When everyone else, their necks stiff, had declared their intention of retiring, Payton alone had remained on deck, insisting on watching the dazzling light show until it ended, or the sun rose, whichever came first. And Drake, who'd gone into the foc's'le with the others, had suddenly reappeared, a blanket and a pillow in either hand.

Payton had thought, for one dizzying, glorious moment, that he intended to join her on deck. But he soon dashed those hopes, and awakened a different kind, when he'd fussed over her, insisting she keep warm, and use the pillow as a cushion for her head against the hard wood of the quarterdeck.

And Payton had been as touched as if he really had joined

her, for it was *his* blanket he'd brought her, and *his* pillow. They smelled of him, that odor that was peculiarly Drake's, of salt air and fresh laundry and clean man, an odor she'd gotten used to in the years they'd traveled together in what was, at times, very close quarters, indeed. She had lain on the deck, wrapped in *his* blanket, her head on *his* pillow, and marveled at his sacrifice, since it meant he was sleeping on his hard pallet in the forecastle with no such comforts.

Of course, her brothers pointed out the following day that he'd been far too drunk to miss them. They'd all been imbibing heavily that night, Drake heaviest of all, and if, in a moment of morbid sentimentality, he'd loaned Payton his blanket and pillow, it was only because he'd been too intoxicated to know what he was doing. Drake had very nobly denied the veracity of this, but to Payton, it hadn't mattered: even if he'd been drunk, he'd still thought of her. Drunk or sober, to be thought of by Connor Drake at all was no very small thing.

There'd been other examples of Drake's superiority to all the men of Payton's acquaintance, of course. That time they'd been involved in that brawl in Havana, and a pirate had seized Payton about the waist, and tried to toss her into the bay: Drake had shot him through the eyes with what Payton liked to think was almost loverlike savagery. And, more intimately, an evening when Drake had been recuperating from a disastrous love affair with a native girl—she'd turned out to be married; granted her husband had several other wives in addition to her, but their union was still legal—and had been drunkenly bemoaning the fact that he was never going to find a wife, and Payton had volunteered her services, if by the time she was of marriageable age, he still hadn't found anyone. Despite her brothers' guffaws at the idea of Payton marrying anyone—and their speculations as to Payton's abilities as wife and mother—Drake had quite gallantly kissed her hand, and told her he had every intention of taking her up on her offer.

That had been, by Payton's reckoning, only four years ago. But here she was, of eminently marriageable age, and no proposal was forthcoming.

Because, of course, he'd found a bride so much more appealing.

Looking across the table at Miss Whitby, Payton had no choice but to admit it to herself: penniless or not, Becky Whitby would make any man an enviable wife. She was everything a woman ought to be: soft, feminine, sweet, gentle. Miss Whitby never cursed, or found lice in her hair, or freckled. Miss Whitby never roughhoused, or stabbed waiters with chopsticks, or declared to anyone's grandmother that she hated their grandchild's intended spouse. Miss Whitby, to Payton's certain knowledge, did not even know how to load a derringer, let alone fire one.

Miss Whitby was perfect.

. Which was why Payton took the silk ribbon from her menu and slipped it, still in its bow, over her hand, to wear about her wrist. In this way, she hoped to bear a constant reminder to herself that what she wanted was most definitely out of her reach. Captain Connor Drake had never considered her anything more than the little sister of his three best friends. He had never thought of her as a woman, or even as female. He was marrying Miss Becky Whitby, and that was all there was to it.

And the sooner she got that through her thick little head, the better.

The ribbon helped. She looked at it every time one of her brothers rose to make a toast to the happy couple, toasts that became progressively bawdier as the night wore on. She looked at it every time Miss Whitby tittered and hid her face behind her fan. She looked at it every time Drake reached for his glass just as Miss Whitby reached for hers, and their fingers touched, and Drake, looking every hour more like a man approaching his execution than the happiest day of his life, murmured, "I beg your pardon."

She looked at it so much, in fact, that finally Hudson noticed, and said, "Gad, Payton, are you so hard up for baubles you've got to start wearin' the party favors?"

Fortunately, no one heard him. It was a gay and boisterous

party, with everyone talking at once. Payton, from years of long practice, was able to separate Drake's voice from all the others. He was speaking to his fiancée and grandmother. Payton would have supposed that, since these two ladies who shared such important places in Drake's life had just met, their conversation would necessarily revolve around getting to know one another: Lady Bisson might perhaps share an embarrassing incident from her grandson's childhood. Miss Whitby would then relate some equally embarrassing incident from her own. In this way, Payton knew, from having watched her brother around his wife's family, in-laws got to know one another.

But that was not the case here at all. Lady Bisson was absolutely silent, opening her mouth only to spoon soup into it now and then. And Miss Whitby was just sitting there, hanging on Drake's every word.

And what was Drake, the night before the most important day—or what ought to have been, at least—in his life, discussing? Not his plans for their future. He wasn't telling his grandmother how they met (he couldn't know that Payton had, albeit unknowingly, already performed that function). No. He was telling them both about his last voyage to the Sandwich Islands. Payton could hardly believe it. He was going on and on about the island natives, as if they were the most interesting topic in the world, and he was doing it in a strange voice Payton had never heard him use before, a voice completely devoid of whatever it was that made Drake's voice so distinctive, so that, whenever he was talking, she could easily trace his whereabouts on any ship, no matter what its size.

Payton knew a thing or two about the natives of the Sandwich Islands, and in her opinion, while they were quite interesting, they did not bear discussing just then, when so many other, more important topics might be explored—like whether or not the groom intended to give up his career upon the sea now that he'd inherited a baronetcy, or just why, precisely, he'd decided to marry this woman he hardly knew anything about, beyond the fact that she had a pretty face and a re-markably bouncy bosom.

Payton became so incensed as she listened to Drake ex-pound on what he called the charming rituals of the Sandwich Island natives, that she finally interrupted with the tart sug-gestion that he tell his grandmother all about the charming Sandwich Island ritual of imprisoning any woman suspected of having performed a licentious act, and then forcing her, by night, to service the local military officers. Wasn't *that* charm-ing?

That shut Drake up. Unfortunately, it also shut up everyone else within earshot. Payton, who'd really only said it to force Drake into using his normal speaking voice, and not that de-tached, polite tone she hardly recognized as belonging to him, blinked a few times. Drake sat frozen, a forkful of lobster halfway to his mouth. Lady Bisson leaned past Hudson to peer at Payton through her lorgnette, as if she were an interesting scientific specimen. Georgiana had sunk her face into her hands, and Ross, Raleigh, and Hudson were looking every-where but in Payton's direction. Only her father and the odious Miss Whitby looked at all pleased—Sir Henry because he was always proud of his little girl, no matter what came out of her mouth, and Miss Whitby because Payton had made such a perfect fool of herself . . . again.

But Payton wasn't about to back down. Dabbing the corner of her mouth with her napkin, she said primly, "Well, it's true." She sent a reproving look at Drake. "You shouldn't lead people to believe it's all bare breasts and waterfalls."

The silence that followed this piece of information lasted maybe a heartbeat, but to Payton, it seemed like a decade. Then Hudson, who could stand it no longer, let out a terrific whoop of laughter, which Raleigh echoed with one of his own. Soon, everyone—with the exception, Payton noted, of Lady Bisson and Miss Whitby—was laughing.

Including Drake.

Only Payton hadn't meant to be funny.

Still, it was very hard not to laugh when so many people around her were doing so.

Payton tried not to smile, but she couldn't help it—especially not after Hudson pounded her on the back, causing her to drop a large portion of lamb cutlet into her lap.

Well, she'd been looking for an excuse to leave the table, anyway. One of the many disadvantages of wearing a corset, she soon realized, was that it did press rather insistently against the bladder. She felt the need for a moment to herself, and not just to wipe the gravy off her skirt.

She was coming downstairs again, having realized a little belatedly that she was more than just tipsy, but downright drunk—how was she ever going to remember how to dance when the time came? Georgiana had spent hours teaching her the latest steps, and now it was all going to be wasted—when a gravelly voice arrested her on the landing. She looked down to find Drake's grandmother waiting for her at the bottom of the stairs.

"Well," Lady Bisson said, as if there'd been no interruption of the conversation they'd been having in the drawing room. "What are you going to do about it?"

Payton stared at the old woman. Earlier in the evening, she had taken Georgiana aside and shared with her the mortification of her interview with the woman who'd turned out to be Drake's grandmother.

"I shouldn't worry about it," had been Georgiana's surprising response.

"*What?* Georgiana, I told her I hate her grandson's future bride! And you say I shouldn't worry about it? Don't you see what I've *done*?"

"Yes," Georgiana had replied mildly. "You were honest with a woman who was very dishonest with you. If she chooses to share what you told her with Drake, or with Miss Whitby, then that's her business. You can always deny you said it."

"You mean *lie*?"

"Yes, lie. You're quite a convincing liar, Payton." Georgiana's smile had been knowing. Too knowing for Payton's comfort.

*That* conversation had been very nearly as bad as the one Payton had had with Lady Bisson. But now, if she wasn't mistaken, the old lady was looking for *another* one. Whatever for?

To torture Payton, no doubt, for having maligned her future granddaughter-in-law.

"Do?" Payton echoed unintelligently. She thought Lady Bisson must be referring to the wrongfully incarcerated women of the Sandwich Islands, and said, "Well, I don't think there's much anyone can do, of course, except lobby for reforms—"

"Not about *that,* you little fool!" Lady Bisson rapped her cane upon the floor. "About the fact that my grandson is marrying a woman whom you, as you put it, hate."

"Oh," Payton said, taken aback. "Well, nothing."

"Nothing?" Lady Bisson looked significantly surprised. Leaning on her cane, she watched as Payton came all the way down the stairs, then stood looking down at her—Drake had obviously inherited his height from his grandmother, who, despite her age and infirmity, was quite an imposing figure. "That's hardly the answer I expected to hear from a woman who has been around the world not once, not even twice, but, I understand, seven times."

"There's nothing I *can* do." Payton remembered not to shrug. "He chose her." Quite suddenly, it was all she could do to keep her voice from throbbing. "He loves her."

"Does he?" Lady Bisson's voice did not throb, or even tremble. It was as even and cool as ice. "Do you believe that, Miss Dixon? Do you really believe that?"

Payton, confused, looked about the hall for help. None was forthcoming. A few of the servants were pushing the suits of armor closer to the walls, to make way for the dancing to come later, and in the corner, the orchestra was tuning up, but no one offered Payton any answers.

What was wrong with this woman? Why did she keep pestering Payton about her grandson? It was *Miss Whitby* she ought to be bothering about it, not Payton. *Miss Whitby* was the one Drake was marrying. Payton tried to remember if Drake had ever mentioned a grandmother before, and dimly recalled a conversation in which he'd admitted he had one, but that she lived in Sussex and seemed to favor his brother over him. This had to be the Sussex grandmother, then, his mother's mother. Now that Drake's brother was dead, she seemed to be concentrating the full of her attentions on her only remaining grandchild.

"If he doesn't love her," Payton said finally, "then why is he marrying her?"

"The very question I ask myself," Lady Bisson said, giving the marble floor a rap with her cane. "Connor Drake is a man of independent means. A virile man, in his prime. Why should he marry a woman he doesn't love, or even seem to like? She hasn't anything at all to recommend her—"

"Oh," Payton interrupted. "But she's very beautiful."

"Nonsense!" Now Lady Bisson revealed she didn't need the cane at all, by raising it and waving it in Payton's direction, so violently that Payton ducked, and just in time, too. The stick came perilously close to her head. "You're just as pretty, and *you've* got money! Twenty thousand pounds your father's settled on you for the day you marry, that's what I heard. And five thousand a year, after he passes. *And* you inherit an equal share in the business with your brothers." Payton raised her eyebrows. Lady Bisson had heard *a lot* for someone she hadn't met until a few hours earlier. "So why isn't he marrying *you*? That's what I want to know. Why isn't he marrying *you*?"

Since that was so very close to what Payton had been asking herself all evening, she could only murmur, "I really think we ought to be getting back to the table, my lady—"

"What kind of answer is that? That's no answer! It's up to *you*, you know. *You're* the only one who can put a stop to it."

That did it. Payton had had enough. She stamped her foot hard on the marble step and said, not caring a bit if Lady

Bisson thought her impertinent, "I shall do nothing of the sort! He wouldn't be marrying her if he didn't want her. And since he wants her, I, for one, will do nothing to stop him from having her. In fact, I'll do everything I can to see that he gets her."

"Oh, my." Lady Bisson's voice dripped unpleasantly with sarcasm. "You mean you love him too much to deny him something he wants?"

Payton glared at her. "Something like that," she said. It was strange, but she didn't feel the slightest hint of embarrassment at admitting to this woman that she loved her grandson. It didn't seem a bit unnatural. It was a fact, plain and simple. Payton could just as easily be admitting she had a touch of quinsy. And like quinsy, she'd be getting over it one day. It might not be until she was a hundred years old, but she'd get over Connor Drake someday. See if she wouldn't.

"How self-sacrificing of you, my dear." Lady Bisson was sneering now. "You're a fool, you know. Self-sacrifice never got anyone anywhere. It certainly won't get you the man you love."

Payton stood her ground. "Since the man I love doesn't want me, that's a moot point, isn't it?"

"Oh, I see. You don't want him unless he wants you, is that it? Don't you know by now that half the time, men don't know what they want until it's too late?"

"What do *you* know about Drake?" Payton knew she was being unforgivably rude, but she didn't care. "You hardly know him at all. You always liked his brother better—"

"Well, of course I did. His brother stayed home. I never had a chance to get to know Connor. He left home when he was still just a boy, and then he was always away at sea. But he's a man now, and I know a thing or two about men—a lot more than you do, for all the time you've spent adrift at sea with them. And I'm telling you, Miss Dixon, he doesn't want that woman. Marrying her will only make him unhappy. And if you love him as much as you say you do, then you'll stop this travesty of a wedding from taking place."

Payton hadn't the slightest idea how to reply to this extraordinary statement. It seemed to her that Lady Bisson must have gone mad. Because Payton had no clearer idea of how to stop Drake from marrying Miss Whitby than she had of how to stop the moon from pulling out the tide.

Thankfully, Payton was saved from having to make any sort of reply since the doors to the dining room suddenly opened, revealing the subject of their conversation himself.

"Ah, Grandmama," he called out. "There you are. Come back to the table, would you? Ross Dixon is preparing to make some kind of speech. He says it's dreadfully important, and that you've got to hear it."

Lady Bisson, after fixing Payton with one last, disapproving stare, stalked back into the dining room. Payton followed more slowly. At the door, Drake, who'd waited to escort her—and not his grandmother, she noted, with a certain muzzy confusion—bent down to whisper, "I'm so sorry. Was she harassing you?"

Payton, too shocked at being noticed in such a manner to dissemble—and much too aware of the proximity of his starched shirtfront, all she could see from the abashed angle at which she hung her head—nodded.

"I was afraid of that." Drake's fingers were very warm as he grasped her arm, just above the elbow, and guided her back to her chair. "You'll have to forgive her. She was deeply upset by Richard's death—it was so sudden. I don't think she's recovered sufficiently. I really ought to have waited before . . ." His voice trailed off, but Payton knew he meant that he ought to have waited for a sufficient period of mourning for his brother before marrying.

"Well," he said. They had reached her chair. On either side of it, her brothers were tossing candied cherries at one another. Drake did not appear to notice; he was too deeply engrossed in their discussion. "But that can't be helped, now, can it?"

Payton didn't want to cause a scene, not right there in front of everyone—and not so soon after that last scene she'd just caused. But still, she was sufficiently irked—and, if truth be told, had consumed enough champagne—to demand, in a voice that wasn't quite steady, "*Why?* I don't understand, Drake. *Why* are you in such an all-fired rush to get married?"

But Drake only reached out and touched the tip of her nose. "Don't," he said, and this time, his smile was neither brittle nor forced, "worry your little head about it, Payton. Ah, look. Your brother's making his toast now."

Payton wanted to scream that she didn't care what her brother had to say, that Ross could take his bleeding toast and shove it up his arse, for all she cared. But she happened to look up and notice, just at that moment, Miss Whitby's gaze on her. Miss Whitby's eyes were as blue as her future husband's, but lacked the warmth that his so often held—when they were not skewering one with their intensity. At that particular moment, Miss Whitby's gaze was icy cold, no doubt because Drake had had his finger on someone else . . . but on someone else's *nose,* for pity's sake. The man was forever pressing down the tip of her nose, as if she were four bloody years old!

But that didn't seem to make any difference to Miss Whitby, who was leveling an extremely waspish look in Payton's direction.

"Attention." Ross had stood up, and was banging on his wine goblet with a spoon. He was so drunk that he'd begun to sway gently on his feet. Georgiana was gazing up at him a little trepidatiously, as if at any moment she expected him to come toppling down on her.

"Your attention, please. Attention." The diners quieted somewhat, and turned their faces toward the eldest Dixon son. All except for Miss Whitby, of course. She continued to stare at Payton. "Thank you. Thank you. I'd like to take this opportunity to say, if I may, that on behalf of my brothers and I—I mean, me—oh, and my father—"

"And Payton," interrupted Raleigh.

"Oh, and my sister, Payton. On behalf of all us Dixons, we—"

"No, no, no." Sir Henry, not quite as drunk as any of his

children, pulled on his eldest son's coattails with enough force to bring him plunking back down into his chair, where he sat, blinking confusedly. "That's not the way to do it. Here, let me." Sir Henry took the glass from his bemused son's hand and stood up to make the toast himself.

"A little less than fifteen years ago," he began, with a solemn bow toward Drake, who'd taken his seat at the head of the table and was gazing fondly at his employer, "a stunted little whelp of a lad came to me, lookin' for a job. I felt right sorry for the li'l weevil—" This was met with general laughter, at which Sir Henry blinked a little confusedly. Still, he carried on. "So I made 'im a cabin boy. Since then, he's grown into one of the finest sailors I've ever known—no, I should say one of the finest *men* I have ever known. Why, he can ride out a sou'wester with the best of 'em, and tack up a topsail in no time flat. Not only that, but he's an unerring navigator, the only man I know who's actually managed to render a reliable map of those treacherous islets and reefs that make up what we call the Bahamas—"

"That's the only reason we like 'im," shouted Hudson drunkenly. "For 'is damned map!"

"Finally," Raleigh announced, with a hiccup, "we'll have an edge up over that blighter Marcus Tyler!"

"Marcus *Bloody* Tyler," Hudson corrected him.

Sir Henry sent his two younger sons an irritated glance. "Connor Drake is a man I'm proud to have in my employ," he continued, as if he hadn't been interrupted. "A man I would be proud to call son. And it's for that reason that I would like to offer Captain Drake a full partnership, equal to that of my own boys, in Dixon and Sons—"

A general gasp went up from the guests gathered round the dining table. And not only the guests seemed astonished. A quick glance at Drake revealed that he too seemed stunned.

But he could never have been as stunned as Payton was when she heard her father's next words.

"In addition, as my way of thanking him for his years of faithful service, I'm hoping Captain Drake will accept, as a small token of my gratitude, the Dixon ship *Constant,* of which he may take immediate command, as it is docked in Portsmouth, waiting to take the captain and his bride on their honeymoon to Nassau—"

If anyone thought it at all odd, a shipping merchant offering a baronet partnership in his business, as well as a boat he could have purchased five times over with a fortune the size of which Drake had inherited, one wouldn't have known it from the way the people gathered round his dinner table behaved. Sir Henry's announcement was greeted with cheers and applause.

Except, of course, from the youngest Dixon. Payton sat where she was, completely and utterly stunned.

Her ship. Her father had just given Connor Drake—who was not even a blood relation—full partnership in the family company. And *her* ship.

And not just any ship, either, but the *Constant,* the newest and fastest ship in their fleet. The ship that by rights ought to have been Payton's, the one she'd asked for not once, not even twice, but several dozen times over the past few months.

The ship that—except for an act of nature, over which she had no control, that had determined that she would be female instead of male—*would* have been Payton's when she turned nineteen.

For a moment, she simply sat there, dazed. When she did finally manage to tear her gaze away from her father, she swung it accusingly toward Ross. That traitor. He'd done it. He'd always said he would, but Payton had never believed it. Even when the gowns and other assorted fripperies for her coming out had started arriving, she hadn't believed it. Her brother would come to his senses soon. She knew he would. He had to. Payton Dixon wasn't cut out to be anyone's wife. She was cut out to be one thing, and that was commander of the *Constant.*

But he'd done it. He'd actually gone ahead and done it. Skipped over her as if she didn't even exist and given what was rightfully hers to his friend.

Shifting her gaze toward that friend, Payton found Drake's

attention already focused on her. While everyone about him was shouting congratulations and raising their glass, Drake alone sat without a smile. For the first time, Payton thought she could read what was behind those inscrutable blue eyes of his. And when his lips parted, and he mouthed two words at her, she knew she had not read his expression wrong. *I'm sorry,* he said.

The worst of it was, regret was not what she'd read in his eyes. Instead, she saw an emotion Payton could not abide—not when it was directed at her.

Pity.

Well, that was enough. The man she loved was not only marrying someone else, he had also managed to take away the only other thing in her life that she had ever wanted—besides him, of course. And he had the gall to sit there and *pity* her!

She couldn't stand it. She would not sit there and endure it, not for a minute more. Rising, Payton threw her balled-up napkin onto the table and stalked away.

But not before she'd caught a glimpse of the triumphant look on Miss Whitby's face.

# Chapter Five

*N*o," Payton said, for what she was sure was the hundredth time. "I will *not* come downstairs, Georgiana. I haven't any desire to be in the same room with my brothers right now, thank you. In fact, if I had my way, I wouldn't even be in the same county—the same *country*—as any of them. But since you won't let me go back to London tonight, I guess I'll just have to stay up here in dry dock until I *rot*."

Georgiana stared down at her intractable sister-in-law, who two hours earlier had flung herself across the canopy bed in the guest room to which she'd been assigned, and had refused ever since to get up.

"Really, Payton," Georgiana said. "While I can understand your disappointment, I think you're being too hard on Ross. You can't have honestly expected him to give you a *boat* for your birthday. I mean, not *really*."

Payton, sprawled on her stomach, oblivious to the fact that her skirt was hiked up to her knees, pinned her brother's wife with a disgusted look. "Not a boat. A ship. And yes, I *really* did," she said. "Hudson got a ship for *his* nineteenth birthday. Raleigh got a ship for *his* nineteenth birthday." She struck a pillow with her fist. "Can you really blame me for thinking maybe, just maybe, there was some justice in the world, and that *I* might expect a ship for my nineteenth birthday?"

"But Payton, really." Georgiana shook her head. "It's just a boat, after all."

"It's *not* just a boat. It's the *Constant*." Payton could not think of a way to impress upon her sister-in-law the importance of this fact. "Don't you see? I *deserve* her, Georgiana, after everything I've done for this company. And Ross went and gave her to Drake. It's not *fair*."

Georgiana sat down on the mattress and smoothed some of her sister-in-law's hair from where it had fallen into her eyes. "But darling," she said, speaking gently. "Women don't become ship captains."

"*Some* do," Payton said.

"Well, certainly, *some* do. But only out of necessity. And those women aren't . . . well, they aren't *nice*."

"How do *you* know? Have you ever met a woman ship captain, Georgiana?"

"Well, no. But the simple fact is, Payton, it isn't at all *seemly* for a woman to go off to sea with a boatload of sailors, and no male kinfolk to protect her—"

"Protect her from what?" Payton glared at her sister-in-law. "Don't think I don't know what you're talking about, Georgiana. But I think it would be pretty asinine for a crew who'd been hired on by a woman to turn around once they were out to sea and rape her. I mean, after all, she's paying their salaries. It isn't very likely they'd be able to collect their pay after doing something like *that*."

"But supposing they couldn't help themselves." Georgiana tapped her fan agitatedly against the bedpost. Discussions like this, which occurred all too frequently with Payton, tended to make her nervous. She sometimes found herself longing for the days before she'd married Ross, when words like "bloody" and "rape" had never once been uttered in her presence.

"Men aren't like women, Payton," Georgiana said. "We can control ourselves." She shrugged her bare shoulders. "Men can't."

"All the more reason," Payton said, "that *we* should be the ones in charge."

Georgiana looked skeptical. "Payton, you've traveled the world. You've seen cultures and lands I've only read about. Can you tell me that you honestly think you can put away to sea with a crew of men—hard-bitten, brutal sailors—and trust that nothing *untoward* will occur?"

Payton said passionately, "*Yes*. Because while I do believe that men as a whole are a sorry lot, as *individuals* they can be appealed to rationally—"

"Oh, Payton, really."

"Well, all right, then. I'll appeal to their rational sides, but I also intend to carry a loaded pistol with me at all times."

Georgiana looked down at her sister-in-law with a sad smile. "I admire your tenacity, Payton. I really do. But I think it might be better if you just forgot about this wild idea of becoming a lady sea captain, and came downstairs with me to have some champagne. Everyone is having a lovely time below—well, except for Matthew Hayford, who was crushed when I told him you wouldn't be coming down."

"Matthew Hayford," Payton echoed bitterly. "I suppose you'd be happy if I *did* go down. Matthew might propose, and take me off your hands."

"Well, Mr. Hayford is a very sweet boy, Payton, but he's hardly the kind of man a girl like you ought to be marrying." Georgiana fussed with the buttons on her elbow-length gloves. "He's only an officer, after all, dear. You need someone with a title, and a bit of land. I can't think why Captain Drake didn't invite any peers here tonight. Why, Matthew Hayford doesn't even own his own house!"

"If he ever got his own commission," Payton suggested wickedly, "we could live on his ship."

"Live on a ship." Georgiana sniffed. "The very idea! Here, Payton, why are you wearing that ribbon? Take it off."

Payton looked down at the pink silk ribbon round her wrist.

"No," she said.

"What do you mean, no? Why are you wearing it? Isn't that the ribbon from the menu?"

"Yes. And no, I won't take it off. I'm using it as a reminder."

"A reminder of what?"

Rolling onto her back, Payton lifted one of the pillows and dropped it across her face. "I don't want to talk about it," she said, her voice muffled by the heavy down.

Georgiana rolled her eyes. "I don't know what the captain could have been thinking, seating you between your brothers. I specifically told him to seat you between Captain Gainsforth and Mr. Raybourne. Out of all his guests, they're the most eligible. I'd rather hoped to give you a taste of what it will be like next season in London. But no, he had to go and seat you between your brothers. And *they* had to go and let you get drunk. Despite what you like to think, you're not a man, Payton. You can't hold liquor the way your brothers do."

Payton lifted a corner of the pillow. "I'm not drunk."

"When we go up to London for your first season," Georgiana said, "you're to remember that social functions are not drinking contests. You're not to attempt to drink your suitors under the table, do you understand? Lord, I take it back, what I said about being angry at Captain Drake for not inviting any peers. That's just what we *don't* need, someone who'll go carrying tales about you back to London." She made a clicking noise with her tongue. "I suppose, what with his brother hardly cold in his grave, it would have been very bad taste indeed to have a large wedding. Well, even if Richard weren't dead, it still would have been in poor taste—"

"Why?"

A knock sounded on the door to Payton's bedchamber. She knew it could only be one of her brothers when the knob turned before she'd had a chance to call "come in." Ross stuck his head in.

"Oh," he said, upon seeing his wife. "There you are." He pushed the door open further and revealed a shirtfront completely covered with a dark brown, glistening stain.

"Aha!" Payton sat up. "No more'n you deserve, you stinkin' lump of hardtack."

Georgiana gasped. "Ross! Whatever happened?"

"It's not blood." Payton's brother began peeling off his evening jacket. "It was Hudson. He threw a bowl of chocolate cream at me. I think he intended it for Raleigh, but I got in the way."

"Good God." Georgiana sprang from the bed, and went to help her husband out of his evening wear. Her face was tight with annoyance. "Really, Ross, you've got to speak to them. They're going to ruin Payton's chances of ever finding a suitable husband with their foolish antics. Someone has got to do something."

"I've already thought of that." Ross held out his arms while his wife's nimble—and sober—fingers flew over the studs that held his shirtfront closed. "I'm sending them both on the Far East run. By the time they get back, Payton'll be engaged."

*"What?"* Payton climbed down from the bed. "What are you talking about? You promised *I* could go on the next Far East run! First you take away my ship, and then you take away my run?"

Ross looked over his broad shoulder at her. "It was never your boat," he said calmly. "I can't think what on earth ever led you to believe it was. And as for the Far East run, you can't go. Georgiana says you've got to drop anchor in London until you find a husband."

Payton let out a stifled scream. "For the last time, *I don't* want *a husband*!"

"Payton, darling." Georgiana wrenched the stained shirt from her husband's enormous frame. "Don't shout so. We discussed this. You're going to stay in London with me and find a nice viscount to marry. Maybe a duke, if we're lucky."

"I don't want a duke!" Payton declared. "I want—I want—" She broke off, shocked at herself. Good Lord, what was happening to her? She seemed to be coming unglued at the seams. She had practically admitted—and in front of one of her brothers, no less—who it was she really wanted.

"Payton, I know what you want, darling." Georgiana spoke gently. "But you know you can't have it."

"*Why?*" Payton demanded.

"You *know* why, darling. It's why we're here."

"But *that's* what I don't understand." Payton shook her head until both her hair combs came out, this time. "Why is he marrying *her?*"

"Are you two," Ross asked curiously, "talkin' about Drake?"

"*Yes,*" said his wife, exasperated, at the same time that Payton shouted, "*No!*"

Ross let out a snort. "I thought," he said, "it was bloody well obvious why he's marryin' 'er."

"Ross," Georgiana said warningly.

"No," Payton said. "I'd like to hear this. Why is he marrying her, Ross? Is it because of her looks? Because of her sweet disposition? Because all she ever says is 'Yes, dear,' and 'No, dear,' and 'Anything you say, dear'? Well, I'd like to know what's so bleeding great about that! If you ask me, it's bloody damn well boring!"

" 'S'got nothing to do with all that," Ross said disgustedly. "I thought it was obvious. It's because—"

"Ross!" Georgiana cried, her fingers flying to her cheeks.

"—she's carryin' 'is brat."

Payton blinked. She did not think she could have heard her brother aright. She thought he'd said the word "brat." But surely that wasn't accurate. He must have said "rat."

But "rat" didn't make any sense. Why should Miss Whitby be carrying Drake's rat? Drake didn't even have a rat. He didn't especially like them, although he had never, like her brothers, killed any with the heel of his shoe, preferring, like Payton, to let the shipboard cats take care of the problem.

He must have said "brat."

And yet that didn't make any sense, either.

"*Brat?*" she echoed.

Georgiana flashed her husband an aggrieved look. "*Really,* Ross. I asked you not to—"

"Well, why shouldn't she know?" Ross, shirtless, shrugged. "She's nineteen, for pity's sake. And if you're going to be shovin' 'er out into the marriage market, then she'd better bloody well get an idea of how these things work. Besides, it's not like Payton's exactly unfamiliar with the facts of life. Mei-Ling taught 'er all about 'em. Didn't she, Pay?"

Payton was still too stunned to make any sort of reply, so Ross went on casually. "Well, you remember what happened at our wedding breakfast, don't you, Georgie? How Payton so impressed your sisters by tellin' 'em that if they took a sea sponge and cut it up and soaked it in some muckety-muck or another, and then stuck it up their—"

"*Ross!*" Georgiana had turned a delicate shade of umber.

Ross shrugged, then grinned down at his little sister. "Too bad you didn't impart that little bit of information to Miss Whitby, eh, Pay?"

"Ross. Really." Georgiana turned her concerned gaze on Payton. "Payton? Are you all right?"

Indignant at the chilly look his wife had shot him, Ross demanded, "What the hell did *I* do? *Drake's* the one who couldn't keep his trousers buttoned, not *me.*"

Suddenly, Payton felt extremely warm. It was midsummer, true, but up until then the house had seemed pleasantly cool, situated as it was on a hill, where a soft breeze continuously moved through the many open windows. Now, however, it was as if the wind had died altogether, and the walls of the manor house were closing in on her. She had a distinct feeling that some of the lobster she'd swallowed was creeping back up.

"What do you mean?" she managed to ask. "Are you saying . . . Are you saying Miss Whitby—"

She broke off, staring at her sister-in-law with wide eyes. Georgiana's face was filled with pity. She left her husband standing shirtless and confused, and went to put her arms around his sister.

"I'm so sorry, darling," she said, gathering Payton to her. "I made them promise not to talk about it in front of you. Really, it isn't at all the sort of thing a girl your age should know anything about. But I didn't realize then how much you—Well, I know now that it's better that you know. I'm sure it doesn't make it any easier for you, but now at least you know why—"

It was fortunate that Ross had been standing behind his wife, and so was in a position to observe his sister's face. Having traveled with her under every conceivable circumstance and condition, Ross knew Payton's expressions well, and the one that came over her face just then was one that was all too familiar to him. In a flash, he had the washbasin off its wooden stand and was holding it beneath Payton's head just as she let loose every bit of her supper, and a good deal of the champagne she'd had, as well.

*Chapter Six*

*M*uch later, sitting on the window seat in the cool darkness of the guest bedroom she'd been assigned, Payton rested her chin in her hands and gazed at the long shadows the moonlight had cast across the garden below.

She was mightily disgusted with herself about the way she'd reacted to the news her brother and sister-in-law had imparted. Really, she was nothing but a great baby, sometimes. It wasn't any wonder, really, that Ross had passed her over for command of the *Constant*. She hadn't exactly acted with great dignity in her disappointment over that. True, she hadn't thrown anything, or smashed any windows, as any one of her brothers might have. But she'd gone to her room and *sulked*. Sulkiness was a trait Payton despised almost as much as swooning. Mature women didn't sulk. They might get a little quiet, in order to express their disappointment, but they never *sulked*.

And they certainly didn't *vomit* when they learned a man they admired happened to have sired a baby with someone else.

She had just never suspected—it had never even entered her mind—that something like *that* was behind Drake's decision to marry Miss Whitby. Stupid of her, she knew. But honestly, she'd never have thought it of Drake. Not that she doubted his virility; she knew perfectly well where it was he and her brothers disappeared to every time they reached port after an extended voyage.

But it was one thing to frequent brothels. It was quite another to make love to a girl who was staying in the room down the hall from one's own.

And what about Miss Whitby? Payton had despised Becky Whitby pretty much from the first day she'd met her, for her sugary sweetness, her vapidity, her general air of a beached haddock.

But Miss Whitby wasn't sweet at all, let alone vapid. She had known what she wanted, and she had gone after it, in the most devious, underhanded way possible—at least to Payton's way of thinking.

It all made sense to her now. Why it hadn't occurred to her before, she couldn't imagine. She supposed because she really was such an ignoramus about these things. Oh, she knew all about the mechanics of lovemaking—one couldn't spend as much time in the company of sailors as she had and not come away with *that*—and, thanks to Mei-Ling, she knew a good deal about things like preventing pregnancy, as well.

But she had never actually been in a position to *try* any of those mechanics—let alone those preventive measures—herself. After all, up until last year, she'd been mistaken for a boy a good deal of the time. No one had exactly been making love to her.

But apparently, there'd been a good deal of lovemaking going on behind her back, and Payton had only herself to blame for it. Hadn't *she* been the one who'd invited Miss Whitby to stay with them in the first place? They'd all lived under the same roof for weeks, Payton in blissful ignorance of the fact that all sorts of illicit trysts and moonlit embraces were apparently taking place after the lights were put out. Payton, a sound sleeper, hadn't had the slightest idea any of this had been going on. Drake and her brothers could have been entertaining half a dozen whores a night, and she never would have been the wiser.

How could she even have suspected it? No one had ever snuck into *Payton*'s bedroom after dark. No one had ever so much as tried the knob!

And why would they? She was such a hideous, unfeminine thing. Who would want *her*?

When she'd wailed this a little earlier in the evening, as Georgiana had been bathing her face and trying to get her out of her corset, her sister-in-law had responded by cooing, "Oh, there, there. That isn't true. Lots of men will want you. Lots of them."

But that was the thing. Payton didn't want lots of men. She wanted one man. And he was marrying someone else upon the morrow.

So why did she still want him? How could she still want that no-good dockside dog?

Maybe because no matter what they said, no matter how much opportunity he might have had, no matter how much he and Becky Whitby might have been thrown together, Payton couldn't bring herself to believe that Captain Connor Drake was capable of doing something so low, so base, as what Ross had accused him of doing. Get a poor orphan girl with child? *Connor Drake?* Impossible! Even if that orphan girl *was* in her mid-twenties, at least, and had hair the color of a gaslight flame, and a figure that caused men passing on the street to walk into lampposts. Connor Drake was not the sort of man who'd allow himself to take advantage of any woman. He wouldn't do it. He *wouldn't*.

"He wouldn't *do* something like that," Payton had informed her sister-in-law, when she'd folded back the bedcovers and urged Payton to climb inside them. "It isn't true." She'd looked at her brother, who'd been dispatched to fetch her a soothing toddy, and had just returned with it. "Did he *tell* you it was true?"

Ross shook his head. He had not understood a single thing that had been going on since he'd come upstairs, and had decided long ago that he probably never would. "You mean did Drake tell me he'd gotten Becky Whitby full in the sail?

Well, no, not in so many words. But, dammit, Pay, why else would he be marrying the wench?"

But Payton ignored the question. "He didn't do it," she insisted. "I *know* he didn't do it."

"All right, Payton." Georgiana extinguished the flame on the candle by Payton's bed. "All right. You drink this, and then go to sleep. You've had enough excitement for one night. You'll feel better in the morning."

Even through the closed door after they left, Payton had been able to hear her eldest brother asking bewilderedly, "Whatever's gotten into Payton? I've never seen 'er get so fouled at the block before. Not even the time that damned pirate La Fond snuck on board and tried to slit Drake's throat—"

"It's your fault," was Georgiana's angry reply. "You and those brothers of yours. *They* encouraged her to drink more than was good for her, and *you* had to go and tell her about Drake. And after I *told* you, repeatedly, not to!"

"Hmph. I don't see why Payton should care a jot about Drake and Miss Whitby. Let him marry the little slut. He'll soon regret not waiting until he's found a perfect gem of a woman, like I did—"

There was the sound of a ladylike slap, followed by an urgent, *"Don't,"* from Georgiana. "Ross, I *mean* it. Put me down. I'm *extremely* put out with you right now—"

"Do we have to go back to that damned party now?" Ross wanted to know. "I can think of something I'd like considerably better—"

Their voices faded into whispers and soft laughter, and then Payton heard the door to their bedroom close. Despite their differences and near-constant bickering, she knew that her brother and sister-in-law really were deeply in love. And she knew with equal conviction that she and Drake could have been equally happy with one another, were it not for two things: the fact that he didn't seem to be aware of her existence...

And, of course, Miss Becky Whitby.

It was well after midnight, but despite the toddy, Payton couldn't sleep. She could hear the music from the dance below drifting up through the open casement windows, along with the occasional ripple of laughter, and crash of crystal (Hudson and Raleigh's handiwork, no doubt). She wondered how long it would be before the orchestra packed up and went home. The wedding ceremony was at ten o'clock—less than twelve hours away.

Less than twelve hours. Connor Drake had less than twelve hours of bachelorhood left.

And what was she doing? Just lying there. Sulking.

Well, and what was she *supposed* to do? Go downstairs and throw herself at him? Even if she didn't believe he'd got Becky Whitby with child, he was obviously marrying her for *some* reason. It was undoubtedly a good reason, or he wouldn't be doing it. Connor Drake wasn't the sort of man to do anything without considerable deliberation; that's what made him such a good navigator. Her brothers jokingly accused him of being too methodical, of plodding, even, but he'd never run a ship into a reef, even in areas where reefs lurked beneath the waves as densely as schools of silverfish. So for whatever reason he was marrying Becky Whitby, he knew what he was doing. Payton wouldn't—she couldn't—second-guess him.

Not like that scary grandmother of his. What was it she'd been spewing on the stairs? That she, Payton, was the only one who could stop him? Lady Bisson obviously didn't know anything about the baby—if there even *was* a baby, which Payton refused to believe. If there was a baby, Lady Bisson surely couldn't blame her grandson for doing the only proper thing. There were men, Payton knew quite well, who'd use a girl and cast her away, regardless of the consequences. Connor Drake wasn't like that. If he'd gotten Becky Whitby pregnant, then he'd marry her. He wouldn't try to pay her off, let alone abandon her. He was too much of a gentleman for that.

That he ought to have been too much of a gentleman to have impregnated her in the first place was the thought that had finally made Payton sit up, climb from her bed, and pad barefoot to the window. She needed, she felt, some fresh air.

Resting her chin in her hands, she gazed out across the moonlit garden. The scent of honeysuckle was heavy in the air. A vine of it was growing up a trellis just beneath her window. Becky Whitby, she thought to herself, was a lucky girl. She'd get to live in this house, and smell the heavenly scent of honeysuckle every spring. What lucky star, Payton wondered, had Becky been born under, that she got to marry Connor Drake, and live in this house, and smell that honeysuckle every spring?

And what unlucky star had shone the night Payton was born, making her destined to lose both her only dream *and* the man she loved in a single night?

Even worse, she'd lost the dream to the man!

It wasn't bloody fair.

How long Payton would have sat there feeling sorry for herself, she didn't know. Probably not long. Payton's spirits were naturally high, and it wasn't long before she'd begun drumming her fingers along with the dance tune the orchestra had begun to play. True, there was a very good chance that tomorrow she was going to have to watch the man she loved marry someone else. And true, it was beginning to look as if Georgiana was going to get her wish, and Payton would have to endure a full season in London.

But she couldn't help thinking that there was an equal possibility her prayers would be answered, and the odious Miss Whitby might die during the night. And if she died, there was a chance that Drake would be too heartbroken to put out to sea again. Payton could very generously offer to take the *Constant* off his hands. And maybe, in a year or two, when he'd had a chance to get over his grief—

It was while Payton was engaged in this delightful fantasy that she smelled, mixed in with the sweet scent of honeysuckle, the faint odor of cigar. And not just any cigar, but the kind Drake smoked of an evening, whenever they were wind-becalmed.

Jerked out of her pleasant dream, Payton grasped the windowsill with both hands and leaned out of it, peering into the blue darkness. It was then that Connor Drake stepped out from behind a pear tree and into the moonlight. He didn't notice her, of course, but she could see him quite clearly, a tall, broad-shouldered man, his hands in his trouser pockets, a thin wisp of smoke trailing behind him as he paced, his gaze on the clay pathway beneath his feet. He was clearly alone, and lost in his own thoughts—thoughts that didn't appear to be so very pleasant, if the slump in his shoulders was any indication of their nature.

But what did *he* have to be unhappy about? In the past two months, the man had got himself a title, a beautiful bride, and his own command. *Payton*'s command. While she had . . . what?

Nothing. Absolutely nothing.

The injustice of it all hit her like a wet sail in the face. How dare he? How *dare* he walk around, looking so mournful, when he had everything, *everything* a man could ever want?

It was without conscious thought that Payton stood up on the window seat, lifted the hem of her nightgown, and began backing down the trellis.

It wasn't such a shocking thing to do, really. The window wasn't that far from the ground. The mizzenpost, to and from which she climbed on a daily, sometimes hourly, basis, when they were at sea, was much higher—though it had to be admitted that, generally, she didn't climb it in a nightdress.

Still, she was well used to going about barefoot, and when she really thought about it, it wasn't Georgiana at all who deserved the nickname "little monkey." By rights, it was Payton who deserved it most.

The trellis was decorative, and had been attached to the house for the purpose of being climbed by plants, not humans. Still, Payton scrambled down it without incident, having to jump the last few feet when a large and thorny-looking rosebush loomed into view. She landed unscathed on the soft clay path, and unnoticed by the revelers beyond the open casement window just beside the rosebush. Straightening her nightdress, which was one of the high-necked, excessively virginal ones Georgiana had purchased for her upon learning with a shock that Payton had been in the habit of wearing exactly nothing to bed, she looked about, and spied Drake wandering, his back to her, toward a small stone fountain some half-dozen yards away.

He appeared to be deep in thought. Well, and why not? He was probably anticipating his happy, happy life as husband, father, and master of the *Constant*.

We'll just see about that, she said to herself, and strode toward him, her fists clenched.

In her anger, however, Payton forgot one very important thing. She forgot that Connor Drake was a man who'd been half his life at sea. And most of those years at sea had been spent on waters that were infested with every imaginable kind of piratical vermin. It did not pay to sneak up on a man who was used to keeping midnight watch on a quarterdeck in the South Seas. He would as soon run you through as throw you overboard.

Payton, thoroughly grounded by her rage, had forgotten all about that. But Drake, lost in his own thoughts, had not. When she reached up to tap him, not very gently, on the shoulder, he spun around fast and, a split second later, had Payton by the throat.

"Bloody hell, Drake," she managed to choke. "It's only *me*."

He released her instantly, at once furious and contrite.

"Payton." Even in the moonlight, his gaze was unnaturally bright on her. "What are you doing out here? Are you mad? Is everything all right? Did I hurt you?"

He certainly had. She felt as if his fingers had left a ring of fire around her neck. Massaging either side of her neck where he'd gripped her, she croaked, thinking she'd only gotten what she deserved for being so foolish, "Damn you. Who did you think I was, anyway? Did you think the Frenchman had snuck onto your grounds and was plotting to assassinate you?"

"You're *not* all right." He shook his head. "I'll send for a surgeon."

"Surgeon?" she echoed. There. That was a little better. She wondered if she'd ever be able to swallow again. She coughed experimentally. Everything *seemed* to be in working order. "I don't need a surgeon."

"Georgiana, then. Let me get Georgiana—"

She glared up at him, really annoyed now. She was certain she was going to be able to swallow again someday. It just might take a while. She'd have to, she realized, wear something with a high collar to the wedding, or his finger marks would show. She was sure they'd left bruises. "What good would waking Georgiana do?" she demanded.

He stared down at her, seemingly unable to explain his justification for waking her sister-in-law. But Payton had a pretty good idea why he wanted to get Georgiana. He'd read the rage in her eyes. His back was to the moon, and his face was lost in shadow, but she thought she knew what he was thinking. And that was: *Oh, no. Not this. Not now.*

He obviously had far more important things to deal with than the enraged little sister of his best friend. Well, too bad. He was going to have to deal with her, and right *now.*

"Payton, I'm sorry," he said.

She just stared at him, her hands on her hips. "I told you, it doesn't hurt."

"Not about your throat, though I'm sorry about that, too. I meant about the *Constant.* I know how much you wanted her—"

"You could," Payton said stiffly, "have said no."

"How, Payton? How could I have said no? They were all sitting there, looking so happy, your father, your brothers—"

"*I* wasn't looking happy, was I?"

"I was planning on telling them tomorrow," he said. "After the ceremony. I'll tell them I don't want it then, when there's no one about."

This surprised her, genuinely surprised her. Moved, she decided she might not have to hit him, after all. She realized she could no longer smell the honeysuckle. Instead, all of her senses were filled with him: the lingering scent of the cigar he'd thrown away as soon as he'd realized who she was; the way his rough fingers seemed to have burned her skin; the breadth of him encompassing her complete field of vision, so that unless she turned her head, she could see nothing but him. Behind him, the fountain burbled. When the wind blew gently, some of the spray struck her face.

"And will you tell them," she asked politely, "to give it to me, instead?"

She thought he smiled. "No. You're on your own there, Payton."

Her jaw dropped. She couldn't believe her ears. *"Why?"* she demanded. "If you're so willing to give her up, why won't you tell them to give her to me?"

"Because I happen to agree with them. You haven't any business commanding a sailing ship."

This hurt far more than his fingers, wrapped around her throat, had. "What do you mean? Drake, you know I could do it—"

"I haven't any doubt you could do it. What I doubt, and very highly, I might add, is that any crew would ever give you the chance. Payton, you're a young girl—"

"I'm almost nineteen, for pity's sake!"

His voice was hard, but filled with amusement, just the same. "Like I said. Do you really believe men—and I mean men like your brothers, Payton, men like me—are going to obey the orders of a nineteen-year-old girl?"

"If she's the one handing out their pay, then the answer is *yes.*"

"Payton." He shook his head, chuckling a little. "You startled me nearly to death, you know, sneaking up on me like that. Are you *sure* you're all right?"

She couldn't believe he was laughing. "Don't try to change the subject," she snarled. "This may be a great joke to you, Drake, but to me, it's my life. If I don't get my own ship, I'm going to have to marry a *duke.*"

This stopped the chuckling at once. "Which duke?" he wanted to know.

Payton, taken aback by his sudden vehemence, blinked a few times. "No duke in particular. Not yet. Georgiana just said I was going to have to marry a duke or a viscount or someone. She said I can't marry Matthew Hayford—"

"Do you want to marry Matthew Hayford?"

Again, he spoke with some urgency. Lord, what was his problem? He'd gone positively dense since she'd spoken to him last.

"No," Payton explained patiently. "Of course not. I'm just saying that even if I wanted to, I couldn't. I haven't any say over my own destiny. But Drake, listen, I have an idea." She did, too . . . a far better idea than her original one, of hitting him. Her sister-in-law had recently impressed upon her the somewhat radical idea that a woman could get her way more easily with fawning than with fists. She thought she'd give the theory a try. "Instead of handing the *Constant* back to my brothers," she suggested sweetly, "you could just sign her over to me."

Now it was his turn to shake his head. "Payton, I already told you, I agree with your brothers—"

"Oh!" She whirled away from him, her disappointment an almost physical pain. Georgiana was wrong. She ought to have hit him, when she'd had the chance.

Drake's deep voice cut through her indignation. "Payton, is that a *nightdress* you're wearing?"

She threw him an aggravated look over one shoulder. "Yes. What of it?"

"Did you come down the stairs dressed in just *that*?"

"What do you think I am, stupid? I didn't come down the stairs at all. I climbed out the window, of course."

Drake sat down with surprising heaviness on the side of the fountain. "Payton," he said, with what struck her as infinite weariness. "You'll kill yourself someday."

She suddenly felt a little tired herself. It was hard going, this constant fighting. It wore at her a little. She joined him on the side of the fountain, feeling the marble smooth and cool—and a little damp—against her buttocks, through the thin lawn of her gown.

"I rather doubt it," she said, referring to his earlier statement. "I'm a very good climber. You might recall all those coconuts I managed to knock down, that time we were all wrecked on Inagua."

She saw him nod in the moonlight. "Of course," he said tonelessly. "How could I have forgotten?"

Payton squinted at him. This was not the Drake she knew. He seemed older, somehow. Drake had always been old—a decade her senior—but he had never *seemed* old . . . at least, not this old. And while he had never joked and laughed quite as raucously as Payton's brothers, he had never before seemed *sad* to her. He did now.

What did *he* have to be sad about? Nothing. *She* was the one whose life had gone so off course.

"Well," she said. She noticed that one of his hands—his left one—lay on the marble between them. It was a large hand—hers could easily have disappeared into it—covered with skin hardened and browned from years of hauling rigging. There were, by her estimate, about eight inches of marble between her and that hand. Eight inches of marble, and the odious Miss Whitby, of course. She traced a circle through the light mist that coated those eight inches.

"What is it, Payton?" His voice was gentle. When she looked up, surprised, he smiled. "I know you. There's something else, isn't there?"

The question caught her off guard. Of course he *would* ask it. Of course he had to be wondering. While shipboard, it would never have come up—she'd often kept him company when he'd pulled midwatch, and he'd never once asked her whether there was something she wanted. But they weren't at sea now. They were in England. Civilized, boring England, where young ladies didn't sit up with gentlemen after midnight—or anytime, really, unchaperoned. Not if Georgiana had anything to say about it, anyway.

So what *did* she want from him? She had asked for the *Constant.* He had said no. So why didn't she go inside? It was damned uncomfortable, sitting there by that fountain. It was past midnight, and she was clad only in a nightdress, the spray from the fountain was dampening the back of it.

"You're cold," he said suddenly.

It was a statement of fact. And before she could deny it, he was taking off his evening coat, and wrapping it about her shoulders.

"Here," he said. "What were you thinking, coming out here without a robe? Or a shawl, at the very least. I bought you that silk shawl in Canton. Why aren't you wearing it? Did you lose it? You're never happy unless you've lost everything you own. I sometimes suspect you of having Bedouin blood in you."

Payton, overwhelmed by the warmth emanating from the satin lining of his coat, and the equally compelling warmth in his deep voice, heard herself asking, as if someone else were speaking for her, "*Why,* Drake?"

His cool, strong fingers were still working at the collar of his coat, turning it up around her ears. "Why what?" he asked lightly.

Oh, God, she thought. Shut up, Payton. *Shut up.* But to her horror, she kept right on talking. She asked, "Why are you marrying her?" Some of her short curls brushed his knuckles with feather-light softness as she shook her head. "I don't understand it. You always said—" Her voice broke. Oh, Lord, what was happening to her? Was she *crying,* for pity's sake? But she never cried! "You always said you'd marry *me.*"

She couldn't see him very well. He was just a dark blur, surrounded by a brighter blur of blue moonlight. But she could feel him. The hands that had been turning up his coat collar moved to cup her face. His palms were rough against the smooth skin of her cheeks.

Strangely enough, his voice, when he spoke, was as raw as hers. "I know."

"You *promised,*" she said, through gritted teeth.

"I know."

"Then *why*? *Why* are you marrying *her*?"

If, five minutes earlier, someone had told Payton she'd be sitting in Connor Drake's garden with his hands cradling her face, she'd have advised him or her to take a running dive off the foredeck. But there she was, with moonlight pooled all around her, and a fountain splashing gently beside her. Somewhere in the garden, a nightingale was trilling scales, seemingly for the pure joy of being able to do so. The smell of Drake, so familiar to her from that pillow he had lent her so long ago, rose up from his coat and enveloped her. His hands, despite their roughness, were warm against her cheeks. It seemed only natural to lean toward him, to try to snatch, if she could, just a little more of that intoxicating, masculine smell, that irresistible warmth . . .

No one could have been more surprised than Payton when Drake leaned forward, too, almost as if to meet her. Because that's exactly what happened. She had swayed toward him, just the slightest bit, the way seaweed swayed with the tide, and found, to her utter shock, that he had swayed forward, too. Suddenly, their faces were only an inch—maybe even less—apart.

And before she could draw away, embarrassed, Drake tightened his grip on her, not letting her go anywhere.

And then she had more of his heat than she'd gambled for, because his lips were on her mouth. Just like that.

And this was not one of those brotherly pecks that she'd grown used to receiving from Drake, on the rare occasions in the past when he'd kissed her. Those had usually fallen somewhere in the vicinity of the top of her head, or, occasionally, on the tip of her nose. This one was smack-dab on the lips. And it was immediately followed by another one. And then another. He hadn't, she could tell, shaved recently. The sharp ends of his whiskers burned the skin around her mouth. He tasted like whisky. He'd been drinking, and heavily, too. Funny how she hadn't noticed he was drunk . . .

But he had to be. Because why else would he be kissing

her like this? She had seen people kiss before—she'd caught Ross and Georgiana in the act once or twice before—and it hadn't been like *this*. *This* wasn't kissing. This was *devouring*. His lips had pried hers open, and his tongue had slipped into her mouth. Fortunately, Mei-Ling had once described this style of kissing to Payton, so while it was *surprising* that Drake was employing it—even more surprising that he was employing it on *her*—Payton at least had a fairly good idea what he was up to, and didn't even think about driving her fist into his solar plexus, which was what she certainly would have done, had it been any other man but Drake kissing her.

Or maybe not. Because what Drake was doing was excessively pleasurable. Payton hadn't quite believed Mei-Ling when she'd assured her that having the right man's tongue in one's mouth was enjoyable. But she believed her now. His kiss was doing all sorts of things to her—mostly making her want more of him inside of her than just his tongue. This was, of course, the purpose behind that kind of kissing, or so Mei-Ling had informed her.

Payton was pleased that she could now report back that yes, indeed, it worked, exactly the way it was supposed to. Because she had already lifted both her arms and wrapped them around Drake's neck, eager to bring him closer to her, and perfectly heedless of his evening coat, which fell, neglected, to the fountain's marble rim, one sleeve dangling into the water. Her fingers were in his soft, straight hair—fine as baby's hair, she realized, with surprise—straining him closer. Somehow, she'd gone from sitting to kneeling on the fountain's edge—possibly because his hands had left her face, and had gone to grip her waist instead, his fingers sinking through the thin material of her nightdress, half lifting her from her seat as he suddenly stood, and pulled her against him.

The explosive reaction of her body to that first meeting of starched white shirtfront and soft, lace-inset bodice was completely unexpected—at least by Payton. Suddenly, she was melded against what, if it hadn't been for the fact that she could feel heat emanating from it, she might have mistaken for the mainmast of a frigate, it was so straight, and so completely unmalleable.

This, she thought, is what Drake feels like, then. She wasn't particularly surprised. She had been tossed about enough by her brothers to know that men felt very different from women—and very different, even, from one another. Neither Ross nor Raleigh was as hard as Drake. Hudson might have been, but thankfully, she'd never been pressed up this close to Hudson, so she had no real information to make a comparison.

One of Drake's hands had dipped down to grip her bottom, a peculiarly singular sensation, since she didn't have anything on beneath her nightdress. She gasped, startled by the sudden heat from his hands . . . and in a place where she had never felt the heat of a human touch before.

But if he heard her swift intake of breath, he gave no sign. He'd brought his lips away from hers and was kissing her throat now, where his hands had gripped it so roughly not a half hour ago. Every so often, his mouth came dangerously close to the place where her lace collar, which she hadn't bothered to fasten, fell open. She hadn't realized before how it was that he'd known earlier that she was cold, but she sussed it out the minute her breasts came into contact with that wall of hard muscle behind Drake's shirt: her nipples were as stiff as if the temperature had plummeted to arctic weather conditions. Lord, how embarrassing!

But Drake didn't seem to mind—probably because she wasn't the only one suffering from such a malady. The hand on her buttock had tightened, bringing her pelvis into solid contact with the front of his trousers, where something very hard and a good deal larger than Payton had been expecting was pressing, seemingly eager to be set free.

Now *this*, she thought to herself, was simply too much to be believed. It was one thing to be kissed by Connor Drake—it was a wonderful, magical thing—but *this* went beyond the pale. All of that was for *her*? It wasn't possible. She was Payton Dixon, remember, who five minutes earlier Connor

Drake hadn't so much as ever even *looked* at twice, let alone harbored something like *that* for.

She was so bemused by this discovery that it seemed only natural to reach down and run curious fingers over it. She felt the need to reassure herself that what she'd felt was absolutely real. She certainly didn't *mean* anything by it, although, when she looked back on it, she supposed she could see why Drake reacted he way he did.

Still, it was a little humiliating when he abruptly thrust her from him, then backed away, as if she'd suddenly burst into flames.

# Chapter Seven

*U*nsupported, she practically toppled into the fountain. And she did bark her shin rather sharply against the marble rim as she tried to regain her balance.

"*Ow*," she said, through lips that felt raw from where his razor stubble had grazed them.

Her shin hurt, it was true, but what hurt more, what felt like someone had suddenly thrown a bucket of icy water at her, was the horrified look on Drake's face. He no longer stood with his back to the moon, and she could read his expression only too well. His chest rose and fell as rapidly as hers, but he was pale, as pale as the marble upon which they'd sat. And that was saying something, because ordinarily, Drake wore the darkest of tans.

Lifting her injured leg, Payton massaged the place where she'd barked her shinbone, eyeing Drake uncertainly. Evidently, she had committed a crime of some sort. Apparently, young ladies did not go around running their fingers over the fronts of gentlemen's trousers.

Well, bloody hell. She *knew* that. But he'd had *his* hand *all over* her backside. Had *that* been called for? And *she* wasn't the one who'd started the whole kissing thing in the first place.

That kissing thing. Why, oh, why had he stopped kissing her? It had been the most glorious moment of her whole entire life, and she'd had to go and ruin it by touching him *there*. What was wrong with her? Mei-Ling had told her once that there were some women who liked making love so much, they'd do it every chance they got. She'd never had reason before to suspect she was one of those women, but it seemed all too apparent now. That was the only explanation for what she'd done.

Damn. That explained *a lot*.

Seeing that Drake was still staring down at her—though from a safe distance of about six feet away—Payton made a very unladylike face and said, "I suppose you're going to feel obligated to tell Ross about this. Well, I would thank you very kindly if you'd keep it to yourself. It's embarrassing enough as it is without me having to endure a lecture about it from *him*."

Drake only stared at her some more. He was actually breathing quite a bit harder than she was. His broad shoulders were practically heaving. "Payton," was all he managed to gasp out before she continued.

"Oh, I know, you probably think I'm in need of proper guidance and all of that, but I assure you, nothing like this will ever happen again." The pain in her shin was lessening. She put her foot down and continued. "Frankly, you're as much to blame as I am. You started it. I don't suppose Ross would feel much like being partners with you if he knew you were going around, putting your tongue in his sister's mouth."

She knew this was perfectly untrue, that if she told her brothers what Drake had done, they'd either refuse to believe her, or find a way to blame *her* for it, most likely by saying it was what she deserved for climbing out windows after midnight in her nightdress.

But there was no reason *Drake* had to know that.

"What's the matter with you, anyway?" she demanded, lifting a hand to touch her mouth, which was still tingling from where he'd ravaged it. "Maybe you've forgotten, but you're supposed to be getting married in the morning."

"I know it." He turned his back on her suddenly, and strode away.

For a second she thought she'd gone too far, that in her effort to cover up her own embarrassment over what had occurred—and disappointment that it had stopped—she'd driven him away completely. She was hanging her head, feeling tears—which she'd managed to hold at bay up until then with her feigned indignation—fill her eyelids, when he came striding back. Apparently, he was pacing, as he had a tendency to do when he was disturbed about something, and not, as she'd originally thought, walking away.

"Don't you think I know that?" he demanded, furiously enough to startle her. Lifting a hand, he dragged it through his overlong hair, making the ends stand up a bit. "Don't you think that's exactly what—You've got to forgive me, Payton."

This wasn't quite what she'd been expecting him to say. She'd expected him to yell at her. She'd expected him to hurl accusations at her. She'd been ready for them. She was already bristling with defensiveness.

But then he'd had to go and ask her forgiveness. Not just ask her forgiveness, but ask it in that voice, filled with self-loathing, with that look on his face . . . Lord, if she hadn't felt like crying before, she felt like it now.

"What I did," he went on, in that same tone, "was unpardonable."

He'd come up to her now. She wouldn't look him in the face, because she knew if she did, and saw that expression he wore, she'd never be able to keep from weeping. Instead, she kept her chin down, and studied the tops of his shoes. They were black shoes, very shiny and expensive-looking. And why not? He was a rich man now.

"Payton. Look at me."

She shook her head mutely. He went on, anyway.

"That should never have happened." His voice was hard now. He was angry, really angry. "It was my fault entirely. I can only ask your forgiveness, and assure you that it will never, ever happen again . . ."

That brought her head up. She looked up at him, tears glistening in the corners of her eyes.

"Why not?" she asked, her voice catching, although she thought she already knew the answer. He was never going to kiss her again because she was such a wicked, wanton thing. Men didn't like girls who were forward, girls who chased after them or went around thrusting their hands at the front of their trousers. She'd seen the look on Drake's face when she'd touched him there. That had not been a particularly happy look. He'd been surprised, maybe, and something else she couldn't identify. But not happy.

"You know why not, Payton," he said, roughly. "Because tomorrow morning I'm getting married, and then . . . then I'm going away."

"But you'll be back," Payton said. She raised a wrist and wiped at the tears that had escaped—damn it!—down her cheeks. "You'll be back, and what's to stop this from happening again? I really think it—" She *had* to say it. "I really think it might just be better if you didn't marry Miss Whitby, after all."

"I've *got* to marry her, Payton. And this won't happen again, because we won't be seeing one another again, you and I."

She blinked at him bewilderedly. "We won't? Why not?"

"I told you." He spoke with infinite gentleness. "Because I'm going away. I'll be operating the Dixon and Sons office in Nassau. Becky and I will be living in New Providence—"

"New Providence?" A spark flickered deep inside her, making her forget all about her tears. "You're . . . you're upping anchor and moving to New Providence?"

"Yes, Payton. I thought you knew that."

"You're marrying that woman." Her fingers, as if of their own accord, curled into fists at her sides. His words had fanned the spark into a very healthy flame. "You kissed me like that, knowing all along that you're marrying that woman, and moving to New Providence?"

Drake looked a little alarmed now. He even stepped backward a pace. "Payton—"

"After kissing me like that, you're marrying Miss Whitby and *moving to New Providence*?"

Payton couldn't remember ever having felt quite so angry. Maybe the time she'd seen those men in port in Shanghai, kicking that dog. Maybe then.

Certainly like then, she was completely unable to control her temper. Her retaliation, when it came, was every bit as quick as it had been against those men back in China. Pulling back her right fist, she sent it plummeting, with strength honed from years of hauling rigging right alongside her brothers and their crews, into Drake's shirtfront, just above the waistband of his trousers, exactly where Raleigh had instructed her was the ideal place to punch a man, as it wreaked havoc with his innards without unduly harming the knuckles of the puncher.

"*That's* what I think about you," she informed him, and was pleased to see that the blow had taken him completely unawares. He let out an *oof* and doubled over. He had, in fact, to reach for the rim of the fountain to keep from falling to his knees. "You," Payton continued, "New Providence, the *Constant* and bloody Miss Whitby!"

Without another word, Payton turned tail and stalked back toward the house.

# Chapter Eight

She was still within calling distance when Drake straightened. After inhaling a few gulps of the fresh morning air, he even felt capable of speech again.

Still, he did not call to her. What would have been the point? It was bad enough that he'd allowed himself to lose control once. He could not risk it happening again.

He watched her, a ghostly figure in her flowing white nightdress, as she made her way not back toward the window from which she'd climbed down, nor toward the front of the house, but around the back, where the servants' entrance lay. For someone who'd only arrived at the house that afternoon, she already had a solid grasp of its layout.

Well, that was Payton. She was as good a navigator as any of the Dixons, with an unerring sense of direction. She could find her way through the thickest fog, the blackest night. She would certainly find her way safely to her bed. It had been foolish, really, of him to have moved Gainsforth and Raybourne to rooms at the opposite end of the house from Payton's. She was a young lady who could certainly take care of herself.

His newly tender gut was testament to that.

But, he thought, as he lowered himself to the rim of that same fountain upon which, just moments before, he'd so forgotten himself, he'd more than deserved the blow. What had he been *thinking*? What had come over him? Never in his life had he done something so rash, so wholly without scruple, as kissing Payton Dixon like that. It defied logic. He'd known this girl for almost the whole of her life. He'd watched her grow from a pantalooned toddler to pigtailed adolescent. And now, simply because someone had put her in a corset, he was lusting after her as if she were a dockside doxy and he was a sailor who'd been too long from port.

Which was certainly not the case. He had plenty of women. More of them, truth be told, than he knew what to do with. Hell, he was marrying one of them upon the morrow. If he wanted to, he could have had Becky Whitby nine different ways that very night . . .

But, no. He'd had to go and molest his best friends' little sister. Bravo, Drake. What did he intend to do for an encore? Kill their father, perhaps?

He didn't know what was wrong with him. It seemed as if all night he'd felt a fever coming on. It had started, as near as he could tell, the moment Payton Dixon had appeared in that white satin thing. Her father ought to have been horsewhipped for allowing her to wear it; Ross ought to have been incarcerated for agreeing to pay for it. There wasn't enough material in that dress to cover a *cat* decently, let alone a living, breathing girl.

But wear it she did. And attracted the attention of every single male guest in the household—at least those to whom she was not related by blood. He'd seen the expressions on the faces of his men, men who the summer before hadn't cast Payton Dixon so much as a second glance when she'd strode by in trousers and a broadcloth shirt. But suddenly, the Honorable Miss Payton Dixon was very interesting, indeed.

What choice had he had, really? As host, it was his duty to protect his guests. He'd ordered McDermott to rearrange the bedroom assignments, and had purposely placed her between her brothers at the dinner table. But it hadn't done any good. All through dinner, every man in the place had stared at her, waiting, Drake was quite certain, for a chance to get her alone. He'd left the table that first time she'd excused herself, as soon as he was able, in order to assure himself she'd reached her room unmolested. Thank God her brother had made that toast, or she might have spent all night on the dance floor. She might *still* be in there, dancing with Matthew Hayford, or some other young buck.

And it was too bad, he supposed bitterly, that she wasn't. Otherwise, what had happened just now might never have occurred. Lord, how he wished what had happened just now had never occurred . . . He wished the whole *day* had never occurred.

Who, he wondered furiously, had put a corset on Payton Dixon? That sister-in-law of hers, no doubt. If it hadn't been for her, he—and every other man at Daring Park that weekend—might never have noticed that the Honorable Miss Payton Dixon had grown into a woman . . . and not just any woman, either, but the most damnably beautiful woman he'd seen in a good long while . . . and that included those beauties they'd encountered in Tahiti.

And yet *not* beautiful, because there was something about Payton Dixon's looks that defied conventional beauty. Certainly by Western standards, Becky Whitby was the more strictly beautiful of the two, with her graceful height, alabaster skin, and long auburn hair. Payton's attractiveness lay in the way she held herself, the confidence with which she stepped, the graceful strength in her every movement. It was in her inability to conceal what she was feeling, the way her emotions were right there, in those enormous hazel eyes, for anyone to see. It was in the blunt frankness, the intolerance for artifice, with which she responded to everyone, from the lowliest housemaid to his own admittedly intimidating grandmother. Payton Dixon might be intimidated, but she would never be bullied.

He wished he could say the same of his future wife.

Still, there were men who admired women like Becky Whitby. Lord, what was he thinking? He *himself* had admired

Becky Whitby immensely, and not just because of her beauty. There was something undeniably appealing about a beautiful woman who was so helpless, so wholly incapable of taking care of herself, so in need of the supportive arm of a man upon which to lean. Drake, like Hudson and Raleigh Dixon, had been powerfully drawn to Becky Whitby. She had aroused in him a desire to protect, to shield her from the dangers and hardships in the world, the way one might wish to shield a child.

But that had been before the start of this infernal fever. The fever had changed everything. Now he couldn't help wondering if childlike helplessness was really what he wanted from a wife. Did he actually want to spend the rest of his life with someone he was going to have to coddle and protect? Wouldn't it be infinitely preferable to share his life with someone who could go through it with him as an equal partner? A lover, yes, but also a friend, to whom he, in turn, could go to in times of need for support and advice.

This was not, he knew, the sort of relationship most married men had with their wives. It was not the sort of relationship he had ever suspected might exist . . . until recently. Most men married anticipating that they would have to support their wives, both financially as well as emotionally, for the rest of their married lives. Marriage was recognized by neither the common populace nor the law as a partnership between two equals. Nor, Drake supposed, ought it to be, under most circumstances.

But those circumstances had never before included a woman like Payton Dixon.

It was a fever. He didn't know what else it could be. He'd contracted any number of diseases in his journeyings around the globe, fevers and agues that had very nearly killed him more than once. But this . . . this wasn't like any of those. It was a slow-burning fever that seemed to get hotter every time Payton Dixon drifted into his line of vision. It defied explanation. No physician in the world could diagnose its exact nature, let alone prescribe a cure. He could only suffer . . .

And suffer some more. In silence. Impotent silence.

Because he'd made his bed. Or rather, his bed had been made for him. And all he could do now was lie in it.

But it wasn't that simple. When was it ever? Because instead of simply lying down, like the dead man he was—the dead man he *had* to be, to her—he'd gone and kissed her.

He couldn't just have walked away. He couldn't just have left her there. Oh, no. Not Captain Connor Drake, baronet and newly appointed full partner of Dixon and Sons Shipping. No, he'd had to go and kiss her. It was no use making excuses, either, like that the moonlight had gone to his head, or that she'd been crying—*Payton Dixon,* whom he'd never seen cry. Well, except for once, when she'd been stung by that Portuguese man-of-war. No, he'd known full well what he'd been doing. Just as he'd known full well that his was the first mouth to ever touch hers.

Who did he think he was fooling? He'd *relished* the knowledge, just as he'd relished her reaction, which he'd known, as he'd never known with any other woman, was purely instinctual . . . How could it have been anything but? Payton Dixon was too ingenuous to dissemble.

It wasn't until she'd laid her hand so boldly over his erection that he'd come to his senses. Her interest in *that* had been as genuine as the ardor with which she'd responded to his kiss. Which was probably why he'd kissed her in the first place. Somewhere, deep down inside, he'd had to prove to himself that he was wrong, that he wasn't making a mistake marrying Becky Whitby. He'd had to prove that as appealing as Payton Dixon might be in her scanty ballgown and upswept hair, she was still just a child, still not fully a woman.

Well, he'd proved it, all right. Proved he was completely wrong, that she was every inch of her a woman, a woman like no other he'd ever encountered in his life. A woman who had a very good idea of what she wanted, and had made it perfectly clear that what she wanted was him.

Well. It served him right. It served him right that all these years, the woman of his dreams had been right there, right there at his side, and he hadn't noticed, not until it was too late.

Far too late.

He buried his head in his hands.

"Connor?"

The soft, lilting voice sent him straightening up again, as quickly as if someone had prodded him in the back with a knife point. He saw her coming toward him along the garden path. He stood up, slipping his hands in his pockets to hide the evidence of his arousal that still hadn't completely waned.

"Becky," he said pleasantly. "Is everything all right?"

"I was about to ask you the same thing." Becky Whitby pushed a straying curl of auburn hair from her forehead. Her skin glowed in the moonlight. Her step was as light as the spray of water from the fountain behind him. "Everyone is wondering where you'd run off to. You keep disappearing."

"I'm sorry." God, it seemed like all he ever did these days was apologize. "I needed some air."

Becky raised a delicate eyebrow. "Did you stain your coat?"

He stared at her. "I beg your pardon?"

She pointed behind him. "Your coat. It's soaking, you know."

He looked, and saw that the coat he'd wrapped about Payton's shoulders had fallen half in, half out of the water. He retrieved it. "Stupid of me," he said. "I hadn't noticed."

"No." Becky smiled at him. Her smile was gentle. "I can see that. Connor . . ."

"Yes?"

"You needn't go through with it, you know." Now the smile was not only gentle, but brave. "I want you to know that. If you want out of it, there's still time. I could go away . . ."

He glared at her. "And live on what? You won't take my money. How would you survive?"

The smile wavered, just a little. Still, she thrust out her chin and said, "I'd get by. I always have."

For one moment—for one wild, miraculous moment—he let his imagination roam unchecked, and actually entertained the notion of calling off the wedding. What did he have to lose? Nothing. Nothing at all. His grandmother had made it clear that she'd be more than willing to weather the social stigma such an action would necessarily incur. And he'd be a free man. Free to do what he chose, go where he chose . . . court whom he chose.

But no. If he called off the wedding, he'd be considered worse than a cad, regardless of the truth behind the reasons why. No one, not even a family as eccentric and unconventional as the Dixons, could afford to be seen with him, let alone keep him in their employ, not if they wanted to continue beating out their chief rival, Tyler and Tyler Shipping, for those valuable commercial accounts.

And, more importantly, Ross Dixon would never allow his little sister to be seen in the company of a man who'd left a bride at the altar. They were best friends, it was true, but even friendship had its limits.

No, as far as Payton Dixon was concerned, Drake was a dead man, whether he married Becky Whitby tomorrow morning or not.

"No," he said, as politely as if he were declining a second helping at the table. "That's all right. I think we'd better go through with it, just the same."

There was no way he could miss the relief that crept into her voice, the flush that seeped into her cheeks, as she responded, "Oh, I'm so glad. I've had such ideas on how we might decorate this old place. You know, bring it up to date. It's dreadfully fusty, you know, Connor."

He didn't have the heart to tell her that after tomorrow, she'd never see Daring Park, fusty or not, again. He'd let that wait until after the wedding. After all, it wouldn't do to have her backing out of it, and going about, telling tales.

"Of course," he said. "Now, hadn't you better get back inside? It's bad luck, I understand, for the groom to see the bride before the wedding, and it's past midnight, you know."

Becky's eyes widened. "Oh," she cried. "You're right! Good night, then, darling."

"Good night."

She lifted her skirts and darted back the way she came, a light and graceful figure in the half-darkness. Drake stood where he was, and watched until she'd disappeared into the house. Only then did he exhale, and lift his face to the night sky.

How he wished, as he'd done a hundred times already that day, that they had, none of them, ever met Becky Whitby. How he wished he were standing at the wheel of the *Constant*, the rolling deck beneath his feet, the cool winds of the South Seas on his face.

She'd forget him, he knew. Oh, not for a while. Women did not, he thought, ever forget their first kiss. But there'd be other kisses. No one who looked at Payton Dixon could be insensible to that. By next month, perhaps, she'll have forgotten, in the rush of new beaus she was bound to attract.

It would take a century for him to forget her. If he ever *could* forget a woman who could kiss like that.

And who could deliver such a purposeful right hook.

It might not, Drake decided, be such a bad idea to have a drink.

He went to find his comfort in a bottle, since he knew he'd find it nowhere else.

# Chapter Nine

$\mathscr{P}$ayton cracked open an eye and saw that the grey light of morning was seeping in through the window casement. She'd forgotten to draw the curtains the night before and had neglected to close the window, and now tendrils of thick morning fog crept into her room, making everything—most especially her bedsheets—a little damp.

Payton yanked on those bedsheets, and, with a groan, brought them up over her head. It was morning. And not just any morning, either. The morning of Drake's wedding.

And the morning after she'd made such a perfect ass of herself.

Huddled in a cocoon of sheets, Payton squeezed her eyes shut, trying to force herself back to sleep. She hadn't slept at all well. She'd spent half the night, it seemed, trying to find a comfortable place to lay her head. She had pounded the soft pillows into every imaginable position, and it hadn't done a bit of good. She had even dragged half her bed clothes down to the floor, and tried sleeping there, for a change. After all, she'd slept well enough on board the hard deck of many a ship on nights it had been too hot to sleep in the foc'sle.

But it didn't do any good. It wasn't that the bed was uncomfortable, or the floor any more or less so. It was because her mind was too full to sleep. Her mind too full, and her heart too heavy.

It hadn't been exactly edifying, finding out that she was such a fool. Certainly, it was something she'd always suspected, but to have it thrust in her face as dramatically as it had been the night before . . . well, it was enough to keep her awake for a few solid hours, wishing there was some way she could undo the damage. If only, she kept thinking, she could go back to that moment right before she'd climbed down from the window. Knowing what she did now, she'd never have left her room. Granted, that meant she'd never have been kissed by Connor Drake. But at this particular point, she no longer cared about that.

Oh, it had been thrilling—the most glorious moment in her life. She would never forget it, not until she was cold and dead in her grave. And that was the problem. At least before, she hadn't known what she was missing. Now she knew, and it was going to be *that* much harder to sit in that church pew and keep her mouth shut while she watched him marry somebody else.

All through the long hours of the night a single question had reverberated through her head: *Why?*

It was the same question she'd asked Drake, and she hadn't gotten an answer. *Why* was he marrying Becky Whitby? Because he had to, he'd said. Which wasn't an answer. It wasn't an answer at all. Of course he *had* to. Only a cad would abandon his bride this close to the altar. But that didn't explain why he'd asked her to marry him in the first place.

It certainly wasn't because he was in love with Miss Whitby. Payton had known that for certain, the moment he'd kissed her. Not that she fancied he was in love with *her*. She was fairly certain that before last night, he'd never even thought of her in *that* way. She'd only been the amusing little sister of his three best friends.

But now, finally, maybe he'd noticed she was no longer a child. Too bloody late.

She refused to believe he was marrying Becky Whitby be-

cause he'd gotten her with child. Payton had lain awake the
other half of the night—the half when she hadn't been kicking
herself for being such a fool—trying to remember those weeks
when they'd all lived together at the town house, and she
couldn't pick out a single moment when Drake had shown any
preference, marked or otherwise, for Becky Whitby. There
hadn't been any looks exchanged over the breakfast table. She
had never caught them whispering together. If the two of them
had ever been intimate, then they were the most superb actors
in the world. And while she wasn't sure about Miss Whitby,
she was quite certain Drake was no dramatist. If he were, what
had happened in the garden would certainly have had quite a
different outcome.

What had happened in the garden, she'd decided, around
four o'clock in the morning, had been the result of emotions
rubbed raw, of instincts taking over where reason normally
ruled. Drake might have been drunk—most certainly he'd
been *a little* drunk, at least—or he might simply have been
carried away by the moonlight and the nightingale. In any
case, he hadn't been acting rationally, and neither, needless to
say, had she.

But that didn't mean that there hadn't been emotion there.
Maybe not love, on his part. But *something*. There was no
denying they were friends, *good* friends of long standing,
who'd not only saved one another's lives but, more importantly, had been there for one another when the situation
hadn't exactly been life-threatening: those becalmed seas,
when not a hint of wind blew for days at a time, could drive
anyone to madness, but they had weathered plenty of those,
with humor and imagination.

Wasn't *that* what love was all about? Not only weathering
the storms, but also making it through those long periods of
stagnation without going mad, or growing to despise one another?

And it wasn't as if they didn't share a mutual attraction to
one another—she knew for absolute certain he'd been at-

tracted to her. She'd felt the evidence of that attraction, long and firm, against her hand.

So if there was friendship—true friendship—and attraction, how far, really, were they from love?

Not that it mattered. Because today he was marrying Miss Whitby, and leaving for New Providence. She might see him again, someday. Maybe he would come back to England for *her* wedding. Under the covers, Payton let out a bitter little laugh. Her wedding. What a joke. She was never going to be a bride. If she couldn't have Drake, she didn't want anyone. Period.

Rolling over, Payton lowered the sheets enough so that she could squint at the clock on the mantel. Eight o'clock. She pulled the covers back over her head with a groan. Lord. Less than two hours until they'd have to leave for the village church.

Payton was up, bathed, and dressed before the clock on her mantel chimed nine. The maid who'd brought her bathwater had chipperly informed her that coffee was being served downstairs, and if it would please the young lady, she could bring her a cup. As it happened, it pleased the young lady very much. Payton was not the least bit anxious to run into the master of the house, much less his bride-to-be. She'd happened to notice, as she was bathing, the band of pink silk ribbon she'd tied round her wrist the night before. It still hung there, a reminder of her foolishness. She removed it—but only to retie it around her ankle, where no one but her maid would see it. She had a feeling she was going to need reminding, throughout the day, just who, precisely, Connor Drake belonged to.

Because it sure as hell wasn't her.

But Payton, she soon learned, wasn't the only Dixon who didn't make it down for morning coffee. A loud thump on her door, followed by the portal opening before she'd had a chance to answer, revealed a half-dressed Hudson, blinking painfully in the morning light.

"Pay," he complained, in a voice that was gravelly with

sleep. "Do up my cravat for me, *please*. I don't know what's wrong, but my fingers are swelled up like sausages. I can barely move 'em."

Payton lifted one of her brother's massive paws and examined it critically. "Who'd you hit?" she asked.

"I didn't hit anyone." Hudson screwed up his ill-shaven face. "Leastways, I don't *remember* hitting anyone."

"Well, this bruise didn't get there by itself." Payton flung away the damaged limb. "What time did you and Raleigh bed down last night, anyway?"

Hudson blinked. "Bed?" he asked. "What's that?" And Payton got a whiff of what it was he'd been up all night doing.

"Lord, Hud," she said, fanning his breath away. "What did you do? Swallow a distillery?"

From the doorway came another thump, and then Raleigh came in. Unlike his elder brother, he was fully dressed. He looked, however, like hell. Payton exercised no restraint in telling him so, but Raleigh took the abuse with uncharacteristic docility. In fact, he walked straight past her, pulled back the bedclothes the maid had neatly tucked in place, and climbed into Payton's bed, boots and all. When she asked him what in the hell he thought he was doing, Raleigh only groaned from beneath a pile of pillows he'd pulled over his head. "*Must* you talk so loud?"

"Get out from under there," Payton snapped. "We've got to be at the church in an hour."

"It's not fair. Your bed's much nicer than my bed." Raleigh sniffed indignantly. "My bed was hard as rock."

"It *was* a rock, you great arse." Hudson was still having trouble holding his eyelids all the way apart. "You fell asleep on the carriage drive."

"And woke up bloody soaked." Raleigh was invisible beneath the pillows and sheet . . . all except for the tips of his boots, which stuck out over the end of the bed. "Damned dew. I *hate* it. And those bleeding awful birds, with their infernal singing. My head's *pounding* because of that blasted tweet-tweet-tweeting. Started up at two, and only got louder. Lord,

I can't *wait* until we're at sea again. Life in port is nothing but torture."

A third fist pounded on the door. This time, it was not a Dixon who peered round the jamb at her, but the barely recognizable face of the groom. He stood bare-chested in the hallway, supporting himself with one hand braced against the wall. Clenched in his other hand was his shirt, waistcoat, and jacket, the sleeves of which dragged along the floor behind him. The lower half of his face was dark with unshaved whiskers. His eyes appeared a brighter shade of blue than usual, since they peered out from purple rings of sleeplessness.

Those eyes drew Payton's gaze and held it. If she'd expected a last-minute appeal to run away with him, she was to be sadly disappointed. Instead, he parted painfully dry lips and croaked, *"Help."*

Payton inhaled, prepared to start screaming. No. This was just too much. As if it wasn't bad enough that she'd had to sit there and watch her brother hand this man her ship; as if it wasn't enough she was going to have to sit there and watch him marry someone else in an hour: she had to help him *dress*, as well?

She wouldn't.

She *couldn't*.

Behind her, Hudson started to chuckle.

"Hoo," he laughed. "Hoo-ha! Come have a look at Drake, Ral. He looks like something that's been dredged up from the bottom of the Thames."

"Is that Drake?" Raleigh flung back the covers and sat up. "Can he talk that bloody cook of his into giving us some food? She says we've got to wait to have breakfast till after the wedding. But if I don't get something into my gut now, I'll be a dead man by the time this bleeding wedding's over."

Payton, who'd been barring Drake's way into her room by keeping a hand planted on either side of the door, searched his face. If she'd thought it etched with pain yesterday, when she'd seen it at the dinner table, that was nothing compared to today. The grooves running from the down-turned corners of his mouth to his nostrils looked deep enough to dive into. And those purple smudges under his eyes were the results of sleeplessness, not Hudson's swollen fingers.

Still, Hudson's assertion that his old friend looked like something that had been dredged up from the bottom of the Thames was an opinion with which Payton couldn't agree. Even suffering from a hangover, Drake was still far too good-looking for Payton's ease of mind. A *hundred* nights without sleep would not have been enough to wither those melon-sized biceps, or soften that rock-hard belly, down which thick blond hair snaked, disappearing into the waistband of his trousers. He could have drunk an entire case of whisky, and his skin would still glow healthily bronze, his teeth still flash white as ivory.

It wasn't fair. It wasn't fair that he should look this good. Because how was she supposed to despise him when just looking at him, standing there in the dim morning light, with his soft blond hair hanging wetly down the back of his neck, made her knees go weak?

"Well," she said, as ungraciously as possible. "I suppose you might as well come in, too. Everybody else seems to feel I'm his own personal valet. Why should *you* be any different?"

She stepped aside, and Drake came in, lifting the garments he held. "I can't get any of these on," he said bewilderedly. "My fingers don't seem to work."

Hudson looked positively delighted that someone was suffering from a malady similar to his.

"I've got the same problem! Can't make a fist." He thrust his hands beneath Drake's nose. "See? Weak as a kitten. Payton says it's from hitting someone, but I can't remember hitting anyone. Do you remember me hitting anyone?"

"Can't say that I do, old man." Drake looked everywhere but at Payton. "I drank a little too much myself, last night."

She glared at him. If he was thinking of using alcohol as the excuse for what had passed between them in the garden, he needed to think again.

"I think we *all* went a little out of our heads last night," she said firmly. "Some of us more than others."

On the bed, Raleigh, who'd fallen back against the pillows, moaned. "All except Ross," he said bitterly. "I saw Ross this morning, and he was fit as can be. Went to bed early, Ross did. I wonder why." He chuckled nastily, then groaned again. "You mustn't ever get married again, Drake. Another night like this past one will kill me."

Going to the tray the maid had brought up for her, Payton poured a cup of coffee for Drake, mixing in a good deal of sugar and milk. Strong sweet drinks were the shipboard prescriptive for men who'd been narrowly missed by one of Captain La Fond's cannonballs, and that was exactly the expression Drake wore just then, a sort of stunned disbelief that he had suffered through what he had, and lived.

"Here," she said, not at all politely, as she thrust the cup at him. "Drink this."

He brought the cup obediently to his lips, then made a face, and looked around frantically for a place to spit out what was in his mouth.

Payton said, "Swallow," in a commanding voice. He did so, but then made a gagging noise.

"Christ, Payton," he exclaimed. "What *was* that?"

"Exactly what you need," she replied. "Drink the whole cup."

"No . . ." He was almost whimpering. "Please."

"Drink it," she said firmly. "Or I'll have Hudson hold your nose, and we'll force it down your bleeding throat."

Hudson feigned alarm. "Don't do it, Drake," he cried. "It's probably poisoned. She hasn't gotten over losing the *Constant . . .*"

Payton narrowed her eyes at her brother. "While the idea is certainly tempting," she said, "I'm only trying to keep him from passing out. Do *you* want to be the one who has to carry him down the aisle?"

Hudson cleared his throat. "Drink the bloody stuff, Drake."

Drake peered despairingly into the depths of the coffee cup she'd handed him. He took a deep, patient breath, then downed the whole of its contents, his broad shoulders shuddering in disgust. Payton averted her gaze. The skin stretched over his shoulders was sun-kissed and would doubtless feel, if she happened to run her hands over them—which, of course, she never would—like silk. Silk laid over iron.

Lord, why didn't someone just shoot her, and put her out of her misery?

When he finally lowered the cup, gagging, Payton said, "Good," and took it away. He didn't look much the better for it, but she supposed it must have done him *some* good, since when she instructed him to hold his arms out, he was able to do so. Before, it had appeared to take him considerable effort even to lift them.

Payton took hold of one of his limp hands and stuffed it through a sleeve of the shirt he held. "I sincerely hope that when I get married," she muttered, "*my* husband won't be so reluctant to enter the union that he feels it necessary to drink himself into a stupor the night before."

"Well, of course he will, Pay," Hudson said, mildly astonished. "No man *wants* to get married."

"Really?" She spoke between gritted teeth. "And so Ross married Georgiana because . . . ?"

"Same reason Drake's marryin' Miss Whitby," Raleigh informed her, from the bed.

This caused a good deal of chortling on the parts of both her brothers. Drake, Payton noticed, did not laugh, or even crack a smile. She was in a position to know, since she was standing in front of him, her fingers flying over the buttons of his shirt. It was important to her that she finish dressing him as quickly as possible, since his proximity was having a disturbing effect on her. It had caused all of the hair on her arms—fortunately hidden from his sight by the balloon sleeves of her blue and white morning dress—to stand on end. And that was not all. She was now quite certain the reason her nipples had gone so hard the night before had not been because of the cold at all, but because of something *he* had done to them. She couldn't tell *how* he'd done it, but it was happening again. The man had to be some kind of witch doctor. Either that, or the mere sight of his partly clad body was enough to send her into a shocking state of arousal.

It wasn't fair. He was using weapons on her against which she hadn't the slightest defense. She was careful not to lift her gaze from her work. She did not want to have to meet that searching gaze, on top of everything else.

"Now, be fair," Hudson admonished his brother, mockly indignant. "*That's* not why Ross married Georgiana."

"No?" Raleigh had kicked all of the sheets off Payton's bed, and now reclined upon it like some kind of hairy odalisque. "Then why'd he do it?"

"Because he couldn't get her any other way," Hudson declared.

"Oh, *that's* right."

Payton directed Drake's arms through the openings in his waistcoat. "You're all," she said, "nothing but a packet of horn-fisted galley-growlers."

"Oh, what are you bein' so missish about, Pay?" Raleigh demanded. "I swear, for someone who thinks she'd make such a fine ship captain, you don't have very much sympathy for your crew. If I didn't know better, I'd say *you* were as hungover as any of us. That's twice now you've damn near snapped our heads off."

Payton glowered at him. "Care to try for a third?"

"Oh, don't mind Payton," Hudson said. "She's just sore because on top of giving Drake the *Constant*, Ross won't let 'er go on the Far East run with us."

"I," Payton declared, "wouldn't want to go to the *corner* with any of you, let alone the Far East."

Hudson lowered himself onto the window seat from which Payton had climbed the night before. "While you and I are havin' the time of our lives, Ral, out on the open seas, Payton's goin' to be up in London, tryin' to decide just how much of her brand-new bosom she should let show when she does her curtsy at St. James . . ."

"I say all of it," Raleigh advised. "After all, the king's

eyesight is not as good as it once was, and it's not as if she's got a whole *lot* up there. She should just open up her dress and let gravity take its course. That ought to do the trick. They'll be lining up in *droves . . .*"

Something fell from Drake's hand, and landed, with a clatter, upon the floor.

"I say," Raleigh complained loudly. "*Must* you make all that racket? My poor head can hardly take much more."

"What was that?" Hudson had lifted a booted foot, and was looking beneath it, at the parquet floor. "A button?"

"Not at all," Drake said. Payton glanced up, and noticed, with relief, that he'd closed his eyes. "It was just the ring."

"The ring?" Hudson leapt to his feet. "Bloody hell, man, why didn't you say so? Raleigh, shake a leg. He's gone and lost the ring."

Raleigh rolled over. "So what? No ring, no wedding. We'll all be able to sleep in."

Hudson strode over and laid the back of his boot upon his brother's rear end. "Out of bed, you lazy sod." He gave Raleigh a terrific shove, sending him flying off the far side of Payton's bed. "Help me look for the bleeding ring."

"I'll show *you* a ring," Raleigh declared, rising up to launch himself at his brother.

As the two men fell, wrestling, to the floor, Payton calmly reached down and retrieved the ring from where it had rolled beside her foot.

"This," she said, holding up the small gold circle, "is what you're missing, I believe, Captain."

Drake opened his eyes. "Oh," he said. Was it her imagination, or did he sound disappointed? "So it is. Thank you, Miss Dixon."

He held out his hand. For a moment, Payton admired the way the diamonds on the band—there were five of them, in all—glowed, even though the light in the room was so dim. It was a finely crafted ring, a ring that had been in his family, she understood, almost as long as those suits of armor downstairs. She didn't think about how it would look on her own finger. She would probably have lost it within a month of gaining ownership, or knocked one of the diamonds out. She was not the sort of girl, she knew, who ought to be given diamonds.

She dropped it into Drake's hand. His fist closed over it, and then he shoved both fist and what it contained into his trouser pocket.

"Thank you," he said, in his deep voice.

Payton felt the hairs on the back of her neck rise. *Damn!* What *was* it about this man that affected her so? Why couldn't she hate him, like she wanted to?

"Well," she said, dropping her arms and taking a hasty step backward. "There. You're finished."

Drake looked down at himself. He would make, Payton supposed, any girl proud to marry him. His wedding clothes included a fine morning coat of light gray, worn over a waistcoat of darker gray stripe. His trousers were the same dark gray as the stripes. The tails of his morning coat reached almost to his knees. He looked a very fine figure of a man— well, except for the circles under his eyes and the fact that he was still badly in need of a shave—but Payton couldn't help thinking she liked him a good deal better when he was dressed in nothing more than a pair of trousers, which was the way he'd arrived at her bedroom door that morning.

"I think you've forgotten something," Drake said quietly. Too quietly. She didn't think she'd heard him aright. Hudson and Raleigh had gone crashing to the floor on top of one another, and it was rather difficult to hear much of anything besides their swearing.

"What?" Payton asked suspiciously.

Mutely, Drake held up a long white band of linen.

His cravat.

It was perhaps fortunate for the captain that at that moment, the bedroom door opened, and Georgiana, looking very shocked indeed, walked in. Otherwise, Payton might surely have twisted that cravat round his neck, and kept on twisting it, until he choked, she was that put out with him. As it was, however, Georgiana's shocked exclamations soon put an end to any and all activity in the room.

"What," she cried, "is this? Payton, why is Captain Drake in your bedroom?"

"It's my fault." Drake seemed to feel duty-bound to come to Payton's defense. "I needed help dressing, and I couldn't find Ross—"

"Because he's down at the church," Georgiana declared. "Someone had to go and supervise those gardeners of yours. You know they've done the whole thing wrong. They used pink roses instead of orange blossom." She held up a basket of flowers. "All of your boutonnieres are pink, you'll be alarmed to know. Hudson, Raleigh, would you please *stop that*?"

Both men collapsed in a tangle of arms and legs. Raleigh lifted his face from the vise-like grip in which his elder brother held his head and said, in a strangled voice, "Hudson started it."

"I don't care who started it." Georgiana thrust the basket of boutonnieres at Payton and strode forward to accost her brothers-in-law. "You have no business being in your sister's bedroom. Get out! Get out right now! Take Captain Drake back to his room, and see that he shaves. And remember your sister is *not* your valet, nor are you to loan her out to your friends to serve as theirs."

Grumbling, the brothers rose to their feet, and staggered out of the room. Drake tried to stay for a few seconds more, apologizing all the while, but Georgiana only shooed him away, politely, but quite emphatically. When all the men were gone, she slammed the door, and turned toward Payton.

"Good Lord," she said. "If he actually makes it to the church this morning, I'll die of shock. I never saw the captain look so ill in my life. What happened to your hair?"

Payton glanced at herself in the mirror above the dressing table. Her hair was curling riotously all over her head. Other than that, however, she thought she looked passable—especially for someone who hadn't slept a wink. Drake had helped with that: his presence had brought a pink glow to her cheeks, and her lips, still raw from where he'd savaged them the night before, were quite red.

Payton settled down upon the window seat while Georgiana picked up a hairbrush and attacked her curls.

"It's criminal, you know," Georgiana was saying, "that Becky Whitby is marrying today, and there isn't a soul from her own family to watch it. Positively criminal. I know how nervous I was on my wedding day, but thank goodness I had my mother and sisters to support me. Miss Whitby hasn't anyone. I went to her room first thing this morning, to help her dress, but do you know, she sent me away?"

Payton, watching as the sun, which had finally put in an appearance, began burning holes through the fog, murmured, "No, really?" even though she wasn't really listening. She was thinking about Drake, of course. How could she not? The sun was hitting all the places in the garden where they'd stood together, not ten hours earlier. It was already warming the marble that had been so cold and wet against her bottom.

"That's right. She sent me away. She said she wasn't feeling well. Well, that might have been . . . well, never mind. Of course, I went back, later, with a cup of tea for her, and by then she was fine. It occurred to me, you know, Payton, that she might not take it amiss if we offered your father's services to her. To give her away, you know. I mean, it isn't as if she has anyone else to do it. And do you know, I think she quite fancied the idea."

Payton, sitting in the window, grunted. The sun had burned away almost all the fog in the garden in a surprisingly short period of time. She could see all the clay walkways now, including the one that led to the hedge maze, several dozen yards away from the fountain where she and Drake had kissed the night before.

Kissed. Where they had *devoured* one another the night before.

"Although I have to say," Georgiana went on, as she tucked some pink rosebuds from the basket into Payton's hair, "I do think Miss·Whitby is a little *old* to wear her hair down at her wedding. I mean, she isn't exactly your age, Payton. I'm sure she isn't yet thirty, but I'd be very surprised indeed if she hasn't seen twenty-five at least. I'm not saying I think she's *lied* to anyone . . . I believe she told Captain Drake she was two and twenty. But *I'm* two and twenty, and I can't help feeling that Miss Whitby is older than I am . . . and *I* certainly didn't wear my hair down when I married your brother . . ."

Through the window, Payton noticed someone moving about the hedge maze. She was very farsighted, which accounted for her so often being up the mizzenpost when they were at sea, and she hadn't any trouble at all in recognizing the two people who came out the far end of the maze. One of them was precisely whom they'd been discussing: Miss Becky Whitby. The other was someone who was just as easily recognizable, but not because he was wearing a wedding gown.

No, Payton recognized him because she'd been taught all her life to despise and abhor him.

# Chapter Ten

Georgiana!" Payton cried, jerking her hair from her sister-in-law's hands. "Look!"

Georgiana let out a yelp. "Payton! Payton, where are you going? Get back in here!"

But Payton was already halfway out the window. Only Georgiana's firm grasp around her waist—and, if truth be told, the yards and yards of petticoats she wore—kept her from climbing all the way down.

"Georgiana," she cried, struggling. "Let go! Let go! Don't you see? Oh!" She realized that only Miss Whitby was in the garden now. Her gentleman escort had disappeared back into the hedge maze. The bride was walking, the light wind picking up her veil and sending it billowing out behind her, quickly back toward the house, looking all about her, as if nervous someone might have seen her secret assignation.

Which, of course, someone had.

"Stop!" Payton yelled. "Becky Whitby! Stop right there!"

While it was true that Payton Dixon had spent a good deal of her life performing labors commonly only practiced by men, and that she was very strong for her sex and size, she was still a good deal smaller than most women. It was for that reason that Georgiana managed to haul her back into the bedroom, using her superior weight as a counterbalance. In fact, she succeeded in sending both of them tumbling backward, and causing them to land in a blizzard of lace-trimmed petticoats and pantaloons.

"Georgiana!" Payton cried furiously, as she tried to scramble back to her feet. "What are you *doing*? You don't know what I just saw!"

"No, but I do know you're acting like an utter lunatic." Seated on the floor, her legs splayed, Georgiana still managed to keep a firm grip on the back of Payton's skirt. "You can't go around climbing out windows, Payton. It isn't *done*."

"I'll tell you what isn't done," Payton began, but before she had a chance, the bedroom door opened, and her eldest brother, Ross, walked in.

Ross looked more than a little surprised at finding his wife and sister sprawled on the floor in a sea of skirts and underthings.

"I beg your pardon," he said. "Am I interrupting something?"

In her shock at being discovered in so ignominious a position by her husband, Georgiana loosened her hold on Payton, who seized the opportunity and headed straight back toward the window. This time, however, it was Ross who stopped her, and he did so by slipping an arm around her waist and lifting her bodily from the windowsill, then striding across the room to deposit her upon the unmade bed, where he held her down quite easily with one hand pressed to the top of her head.

"Ross," Payton cried indignantly. "Let me up. You don't understand! You don't understand what I just saw!"

Georgiana had, by this time, climbed to her feet and brought some order back to her skirts.

"Honestly, Payton," she scolded. There were bright spots of color on either of her cheeks. She was obviously appalled at having been discovered in so improper a position by her husband, even though Payton had a pretty good idea that her brother and his pretty young wife had been practicing some improper positions of their own the night before. "What *could* you have been thinking? Ladies don't go scrambling out windows. They use doors. We're not on the *Constant*, you know."

"I wish to hell we were," Payton said with heartfelt earnestness.

"And ladies don't curse," Ross said. He flicked an inquisitive gaze toward his wife. "Do they?"

"Certainly not." Georgiana shook her head. "Oh, Payton, really. Look at you. I'm going to have to start your hair all over now."

Payton had had about as much as she could take. "*Bugger* my hair!" she shouted.

Georgiana gasped, and even Ross looked stern. "Payton," he began threateningly.

"Now that I've got your attention," Payton said, a little more calmly, "would you please listen to me? This might be somewhat important."

Ross noticed that Georgiana was looking at him accusingly. "*What?*" he demanded.

"Oh, nothing." Georgiana looked away. "I was just wondering where she could have picked up that kind of language."

"Well, not from me!" Ross, though clearly outraged, still did not let go of Payton. "I don't allow swearing on my ships. If she picked it up anywhere, it was in port somewhere."

"Sir Marcus Tyler," Payton said.

"In port?" Georgiana glared at her husband. "And in which port, pray tell, is the term she just used employed with any frequency? That particular word isn't Chinese, you know. Nor is it Tahitian, Jamaican, or French. She obviously learned it from an Englishman, and I suspect it might have been an Englishman in her very own—"

Ross held up his free hand. He was staring down at Payton curiously. "Wait a minute. *What* did you say?"

Payton said, again, very slowly, "Sir . . . Marcus . . . Tyler."

Georgiana looked from brother to sister. "Sir Marcus Tyler?" she echoed. "What are you talking about?"

"You saw," Ross said, "Marcus Tyler? Here? At Daring Park?"

Payton nodded emphatically. "Coming out of the hedge

maze. He and Miss Whitby were *talking*. Then they both went away. In separate directions."

Ross shook his head, the way a dog did when it had water in its ears. "No, no," he said. "You must be mistaken. What would Sir Marcus be doing here? Drake would sure as hell never invite him."

"Right." Ross had let go of her, and now Payton was able to sit up. "I'm thinking Miss Whitby did."

"Why would Miss Whitby invite Marcus Tyler to her wedding?" Ross, clearly bewildered, sat down beside Payton on the bed. "She doesn't know Marcus Tyler."

"How do *you* know she doesn't know him?" Payton shook her head. "What do any of us know about Becky Whitby, except what she's told us?"

Georgiana, still standing, said, "Wait. I don't understand. Payton, are you saying you saw Sir Marcus Tyler, the owner of Tyler and Tyler Shipping, outside in the hedge maze with Becky Whitby just now?"

Payton looked up at her. "Yes," she said somberly.

Georgiana was not a slow woman, but she was new to the family, and needed occasional clarification. "Forgive me if I'm wrong, but isn't Tyler and Tyler—"

"Our chief competitors." Ross shook his head. "Payton, it *couldn't* have been Marcus. It was just someone who resembled him."

"I think I would know what Marcus Tyler looks like," Payton snapped. "After all, I was there last summer, too."

"Last summer?" Georgiana echoed, her pretty forehead knit with bemusement.

"Last summer," Ross confirmed grimly. "Those pirate raids I told you about, on our ships down in the Bahamas. We can't prove it, of course, but we're pretty certain Marcus was behind them. We think he's got Lucien La Fond in his pocket. He denies it, of course, and we haven't any proof, so we can't prosecute. But the raids have all occurred on Dixon ships, not Tyler ships, and most especially Dixon ships carrying cargo belonging to commercial accounts for which Tyler and Tyler is in competition with Dixon and Sons."

"Oh." Now it was Georgiana's turn to sink down onto the bed. "I see. And Lucien La Fond? Isn't he that French pirate captain who hates you so, Ross?"

"Not me," Ross said. "Drake."

"He hates Drake? But why? What for?"

Payton and Ross said, at precisely the same time, "It's a long story."

Georgiana said, "Oh," again, and was silent.

"It couldn't," Ross said, after a moment or two, during which the three of them sat, thinking, "have been Marcus Tyler, Payton. The whole idea's ludicrous. Miss Whitby doesn't know him. I mean, my God, she lived in our house. She heard how we spoke of him."

"Exactly why," Payton said, "she'd have kept her mouth shut if she did know him. She probably thought that if we found out she was friendly with Sir Marcus, we'd give her the old heave-ho."

"But if she's friendly with Tyler," Ross said, "why wouldn't she have turned to *him* for help, after she was robbed? Why throw herself on *our* mercy?"

Payton said, "Perhaps because she's a Tyler spy."

Georgiana cleared her throat. "Um, Payton. Forgive me, dearest. But are you certain you aren't letting your imagination run away with you? Perhaps what you saw was just . . . wishful thinking."

Payton stared at her sister-in-law. "What are you talking about?"

"Well, darling, we know you aren't very fond of Miss Whitby. And you're quite understandably . . . *attached* to the captain. I mean, you've known him forever. It's only natural you would come to feel . . . *something* toward him. Don't you think it isn't the slightest bit possible you only *thought* you saw Sir Marcus in the garden with Miss Whitby?"

Payton said, "No."

Ross raised his eyebrows. "Payton's got damned good eyes, Georgie. She can spot a whale miles off."

"I'm not denying that if Sir Marcus were in the garden with Miss Whitby, Payton could have spotted him. All I'm saying is perhaps Payton only *wanted* to see Sir Marcus in the garden with Miss Whitby, because that way there'd be a good reason to urge Sir Connor to call the wedding off—"

"Georgiana!" Payton burst out. "This has nothing to do with *that*! I saw him, I swear it! I saw Marcus Tyler in the hedge maze!"

Even to her own ears, she sounded like a crazy woman. Ross noticed, but didn't react right away. Instead, he stood up, and very calmly reached into his waistcoat and drew out his pocket watch. When he saw the time, he gave a low whistle. "If we're going to get to the church before the ceremony begins, we'd better go."

Payton, feeling tears in her eyes, stared up at him astonishedly. "Ross . . . you can't mean . . . you don't *believe* me? You think I'm making it up?"

Ross cleared his throat uncomfortably. "Well, Pay, you have to admit, it's a little convenient, your seein' Miss Whitby with Marcus Tyler the day she and Drake are about to sail off on the ship you thought you were goin' to get for your birthday." Ross shook his head. "I know you want that boat, but really, Pay. You've gone a little too far. Even if he does call the weddin' off, he still gets to keep the *Constant*. You're not gettin' your hands on it, wedding or no wedding."

"But Ross—"

"That's enough, now. You've told some whales of a tale in the past, but this one tops 'em all. Next thing you'll be telling me is that *you're* marryin' Drake." This seemed to strike him as extremely amusing. "Right! *You're* marryin' Drake, in order to get your hands on the *Constant*! Wait'll I tell Hudson and Raleigh!" He laughed for some time before finally reaching down to hold out a hand to his wife. "Come along, Georgie, before she thinks of a new one . . ."

Obediently, Georgiana took her husband's hand and stood.

Payton, on the other hand, stayed exactly where she was.

"Ross," she said angrily. "I am not making this up. Don't you think we ought to at least tell Drake? I mean, don't you think he has a right to know?"

Ross was still chuckling to himself over his little joke—which Payton couldn't say she'd found very funny. "Payton, you didn't see Marcus Tyler with Miss Whitby in the garden just now. I'm sure you saw her with someone, but it was probably just one of the gardeners."

"One of the *gardeners*!" Now Payton did stand up—stood up and put both hands on her hips. "Are you trying to be funny? Because unless Drake's started dressing his gardeners in frock coats and stovepipe hats, I don't think that's who I saw—"

"Well, I do." Ross looked down at her. He attempted to look stern. "Listen to me, Payton. I know you don't like Miss Whitby. But I must say, I don't find it very sporting of you, making up these outrageous stories about her—"

Payton exploded. "I am not *making it up!*"

Georgiana was chewing on her lower lip. "Well, Payton," she said, after releasing it. "You are . . . *fond* of the captain."

Payton narrowed her eyes at her sister-in-law, daring her to go on. "So?"

She shouldn't have dared her. Georgiana went on, although, to her credit, it must be admitted that she did so reluctantly. "Well, it only seems natural that, as . . . *fond* as you are of Captain Drake, you might want to . . . well, I don't know. Stop him from marrying someone else, perhaps."

For the first time since her brother had brought Georgiana home, Payton thought she might just have to kill her. Up until now, everything had been going well, but a girl simply couldn't say something like that to another girl, and not expect reprisal of some nature.

Especially for having said it right in front of her brother.

Ross snickered. "Now, now, Georgie," he said, patting his wife's shoulders. "Let's not go too far. Payton doesn't like Drake in *that* way."

"No," Georgiana said slowly. She must have seen the murderous glint in Payton's eyes. "No, I'm sure she doesn't."

"We all know Payton isn't overly fond of Miss Whitby, however. I'm certain that if she's loath to see Drake get married, it's only because of that."

"Oh," Georgiana said. "Of course. I only meant that Payton's . . . affectionate nature might make her feel that perhaps Miss Whitby isn't the most suitable bride for someone for whom she entertains such . . . sisterly feelings."

That was a little better. Payton decided she might not kill her sister-in-law, after all. The truth of it was, she was getting to be rather useful. The corset had certainly done its work, hadn't it?

"Right. And besides." Ross draped a heavy arm over his sister's shoulders, and gave her a squeeze that was as much affectionate as it was restrictive. "Drake knows that if it ever entered his head to lay a finger on Payton here, we'd be forced to chop 'im up and feed 'im to the sharks. Right, Pay?"

Payton swallowed, and uttered a swift and silent prayer of thanks that she hadn't been observed with Drake in the garden the night before.

"Um," she said. "Right."

# Chapter Eleven

The vicar, standing before them on the dais, prayer book in hand, cleared his throat. He was a big man, who evidently hadn't turned down an offer of dessert in quite a while. He seemed an enormous figure in his little sunlit church. Small—hardly big enough to fit fifty people—it was nevertheless quite a beautiful chapel, with its stained-glass windows, and the scent of rose blossoms hanging so heavy in the air.

Still, big as the vicar was, he was dwarfed by the four gentlemen standing to his right. Drake, Ross, Hudson, and Raleigh each stood a little over six feet tall, and with their deep tans and broad shoulders, radiated manly good health—well, except for the pallor of sleeplessness worn by Drake and the two middle Dixons. None of them looked very comfortable—they were all of them used to wearing considerably less clothing—but they were undeniably handsome.

Of the four of them, Payton supposed that Ross looked the least unhappy. He even, as Payton gazed at him, managed to give her a little wink, causing Georgiana to frown.

Drake looked the sickest. He looked, in fact, as if he might lose his breakfast at any moment. If he'd even *had* breakfast, which Payton supposed he hadn't. Well, except for that cup of coffee she'd made him drink.

Since she was seated in the first right-hand pew, he stood

directly in front of her, not four feet away. She felt his gaze on her, though she refused to look up. Only the blush she could feel suffusing her cheeks gave away the fact that she was aware of his gaze, and she tried her best to tamp the color down. Think about something else, she'd urged herself. *Anything else.*

The letter. He hadn't acknowledged it. She'd scrawled a few words—a warning about what she'd seen—on a piece of foolscap, and stuffed it into Hudson's hand as soon as she'd entered the church. "Give this to Drake," she'd hissed, careful not to let Ross see her. "It's important."

Hudson had been busy leering at Drake's attractive cousins, whom Ross and Raleigh had had the privilege of ushering to their seats. "Right," he'd said. "Anything you say, Pay."

But if he'd succeeded in getting her note to Drake, Drake had obviously not taken it very seriously. There he stood not looking exactly as if he felt well, but surely not looking as sick as a man who'd just learned his bride was a spy for his mortal enemy ought to look. Hadn't he been able to decipher her handwriting? Payton knew she didn't write as beautifully as Georgiana, but her cursive was surely legible . . .

A lace-mittened hand settled upon her right knee, which Payton had been jiggling nervously up and down. When she looked up, she saw Georgiana smiling down at her.

"Don't," Georgiana whispered from the corner of her mouth. "You're shaking the whole pew. Lady Bisson keeps looking this way."

Payton turned her head a little. Georgiana wasn't lying. Lady Bisson *was* looking their way. Or Payton's way, at least.

And there wasn't the least bit of warmth in that look, either. In fact, if half a dozen poisoned darts suddenly embedded themselves into the back of Payton's neck, she'd have no doubt at all who'd launched them.

"I can't help it," Payton whispered back miserably.

"You can, and you will." Georgiana removed her hand. "He can take care of himself, you know. He's a grown man."

Payton felt her cheeks turn crimson. "I know that. You

think I don't know that? But if you'd just have let me see him, just for a minute—"

"Too late now." Georgiana looked past her, nodding graciously at a mutual acquaintance.

"Well, you could have at least let me confront Miss Whitby—"

Georgiana let out a sound that might have been a snort. But that was ridiculous. Georgiana was far too ladylike to snort. "And had you blacken her eye before the ceremony? I think not."

"I wouldn't have hurt her," Payton insisted. "I just wanted to *talk* to her . . ."

"Certainly you did." Georgiana turned her face back toward the front of the church. "The vicar's looking this way. Be quiet now. We're in a house of the Lord, remember, so try not to swear."

Payton fell silent, chagrined. A house of the Lord. *Do you hear me, Lord?* Payton raised her eyes toward the raftered ceiling. *I just wanted to thank you very much. No, truly. This is just the nicest thing you've ever done for me, forcing me to sit here and watch Drake marry that harpy. Really, I don't know what I've done to deserve this, but thanks for singling me out for this honor . . .*

Did God approve of sarcasm? Payton didn't know. But it was all He was going to get out of her, for the time being.

It wasn't until the church organ suddenly wheezed that she looked away from the ceiling, startled by the noise, and inadvertently met Drake's gaze.

Then froze, locked into that hypnotic stare. His eyes—the color, she'd often thought, of ice—seemed to bore into hers. It was unnerving, having those eyes, so unnaturally bright in that dark face, on her. What, she wondered sluggishly, in the part of her brain that hadn't automatically shut down the minute that gaze locked on hers, does he want? Why is he staring at me like that? Did he get my note? Is that it? But if he got it, why is he still going through with the wedding?

She scanned his face, but could find no hint as to the reason behind that enigmatic stare. Maybe, she thought grimly, this is his way of saying good-bye. Good-bye forever.

Then, all around her, people in the pews began to stand. For the only time in her life, Payton broke eye contact with Connor Drake first, and swiveled her head to look past the bunch of rose blossoms tied to the end of her pew. Between the time she'd slipped into her seat and now, looking back down the aisle, someone had laid down a carpet of white crepe for the bride to walk along during her approach to the pulpit. At the end of that long carpet stood Payton's father, beaming proudly, blissfully ignorant of the secret pain his daughter was going through, with Miss Whitby, resplendent in ivory lace, a long veil lowered over her face, on his arm.

Beside Payton, Georgiana tugged on her sleeve. *"Stand up,"* she leaned down to hiss.

Obediently, Payton climbed to her feet.

Georgiana studied her young sister-in-law's profile carefully. She was really very worried about Payton. It was clear the girl fancied herself in love with Captain Drake—or Sir Connor, as they were to call him now. It mustn't be at all pleasant, Georgiana supposed, watching the man you love marry someone else. Georgiana wouldn't have stood for it, herself. Why, if Ross had taken it into his head to marry someone other than her, she would have lain down in the middle of the church, kicking and screaming, if that's what it would have taken to stop the ceremony. That Payton was restraining herself from doing so struck Georgiana as admirable in the extreme.

The organist launched into a wedding march. Slowly, Sir Henry Dixon and Miss Whitby began to make their way down the aisle.

Georgiana glanced at Captain Drake, to see how he was bearing up. Really, for a groom about to marry such a lovely young lady, he did not look at all well. Georgiana, of course, hadn't missed the way he'd stared at Payton, for most of the time she'd been seated there in front of him. Georgiana fancied herself the most practical of women, without much imagination, but she'd caught herself feeling quite certain that there'd been *something* in Captain Drake's face, as he'd looked down at her little sister-in-law. Something not unlike . . . well, longing.

Oh, it was silly, she knew. After all, Captain Drake—oh, bother. *Sir* Connor—was more than a decade older, and a hundred times more sophisticated than Payton. It was hardly likely that a man like him would fall in love with a girl who, up until a few weeks ago, he'd probably never actually seen in a dress.

Still, there'd been something in his face. It had disappeared the moment Payton looked up. Like a gate crashing down over an entrance, Captain Drake had schooled his features back into stony impassability. But not before Georgiana had seen . . . and for the first time, she began to suspect that perhaps . . . just perhaps . . . some of her sister-in-law's feelings might be returned.

But it was too late now. Because here came the bride.

And she was lovely, Miss Whitby was, in the gown Georgiana had chosen for her. It was scandalously low-cut in the front for a bridal gown, and Georgiana saw with disapproval that Miss Whitby had not, as Georgiana had suggested, inserted a piece of lace over the place where her décolletage dipped lowest.

Common, Georgiana thought. That's what Becky Whitby was. Quite common. How she'd ever lured a man like Captain Drake into her bed, Georgiana couldn't imagine. She supposed she had only herself to blame for that. She should never have allowed the creature into the house. Payton was forever collecting injured animals and birds and nursing them back to health again. Miss Whitby had, at first, seemed like one of those birds, a dove with a broken wing, or some such. Georgiana hadn't noticed how common she was until it had been too late, and Captain Drake had already announced his plans to marry her.

Poor Payton. She'd never really stood a chance, with a woman like that in the house. Well, it would be a good lesson for her: there were sirens everywhere, not just perched on rocks at sea.

Georgiana sent an anxious glance in her sister-in-law's direction when Sir Henry presented Captain Drake with Miss Whitby's hand, then stepped aside, to take his seat beside Lady Bisson in the pew across the aisle from theirs. But Payton didn't flinch. She didn't move so much as a muscle. When Captain Drake and his bride turned to face the vicar, Payton sat down calmly with the rest of the congregation, laying her fingers in her lap, not even curled into fists, as one might have expected, with a girl who was so quick to strike out at things . . . and people. Georgiana could not even detect a tear on Payton's smooth, tanned cheeks.

*She's weeping,* Georgiana thought, *on the inside,* and felt such pity for her young sister-in-law that she reached out and took the hand closest to her.

Payton did turn her head then, but only in surprise that her sister-in-law had taken her hand. *Why,* she wondered, *is Georgiana being so nice to me?* Not that it mattered. She had known, the minute she'd seen the sunlight streaming in through the round stained-glass window above the vicar's head, setting Miss Whitby's red hair, beneath her veil, ablaze, exactly what it was she had to do. After all, how did the saying go?

*Red sky at night, sailors' delight. Red sky in morning, sailors take warning.*

Well, it was morning. But it was Miss Whitby herself who had better take warning.

Payton wasn't afraid. What did she have to fear? She'd already sat through the worst thing she could ever imagine, watching her own father walk her bitterest enemy down the aisle, to deliver her to the arm of the man she had loved for as long as she could remember. What could possibly be worse than that?

A sort of calm descended over her. She listened to the vicar's monotone as he explained to the gathered assembly that they'd been asked there in order to witness the union of one Rebecca Louise Whitby and Sir Connor Arthur Drake. She almost let out a hysterical bark of laughter upon hearing the Arthur. She'd had no idea Drake's middle name was Arthur, but she supposed she had no room to talk. Her middle name was Fulton.

Beside Payton, something suddenly clutched at Georgiana's heart. Seeing her sister-in-law's expression change so dramatically from tense to calculating, she knew good and well exactly what Payton intended. She clenched the hand she held, driving her nails through the kid leather of Payton's gloves. But Payton only looked at her and smiled. Smiled, with those hazel eyes of hers so clear and cool, they seemed fathoms and fathoms deep. *No, Payton,* Georgiana thought frantically. *No!*

When the vicar finally—after what seemed to Payton like hours—inquired of the assembly at large if there was anyone there who had knowledge of any sort of impediment to the match, let him speak now, or forever hold his peace, Payton felt Georgiana's hand, still resting over hers, convulse. She clutched Payton's right hand firmly, and shot her a look that was so very forbidding, had Payton been four years old again, she might have been quite frightened.

But Payton was nearly nineteen. So instead of being cowed, she merely lifted her free hand, and waved it at the vicar.

The vicar, who, expecting no interruption of his service at that point—he had doubtlessly married hundreds of couples, and never had a positive response to that particular question before—had glanced down at his prayer book to see what he ought to say next, when he became aware of a startled ripple through the assemblage, and glanced up . . .

And saw Payton's hand very firmly in the air. He also saw that the young lady seated beside her was trying very hard to pull that hand down. Well, he'd noticed the two of them whispering together already. He ought to have known they'd be trouble.

"Um," he said, in a somewhat distressed tone. "Yes, miss?"

Payton was aware that not only Drake and Miss Whitby had turned round to look at her, but all three of her brothers were staring daggers at her, as well, Ross most particularly. She didn't care. She stood up and said, "I believe there *is* an impediment, sir."

The vicar swallowed. It was growing quite warm in the church, what with all the sun spilling in through the stained glass. He wasn't at all certain he was in any fit state to handle this sort of interruption.

Fortunately, it looked as if he wouldn't have to. One of the groomsmen, the eldest one, suddenly stepped forward, his expression one of abject embarrassment.

"Never mind," he said to the vicar, as well as the congregation. "Please go on. She just needs a bit of air."

To the vicar's astonishment, the man then wrapped a single arm around the girl's waist, lifted her feet off the floor, and began to carry her bodily from the church. Before he could say a word about it, however, Lady Bisson, the groom's formidable grandmother, stood up, her expression dark as a thundercloud. Rapping her cane sharply upon the flagstoned floor, she snapped, "Put that girl down at once!"

Ross stumbled, and very nearly dropped his sister altogether. "W-what?" he stammered.

"You heard me." Lady Bisson was now shooting her poisoned darts in Ross's direction. "If the girl says there is an impediment, then I for one want to hear what it is."

Payton elbowed Ross forcefully in the ribs. "See? Put me down, you bloody sod."

The vicar noticed that a number of fans that had been produced by ladies hoping to combat the heat began to move quite a bit faster at the words "bloody" and "sod." He cleared his throat.

"Now, see here, young lady," he said. "Kindly remember that you are in a house of the Lord."

Payton, whom Ross had deposited, none too gently, back on her feet, adjusted the bodice of her gown and said, "Oh, I do apologize, Vicar. It's just that my brothers can be *such* galley rats sometimes."

"Er, yes." The vicar thought fleetingly about the roast his

cook had been preparing when he'd left home that morning. He hoped this delay wouldn't cause it to be overcooked. "Now, what was that impediment of which you spoke?"

"Oh," the young lady said. She was quite an extraordinary-looking little thing, he saw. Slender as a reed, she was quite tanned, with disgracefully short brown curls sticking out of the sides of her bonnet. Across her nose was a layer of—he was almost certain of it—*freckles*. And while she wasn't precisely beautiful—the bride, Miss Whitby, was the only woman in the church who could have been called *that*—she was in no way unattractive. In fact, she was quite arresting, with her large, intelligent eyes, and boyish, husky voice.

"The impediment," the girl went on, "is only that I believe Miss Whitby to be in secret alliance with Sir Marcus Tyler, Dixon and Sons Shipping's arch rival. I saw them together this morning, in Captain Drake's hedge maze."

There was a collective gasp from the congregation, although few of them, including the vicar, had the slightest idea why such a thing connoted an impediment to marriage.

And then Miss Whitby astounded everyone further by dropping her bouquet and sinking, in a dead faint, to the stone floor.

# Chapter Twelve

$\mathcal{A}$re you sure I can't get you something, miss?" asked the innkeeper's wife. "A glass of wine, perhaps?"

Payton, sitting in quite an unladylike position with her back against one arm of the leather chair and her legs draped over the other, looked past Mrs. Peabody, at the others gathered in the private sitting room.

Ross was still too angry to sit down. He kept pacing up and down in front of the fireplace. Georgiana had collapsed some time ago upon the settle, and except for having laid a handkerchief across her face, had not stirred once in the past half hour. Hudson and Raleigh had taken up positions on either windowsill, and took turns alternately glaring at Payton and sneaking glances through the mottled glass, hoping for a glimpse of the fetching barmaid they'd spied on their way in.

Only Sir Henry, mulling over his musket-ball collection, seemed oblivious to Payton's status as a social pariah, and occasionally leaned over from the table at which he sat and asked her if she didn't think the ball attributed to the nefarious pirate Lucien La Fond didn't look a good deal similar to the one attributed to Blackbeard. He was worried he might have been cheated, a little.

"Miss?"

Payton smiled queasily at the innkeeper's wife, and shook

her head. She couldn't imagine eating or drinking much of anything while under the malevolent glares she seemed to be engendering. Anything that touched her lips was bound to taste like sand.

"Very well, then."

Mrs. Peabody took away the tray of sliced meats and cheeses that had sat untouched on the table since noon. If it struck her at all strange that, out of a family of such hearty-looking eaters, not a single one had sampled her best luncheon platter, she didn't say anything. She recognized a family in turmoil when she saw one. She rather fancied that the young lady was the root of all the trouble. Young ladies often were. Perhaps, Mrs. Peabody thought, the young lady had been caught whilst trying to run away with her lover. A penniless lover, of whom her obviously well-off family did not approve. A romantic at heart, Mrs. Peabody felt quite bad for the Honorable Miss Dixon, who had so many alarmingly large brothers, and a father who didn't appear to have the firmest grasp on sanity. She decided that if the young man came in the night, and tried to rescue the young lady from all those brothers, she'd do what she could to help.

Mrs. Peabody, however, like so many people that day, was bound to be disappointed. Because the young man—who was not as young as Mrs. Peabody might have imagined—was not going to come, and he was most certainly not going to try to rescue the young lady. He was by now a good many miles out to sea, and he was in the company of a much prettier young lady who, at the end of their journey, would be his wife in deed, if she was not already so in name.

But Mrs. Peabody, in her romantic imaginings, wasn't *completely* wrong:

Payton *was* the root of all the trouble in the family.

"The convent," Ross declared suddenly, stopping in his tracks and pointing an accusatory finger in Payton's direction. "That's where I'm sending you, the minute we get home!"

"No convent would take 'er," Raleigh drawled, from the windowsill.

Hudson agreed. "She's too foulmouthed for any convent, Ross. The nuns'd send her packing at the very first 'bugger' that came out of her mouth."

"Well, what am I to do with her, then?" Ross turned around, and continued pacing the length of the hearth and back again. "She's made a laughingstock of herself. I'll never be able to get her married off now. It's going to be all over London in a matter of weeks, the way she stopped Drake's wedding."

Payton, who'd been listening to complaints along this line for the better part of the afternoon, could contain herself no longer.

"Well," she said, from the depths of her armchair, "at least I was right. I *did* see Miss Whitby talking to Marcus Tyler in the hedge maze."

Ross's voice was so loud, it sounded like thunder. "I don't recall giving you permission to speak!"

Payton, disgusted, looked back at the roof beams, which she'd been examining at some length for the past hour. There didn't seem to be anything she could say to make her family understand why she had felt compelled to stop Drake from marrying Miss Whitby. They all thought she'd done it out of some perverse need to avenge herself for the loss of the *Constant*. Payton hadn't tried very hard to dissuade them from this notion. She certainly couldn't tell them the truth— that she loved Connor Drake to distraction, and even if she *hadn't* spied Becky Whitby in the hedge maze with Marcus Tyler, she probably would have tried to stop the wedding anyway.

What were they so angry about, anyway? It's not like it *mattered*. As soon as the couple set foot in Nassau, they were going to be married by the first clerk they could find. Or at least that's what Drake had said.

So what was everybody so angry about?

Of course, Payton *had* been a little afraid, when Miss Whitby had first fallen down upon the chapel floor, that the good Lord had finally answered her prayers, and had struck the bride down dead. But she realized she hadn't been so lucky when she saw how easily Miss Whitby was revived after Raleigh and Hudson—who'd happened to catch the bride as she fell—carried her into the vicar's study. The vicar's wife had simply waved some smelling salts under her nose, and Miss Whitby woke, albeit haltingly. Even semiconscious, Miss Whitby had looked quite beautiful, lying there with her ruby lips parted, her heavy bosom rising and falling as she breathed in shallow gasps.

Of course, the minute Payton saw she wasn't dead, she knew the bride was faking a faint. If the smelling salts had not brought her round with satisfying speed, Payton had already volunteered to pinch her back into consciousness. Miss Whitby must have overheard this muttered threat, since she'd immediately opened her jewellike eyes and inquired breathlessly, "Oh, where am I? What happened?"

It was the vicar's wife who'd said, kindly, "You fainted, my dear. You're in the village chapel. May I get you something? Some brandy, perhaps?"

Miss Whitby declined that offer, then, blinking groggily, looked up at Drake, who stood a little apart from everyone else, and cried, "Oh! How I've wronged you!"

Miss Whitby then turned her face away, as if she couldn't bear to look him in the eye.

"There, there, my dear." The vicar, not wanting to be left out of the little drama unfolding before him, had taken over for his wife, and now knelt beside the couch where Miss Whitby lay, and patted her hand. "There, there. I'm sure you've a perfectly reasonable explanation, haven't you? Am I right? A perfectly reasonable explanation for the charges against you?"

Miss Whitby nodded. "I . . ."

Everyone leaned forward, eager to hear Becky Whitby's perfectly reasonable explanation of why she'd been in the hedge maze with Sir Marcus. All except for Payton, of course, who had by that time realized that Miss Whitby fully intended to lie. She stood back, a little apart from the group—almost as far back as Drake, who also hadn't leant forward, and his grandmother, who had pressed her lips so tightly together, they had all but disappeared. This, Payton figured, was going to be good.

Miss Whitby did not disappoint. It *was* good, a riveting story, actually, which featured her, Becky Whitby, as its heroine, and Sir Marcus Tyler as its cold-hearted villain. If Payton had tried, she couldn't have made up as good a story. Lord, Payton thought in disgust. Wasn't there *anything* this girl couldn't do?

Sir Marcus, it appeared, had approached Miss Whitby one morning in Hyde Park, early on during her stay at the Dixon town house, whilst she'd been out riding the mare Miss Dixon had so generously loaned her. Sir Marcus had had a proposal to make to the penniless orphan, and it was a proposal any penniless orphan would have been hard-pressed to turn down: in exchange for supplying him with a certain piece of paper, which could be found in the possession of Captain Connor Drake, current guest—as Miss Whitby was—in the Dixon household, he was prepared to pay her the astonishing sum of five thousand pounds.

"And what," the vicar had very rightly asked, "*was* this piece of paper that was worth such a vast sum to Sir Marcus?"

"Well," Miss Whitby said with a sniffle. "I hardly know. But Sir Marcus described it in such a way as to lead me to believe it might be a map."

"A map?" The vicar had looked very perplexed, indeed. Sir Marcus Tyler was prepared to pay what amounted to a small fortune, all for a single map?

"Well," Miss Whitby went on to explain tearfully, "it's the only map of its kind in existence." A map, she told them, that Sir Marcus had said Captain Drake had drawn up the summer before.

At this point in Miss Whitby's narrative, Ross had sworn quite colorfully, and Hudson and Raleigh had groaned. Only Drake appeared unmoved, leaning against the mantel, his arms, like Payton's, still folded across his chest.

The map Sir Marcus wanted, Ross explained to the bewildered vicar, when asked, was a map of the seven hundred or so islands of the Bahamas. No such map, other than Captain Drake's, existed: the islands were simply too scattered, the area too full of dangerous reefs, for anyone to have ever fully explored it.

Before Captain Drake's expedition, the previous summer, that is. The map was of inestimable value to merchant shipping companies, like Dixon and Sons, who did business in the Bahamas. But even more so, its existence was sorely resented by the piratical scum that made their homes in and about those seven hundred islets. Previously, they'd been able to disappear between the shoals, without fear of pursuit, since no clipper-sized ship dared risk running aground upon some islet or reef. With Drake's map, however, anyone could navigate, with a pirate's ease, in and out of the treacherous waters.

Dixon and Sons, being Drake's employers, owned exclusive rights to the map, and their competitors—Sir Marcus Tyler, for instance—would stop at just about nothing to get their hands on it.

Even attempting to bribe a pretty, penniless orphan like Becky Whitby.

"I see," the vicar said slowly. "And did you give him the map, then, child?"

Everyone—with the exception of Drake and the Dixons—leaned forward to hear the answer to that one. But Payton already knew what Miss Whitby was going to say. The map was resting in a safe in her father's administrative offices. A few copies had been distributed to the Dixon and Sons Shipping captains who sailed in those waters, but unless Drake had carelessly left a copy lying around his room, there was no way Miss Whitby would have been able to get her hands on one.

And Connor Drake was many things, but careless was not one of them.

But the rest of the people in the room weren't aware of that, and let out a collective sigh of relief as Miss Whitby, shaking her head, said, "Oh, no! But I didn't want to anger Sir Marcus, you know, so I put him off for as long as I could. I kept telling him I was looking for it, and couldn't find it. He kept telling me to look harder. When I finally left London for Daring Park, I was so happy—I thought at last I was rid of him. But as you know from Miss Dixon, he followed me even here, and sent a note, demanding to see me this very morning. I—I was too frightened to say no to him. I slipped outside after breakfast to tell him I still hadn't found the map. We're leaving—" She lifted wounded blue eyes toward Drake at that point. "We *were* going to leave for New Providence straightaway after the wedding breakfast, so I thought I might never have to see Sir Marcus again. But I suppose he would have found me, even there."

Miss Whitby's tone was so mournful, her voice so filled with shame, that for a moment, Payton found herself actually feeling sorry for her. But a glance in Drake's direction showed her he was suffering from no such weakness. He was regarding his bride-to-be—if she still *was* his bride-to-be, which Drake's expression left somewhat in doubt—stonily, the corners of his lips at a definite downward slant.

"Well," the vicar said. "This is all very illuminating. But what I don't understand, child, is why didn't you turn to your friends for help when this man first approached you? Surely, the Dixons were very kind to you. Why couldn't you have gone to them, and told them of Sir Marcus's offer? You clearly had no intention of taking his money. You seemed to know that what he was asking you to do was not only illegal, but immoral, as well. So why didn't you tell anyone about it?"

Here Miss Whitby had hung her head. It shamed her to say it, she confessed, with a sob, but Sir Marcus's offer had not only included five thousand pounds if she produced the map. It also included a punishment if she did *not*. And that punishment was that Sir Marcus intended to reveal something to her new friends that Miss Whitby wanted very much to keep hidden from them.

This bit of information, of course, caused everyone in the

room to hold his or her breath, anticipating a very succulent piece of information, indeed. But unfortunately, the vicar deduced that the only persons to whom it was necessary for Miss Whitby to reveal it were himself and the man who'd intended to marry her—rather to the fury of that man's grandmother, who did not take it at all well when the vicar attempted to shoo all other parties from the study—including his own wife, who looked considerably put out at not being able to hear the end of Becky Whitby's poignant story.

Out in the churchyard, where the congregation had gathered to discuss the morning's extraordinary events, no one actually walked up to Payton and offered his congratulations. She rather fancied Lady Bisson might, since she'd done exactly what that lady had asked her to do—stop her grandson's wedding. But Lady Bisson didn't say a word. Instead, she walked into the graveyard, and stood gazing at Sir Richard's tomb, looking not a little forbidding.

Still, Payton had thought *somebody* might have offered her some congratulations. After all, she *was* a bit of a hero for having saved not only Drake, but Dixon and Sons' interests in the Bahamas, as well. But nobody said a word. Payton, feeling for the first time that perhaps she'd done something wrong, felt tears smart her eyes. Well, damn them all! What did she care what they thought, anyway? All that mattered was Drake. Somebody had had to save Drake. She'd been proud to do it, *glad* to do it. She'd do it again, too, if she had to.

So it was something of an anticlimax when the vicar emerged from his study to inform them that the couple were leaving at once for Portsmouth, where they would board the *Constant* and head for the islands, where they would be wed, instead of pursuing marriage in England, where there appeared to be too many . . . complications.

Complications. Never in her life had Payton thought Connor Drake might refer to her as a complication.

But it appeared that he had. Not only that, but he was fleeing the country, apparently in an effort to rid himself of her.

There'd been talk, of course. A good deal of talk, first about what it could have been that Sir Marcus knew about Miss Whitby that was bad enough she'd go to such extraordinary lengths to avoid his revealing it to her friends—but that, when revealed to her intended, had not affected his decision to marry her in the least. It could not, Payton heard guests hypothesizing, have been that Miss Whitby was pregnant with the captain's child, because surely, as this hasty marriage illustrated, he knew that already. So what could it have been? Something Miss Whitby didn't want anyone else besides Captain Drake to know.

But what was so bad about the fact that she was marrying, as the French said, *enceinte*? It was a little shocking, of course, but it happened. It would have been a good deal more shocking if Captain Drake had refused to marry her, for all she was carrying his child. But the fact that he was ready to admit the child as his was no reason for shame. Such weddings took place every day.

The whole matter was decidedly perplexing, and extremely unrewarding for those guests to whom a good piece of gossip was worth its weight in gold. They went away disappointed—though none as disappointed as Lady Bisson, who called for her carriage and left for Sussex without another word. Still, it had to be admitted, although they weren't privy to the details, the performance itself had been quite memorable. And the part Payton Dixon had played in that performance was something few guests were likely to forget. It seemed that the Honorable Miss Payton Dixon would go down in history not as one of the first lady ship captains, but as the girl who had tried to stop Sir Connor Drake's wedding.

It was not a title Payton much relished.

Her family was none too pleased about it, either.

"If the convent won't take 'er," Ross said at length, "perhaps America will."

That was enough to drag Hudson's attention away from the window.

"You can't be serious, Ross," he said. "Send Payton all the way to America?"

"Why not?" Ross, still pacing, seemed to like the idea. "We've got cousins in America, I understand. Boston. I say let's send Payton to Boston. No one there will have heard of Connor Drake. We ought to be able to marry her off to an American."

That was the last straw. Payton drew in a deep breath and shouted, "I will *not* marry an American—"

Nor anyone else for that matter, she meant to add, but Ross cut her off.

"You have no choice in the matter." Ross, now that he had come up with a workable plan, was quite pleased with it. "No Englishman will have you after the spectacle you made of yourself today. But an American would, and right gladly, I'd think, with your money. And," he added grudgingly, "you aren't as ugly as Raleigh's always makin' you out to be. Leastways, to an American you ought to be passably pretty."

"I won't go!" Payton roared. "You can't make me go!"

"You will," Ross assured her, "and I can."

"I say, Ross," Raleigh said mildly. "I have to agree with Payton here. This seems a little extreme. Send the girl all the way to America, just because she—and very rightly, I might add—tried to save Drake's arse? I think you're being a bit harsh."

"Right." Hudson stood up. "She was only tryin' to help out a fellow seaman."

"That's precisely the problem," Ross insisted. "Payton isn't a seaman. She's supposed to be a marriageable young lady. But she can't seem to remember that, now can she? But maybe if we get her away from the sea—"

"I won't go!" Payton cried. "So bugger off, you bleeding sod!"

At that, Georgiana removed the handkerchief from her face and sat up. "Ross," she said in a very small voice. "May I see you in the other room, please?"

Ross held a hand, palm out, to his wife. "In a moment,

Georgie. First I've got to thrash Payton within an inch of her life."

Georgiana laid the handkerchief to one side. "No, Ross," she said. *"Now."*

But whatever it was Georgiana was going to tell her husband in the other room was left to the imagination of all concerned, because at that very moment, the door to their private sitting room fell open, and a white-faced young man, panting very heavily, collapsed upon the floor before them.

"Cap'n Dixon," he cried, reaching a hand out toward Ross. Like a man dying of thirst he reached his hands toward whatever water was on hand. "Thank God I've found you!"

Mrs. Peabody appeared in the hallway beyond the door through which the young man had crashed. Horrified that this scruffy-looking fellow might be the pretty young lady's lover, and perfectly understanding why her family should be so upset over the prospect of her marrying him, she had followed the youth up the stairs, and now declared, "Oh, I tried to stop him, sir, honest I did, but 'e wouldn't listen. Said 'e 'ad something right urgent to tell ye, and—"

"All right, all right." Ross waved the lady's apologies away. "We know him. It's young Hill, isn't it? You're shipboy, aboard the *Constant*."

"That's right, sir." The boy could barely draw breath, he was panting so hard, but he hadn't forgotten his manners. Seeing that there were ladies in the room, he'd swept off his cap, and now sat on the floor, crumpling it anxiously between white-knuckled fingers. "Jeremiah Hill, sir."

"Well, then, Hill, what seems to be the trouble? Shouldn't you be aboard the *Constant* with Captain Drake? I'd have thought she set sail hours ago."

"That's right, sir, she did. Only not with me on her. I was—I'm sorry to say I missed 'er sailing, sir. I was 'avin' a drop with a friend, and the time slipped away, and next thing I knew, she'd set sail—"

"Well," Ross said severely. "That's a serious offense,

young man, missing your sailing. Captain Drake won't like it. He won't like it a bit."

"I know, sir." Hill ran a trembling hand through his neatly trimmed brown hair. "That's not why I'm 'ere, sir. I mean, I'm not 'ere to beg your pardon, sir."

"Good," Hudson said, offering the boy a tankard of ale he poured from a pitcher on the table. "Because Ross's pardon is hardly worth begging for. He's a mean old chap, our brother. Here, now. Drink this."

The boy took the tankard, and gulped down its contents gratefully. When he had somewhat quenched his parched throat, he wiped his lips on his sleeve and said, "It's what I saw along the docks, sir, when I finally realized I was late, and went runnin' for 'er—for the *Constant,* I mean. She'd already pulled out—wasn't but a speck in the distance—and I realized I'd mucked it up, but good. I was swearin' fit to burn the captain's ear—" He glanced guiltily at Payton and Georgiana. "Beg your pardon, mum. Then, as I was standin' there, I got jostled aside by the biggest bloke I ever did see, a great black fellow, with rings in his ears and nose. And after 'im came all sorts of no-good–lookin' men, the likes of which I only ever saw down Nassau way. They were all makin' 'aste to pull out, sir, on account of—this is what I 'eard one of 'em say—on account of that bastard—beggin' your pardon, la-dies—Cap'n Drake had left port early, and they had orders to follow 'im."

"Damn!"

Ross had gone nearly as pale as the quaking lad before them. He exchanged looks with his two younger brothers. "La Fond?" he asked them.

Hudson nodded. "Sounds like it. He wouldn't dare show his face in Portsmouth, but you can be sure he'll be waiting somewhere offshore."

"But how could he know?" Raleigh shook his head. "How could he have known Drake was sailing today?"

Payton had climbed out of the depths of her leather chair, and now stood, shaking with rage, before them.

"I'll tell you how he knew," she said, her hands in fists at her side. "Becky Whitby told Marcus Tyler this morning!"

This was enough to send even Raleigh, the laziest of the Dixon children, to his feet. "Good God in heaven," he breathed. "She's right!"

"We've got to get out there, Ross." Hudson was already reaching for his hat and gloves. "Madam." This was addressed to Mrs. Peabody. "Have your man bring our carriage round. And hurry!"

Mrs. Peabody, alarmed by the gentleman's imperious manner, scooted off in a flurry of skirts and apron. Things were not turning out at all the way she'd planned them for the pretty young lady. And she was beginning to think she was better off not understanding them, after all.

"Ross," Georgiana said. "I don't—"

"Have we got any other ships in Portsmouth right now?" Raleigh, who'd also started pulling on his gloves, wanted to know.

"Aye, sir." The boy, Hill, had finally climbed off the floor, and now stood twisting his cap. "As soon as I 'eard those men talkin' about Cap'n Drake, I went straight to the dockmaster, an' found out the Dixon frigate *Virago* pulled into port last night. I went and spoke with the cap'n—'e's the one 'o knew you'd've been at Cap'n Drake's wedding, an' 'e's the one that sent me 'ere. 'E said to tell you 'e'll be ready to leave the minute you set foot on board—"

Hudson looked pleased. "The *Virago*, eh? She'll do. Armed with eight thirty-pounders, she is."

A grim-faced Ross tugged on his top hat. "What are we waiting for, then? Let's go."

All four Dixon children turned and hurried from the room, leaving their father, Georgiana, and the shipboy blinking at one another.

"I say, Georgiana." Sir Henry looked up from the musket ball he'd been polishing. "Where did everybody go?"

Georgiana was in no mood to placate the old man. She sank

back down on the settle and, laying the handkerchief over her face once again, quipped, in a very irritated voice, "To the devil."

She was not far wrong.

# Chapter Thirteen

Drake stood on the quarterdeck of his ship, the *Constant*.

And she *was* his ship, not just one he was commanding; she belonged to him now, a thought that kept returning, again and again. And filling him with guilt, because he knew how much Payton had wanted her. More than that, he knew how much Payton *deserved* her, how hard she'd worked for her, how lovingly she'd polished her brass, and how much input she'd had in her design.

And yet there was joy inside him, too, just when he'd begun to think he might never feel happiness ever again. Joy because she was a beautiful ship, the fastest craft on water, as finely made as Chinese porcelain, just as lovely, just as strong.

Yes, she should have been Payton's. And maybe it was true that, deep in his heart, he knew she *was* Payton's, and that he was only borrowing her—taking care of her—until her rightful owner could claim her. And he didn't mind. He didn't mind at all. It was something they could share, something that connected them across the waves, across the miles separating them.

It was enough.

It had to be.

But right then he had more important problems than the *Constant*'s rightful ownership. That ship to the north, for instance. He hadn't been certain at first, but now there was no doubting it: it was following them. And now his crew had figured it out, as well.

"Captain." His first mate, an able fellow by the name of Hodges, approached. "I've just had a report there's a full-rigger bearing down on us out of the north. She's coming on fast and strong, sir."

Drake nodded. "I noticed her at sunup. Perhaps our boy Hill flagged himself a ride, and is trying to catch up?"

The second mate overheard, and gave a chuckle. "I wouldn't put it past 'im. 'E's the type that'd do anythin' to spare 'imself a whippin'."

Hodges shook his head. "He wouldn't be ridin' on this ship, sir. Or, if he is, it isn't voluntary. This ship's not flyin' any flags."

Drake raised a hand to his chin, and stroked it thoughtfully. "Not flying any flags, eh? Who do you think it is, Hodges?"

"Never known the Frenchman to make his way this far north, sir, but if I were a bettin' man, that's who I'd put my money on. Word around the alehouse is he was plenty burned up about the way you fired on him off Cat Island last August."

Drake's smile was rueful. "That pirate never could take a joke. Well, have the men stand ready, in case there's some-thing to this. I'm guessing it's nothing, but it never hurts to be prepared."

"Aye, Captain."

Hodges went away, and Drake turned his gaze toward the horizon, looking, to the disinterested observer, every inch of him the cool, collected officer. His hands behind his back, one booted foot upon the base of the rail, he seemed oblivious to the danger into which they were sailing—or, if not oblivious, confidently uncaring.

This was the way he wanted to appear to his men. Inside, however, Connor Drake was fairly jumping for joy. He couldn't tamp down a sudden thrill of exhilaration. A full-scale battle was about to come under way, and Drake couldn't have been happier about it. Not, of course, at the prospect of bloodshed. A man couldn't be happy about that. But he couldn't help but be happy that things, which had looked so bleak up until now, might well work out, after all. And work out to his liking.

The minute he'd heard the name Marcus Tyler tumble from Payton's lips the day before, things had finally begun to make some sense. He'd had his suspicions, but Payton's observation in the hedge maze confirmed them. It was all he could do not to rub his hands together in glee. It was for this reason that he kept them firmly in check behind him. After days—no, *weeks*—of straining at his own impotence, unable to lift a finger to change the way events were unfolding all around him, he could finally, *finally* take some action.

The first thing he was going to do was blow the ship coming after them out of the water. He hoped her crew would put up a decent fight. If La Fond was commanding them, they would. If, however, they were some of Tyler's hired mercenaries, he really couldn't expect much. They were in it for the money, not the glory—not like La Fond, whose pride was at stake. It *had* to be La Fond, he thought to himself. He *had* to be involved in all of this somehow. Drake was going to be bitterly disappointed if it was proved he was not.

He wasn't really very clear about what he was going to do after he'd blown his pursuers away. If he judged it safe enough, he might just turn the *Constant* right round, and head straight back to England. There were a few things there he'd left unfinished, and he figured, once he'd gotten rid of Becky Whitby, he could go back and take proper care of them.

"You there," he called to the man in the crow's nest. "What do you see?"

"They've got their guns out, cap'n," came the cry. "I'd say they're bound on firin' on us, soon as they're within range."

"Excellent. Hodges! See that the cannons get loaded." Drake took his hands out from behind his back, but only to rest one on the hilt of the sword he wore at one hip, and the other on the butt of the derringer he wore strapped to the other. "Change our heading. I want to try to ram her."

Hodges balked. *"Sir?"*

"Oh, we're not *really* going to ram her, Hodges. Do you think I'd do something like that to this lovely lady? Not on your life. But they don't know that. Let's give them a little scare. If anything, it'll bring us in range to fire on them."

· Hodges touched his captain's arm. "Beg pardon, sir," he said, as quietly as he could, and still be heard over the shouts of the men and the constant roar of the sea. "But you aren't forgetting there's a woman on board? Wouldn't it be better if we tried to outrun 'em? I mean, after all, this is the fastest ship on water, sir . . ."

"Run?" Drake stared down at the shorter man. "When we've ample time to prepare for a fight? Perish the thought, Hodges."

Hodges nodded. "Well, I was only thinking of the lady, sir."

"Well, let me worry about the lady. You worry about getting those cannons loaded."

"Aye, aye, sir."

Hodges went away, and Drake, though still unable to shake his feelings of elation, realized the man had a point. There *was* a lady on board. He decided he had better pay her a little visit.

Becky, almost as soon as she'd set foot on board, had locked herself into the captain's cabin, claiming she felt ill. Well, that was to be expected, he supposed. She wasn't used to sailing, and, like most women, was bound to suffer sea-sickness during their crossing.

And it had to be even worse for her, in her condition. Drake truly did feel pity for her. Yet he couldn't help thinking, as he made his way through the busy throng of sailors, toward the after house, where the captain's quarters were located, that really, *this* was living. *This* was how he'd always intended to spend his life, never dreaming that one day, he might inherit his brother's title, fortune, and lands. He hadn't been happy when he'd learned about it, that day in the lawyers' offices. Connor Drake belonged to the sea, and not to some baronetcy smack-dab in the middle of dairy country. What kind of man spent his life chained to a desk, sitting there adding up column after column of sums, declaring how much milk they'd pulled in from however many Jersey cows they happened to own at any given time? That kind of life had been all right for his brother, Richard. Richard, with his dull wits and hamfistedness, was suited to it.

But not Drake. He wouldn't have been able to stand it. Sit at a desk, when he could be sailing the open seas, commanding his own ship? No, thank you. He'd take the sea, with all its perils, any day of the week.

Of course, he hadn't expected Becky Whitby to understand that. He couldn't have expected any woman to understand it, really. Which was why he'd put off telling Becky as long as he could, why he hadn't mentioned it at all until that point, following Payton's incredible announcement, that they'd been alone together in the vicar's study. He'd thought she was going to faint again, that moment he'd told her he was putting Daring Park up for sale. She had worn an expression of shock their entire ride to Portsmouth. And no sooner had they boarded the *Constant* than she'd shut herself up in his cabin, refusing to speak to a soul.

Well, what was he supposed to have done? He wasn't his brother, Richard, and he never would be. The sea was where he belonged. She'd *known* that. He'd explained that. Drake had been frank with her from the beginning. Well, not about how he intended to sell the house and install her in the villa in Nassau, but about how he would spend most of his time at sea. What difference did it make, really, whether she was mistress of his house in England or New Providence? She was still what she'd always wanted to be: a lady.

Well, not anymore. At least, not if what he suspected turned out to be true. Oh, her story back in the vicar's chambers had been pretty enough. He was almost disposed to believe it. Part of it, anyway.

In the meantime, however, he was still a gentleman, and he would attempt to behave as such. He had a feeling he'd have better luck acting like a gentleman around Becky Whitby, who was no lady, than around Payton Dixon, who most definitely was. Well, of a sort.

He knocked first. After all, it wasn't as if they were man and wife—yet. He couldn't just go barging in there, for all it was his own cabin.

But the knock went unanswered. She either hadn't heard—which was not unlikely, given the pre-battle activity on deck, and the creak of the bow as they made the turn toward the ship coming at them—or she wasn't answering. Well, that too was understandable. She hadn't answered but once or twice since she'd locked herself in the day before. He wasn't certain what it was she was doing in there, besides, if his suspicions were true, vomiting. She'd have been better off battling seasickness on deck, but had ignored him when he'd insisted this. He still wasn't even sure she'd heard him. It was difficult to shout instructions through a door, especially with half his crew snickering over the fact that the captain's bride would not open it to him, and the other half wondering why the captain didn't simply rush the portal and give the girl the thrashing she deserved.

"Miss Whitby," he called. "It's Connor Drake. Open the door, will you? There's something I've got to talk to you about."

Deep within the cabin, he heard her say, quite calmly, "Go away."

"I can't go away, Miss Whitby. You see, we've run into a bit of difficulty—"

"What kind of difficulty?"

"Well, there's another ship—"

"Why should I care about that?"

Why, indeed. "Well, I don't want to alarm you, but she isn't one of ours. There may be cannon fire. I only wanted to let you know—"

So you wouldn't be frightened, he almost said. And run out onto deck like a chicken with its head cut off, and get yourself blown to bits, since, judging from her behavior in the past,

Becky Whitby was not the type to keep her wits about her in moments of danger.

At least, not the Becky Whitby he'd thought he was marrying. This new Becky Whitby, the one who met men like Marcus Tyler in hedge mazes, he hadn't any doubt could keep her head in just about any situation.

"I thank you, sir, for your concern," came the voice behind the door. "Now, unless you've a priest with you, and a plan on finishing what you started, go away."

"I'd be a sight more willing to find a priest if you'd just be honest with me."

"I *was* honest with you!" Miss Whitby bellowed. For a girl who'd been so demure when he'd first met her, she could shout quite loudly when it suited her. "But are we wed? No! And all because that horrid Dixon girl stopped it. I can't believe you're willing to take *her* word over mine!"

Drake couldn't help smiling. Even after nearly twenty-four hours, Drake still could not think of the calm way in which Payton had raised her hand, without letting out a chuckle. Leave it to the Honorable Miss Dixon to make a shambles of the soberest of events. She seemed to have an uncanny knack for locating the closest source of trouble, then throwing herself bodily into it.

Of course, that amusing moment when she'd raised her hand had been followed by a bloodcurdling one, in which the vicar had asked her the nature of the impediment, and Drake had been convinced she was on the verge of revealing his assault on her the night before. Absurd, of course. He ought to have known that was something Payton would never reveal . . . at least, not in front of those brothers of hers.

Oh, they'd have raked him over the coals for laying a hand on their sister, no doubt about that. When they weren't conveniently forgetting her existence, or treating her with the roughness with which they were accustomed to treating one another, they were fiercely protective of her. There hadn't been any real call for this, since, up until recently, not many people had actually been aware that Payton wasn't a boy. But now

that Georgiana had finally got her into a corset, it looked as
if Ross and his brothers were going to have to start fighting
off their sister's admirers in droves—and it had seemed, for a
moment, as if their first victim was to be their best friend,
Drake.

But even as he'd stood there by the altar, bracing himself
for their attack, a part of him was exulting. Because Miss
Whitby could not possibly hear about his disgraceful assault
on Miss Dixon—on the night before he was to be married, no
less!—and not feel compelled to call off the ceremony, leaving
him free . . .

Free to launch similar assaults on the Honorable Miss
Dixon.

But when, instead of a scathing condemnation of his having
kissed her the night before, the words "Marcus Tyler" tumbled
from Payton's lips, a cold fist had gripped Drake's heart. Because he knew that if Payton had thought she'd seen Marcus
Tyler in the hedge maze, then she'd really seen him. Her eyesight was as good as a gull's, and she was incapable, unlike
most other women he knew, of telling a falsehood.

And if Payton had seen Becky Whitby with Marcus Tyler,
that meant they were all in considerable peril. Because Marcus
Tyler, despite what anyone might think, was not merely a shipping magnate, or even a ruthless businessman, who peddled
human flesh without a qualm, something no Dixon would even
dream of, despite the profits that could be had transporting
slaves—or "black gold," as Tyler referred to them. Marcus
Tyler was a villain, plain and simple, with no more morals or
scruples than a great white shark, maiming and devouring anything and everything that stood between him and whatever it
was he wanted this week.

And it appeared that what he wanted this week was Connor
Drake.

Well, Drake was prepared to let him have what he wanted,
but not before he'd removed himself a considerable distance
from his friends. He was only too happy to go head-to-head
with Sir Marcus—but on his own terms, and in his way. And

the farther away he could move the battle, the better his chance of sparing the Dixon family *worse* trouble.

He glanced back toward the bow. There, he could see the ship they were fast approaching, moving inexorably through the choppy waves. "Well," he said to Miss Whitby, "I've known Miss Dixon longer than I've known you—"

"Not long enough, apparently, to realize what a liar she is." Becky's voice sounded shrill, even with the wooden panel separating them. "Are you so dense you can't see why she stopped the wedding? She wants you. She'll stop at nothing to get you."

Drake shook his head. Well, what had he expected her to say? Whatever else she might be, Becky Whitby wasn't blind. She had to have noticed . . . Last night in the garden, she had to have guessed . . .

Unless—and this thought cast a cold chill over him—he was wrong about what had passed between him and Payton in the garden. That what to him had been an extraordinarily emotional, passionate exchange had been, to her, no more than an interesting test of her newly discovered ability to attract men. Was he special, or was she planning on laying her hand over the erection of every man who kissed her?

And those blasted brothers of hers were dead set on marrying her off. They were bound to be pushing her into all sorts of situations in which she might meet eligible bachelors. Who knew how many men she might be kissing in his absence? He had better, he decided, hurry up, if he intended to get back to England before that blasted girl found herself in the same sort of hot water Becky Whitby was in.

"Wait . . ."

For a moment, he thought Becky was going to open the door. But no, she went on, in the tones of someone to whom something brilliant had just occurred. "Wait! It's not *you* she wants at all, but this boat! This stupid boat! Good God, of course! It's all she ever talked about—"

Drake set his jaw. "I suggest," he said coldly, through the

door, "that you strap yourself down, Miss Whitby. We're heading for choppy waters."

Without another word, Drake turned, and headed for the wheel.

"Well," he said, taking the spyglass from Hodges, and laying it to his own eye. "What have we got?"

"Strangest damned thing I ever did see." Hodges spoke with his usual lack of hurriedness. "That's a pirate vessel bearin' down on us, no doubt about that, guns drawn and at the ready. But look over there to the south."

Drake looked, and let out a low whistle at what he saw. "Well, I'll be. A Tyler ship."

"That's what I thought. Now, I ask you, sir, why would a Tyler ship be comin' to *our* rescue?"

"It's not." Drake calmly set aside the glass. "They're both of 'em after us, Hodges."

Hodges's eyes grew round as compasses. "Beggin' your pardon, sir, but while I'd pit the *Constant* against any ship in anybody's fleet, I don't think she could stand an attack from *two* boats, sir, comin' at 'er from two different directions!"

"You're quite right, of course, Hodges." Drake nodded to the wheelman. "Turn 'er around. We're going to have to try to outrun them."

But even as he issued the orders for retreat, he knew it was hopeless. The *Constant* was the fastest clipper in the Dixon fleet, but no ship, no matter how fast she was, could outrun two full-riggers moving with the wind at their backs. He ought to have known, of course, that it was a trap, that Tyler, knowing him as he did, would have assumed he wouldn't run from a fight—not a fair fight, anyway. Now he was trapped, trapped like a rat.

His only consolation was that, while the Honorable Miss Payton Dixon might be hundreds of miles away back in England, laying her hands over the erections of any man who kissed her, at least she was not here, and in any sort of danger.

For that, at least, he had to be thankful.

# Chapter Fourteen

$\mathcal{P}$ayton lowered the glass and cried angrily, "Oh, the cowards! The cowards! Two ships! How is he supposed to beat *two* ships?"

"He's not," Raleigh informed her, taking the glass and applying it to his own face. "That's the point." He worked on focusing the lens. "They can't risk letting him get away, which is why they've pitted two boats against his one. Ah! There he is."

Payton, clutching the side rail, jumped up and down. "Oh, Raleigh, let me see!"

"No. And stop grabbing my arm."

"Raleigh!"

"Aw, calm down, Pay." Raleigh peered through the glass. "The *Constant*'s all right. They'd be fools to damage 'er. She's worth more'n both those ships put together. It's *Drake* I'm worried about."

Payton didn't dare snap at her brother what she wanted to, which was that she was worried about Drake, too. Damn the *Constant*! It was the man she wanted back in one piece, not the ship.

"Why, he's got his sword out," Raleigh reported. "I thought he lost that particular piece of steel back in that bar fight in Havana. I say, Hud!" Raleigh called back over his shoulder to his elder brother, who was stomping about the deck, preparing the *Virago*'s cannons for firing. "Didn't Drake lose that blade of his in Havana last year?"

"Yes." Hudson lifted a torch, and touched the flame to the fuse of the cannon nearest by. "But he won it back in a card game. Ready?"

"Be careful where you aim that thing," Payton urged worriedly, inserting her fingers into her ears.

"Aw, damn, Payton. I'm not goin' to hit your damned ship, all right?"

Damn the ship, she almost shouted. Don't hit Drake! But before she could get the words out, Hudson yelled, "Fire!"

The cannons let out a deafening roar as they catapulted thirty-two-pound iron balls at the ship to the *Constant*'s port side. Only one of the balls hit home, smashing through the unidentified ship's prow.

"I say," Raleigh said, removing the glass from his eye. "Jolly good shot."

Hudson bowed humbly. "Thank you."

"Oh!" Payton removed her fingers from her ears and ran back to the rail, where she leaned out as far as she dared. "Oh, Raleigh, they're boarding her! I can see they've boarded her from here."

"Don't worry, Pay." Raleigh was refocusing the glass. "Connor Drake'll never let 'em take the *Constant*. Leastways, not alive."

"You ignorant boob, what do you think I'm afraid of? Give me that glass. Give it to me!"

Raleigh, keeping the glass easily out of her reach just by stretching to his full height, murmured, "Uh-oh."

"What?" Payton, feeling as if she might burst if they didn't make headway soon, leapt about her brother, bombarding him with questions. "What? Has he gone down? *Has he gone down, Raleigh?*"

"Not yet," Raleigh said. "But you'd better duck."

"Duck?" Payton stood there, staring at him stupidly. "Why?"

A cannonball whizzed past her and crashed, with a thunderous explosion, through the deck just a few feet behind her, splintering wood and creating a gaping, smoking hole. Payton, indignant, cried, "Why, those devils! They nearly blew me up!"

Ross's reaction was not nearly so mild. He leapt down from the mizzenmast, where he'd been issuing orders with lightning speed, and hurled out a few more, along with some choice swear words.

"Light those cannons! Yes, all of them! We'll blow those galley rats out of the water, see if we don't!"

Too late. Because at that moment, something flared on the deck of the *Constant*. The next thing Payton knew, her world was blackened by something thick and heavy, thrown across her eyes.

"Raleigh!" she shrieked furiously. "Let me see!"

"No." In spite of her fingernails, clawing at him frantically, Raleigh refused to remove his hands from her eyes. "It's too awful. It will break your heart, Pay."

Her heart in her throat, Payton finally managed to fling his hand away—just in time to see the *Constant*'s hull disappear in an explosion of black smoke and flame.

She wasn't even aware that she'd begun whimpering until Raleigh's hand settled on her shoulder.

"She was a beautiful ship," he said mournfully. "You were right to want to command her."

Payton's lips were moving. Eventually, she was able to form words. "Ship?" she echoed. "Ship? Who cares about the bloody *ship*? Where the hell is *Drake*?"

They were close enough that Payton could see, without the help of a spyglass, the smoking hulk of what had once been the *Constant*. Its deck—what was left of it—was teeming with men, darting in and out of the thick black smoke from her hull. It was impossible to tell which men belonged to the crew of the *Constant,* which men were from the pirate ship upon which they'd just fired, and which of them were from the third ship—identified by Raleigh as a Tyler ship called, ironically enough, the *Rebecca*. Completely uninjured, protected from the *Virago*'s cannons by the hulls of both the pirate vessel and the *Constant,* the *Rebecca* was evidently standing by, prepared to take on passengers—or captives—if necessary.

"Oh!" Payton cried. "There he is! There he is!"

She could see Drake clearly now, moving about the wreck that had once been his ship, shouting orders to those of his men who'd not yet been captured or killed. The *Virago* was close enough now that if they didn't drop anchor, they'd crash straight into the pirate vessel—close enough that all four of their cannons, when they went off, which they did just then, sent crippling volleys through the hull of the full-rigger between them and Drake's boat.

But they were also close enough that the *Rebecca*, on the *Constant*'s starboard side, was able to fire off a cannonball that knocked off the top quarter of the *Virago*'s mizzenpost. The crew scattered to all sides as sails and rigging rained down upon their heads. Payton narrowly escaped a concussion as a large chunk of mast crashed down directly where she'd been standing, and only because, at the last minute, she leapt over the railing . . .

And onto the deck of the pirate ship.

Which was not, she quickly realized, where she really ought to have been, just then. It was, in fact, the direct *opposite* of where she ought to have been.

But, with a quick glance over her shoulder, she realized that this wasn't the worst of her problems. The collapse of the *Virago*'s mizzenpost was enough of a calamity that for a moment, no one paid attention to her direction. . . .

And that moment was all it took to send her prow directly into the side of the pirate ship. There was an explosion of splintering wood, and some very loud, and quite distinguishable, cursing from Ross and some of his deckhands.

Now there was a three-way tie-up of boats: the *Virago,* the pirate vessel—which, now that she was on it, Payton could see was called the *Mary B*—and what was left of the *Constant,* while nearby floated the unscathed *Rebecca*.

Thrown to her knees by the impact of the two ships ramming into one another, Payton stayed where she was for a second or two. After all, she was on a strange ship. She didn't want to appear too conspicuous.

But the crew of the *Mary B* seemed wholly occupied with ransacking the *Constant* for anything on board they could lay their hands on—and that seemed to include Miss Whitby's trousseau, which Payton could see them removing, lace pantaloon by lace pantaloon, from the captain's cabin in the after house. As for Miss Whitby herself, Payton wasn't certain what had happened to her, but could only assume she had been taken, with the other prisoners, across the plank that had been thrown across the railing round the *Constant*'s deck to the deck of the *Rebecca* . . .

And yes, there she was, her hair a bright spot of red in all the smoke. She was being jounced along upon the shoulder of a tall man in a feathered hat, who had his arms wrapped around her hips and was conveying her on board the *Rebecca*—though not, apparently, against her will, since she was not struggling at all. Which hardly seemed, Payton thought, like Miss Whitby, who had always been something of a screamer . . .

Then Payton realized that the reason Miss Whitby wasn't struggling was—could *only* be—because she was unconscious. Well, of course. Miss Whitby was, after all, a delicate flower of a woman. Wasn't that why Payton and her brothers had felt compelled to rescue her that day outside the London inn? She was a victim. A perpetual victim, from the looks of things, because here she was, in trouble *again*.

Well, Payton wasn't going to make the same mistake twice. The first time she'd rescued Becky Whitby from harm, what had she gotten for her efforts? A big fat nothing. Well, actually *not* nothing. Becky had thanked her very nicely by stealing the love of her life. How was that for gratitude?

Besides, what did *she* care, whether or not Becky Whitby ended up some pirate captain's personal prisoner, shark bait, or just plain dead? She'd been praying for something like that to happen for days—for weeks, even. And now her prayers were finally being answered. Only . . .

Only what if she really *were* carrying Drake's baby? Payton couldn't very well let her die, could she?

Well, could she?

Then she saw what was happening a few dozen yards away from her, and her decision was pretty much made for her. Several men—several really *big* men—were dragging what appeared to be an unconscious Connor Drake over the railings of the *Constant* and onto the deck of the *Rebecca*.

At least, she assumed he was unconscious. Surely he couldn't be dead. A dead man they'd throw overboard, not drag below, which was where they took Drake.

*Oh, my God,* she prayed, frantically looking around to see if anyone else had noticed that Drake had been taken captive. *Please don't let him be dead. Take me instead.*

*Or, better yet, take Miss Whitby!*

But her brothers and the rest of the crew of the *Virago* were still trying to get out from beneath the topsail that had collapsed over them. It was going to take them forever to get untangled from it. And by the time they did, the *Rebecca* and her prisoners would be long gone . . .

Payton didn't actually think about what she was doing. If she'd stopped to think about it, of course, she'd never have done it.

She had just swung a leg over the splintered railing of the *Constant* when a very unfriendly voice growled, "Where in the 'ell do you fink *you're* goin', eh?"

Payton turned, and saw a boy coming out of the *Constant*'s forward house—the forecastle of which was now in flames—holding an enormous net bag full of bread and citrus fruits. He had evidently been raiding the galley, and looked extremely annoyed at finding someone standing in his way.

"What're you, deaf?" he wanted to know, when she didn't answer him straightaway. "I arst you a question, boy. 'Oo are you?"

Payton looked down at herself. She had forgotten that

shortly after boarding the *Virago,* she'd borrowed a shirt, vest, and trousers from the cabin boy, since it was a good deal easier to move about on a frigate's deck in pants than in petticoats. She supposed that, with her short hair—and, it had to be admitted, not very sizable chest—it might be easy to mistake her sex. Still, it wasn't very flattering to be taken for a boy, even by a grimy lout like the one before her.

"You want I should knock that hat off you, boy?" The young man seemed quite irritated by her silence. "I'll do it. Don't fink I won't."

Payton didn't like being threatened—at least not by someone who wasn't that much bigger than she was. Drawing herself up to her full height, she said, "Get out of my way."

The boy's upper lip curled. "Why? Where d'you fink you're goin'?"

Payton pointed to the deck of the *Rebecca.* "There," she said.

The boy dropped the bag full of food. "No you ain't," he said.

"Oh?" Payton eyed him. He was as tall as she was, but looked to be about fifty pounds heavier. "You think so, do you?"

"*Fink* so? Matey, I *know* s—"

But he never got to finish that sentence, because Payton's fist connected solidly with his nose. The nose, her boxing brother Raleigh had once informed her, was the second-best place to punch a man, after the stomach. Many boxers made the mistake of striking their opponent in the mouth, forgetting how deeply teeth can cut a knuckle. Nasal cartilage, being quite thin, had the dual advantage of crumpling easily beneath the fist, and splintering quite painfully into the face when smashed.

Payton was just stepping neatly over her opponent, intent upon rescuing Drake, when she found herself seized around the waist and hauled off her feet. Suddenly, the wooden planks of the ship deck, which had been beneath her toes, were over her head, and her toes were pointing toward the gray, overcast sky.

"Little bastard," a vicious voice swore at her. "I'll teach *you*."

What the gentleman—and she applied that term loosely—meant to teach her, Payton never knew, since into her upside-down world stepped an extremely large black man with several gold hoops through his earlobes, and another through his right nostril. He too was carrying a heavy sackload of pillaged foods. He did not look happy.

"Put 'im down, Tito," he said, in a voice that sounded like monsoon thunder.

"Aw, Clarence." Her captor, of whom she'd yet to catch a glimpse—beyond the fact that he wore boots in an extremely large size—sounded unhappy. "Look what 'e did to Jonesy."

"Never mind that, now. Remember what the cap'n said. No captives, 'cept his woman and Drake. Let 'im down."

"*Clarence*—"

"*Down,* I said."

Payton realized what Tito was about to do just seconds before he actually did it, but it was still jolting when her backside met with the hard planks of the *Constant*'s deck. Wincing, she rubbed her sore behind and looked up at the two men who stood arguing over her.

"I tell you, 'e shouldn't be able to get away wi' doin' Jonesy that way!"

Tito, Payton was surprised to see, was a completely bald, middle-aged white man . . . bald, middle-aged, and quite fat about the middle. Which might explain why he'd been dragging the carcass of an enormous pig behind him, with a heavy hook. Since he was also very tall, Payton decided he was about the biggest man she'd ever seen—at least until she got a good look at Clarence. Then she quickly amended that opinion.

"No prisoners." Clarence shook his enormous head, and his many chins swayed pendulously. "Just Drake and the cap'n's woman. You know we ain't got enough food for more. Wha' wi' the *Mary B* sinkin' fast, we're goin' to have to feed their crew as well as ourn. We've barely got enough to last us till Nassau as it is . . ."

Payton, hearing for a second time that the intention of the attack on the *Constant* had been to capture Drake and Miss Whitby—whom the pirates referred to, oddly enough, as *their* captain's woman, not Drake's, which she thought odd—knew that she couldn't possibly let them leave her behind. Who was going to look after Drake? Not a single one of her brothers had yet cleared the deck of the *Virago*. They were still trying to untangle the cannons from beneath the mainsail.

It was up to her. It was entirely up to her.

But as she was rolling over, preparing to crawl, if she had to, after Drake, her head was suddenly yanked back quite forcefully—she was wearing a knit cap in deference to the winds—and presently, she felt the tip of a knife-point at her throat.

Then she realized it wasn't a knife at all, but the point of the hook that a few seconds ago, had been embedded in the pig Tito was stealing from the *Constant*'s galley.

"Let me kill 'im then, Clarence." Tito's foul breath was warm on her cheek. "Please? The Frenchman won't mind. I *know* 'e won't mind."

There was enough hesitation in Clarence's voice that Payton knew if she acted fast, she had a chance. " 'E's jest a *kid*, Tito . . ."

Payton, the back of her head resting on Tito's massive shoulder, said hoarsely, "You don't mean . . . You don't mean that your captain is *the* Frenchman, do you?"

" 'E is," Tito snarled in her ear. "An' no other. Why? You 'eard of the Frenchman?"

"Oh, of course." It was very difficult to swallow with the business end of a hook stuck at the hollow of her throat, but Payton managed just the same. "There isn't a seaman alive who hasn't heard of Lucien La Fond. Why, he's the scourge of the South Seas! I'd give *anything* to see him, just once. Tell me, is it true he once outran His Majesty's naval forces in the Indian Ocean, using only a single sail, when a storm took out his main mast?"

"It is." She felt the pressure on her throat lessen just the tiniest bit. "I was on that ship, you know."

"Were you?" Payton tried to instill her voice with boyish enthusiasm.

" 'Course I was. 'Oo d'you think 'eld the mast in place, after she broke off?"

"Was that you?" Payton shook her head, which took some doing, seeing as how he was still holding onto a handful of her hair through her cap. "You must be powerful strong. Oh, please, sir, don't you think instead of killing me, you could take me aboard with you? I'd be right honored to sail under such an able seaman as the Frenchman."

"See 'ere," Clarence said, obviously not liking the sound of this a bit. "We're not takin' on no new crew. We've got enough swabbies as it is . . ."

"I'm no swabbie," Payton said scathingly. "My last position was cabin boy for Admiral Kraft!"

"Admiral Kraft?" She sensed that the pirates had exchanged glances over the top of her head. Admiral Kraft was one of the navy's most dedicated eradicators of what he called the pirate scourge. Payton had met him once at a dinner party. She didn't think he'd much mind her bandying his name about so loosely, for all he'd complained to her father some weeks after the party, about how Payton had spent the better part of the evening discussing the family arts with the admiral's soon-to-be-wed eldest daughter, who'd then insisted upon practicing some of these arts with her new husband.

"You served under Admiral Kraft?" Tito twisted her head around so that he could look into her face. "If you're lyin', boy—"

"I'm not lying." Payton met his watery-eyed gaze steadily, though his breath was enough to make her want to vomit. She happened to get a good look at his teeth, and saw why it was his breath stank so. He had very few teeth left, and those that remained were black with rot. "I looked after him right ably, and his daughter, too." Her gaze slid toward Jonesy, who was still slumped upon the deck, both hands over his nose. Blood streamed down his face, and had stained his shirtfront, which hadn't been clean before, a deep, dark brown. "Maybe I can make up for what I did to your boy Jones, there, by taking on his duties. I don't imagine he's going to be good for much for the next few days—"

A series of explosions sounded behind them. Instinctively, Payton ducked as bullets went whizzing past their heads. A swift glance behind her showed that her brothers had given up trying to untangle the *Virago*'s cannons from the mainsail that had collapsed over them, and had decided instead to fire on anything that moved.

She thought about shouting to them to watch where they were bloody well shooting . . . but before she had a chance even to inhale, the air was pierced by a blast from a conch shell, long and urgent. It appeared to be coming from the *Rebecca*. All around her, Payton saw heads lift, and faces turn toward the only able-bodied ship remaining in the area. It was evident from the activity on board that the sails, which had been dropped during the battle, were being hauled back up, and the anchor lifted. Departure was imminent, thanks to a sudden volley of bullets from the *Virago*. Men who'd been filling their arms and pockets with bounty from the *Constant* began retreating, and right quick.

Payton's would-be assassin was no exception. Without another word, Tito dropped her and sank his hook back into the pig he'd been lugging behind him. Payton, in a very good position to view this, swallowed hard when she saw the heavy hook sink, all the way to its handle, into the marbled slab of meat.

*That could,* she thought, *have been* me.

She would never again be able to look at pork the same way.

" 'Ere we go," Tito said with a grunt, as he began dragging the meat toward the full-rigger. "Jonesy, get up."

Clarence had already reached down to lift the sack of food

Jonesy had dropped, shouldering it easily along with the heavy bag he already carried. "Up, boy. It's only your nose."

"Aye, but it bleedin' *'urts,*" Jonesy complained, staggering to his feet.

Payton glanced over her shoulder, just as her brothers let loose another round of bullets. This time, the *Rebecca* answered back with some firepower of her own. Payton, caught in a shower of bullets, jumped to her feet. She hadn't much time, she knew. She had to decide, right then and there, which it was going to be:

Back to safety with her brothers.

Or onto the *Rebecca,* with all its dangers . . . and Drake.

She turned, and started hurrying after the men who, moments before, had been ready to kill her.

"Hey!" she shouted. "Wait for me!"

## Chapter Fifteen

It wasn't hard for him to keep track of time.

There was light in the room in which he was held, light that spilled down from cracks through the ceiling above him. The ship's deck, he knew, was what was above him. In particularly bad weather, waves crashed across the deck, and he was showered in saltwater. When it rained, all he had to do was cup his hands, and he could catch a few mouthfuls of fresh water.

It was a sign of shoddy workmanship that light and water seeped through the cracks between the planks of the ship's deck. That's how Drake had known, from the moment he'd wakened on this hard, straw-strewn floor he'd gotten to know so well, that he was on a Tyler ship. Sir Marcus was notorious for hounding his shipmakers to finish his crafts on time, not necessarily caring what sacrifices might have been made in order to meet some arbitrary deadline.

So he knew, from the light that shifted into his cell, how many days had passed since his ship, the *Constant,* had been attacked by another on the open seas. By counting the number of times his cell door had been opened, and meals delivered, he even had a rough idea of how many hours. He even, judging from the slowly warming air, had a general idea of where they were headed: south.

What he did not know was anything beyond that. The man who guarded his door would tell him nothing. The giant who brought him his meals told him even less.

But Drake had a pretty good idea what had happened. He had been captured, most likely by the pirate Lucien La Fond, who had never been particularly fond of him. While this was irritating, it was not particularly distressing. The Frenchman obviously wanted something—why else had he let his prisoner live this long? And Drake had a pretty good idea of what that something was. So all he had to do, really, was sit back and wait.

His main concern was, of course, for his men. They had fought bravely to protect the *Constant* against the flood of pirates that boarded her. Drake suspected a number of them had given their lives defending her. For that, he blamed himself. He had suspected something of the sort might occur, even before they'd ever set sail. He ought, he knew, to have never allowed Miss Whitby aboard. Doing so had been foolhardy, like agreeing to convey a cargo of cobras. Not that it would have made any difference. They still would have come after him. But they wouldn't have had the information they did now, information that had been dutifully supplied by their informant.

Oh, well. There was nothing he could do about that. He would be forever sorry for the lives lost in this debacle, a debacle that, he suspected, was all of his own making. When he got out of it—and he knew that, one way or another, he would; he always did—he'd try to make it up to the wives and families of those men, any way he could. It was the least he could do, for men who had so unhesitatingly thrown themselves in harm's way.

That map. That damned map. If only he'd never drawn the wretched thing.

It had all started out as a lark. One night the summer before, he and Hudson and Raleigh Dixon had been visiting a favorite brothel in New Providence—certainly nothing to be proud of, but they had been a long time at sea, and men had certain needs, after all. Anyway, they'd finished, and were making their way back downstairs, when Drake happened to notice a familiar figure escorting a young lady into one of the bedrooms. It was none other than the notorious pirate captain Lucien La Fond, whom they'd suspected of having been behind a number of raids on Dixon ships sailing in the area.

Though Drake had always considered the Frenchman a grotesque monstrosity of a man, it was clear Monsieur La Fond felt otherwise about himself, since he exercised even more meticulous care over his wardrobe and personal grooming than Raleigh Dixon. Now, Drake might have been a little drunk, it was true. And the idea, to a more sober man, might have seemed a bit childish. But it occurred to him that it might be rather amusing to wait until the Frenchman was otherwise occupied, and then relieve him of his highly colorful habiliments. Hudson and Raleigh were then to set a very smoky but easily contained fire. Then they would reconvene a safe distance away to watch just what the Frenchman donned in his haste to leave what he would think was a burning building.

This ludicrous plan had succeeded beyond anyone's expectations when, quietly entering the room into which Monsieur La Fond had disappeared, Drake found the pirate—having made rather rapid use of the woman dozing beside him—in a dead sleep. So when the cry of fire rose up through the house, the infamous pirate Lucien La Fond came dashing through the doors of the villa donned in a woman's diaphanous nightdress, with one half of his black mustache—of which he was so inordinately proud—cut off.

Hearing raucous laughter, and seeing no signs of flame, Captain La Fond turned to spy his archenemy, Connor Drake, holding up his velvet coat and breeches in one hand, and a long curl of black hair between the index finger and thumb of another.

"A tout à l'heure, Lucien," Drake called, and then he and the Dixon brothers turned and ran for all they were worth.

A childish prank, to be sure, but word of it spread through town like wildfire. It got to be so bad, in fact, that the pirate captain could not enter an eatery without inspiring snickers and guffaws. Finally, he returned to his ship and set sail, ostensibly for the gentler climes of Key West, but really, it was rumored, to one of the other islands, to wait for his mustache to even out.

Hearing this, and having nothing better to do—they were waiting for a shipment to be made ready for the journey back to England—Drake set out after the pirate, determined to flush him from his hiding place. It was while he was searching for La Fond that Drake decided to begin mapping each area he searched, so as to have a record of where he'd already looked.

By the time he finally found the pirate in a cove just off Cat Island, he had recorded nearly two thousand islets, five hundred cays, and six hundred or so islands, along with all the reefs and shoals to avoid while traveling to each of them, something that had never been done by any man before him—and something he had done only out of abject boredom.

Then, to add insult to injury, Drake had fired off a single cannonball at La Fond's ship, just to let him know he'd been found out. He then sailed triumphantly back to Nassau.

It was enough, Drake supposed, to make any man a little angry. But really, this attacking of the *Constant*—killing innocent men—over it was a little much. If he'd known La Fond was such a bad sport, he'd never have started up with him in the first place.

Though he had thoroughly enjoyed holding up that bit of mustache.

Things had gone entirely too far, though. Now he was locked in the brig of a Tyler ship, and Lord only knew what had happened to the rest of his crew. He couldn't remember much that had happened after they'd been boarded. Something had struck him forcefully on the head, and the next thing he knew, he'd wakened here. He dimly recalled cannon fire, which led him to believe his crew might have been rescued—but by whom, and to what avail, he had no idea.

The only thing, really, that he had to be grateful for was that, if La Fond had to pay him back for last summer's practical joke, he couldn't have chosen to do so at a more opportune time. Drake had been on his way to Nassau to marry a woman he didn't love, and whom he was beginning to suspect might have motives even ulterior to the ones she admitted to in attaching herself to him. La Fond had put a convenient stop to that.

So things were not *very* bad. It would have been another matter entirely, this being held captive by Lucien La Fond, if the pirate had also gotten hold of people Drake actually cared about. Any of the Dixons, for instance. Even the youngest Dixon, who, he thought, in his bleaker moments, was undoubtedly well on her way by now to becoming the belle of London. At least if her sister-in-law had any say in the matter.

And that, Drake told himself firmly, was as it should be. It was a far better thing that Payton Dixon marry some earl or viscount, as Ross's wife intended her to, who might be able to keep her under control and out of trouble, than that she continue to run around in the completely undisciplined manner to which her brothers had allowed her to grow so unfortunately accustomed. That kind of behavior was only going to get her in trouble. He thoroughly hoped a husband was found for her, and quick.

Still, it was odd how, as much as he hoped when he returned to England—if he lived long enough to return to England, that is—Payton Dixon would be safely married, the idea made him feel like yanking the chains with which his wrists were shackled right out of the rings that held them bolted to the wall. He *wanted* her married, after all. For her own good. For *his* own good. She needed a husband to keep her out of trouble. And *he* needed a good reason to stay away from her. Well, a reason beyond the fact that if he didn't, her brothers would kill him.

Whenever he found himself entertaining the idea that *he*

might have married Payton himself, had he not been idiot enough not to notice her until the day before his wedding to someone else, he generally leaned his head up against one of the walls he could reach and smacked his forehead against it a few times. Not so much out of regret, but out of the mere ludicrousness of the idea. *Him*, marry Payton Dixon? Was he losing his mind? She was just a child.

All right, maybe not a child, but still, she was the little sister of his best friends, the best friends he had ever had. As much as they tended alternately to ignore and browbeat her, they all adored her, and would never have allowed her to marry someone like Drake. They knew him too well, and much of what they knew of him wasn't exactly good. He'd frequented *brothels* with them, after all. They'd shared some of the same women, and the ones they hadn't shared, they'd described in graphic detail to one another. Was *that* the kind of man they would ever allow their sister to wed? A man who mightn't feel the slightest compunction about describing to other men exactly what she'd been like in bed?

No. Without a doubt, no. Hypocritical, maybe, but perfectly understandable. This was their *sister,* after all.

And even if they'd been willing to look beyond that—even if he managed to convince them that a man who bragged about his trysts with prostitutes would never talk that way about his wife—hadn't they all, only just a few weeks ago, been best men at Drake's wedding to someone else? True, that marriage hadn't exactly been consummated—in either sense of the word—but the fact remained, the union had been announced in *The Times*. If he lived to return to England, it would only be to great scandal: after all, he was returning without his bride.

No. There was nothing else for it. Payton Dixon had to marry someone, and right quick.

Maybe, if he lived through this, Drake might even get to like the fellow.

Right.

As the hours stretched into days, and the days into weeks, Drake tried to keep his body active, so it would not atrophy to the extent his mind obviously had. He couldn't walk far in his chains, but he could take three steps forward, and three to either side of the rings to which he was chained. As far as prisons went, this was not the worst in which he'd spent time. He had plenty of clean straw, and two meals a day. The food was pitiful, it was true, but it was at least edible. In addition to these luxuries, he was given a bucket of salt water every morning. He tried to keep himself as clean as he could, since cleanliness was next to godliness, or some such balderdash.

He was slowly losing his mind. He was sure of it.

And the morning the door to his cell opened, and, instead of the enormous man who normally brought his meals, Payton Dixon came in, he knew he had gone completely round the bend.

It wasn't Payton Dixon. It couldn't be. Payton Dixon was hundreds of miles away, back in England. But no matter how hard Drake blinked, the image before him didn't change. It looked exactly like Payton Dixon, as she used to look on board her brothers' ships, dressed in boys' clothes. There was dirt on her face, and her short hair was covered with a knit cap, but it was very clearly Payton Dixon.

He was hallucinating, he knew. It irritated him, this hallucination. Why couldn't he have hallucinated a Payton Dixon in that ballgown she'd been wearing the night before his wedding? Or better yet, naked?

Then the hallucination spoke.

"We're headed for Nassau." Payton bent down and placed a tin cup of fresh water and a bowl of mash beside him. Her back to the guard, who was peering in at them without much interest, she spoke softly and swiftly. He could hardly hear her.

"I haven't figured out why, yet, or what they plan on doing with you. Miss Whitby's on board, and she's all right, but I'm afraid it turns out she's Lucien La Fond's mistress. The baby's his, not yours. I hope you aren't too disappointed."

And then she lifted the empty cup and bowl that had contained his water and mash from the night before, and left. The guard slammed the door behind her, and locked it.

And that was all.

That was all. Except that in a single heartbeat, his world had turned inside out. Payton Dixon, whom he'd thought safely back in England, attending balls and tea parties like any other girl her age, was actually on board this ship—had apparently been aboard this ship all along. She was quite obviously in disguise—Payton had never been one for hats, unless it was cold. Besides, she was meticulous about keeping clean. That dirt on her face had been put there deliberately. She was actually trying to pass herself off as a boy.

Was she *insane*?

Where had she *come* from? What did she think she was *doing*? What was she doing on board this ship?

Tentacles of fear, cold and sharp, wrapped around his heart. Whereas before, he hadn't exactly been happy, sitting there day after day, chained to a wall, at least he hadn't particularly had any worries, other than the obvious one, that he was about to be killed. Now he had another, and very much more disturbing worry: that he was going to have to watch Payton Dixon die, right before he himself was killed.

While death did not trouble Connor Drake—why should it?—the thought of watching Payton Dixon die troubled him very, very much. So much that, for a whole hour after she'd delivered his midday meal, he raged against his chains, cursing and shouting, and in general making a nuisance of himself. When the guard opened the door and told him to shut up, Drake threw his bowl of mash at him.

This earned him a very hard knock on the head. Drake was grateful for the pain. It gave him something else to think about, besides Payton Dixon.

All afternoon, he slumped against the wall, blood trickling from the wound on his forehead, and listened for her. He had never thought to do so before, not having had the slightest suspicion she might be somewhere nearby. He strained his ears listening, but did not hear her voice at all. Where *was* she? Had she been on board all along? How had she gotten there? And what were those clodhopping brothers of hers thinking, letting her put herself in such a dangerous position?

All day, he sat and alternately worried and raged about her presence on the ship. When the light in his cell had finally begun to fade, he heard keys scrape in the lock. He scrambled hastily to his feet. Would she come again? Had that morning's visit been a one-time fluke? Had he imagined the whole thing?

No. He would never have imagined Becky Whitby being Lucien La Fond's mistress. Payton Dixon he'd imagine, yes. But not the part about Miss Whitby.

The door opened, and there she was again. Their gazes collided, and this time, he saw her take a quick step backward, as if she was frightened by what she saw on his face. Good. She should be. Because if La Fond didn't kill her, *he* most certainly was going to, just as soon as someone let him out of these chains.

"Go on, 'Ill" the guard growled, placing a hand in the center of her back and pushing her forward. "And be quick about it."

Drake dragged his murderous gaze from Payton's face and fastened it instead on the guard's. Now he was going to have to kill him, too, for touching her.

No sooner had he broken eye contact with her than Payton hurried forward with his evening meal. Another tin of water, another bowl of mash. She squatted down to place it on the floor near his feet. Drake, watching her, felt the blood drain from his face. When she squatted, the seat of her trousers, which were baggy enough to have accommodated someone twice her size, tightened, revealing all too clearly her heart-shaped backside. No boy in the history of the world ever had a derriere like *that*.

Swallowing hard, Drake glanced in the guard's direction, certain he could not have failed to notice the roundness of "Hill"'s hips. But even as he looked, an explosion sounded nearby—not a loud one, like a cannon, but not a small one, like far-off thunder, either—followed by a bellow that sounded as if it had come from a bull.

The guard looked quickly over his shoulder, in the direction of the explosion, and whatever it was he saw, he started running toward it . . . letting the door to Drake's cell swing shut, locking in both the prisoner and his attendant.

Payton looked up, and he saw that there was a smile playing on her lips. It was a shy smile. She was still a little put off by the way he'd glared at her when she'd come in.

"I created a diversion," she explained, straightening. "We should have a little while before Tito remembers I'm in here with you, and comes back. I tried to lift the keys to your wrist shackles, but I couldn't quite get them. They're on his belt, and he's so damned tall. Sorry."

Drake stared down at her. He felt a sudden compulsion to grab her and shake her until her neck snapped. He even reached out and placed a hand, made all the heavier by the iron around his wrists, on either of her shoulders, gripping her, hard, with his fingers.

But when she looked up at him, there was something in those glowing hazel eyes that made it impossible for him to do anything but pull her—not very gently—against him, and bury his face in the graceful curve that showed through the open collar of her shirt, where her neck met her collarbone.

"Payton," he breathed, inhaling the sweet scent of her. "What are you *doing* here? How did you *get* here?"

She flattened her hands against his chest. When she spoke, her voice was muffled against what was left of his shirt. "Drake," she murmured. *"Drake."*

He wrapped his arms around her, straining her closer to him. "You've lost your mind, you know that, don't you?" he said, into her hair. "They're going to kill us both."

"Don't be an ass."

He almost started laughing at that; it was such a genuinely Payton-like response. She clearly cared about him enough to risk her life for him, yet she called him an ass. He'd been treated a lot more respectfully by many a woman who had loved him less.

Then all urge to laugh left him as it occurred to him that maybe Becky Whitby had been right. Maybe it wasn't *him* she'd set out to rescue at all, but something *else* she loved. . . .

Abruptly, he pushed her away from him—keeping hold of her shoulders, however.

"You listen to me, you little idiot." Now he did shake her, hard enough to send her head snapping forward on her slender neck. "The *Constant*'s gone, do you hear? They blew her away. Out of the water. I saw it with my own eyes. What did you think you were accomplishing, coming after her like this?"

Payton lifted her head to stare up at him, no comprehension whatsoever in her hazel eyes. "W-what?" she stammered.

"Besides, even if she isn't resting on the bottom of the ocean floor, she's *mine,* you understand? You'll never get command of that ship, not while I've got breath left in my body. The sea is no place for a woman. If we live through this, and I *ever* hear you've gotten command of a ship—any ship—I'll track you down and wring your neck, do you hear me?"

She blinked. "I hear you. I think you've lost your mind, but I hear you."

"The minute we get anywhere near land—I don't care where—you wait until night, and then you lower a longboat and you row toward it. Understand? And then you wait on land until a Dixon ship pulls into port. Do you hear me, Payton? Do you understand?"

There was no confusion in her gaze now. She fixed him with an irritated glare. "Why don't you say it a little louder, Drake? I don't think the whole ship heard you."

"I mean it, Payton." He punctuated each of his syllables with a shake. "This is not a game. These men are vicious, vicious criminals. If they find out who you are—"

"God." She reached up and pulled down on either side of her hat, which had come loose from all the shaking. "So far

I've been a lot safer with *them* than I have with you. None of *them* have laid a hand on me—"

"The minute they suss out you're a woman, they'll lay a lot more than a hand on you, sweetheart, I can guarantee that." Just saying it, he felt as if someone had kicked him in the chest. He gripped her as tightly as fear gripped him. "I want you off this ship, Payton. I want you off this ship just as soon as you can get off."

"I thought I told you"—she swung up both her arms and, bringing them around beneath his, neatly broke his hold on her by ramming his forearms, hard, with her own. Then, to avoid being captured again, she danced out of his reach—"not to be such an ass."

"Payton." He tugged furiously on his chains, trying to get hold of her. "I mean it. I want you to do as I say."

"What happened to your head?" Payton asked, staring at him curiously.

He reached up and touched the place where the guard had struck him, earlier that day. It was tacky with blood.

"Nothing," he said, bringing his hand down. "Payton. Where are your brothers? How in hell did they let you out of their sight?"

"My brothers, for all I know, are still trying to get the *Virago*'s cannons out from under the mainsail that collapsed on top of them. That's what they were doing last time I saw them, and I haven't seen a sign of them since. I walked over from the *Virago*." She explained it so matter-of-factly, as though it wasn't at all an extraordinary thing to have done. "It collided with the *Mary B,* which was the ship that attacked the *Constant.* I've been working here in the kitchens ever since . . . but that's not important. What's important is, we have to figure out a way off this wreck, and before we get to Nassau." She studied him with those incandescently hazel eyes. "Were you very upset about Miss Whitby?"

He frowned. "*Miss Whitby?* What about her?"

Payton looked heavenward—or in this case, toward the

leaky ceiling. "I *told* you. She's carrying Lucien La Fond's
ba—"

"Oh, right, right." His head started to throb all of a sudden,
and he put his hand back up to the wound. "I heard you the
first time. Payton, I want you to promise me that the minute
land comes in sight, you'll make for it. Promise me you'll do
as I say."

She shook her head. "No. Why should I? You can't order
me around. You're not *my* captain."

It was a good thing she was standing so far from his reach.
His fingers fairly itched to curl around that neck.

"Payton." He was convinced he was in hell. That was it.
He wasn't actually being held captive by Lucien La Fond. He
was actually dead, and this was hell. It had to be. There
couldn't possibly be anything worse than this. He took a deep
breath, striving for patience. "The *Constant* is gone, I'm telling
you. I saw it with my own eyes. It was on fire. I don't know
what you think you're doing here—"

"Uh," Payton said. "I would think that would be obvious.
I'm here to rescue you."

"Payton." He told himself to breathe. Deep, even breaths.
It was like diving. Talking to Payton was like deep-sea diving.
In between dives, you had to keep breathing, deep and even.
"You can't rescue me. My God, honey, you can't even begin
to realize what you're up against—"

"Oh, I see," Payton said. She was examining the sleeves of
her shirt where he'd held on to her so tightly, the material was
actually damp. "Because I'm just a woman, I suppose."

"Payton. That's not what I meant."

"You know, I'm surprised, Drake. Really. Because you certainly never noticed I was a woman before now."

"What are you talking about? Of course I—"

"Oh, sure. That night in the garden you noticed, all right.
But before that, nothing. No acknowledgment whatsoever."

"Payton. This is insane—"

"Oh, no." Her hands were on her hips, her face thrust toward his. "You couldn't marry *me*. No, *I* was objectionable.

But you could marry a woman who was carrying another man's child easily enough."

"What are you *talking* about?"

"Miss Whitby, of course."

He said, through clenched teeth, "Payton. I thought I *had* to marry her."

"If you'd kept your trousers buttoned, you wouldn't have had that worry, would you? But no, you had to go and put—"

Drake could not quite believe he was having this conversation. "For your information," he interrupted, before she could go on—he was very much afraid about what she would say if she was allowed to continue—"I did keep my trousers buttoned. She told me it was Richard's."

That got her attention. She dropped her hands from her hips. *"What?"*

"She told me it was Richard's."

"Richard's? Your *brother's*? She told you she was carrying your brother's child?"

He nodded. "Now, please, Payton. Wait until dark, then *get off this ship*."

But Payton appeared not to have heard him. "But Richard's dead," she said. "How could she be carrying your brother's baby, if he was dead?"

"They met before he died, Payton." He'd been right. This *was* hell. And Payton Dixon was going to torture him until he descended into madness, as well. "In London. He was there for the season, and they met in some shop somewhere. When he went back to Daring Park, he wrote her letters, love letters. She showed them to me. She wrote him about the child, he wrote back, asking her to marry him. He died from being thrown from his horse while he was on his way back to London to see her. That day we met her, outside that inn, was supposedly just a coincidence. She was on her way to the same solicitors, to see if any provision had been made for her in Richard's will—which, of course, it had not."

"Oh," Payton said, in a very small voice.

Drake shook his head. "Now I know that whole little performance, the reticule being stolen, Marcus Tyler having seen her and my brother together, which was why, she told me in the vicar's study, he was blackmailing her for the map—it was all planned." He caught a trace of the smell of smoke. Whatever "diversion" Payton had created, he hoped it wasn't going to end up killing them both. "But at the time, I didn't know that. I believed her. I thought my brother had got her with child. She wouldn't take any money from me. She put on quite a convincing act, Payton. And so I did the only thing I could think of—"

"Oh," Payton said again. Only this time, she folded her arms across her chest. "Marrying her yourself was the *only* thing you could think of? Don't patronize me, Drake. You *liked* her. You thought she was—"

"Payton. Do we have to go into this *now*?"

Her chin slid out obstinately. "Yes."

"I thought she was a pretty girl," he told her, as loudly as he dared, "whom my brother had left in a terrible spot. Yes, I *liked* her. I didn't *know* her, but she seemed like the kind of girl who'd make a good wife, and I certainly wasn't getting any younger, and so I figured—"

"You figured you'd hit two birds with one stone." Payton was glaring at him now. "You'd give a name to your brother's bastard, and you'd get yourself a pretty little mealy-mouthed wife who'd sit at home darning socks for you while you were away at sea."

"All right," he said, with a sharp nod. "Yes, that's exactly what I thought. Now will you please get out of here? Because if they come back and find you here harping at me like a fishwife, they're going to *know* you're a woman."

"Be quiet." She was pacing back and forth inside his tiny cell now, only it took her twice as many steps. Six steps starboard. Six steps back. "You ended up getting a lot more than you bargained for, didn't you? Because the pretty little mealy-mouthed bride turned out to be a spy for Marcus Tyler." She stopped pacing, and stood furiously in front of him. "How could you have been so stupid, Drake? How *could* you?"

Drake licked his lips—cracked from having received so little fresh water over the past few weeks—and said nastily, "Well, maybe, if you had once acted like a *woman,* and put on a *dress* once in a while, I might not have been so quick to succumb to Miss Whitby's charms—"

Payton sucked in her breath. Payton, when she was at her most indignant, always put him in mind of a shipboard cat upon whose tail someone had inadvertently trod. She looked even more like one now, as she puffed out her chest and snapped, "How *dare* you try to turn this around so it's *my* fault? If you couldn't see there was a woman underneath those trousers all along, then all I can say is, you and Miss Whitby deserve each other! I hope you'll be very happy toge—"

It worked. He'd gotten her so riled up that she inadvertently stepped too close to him. In a second, he had her by both shoulders again, only this time, he didn't shake her. He held her fast in a grip of iron, pulling her up onto her toes and lowering his head until his face was just inches from hers.

"Now, you listen to me, Payton Dixon, and you listen hard. It doesn't matter what happens to me, because either way, I'm a dead man. If I don't get off this ship, La Fond'll kill me, and if I do, your brothers'll kill me, for having gotten you into this fix in the first place. Frankly, between the Frenchman and your brothers, I'd take La Fond any day of the week. He'll probably let me die a quicker death, anyway." She was wriggling like a porpoise to get away. He only took firmer hold of her. "We've been at sea for nearly three weeks now. If I know La Fond, he's taking the long way, because he'll think anyone following will assume he'd take the shortest path back to Nassau. So we'll probably be approaching the American coast soon. As soon as you see it—as *soon* as you see it—you wait until dark, and then you slip into a longboat and you cut the lines and you *go!*"

She was still squirming. "Not without you."

"*No!* That is what I do *not* want you to do. *Don't* wait for me, Payton. If I even *start* to suspect that you're waiting around for some chance to rescue me, I swear to God, Payton, I'll—"

She stopped squirming. Her eyes opened very wide. Her lips, he noticed, parted slightly. This was very distracting. She said, in a voice hard with challenge, "You'll what?"

He really felt that what happened next was her own fault.

# Chapter Sixteen

The Honorable Miss Payton Dixon did not fancy herself a theologian. In fact, there had been times when she'd been in serious doubt of God's existence.

Now, however, was not one of those times. Because God— that same God who'd taken Payton's mother from her at birth, and then cursed her further by letting her grow up to have hardly any bosom to speak of—had answered her prayers:

She was in Connor Drake's arms, and Connor Drake was kissing her.

She wasn't quite sure how it happened. One minute his hands had been gripping her shoulders, and he'd been shaking her—shaking her hard, too—and the next, he was kissing her, as passionately and as emphatically as, a few seconds before, he'd been shouting at her.

Payton couldn't help thinking, even as she kissed him back, that this moment, this very moment, made it all worthwhile . . . all of it, everything she'd had to suffer since she'd boarded this miserable vessel. His whiskers, which had turned into a full-blown mustache and beard in the weeks he'd been incarcerated, rasped the sensitive skin around her mouth, and when, a second later, he dragged his lips from her mouth, to press them against her neck, his hot breath burned her throat, making her shudder pleasurably, and her nipples go hard beneath the soft linen of her shirt, and the heavier material of her borrowed vest.

That sensation alone, of his lips on her neck, convinced her: it had all been worth it—the pots she'd been forced to scrub; the buckets of water she'd had to haul back and forth from the after house; the fact that she hadn't been able to take a proper bath in a month; the fact that she had to wait until midnight every night before she could find a quiet corner in which to conduct her personal business, if she wanted to lower her trousers without fear of getting caught not having that particular appendage which the rest of the crew waved so proudly over the back of the ship whenever the urge took them.

It was all worth it. Even the reception she had received when she'd first entered the prisoner's cell—even that was forgiven, now. Oh, it had been sweet enough, at first . . . until he'd started shaking her. *That* hadn't been at all the kind of welcome she'd been expecting. She hadn't exactly thought Drake would be overjoyed to see her, true—he'd surely have been happier, she supposed, to see his precious Miss Whitby— but then, she hadn't expected him to be so *angry,* either. What ailed the man? Here she was, risking life and limb for him, and he hadn't seemed the least bit grateful.

When she'd first seen the murderous rage in Drake's eyes, Payton almost turned around and ran. Except she'd gone to so much trouble—pouring that gunpowder into the dunderfunk mix, timing its explosion just so that she could have a little while alone with him—she couldn't bring herself to go.

Weathering his initial wrath seemed worth it now. His lips on hers made it all worthwhile; the hunger in his kiss, the desperation—like that kiss he'd given her the night before his wedding—was such that she knew, then and there, she'd done the right thing. This man needed her. She was vital to him, she realized. It was right there, in the greedy way he was kissing her, the urgency with which his tongue was prying her lips apart. She'd been a fool not to see it before.

Or maybe she had, and that was why, in spite of everything, she'd never let him push her completely away, no matter how hard he'd tried. She was as vital to him as food and air. He didn't want to admit that—that was obvious. But it was also obvious in the way he was kissing her that he couldn't do without her.

The realization filled her with giddy joy, and she clung to him. He tasted exactly the way he smelled, of fresh clean ocean, salty, bracing. It felt wonderful, more wonderful than she ever would have dreamed, to be in his arms again. The man had been weeks in an airless cell, and yet he still smelled the same, of salt air and clean, healthy male. It was an odor as familiar to her as home. It was *Drake*. There was no sweeter fragrance in the world than him.

Her fingers fisted in his hair, that baby-fine blond hair that felt so wrong on such a large, hard man. Payton could feel that hardness swelling against her, as certainly as she could feel the softness of his hair, the bristles of his beard scraping against her face. She knew what it was this time, that thick stiffness prodding against the front of his trousers, and this time, she sure as hell wasn't going to touch it; not after what happened last time.

But it sort of seemed to her as if this time he wanted her to. Because as he'd been kissing her, Drake had been slowly backing up—taking her with him—until he came up against the wall to which he was chained. Then, slowly, he slid down that wall, still taking her with him, until he was seated on the floor of his cell . . .

And *she* was seated in his lap.

Only she wasn't even sitting, really. *Straddling* his lap was more like it, facing toward him, her trousered legs on either side of his, a position of which Georgiana would most heartily disapprove, but which Payton couldn't help feeling was absolutely right. She tended to think Drake agreed—especially when he breathed her name against her hair. Payton heard it, but more than that, she *felt* it, the deep reverberation of his voice in his chest. He was straining her so tightly to him that it seemed as if when he spoke, the sound went straight through her. His voice, saying her name, made something happen to her spine, loosened it, changed it from rigid bone to a substance more akin to butter. She brought her face away from where she'd buried it against his neck, and looked up at him, wondering how he'd done it, this magic with his voice.

But he soon gave her other things to wonder about. His hands, which had been wrapped around her, moved to grip her shoulders. Then one went to her arm, and the other to her waist. Then she realized the one at her waist had actually dipped down beneath her vest, and then disappeared inside it. She could feel the heat of his hand against her ribs, his fingers separated from her bare flesh by only the thin linen of her borrowed shirt.

And something else was happening. At first she'd thought it an accident, when that hard shaft, pressing so deliberately against the soft twill of his breeches, had suddenly brushed against the seams that kept her trouser legs together. She knew he didn't like to be touched there, and so she'd tried to move away, but the hand on her arm pressed her back down—quite firmly, in fact. So firmly that the swollen head of that shaft stabbed her in the most intimate of places. Intimate and, to Payton, quite unexpected. She let out a little bark of surprise and broke the kiss, rearing back to get a look at this man who was assaulting her so suddenly, and on so many fronts.

"What—" she started to inquire, through lips reddened from his kiss, but then her voice caught in her throat as Drake, his gaze very much below her neck, and unabashedly so, soundlessly and deliberately untied the string that held her shirt collar closed at the throat. Payton, confused, followed his gaze, but saw only her chest, the skin of which Georgiana had declared disgracefully tanned. What interest Drake could have in the skin of her chest, Payton hadn't the slightest idea . . . until the hand that had untied her shirtfront dipped inside it to cup one of her small, tip-tilted breasts.

She sucked in her breath. Never had she felt heat like that, not *there*. As his fingers tightened, his palm grazed the tender bud of her nipple, which had gone rigid—both of them—the minute he'd first started kissing her. It was torture—exquisite torture—feeling that skin so close, yet not quite touching that part of her that was stretching, yearning for his touch . . .

And then she realized why he'd reacted the way he had that night in the garden, when she'd reached for the front of his breeches. He hadn't been angry with her. He'd *wanted* her to touch him there, the same way she was yearning for him to flatten his hand against her breast. He'd probably just been surprised she was so forward.

Well, then he didn't really know her, did he?

Tightening her arms around his neck, she pulled his head down so that she could kiss him again—and artfully thrust the whole of her breast against his hand as she did so. She shuddered pleasantly as his fingers caressed the soft flesh, kneading, exploring it. She might not have had enough bosom to adequately fill the fashionably low-cut bodices of the day, but it was clear that to this man, anyway, what she did have was more than sufficient.

And then it happened again, that prodding of her privates. This time, she wasn't surprised—nor did she try to move away. Just the opposite, in fact. She pressed her pelvis down against that thick hardness, and felt a pleasurable tightening where her legs joined together. Just to make sure she hadn't been imagining things, she pressed again, and got the same reaction—a sweet little throb. Well, not really a throb. More like a tug.

Only this time, in addition to the tug, she also elicited a reaction from Drake—a sort of groan, deep in the back of his throat. She pulled away from him at once, worried she'd hurt him. Maybe, as firm as it felt beneath her, that iron rod wasn't meant to be bounced on quite so energetically—

But again, Drake pushed her right back down on top of him. This time when he did so, he was looking her straight in the eye. For once, Payton was able to meet his gaze without feeling that those blue eyes of his were filled with ice. In fact, he even wore a slight, crooked grin on his face. Well, if he's grinning, Payton thought, he can't be in too much pain.

Far from it, apparently. Because a second later, he'd unbuttoned her vest and completely parted her shirtfront, then lowered his head to stare at her bare chest. Payton, looking down, couldn't see what was holding his interest so closely. All she saw were her breasts, which were so small and firm that they hardly ever moved on their own, not bouncing much even when she was running. Her nipples, too, she thought on the puny side, the areoles very narrow as well as a rather alarming shade of pink. Naked to the brisk sea air, they were both erect, pointing rather saucily toward the ceiling. Payton felt she ought to apologize for both their lack of size and appalling color. She had in fact opened her lips to do so when Drake did something perfectly extraordinary, and surely not at all proper: he lifted a hand, the chain descending from it clanking against the floor, until his fingers cupped her right breast, and then, bending his head, seized the hardened nipple in his mouth.

For Payton, the resulting rush of sensations was overwhelming. The heat from his mouth—the hot brush of his tongue—singed her, causing her back to arch, and a flood of moisture to dampen the gusset of her drawers. What was happening to her? The tug she'd felt between her legs had turned into a pull, and suddenly, she was pressing herself against his erection not because it felt pleasurable, but because it seemed necessary to her very sanity. He was a solid rock to which she could cling in what had become a maelstrom of desire . . .

Her breath caught as his month-old growth of beard razed against the tender skin of her chest as he slid his mouth from one nipple to the other. Both his hands had risen now to imprison her breasts. She clung to his shoulders, feeling him move beneath her, feeling herself begin to move with him, along the length of his enormous erection and back up again, pressing as close as she could without actually taking him inside of her.

And then one of his hands left her breasts, and moved

down, to fumble with the buckle of her belt. Payton hardly noticed. Her breath was coming in short, sharp gasps. She held twin fistfuls of his shirt, still moving against him, oblivious to everything except the pull between her legs, which seemed to have taken over her entire body, and had turned into an ache, an ache only he could fill. She was using him, she knew, using him for her own selfish pleasure, and she felt guilty about that, especially because in some distant part of her mind she seemed to remember that at one time he hadn't wanted her to touch him there . . .

Well, she wasn't touching him there. Not with her hands, anyway.

And then she was exploding, like one of her brothers' cannons. It was as if someone had lit a fuse beneath her and she had been shot up toward the night sky, where she was racing faster and faster toward the stars, until suddenly, she'd collided, in a shower of sparks and twinkling lights, into one of those stars. Her back arched, her fingernails dug into Drake's shoulders, her thighs tightening around him like a vise. She was dimly aware that Drake's hands had left her breasts, and were now holding onto her hips as she writhed against him.

And then she let out a cry, and collapsed against his bare chest.

# Chapter Seventeen

*He* cradled her head against his shoulder, listening to her unsteady breathing, although it was almost drowned out by the roar of the waves through which the *Rebecca* was plowing. Beneath him, he could hear the creak of the ill-made ship as the wood protested against the strain the captain was putting it under, forcing it to travel at such excessive speeds. Above him, he heard the cry of the midwatchman, and the violent flap of a torn seam in a topsail. And against him, he felt her heartbeat go from racing to a slow, even rhythm against his chest.

She was so small that even with her full body weight resting on him, she seemed light as a child. He had to remind himself that she was a fully mature woman—probably nineteen years old by now, if they'd truly been aboard this wretched vessel as many days as his hatch marks on the wall indicated. Nineteen was certainly not ancient, but it wasn't anything to sneeze at, either.

Of course, Payton Dixon might have been nineteen, but she was also a virgin. That made her seem younger than any other woman he'd ever been with . . . in spite of the fact that she'd assaulted him in a manner that hardly suggested any sort of virginal modesty. What kind of virgin *was* she, he couldn't help asking himself, that she was capable of an assault like that?

Which was exactly how he felt. Like he'd been the victim of an assault. Oh, he'd started it. He was more than aware that he was the one who'd started it, with that first burning kiss. And it wasn't as·if he minded what that kiss had brought about. At least, not very much. No man would mind being assaulted in that way, not by a young and pretty girl. He certainly wasn't complaining . . .

Though it might have been nice if he, like Payton, had found some relief. He was still rock-hard, and starting to ache a little. Even through the double layer of their clothing, he could feel the moist heat emanating from between her legs. The temptation to loosen her trousers, tuck her beneath him, and rut upon her with wild abandon was a strong one.

Fortunately, despite the weeks he'd spent chained to this damned wall—and despite his earlier behavior, which he already regretted, and deeply—he was still aware that he was a gentleman. Dimly aware of it, but aware, all the same. And so he shifted her limp body a little—to relieve some of the pressure on his erection—and simply held her, trying hard to think of things other than what it would be like to make love to Payton Dixon.

Which was easier said than done. It had been an entirely new experience to him, being with a woman whose sole motivation was pleasuring herself; every other woman he'd ever been with had had *his* pleasure foremost in mind, not her own. Well, he'd generally paid them, and very well, for the courtesy.

But even the women he had not hired—the native girls, curious about the white men who'd arrived on the tall ships— had never straddled him and rode him as if he were a stallion.

And she was a *virgin*. That was the worst part. She was a *virgin*. *He* ought to have been the one showing her how love between two people was properly made. But she hadn't given him the chance. After he'd started kissing her, she'd attacked him with so much ingenuous sensuality that he'd hardly had a chance to catch his breath, let alone gain the upper hand. Who would have thought that there was that much sensuality packed into the compact little body resting so comfortably against him?

He ought to have known. It had been there all along, after all, in the way he'd occasionally caught her looking at him, her eyes disappearing behind a veil of thick brown lashes as soon as he glanced in her direction. In the way she'd made it her habit to sit near him at mealtimes—never directly beside him, but close enough to overhear his conversations, and put in a saucy remark of her own. In the way she always chose to stand by him . . . not too close. Never too close, lest one of her brothers should be watching . . . but close enough so that occasionally, when he'd turn around, he'd nearly step on her.

How long had Payton Dixon been watching him, measuring him, sizing him up for her own? And how long had he stumbled around in complete ignorance of it, of *her,* never having the slightest clue that everything he'd ever been looking for in a woman was standing right there beside him? It wasn't until that kiss in the garden the night before his wedding that he'd realized its existence, this incredible sensuality with which the Honorable Miss Payton Dixon was fairly brimming over. Discovering it the night before he was to marry someone else had very nearly driven him mad. How could he, even for the best of all reasons, have married a Becky Whitby, knowing there was a Payton Dixon in the world?

Still, in the moments when he dared to envision a future that included Payton—and those moments were rare and far between, since, locked as he was in the hold of an enemy ship, he did not suppose he had much of future, with or without Payton, or any other woman, for that matter—he had never imagined their first time together quite *this* way. When he let himself picture making love to her at all, the deed was always conducted in the large, satin-sheeted bed in the captain's cabin on the *Constant,* with moonlight spilling in through the casement windows, and the gentle lap of ocean waves the only accompaniment. He had certainly never imagined making love to her in the stinking hold of this pirate ship, to the sound of clanking metal links; nor that when the moment finally came, either of them would remain fully clothed for very long . . .

As if she'd read his thoughts, Payton raised her head just then, and said, "I don't think I did that right."

He tried not to smile, since she seemed quite serious. His attempt was not quite successful.

"Well," he replied. His voice was a little wobbly, thanks to the discomfort in his breeches. He cleared his throat. "That would be a matter of opinion, I suppose."

"My guess is that I should have waited until we'd taken our pants off."

"That's generally how the thing is done."

"I couldn't wait, though," she informed him. And then, with a slight movement of her hips, and a quick downward glance at the place where the front of his trousers bulged with the evidence of his arousal, she said brightly, "But it's not too late, is it? I mean, *you* had the self-control to wait. Why don't we—"

Well, what had he expected? There was very little the Honorable Miss Dixon did not take in stride. It could be assumed that sexual transgressions like the one they'd just shared shocked her no more than anything else. Her fingers were actually on his belt when he reached out and took hold of her wrist. "Payton," he said.

The stricken expression that came over her face when she looked up to meet his gaze was heartbreaking to see. "Oh," she said, drawing her hand away as if his belt buckle had grown very hot of a sudden. "I'm sorry. Only I thought—you see, I thought maybe you wanted to." Again the quick glance at the front of his trousers. Then, she said, very quickly, "But that's all right, really."

"Payton." He didn't release her wrist, although she was pulling on it, and trying to roll off him, at the same time. He wouldn't let her. "Listen to me."

"No, it's all right, really. I know I get carried away sometimes. Don't pay any mind to me. I'll just be going now—"

Only a quick flexing of his muscles kept her from escaping. Her catlike agility was startling, but he possessed the superior strength, despite the cumbersome chains round his wrists. In a moment, he had her pinned beneath him, exactly where he'd fantasized about having her. Only now it was to keep her from leaving, not to deflower her.

"No," he growled. "You're not going anywhere until you've listened to me."

She seemed too astonished to reply. Encouraged by this rare silence on her part, he went on.

"Listen, Payton," he said. "That wasn't how it ought to have been—"

"I know." Her voice was filled with self-loathing. "I did it all wrong. Just like in the garden."

He let go of one of her wrists long enough to reach up to stroke some of her thick, short curls away from her eyes. "No. No, honey, you didn't do anything wrong. It's just that this isn't exactly how I wanted it—our first time—to be . . ."

The despair he'd seen in her hazel eyes fled, and was replaced by something he could not put a name to. "You *thought* about it before?" she asked eagerly. "You thought about you and me doing *that*?"

He had to clear his throat again. Really, he was not at all used to having these sorts of brutally frank conversations. But then, when Payton was involved, it was virtually impossible to have anything else. "About making love with you? Yes, of course I've thought about it. And this isn't—"

*"Really?"* She'd begun to squirm beneath him in a manner that was entirely too provocative for his peace of his mind. "When?"

"When what?"

"When did you start thinking about making love with me?"

"When did I—" He broke off and shook his head. "That doesn't matter. What I'm trying to tell you, Payton, is that what you and I just did, that wasn't how I—"

"It matters to me."

If he hadn't known her better, he might have suspected her

of pouting. But Payton Dixon never pouted. Threw punches, maybe, but never pouted.

"I never even knew you *liked* me," she went on, "let alone thought about making love with me."

"If you'd let me finish," he said, between gritted teeth, "I'll tell you about it." He wasn't gritting his teeth out of impatience, but because it was damned uncomfortable, having her squirming beneath him like that, when he was still so hard. Well, hell, what could anyone expect? It had been months since he'd last had a woman. And he'd *never* had one like *this*, who'd sat perched astride him with such insouciance, not caring a whit that her breasts were quite bare. Even now, he could feel her nipples, hardened into little pink pebbles from the ocean breeze that seeped in around them, pressing against his thickly matted chest hair.

"Well, I'm sorry," Payton said, sounding a good deal more indignant than apologetic, "but I've never done anything like this before—"

"I should sincerely hope *not*," he interrupted, horrified.

"And so I'm not sure how I'm supposed to act," she continued, as if he hadn't spoken. "I wish I could be vulnerable and feminine like Miss Whitby, but—"

"You're not supposed to *act* like anything but yourself," he ground out. "And certainly not like Becky Whitby."

"Well." She sniffed missishly. "It took you long enough to realize *that*."

*Now* his teeth were gritted with impatience. "Payton. If we live through this—"

"What do you mean, *if*?" She looked up at him in astonishment, as if he had suddenly slipped into the early stages of dementia. "Don't worry, Drake. We've been in much worse spots. This is nothing. I'll get us out of this."

She said it with such casual assurance that for a moment, the actual meaning of the words escaped him. When it finally did sink in, he was gripped by a chill that had nothing to do with the temperature of the air outside his cell, which had actually been daily growing warmer.

"No," he said, reaching up to lay a hand upon either side of her face. "No, Payton, listen to me."

He'd been a fool, he realized. He'd been a fool ever to kiss her in the first place. He ought to have done everything he could—everything he *had been* doing, before he'd let those lips of hers go to his head—to frighten her away, to convince her that he didn't care for her. Maybe then she'd have done the sensible thing. Maybe then she'd have left this infernally damned ship . . .

But he'd let himself be distracted by the shape of that damned mouth of hers. Fool that he was.

"Payton, you've got to promise me that just as soon as an opportunity to get off this boat presents itself, you'll take it. Don't worry about me. I can take care of myself—"

She snorted at that. "Oh, and you've done an exemplary job so far."

He tightened his grip on her face. "I mean it, Payton. It's only dumb, blind luck that you haven't been found out yet. How much longer do you think you can keep up this charade?"

She shrugged. "Indefinitely. Even Becky Whitby hasn't recognized me. I don't see why anyone else on board should—"

Incredible. He could not fathom how anyone could look at her and not see that she was a woman, in every sense of the word. The very thought of what would happen to her when someone finally did—and it was inevitable that someone would—made his blood run cold.

"Payton, you've got to—"

"Yes, yes." She rolled her eyes. "I heard you the first time, Drake. Let's get back to what you were saying before, when you were talking about how you used to think about us making love."

"*No*. Payton, you've got to promise me—"

But before he could get another word out, footsteps sounded outside Drake's cell. She stiffened at once. "Tito's coming back," she said. "Let me go."

He didn't loosen his hold. "Promise me you'll leave. Promise."

She started squirming again. He noticed that this time, she was careful not to look him in the eye. "Drake—"

His fingers sank through the linen of her shirt, into the soft flesh of her upper arms. *"Promise me."*

"God, all *right,* I promise. Now, let *go*—"

Tito opened the door just as Drake released her. Payton scrambled to her feet, adjusting her loosened clothing. Fortunately, the guard had eyes only for the greasy-looking fistful of food he held.

"Eh, 'Ill," he said, between bites. "Cook wants ye."

Hill—Jeremiah Hill—was the name Payton had told her fellow seamen she went by. In response to it, she reached down and lifted the empty cup and bowl left over from the first time she'd visited him. "I'm coming," she said, to the toes of her shoes.

"Better 'urry." The giant was still chewing laconically. "Stove exploded. One o' them bastards from the *Mary B* musta thrown some gunpowder in it. Never seen anythin' like it. Dunderfunk all over the galley." He swallowed, then lifted the wad of food in his hand, and bit into it again. Grease ran down his beard. "If you're wantin' any supper, you better get there soon, or it'll be gone in no time."

"Right. Thanks, Tito." Payton rose, and without looking at Drake again, left the room.

Watching her walk away, Drake wondered how anyone could ever mistake her for a boy, even dressed in those baggy trousers. To him, it seemed as if her every movement screamed her femininity. The fact that that femininity had always been there, and he himself hadn't noticed it until recently only served to rankle him further. All he could think about was what was going to happen when—and he knew it was a matter of when, not if—her true identity was discovered. He didn't think he could bear it. Never had he felt so helpless, so ineffectual.

Helplessness was not an emotion Connor Drake was used to feeling. In fact, it was quite alien to him. As he sat slumped in his cell the rest of that night, however, he realized helplessness was something he was going to have to get used to. At least so long as he was chained to this wall.

And at least as long as Payton Dixon remained on board this ship.

# Chapter Eighteen

*W*ell, damn him, anyway.

Who did he think he was? Just who did he think he was, ordering her about as if she were his bosun?

Payton, scouring the galley floor the next morning, was almost glad the explosion she'd triggered had sent hardtack crusting nearly every surface in the forecastle. She needed something to do to keep her mind off Drake.

Not that it was working. As she scrubbed, she couldn't help going over and over yesterday's alarming events.

Did he think it had been easy for her, any of it? It hadn't. Especially convincing Clarence to let her start bringing the prisoner his meals. She badgered him quite literally for weeks. In the end, it had not been any effort on Payton's part that changed the cook's mind, but the simple fact that, the *Rebecca* having taken on the crew of the *Mary B* when the *Virago*'s cannons destroyed the ship, food was in such short supply that Clarence no longer dared leave the galley, for fear of every edible morsel within it being stolen. Payton now had to deliver the captain's meals under armed escort, while the rest of the crew stared, licking their lips, at the platters she held.

Of the three of them—Drake, Becky Whitby, and Payton— Payton considered her lot the hardest. After all, Drake was nice and snug, locked in a little room all by himself. Becky

Whitby was living in luxurious comfort in the after house, as Payton had seen with her own eyes the very first morning she'd delivered the captain his breakfast.

No, it was Payton who was the most unfortunate of the three of them, Payton who'd been slaving away since her arrival, peeling potatoes and chopping celery and boiling pig parts.

Was she to be blamed, then, for grasping that tiny share of happiness she'd found in Drake's lap?

She didn't understand why he was so upset. It was extremely unlikely she was going to be found out. In fact, up until that afternoon, her sojourn upon the *Rebecca* had been no different from her stay on any of her brothers' ships—with the exception of the fact that her duties on board the *Rebecca* were significantly more manual—no boxing the compass for her here—and there was no bed reserved for her in the after house. There was no bed for her *anywhere,* in fact, since the crew of the *Mary B* was crowded into the *Rebecca*'s forecastle. Payton had taken to snagging a blanket and stationing herself below, as close as she could get to the room in which Drake was locked. She wasn't able to speak to him through the thick walls, but it comforted her to know he was there, just a few feet away.

So what was he so worried about? She didn't know. But then, what *did* she understand about men? Not a whole hell of a lot, she was realizing.

Why, for instance, would a man be willing to marry a woman he'd thought his dead brother had impregnated? Drake had spoken of duty, but Payton suspected that had Becky Whitby been unattractive, he'd probably have found some other way to satisfy his sense of duty toward his dead brother's child, other than marrying its mother.

And his jibe that had Payton ever bothered to act like a woman herself, he might not have fallen so easily under Miss Whitby's charm had hurt more than he would ever know. Why hadn't he been able to see that the rough-and-tumble ways taught to Payton by her brothers were not her true nature? For close to twenty years, she had mimicked the behavior she saw all around her, only realizing that behavior was inappropriate for someone of her sex when one of her brothers finally married, and an undeniably feminine influence began to be exerted in Payton's direction.

Still, that didn't explain Drake's behavior, back in his cell. Payton was beginning to think there was no rational explanation for that.

*Men.* What was *wrong* with them?

Take that ridiculous promise he'd forced her to make. Good Lord, he couldn't possibly think she intended to keep that one. Leave the ship, without him? Not bloody likely.

It was all well and good for him to tell her to abandon ship. Maybe if she felt a little less for him, she would. Then again, maybe not. Only a lily-livered coward would leave behind a fellow crew member, and save himself. Was Drake asking her to be a coward? Because she wouldn't do it. She was a Dixon. She had a name to live up to. She would never leave anyone behind, not the lowliest cabin boy, not the scurviest dog of a swabbie.

Not even Becky Whitby.

Or at least that's what she'd told herself, before she'd known the true nature of Miss Whitby's relationship with Captain La Fond. Payton remembered that first morning she'd brought the captain his breakfast, how nervous she'd been about what she'd find behind the door of the after house. She had seen Becky Whitby conveyed there, and she had not seen Becky Whitby come out. Would that door open to reveal the girl's bloodied corpse?

But when the door had been flung open at her tentative knock, she'd been relieved. No Becky Whitby in sight, and the man who'd stood before her hadn't looked particularly fearful.

*This* was the infamous pirate captain Lucien La Fond? she'd thought to herself, at the time. The Frenchman, whose very name, mentioned in Kingston or Havana, made men reach for their swords? Certainly he *looked* the part. He was tall enough, she supposed, to intimidate those of average or less stature on his crew. And he was certainly dressed as foppishly as any pirate she'd ever seen, fashion sense being something the mercenaries she'd met had generally seemed to lack. His coat was velvet and a rather shocking shade of turquoise, while his fingers were quite heavily ringed, and the lace on his shirt cuffs so long, they reached almost to his knuckles.

But he was by no means fearsome-looking, as the most famous pirate captain of all, Blackbeard, was rumored to have been. In fact, the Frenchman was rather good-looking, with a full head of black hair, tied back in a ponytail, and a rather dashing black mustache. Just then, however, his facial muscles were tight with worry. He was obviously concerned about something, and kept pacing back and forth in front of a closed door that Payton assumed led to his private sitting room.

She'd wondered what he had done with Becky Whitby. Had he, as she most certainly would have done, thrown the odious Miss Whitby overboard, after having been forced to listen to her weep night after night? Or had she barricaded herself fearfully behind that door? Pirates were a frightful lot, thinking nothing of raping any woman they could get their hands on, but Lucien La Fond looked like the sort who might try, at least, to pass himself off as a gentleman. And his concern for whoever was behind that door appeared quite genuine. When the ship surgeon arrived moments after Payton, the captain accosted him immediately.

"Isn't there anything you can do to make her more comfortable?" he'd asked, his voice, with only the slightest trace of a French accent, sounding a bit desperate. "What about laudanum?"

"But, sir, think of the babe," the surgeon had cried.

"Blast the babe!" the captain had exploded. "I can't stand to see her suffering so!"

The surgeon had shaken his head. "Sir, you cannot mean that. Surely you don't want me to risk the life of your child simply because its mother is suffering from a little bout of seasickness—"

"Lucien?" The voice that had come from behind the silk-padded door was weak, but it seemed to have an electrifying effect on the pirate captain. He threw himself upon it at once, and heaved it open.

"Yes, my love?"

Payton had caught a glimpse of the heart-shaped face as it lifted weakly from the arm of a satin-covered couch. "Is that Mr. Jenkins?" that all-too familiar voice had asked.

"Yes, madam." The surgeon had hurried in after the Frenchman, and then Payton had been unable to see the distressed lady anymore, since her view was blocked by broad, masculine backs.

She hadn't, however, needed to see the woman again. She'd seen enough by then to know who it was. She knew the voice almost as well as she knew her own. The bright red hair that had been streaming over the arm of the sofa only confirmed it.

Only then had it hit her. She was on board the *Rebecca*.

Of *course*.

It had been there all along, staring her in the face, and she hadn't realized it. Had she always been this stupid, or had it only been since she'd fallen so head over heels in love with Connor Drake?

Becky Whitby, whom she'd seen with Sir Marcus Tyler on the morning of her wedding to Drake, was mistress to the pirate Lucien La Fond, whose nautical attacks on Dixon ships had long been rumored to be funded by their chief competitor, Tyler and Tyler Shipping.

That story Becky had told in the vicar's study, about Sir Marcus wanting to get his hands on Drake's map—Payton had put that story down as unmitigated bunk. But what if it were true? Not the part about Becky being an innocent pawn in the whole thing—that she knew was a lie. But the part about Sir Marcus being desperate to get his hands on that map—that part might be true. And it would explain why Drake was still locked up below, instead of having been sliced into shark bait long ago, which would surely have been the Frenchman's first inclination.

Dipping her scrub brush into the cold seawater she was using to clean the floor, Payton pressed her lips together determinedly. She was going to get him out of there. She had to. Just as she knew he would never leave her had the situation been reversed, she could never leave him.

And besides, things weren't all *that* bad. They'd been in far worse scrapes than this, after all. She couldn't remember one, but she was almost sure of it. All she had to do, really, was get them off this ship before they reached Nassau. Payton still didn't know what fate the Frenchman had in store for Drake there, but whatever it was, she knew it wouldn't be a good one. So it was simple, really. She just had to get him off the ship before they reached New Providence.

Of course, he wasn't going to like hearing that very much. Drake had always been a very exacting commander, expecting his orders to be carried out to the letter, and offering swift punishment to those who failed to do so—unless they could give him a good reason why his orders had been ignored. He was exacting, but he was just.

Payton thought she had a good reason why she hadn't carried out his order that she leave the ship. The reason was that, simply, she couldn't. She just couldn't leave him. She didn't suppose he was going to consider that a good reason, but then, what was he going to do about it? Not a whole lot. He was chained to the wall. What could he possibly do to her?

She found out, the very next time she had opportunity to bring the prisoner his supper—this time distracting Tito with a bottle of whisky, stolen from the captain's liquor cabinet—and enter Drake's cell.

Night had fallen by the time Payton was finally able to escape the galley and let herself into the hold, and it took a moment for her eyes to adjust to the darkness in Drake's cell. She hadn't thought to bring a candle—her hands were too full to carry one anyway, since she was cradling all the food she'd managed to smuggle out of the forecastle, tucked beneath her shirt—but moonlight spilled through spaces in the wooden planks overhead . . . enough moonlight for Payton to see that Drake, though he'd obviously noticed her, hadn't bothered climbing to his feet.

This actually shocked her more than anything she'd seen so far aboard the *Rebecca*. Back in the days when they'd sailed with her brothers, Drake had *always* risen when she'd entered a room or come on deck. Her brothers had teased him about it, since Payton, in her bare feet and braids, didn't exactly resemble the sort of fine lady upon whom gentlemen practiced social niceties. But Drake had always ignored them, continuing to rise whenever Payton appeared.

Until now, apparently. Now he just looked up at her from where he sat, slumped against the far wall, his elbows on his knees. Looked up, saw her, and looked away.

Bloody hell! Here she was, with all sorts of food she'd had to go to no end of trouble to scrounge up—fruit, bread, not to mention a few strips of salt pork that felt *quite* uncomfortable against her bare belly—and he had the nerve to snub her like that! Not that she cared about the fact that he hadn't stood. But he could at least *acknowledge* her presence . . .

And then it hit her. Maybe he was ill!

Good God! That had to be it! Those bastards. What had they done to him? She'd kill them all.

Hurrying into the cell, Payton fell down to her knees at Drake's side, pieces of fruit and bread rolls dropping out from beneath her shirt and falling to roll unnoticed across the hardwood floor.

"Drake," she cried, her naturally husky voice breaking. "Are you all right? What did they do to you?"

He swung his head round to face her, but for once, those glowing silver eyes had no effect on her. She was too busy scanning for wounds to notice how his gaze raked her. Had they beat him? she wondered. Whipped him, perhaps? He certainly didn't look his best—even in the dim moonlight, Payton could see that his trousers, which had once been fawn-colored, were now a dingy gray, with twin tears through which his darkly tanned knees jutted. His waistcoat and jacket were long gone—Payton had thought she'd spotted the Frenchman's first mate wearing them, along with Drake's gleaming Hessian boots. All he'd been left with were his trousers and a linen shirt that had once been white and whole, but was now gray and ripped down the middle, so that it revealed all of his chest and most of his strongly muscled stomach.

But though he might not have been dressed as usual in the height of fashion, Payton, looking him over, could detect no injuries. He looked, in fact, incredibly well for a man who'd subsisted, for the past month, on little more than mash and water. Even the beard and mustache did nothing to detract from his overall handsomeness, serving only to emphasize the aristocratic planes of his face. Looking at him, Payton couldn't help but think it sad that Miss Whitby had turned out to be mistress to someone else. The two of them would have made a lovely couple.

Then, when Drake continued to stare at her in utter silence, a horrible thought occurred to Payton. She reached out to grasp him by the shoulders.

"Drake!" she cried. "Did they cut out your tongue?"

The upper lip that just a moment before she'd been admiring, even coated as it was in tawny hair, curled. "No," he replied, his deep voice so low it was nothing more than a guttural growl. "Of course not. Payton, what are you still doing here? I thought I told you to get off this ship."

She blinked at him. "You mean . . . you're not hurt?"

"Of course I'm not. But you're going to find your backside smarting something fierce if you don't get it out of here this minute—"

He made as if to lunge at her, but Payton scrambled away backward on all fours, like a crab. When she'd reached a safe distance, out of reach of his chains, she sat there in stunned silence, watching him with wide eyes.

He was on his feet now, but not out of any sense of gentlemanly duty. No, he was trying to get hold of her, undoubtedly to make good on his promise to wear out her backside. He was making all sorts of horrible grunting noises as he strained ineffectually to break his chains. Payton, who'd only rarely seen Drake lose his temper—and certainly never because of something *she'd* done—could only watch, in horrified fascination. She'd seen her brothers lose their tempers before— especially Ross—but she had never seen any of them quite *this* angry.

She watched him rage for a while. He was cursing fitfully now, oaths that would have burned the ears of any properly brought-up young lady, but which Payton had heard daily and sometimes uttered herself, when provoked. Occasionally she glanced at the door to the brig. She'd closed it behind her, but that didn't mean that his voice wasn't going to carry to other parts of the ship. They didn't have to worry about Tito overhearing them, but there were others on board who didn't have their lips wrapped around a bottle, and who might get curious.

She decided she had to shut him up—if only so that she could talk some sense into him—but she didn't have any idea how to do that without going near him, and remembering the way he'd shaken her the day before, she wasn't about to get anywhere within grabbing distance of those enormous hands. Payton tried to remember what Georgiana had done, the last time Ross had had a similar temper tantrum. She seemed to recall that tears had been involved.

Tears? She was going to have to *cry*?

Oh, Lord. When were her trials going to end?

Pulling her knees up to her chest, Payton let out what she hoped sounded like a sob, and dropped her face down onto her arms, which she'd folded over her knees. She sat like that, twitching her shoulders a little and making sniffling noises, peeking up occasionally to see if Drake had noticed. He had not. He had hold of one of his chains, and was busy trying to yank it from the iron support to which it was anchored to the wall.

Payton, disgusted, thought she'd better cry a little louder, so she let out a louder sniffle, then quickly dipped her head down again when Drake finally glanced her way.

"Payton?" He didn't sound at all concerned, the way Ross always sounded when Georgiana cried. Drake sounded more suspicious than concerned.

Damn it all to hell. Was she going to have to summon up real tears? Payton tried to think about something sad. Her dead mother. No, that wasn't sad. She'd been only a few hours old when her mother died. She didn't remember her, had never even known her, not like her brothers, who sometimes sighed and got a faraway look in their eyes whenever Sir Henry mentioned his beloved wife's name. What else? Mei-Ling leaving her, to go back to her own family. But that wasn't sad, either. Mei-Ling had been so *happy*. The *Constant*? Her family giving away the only thing she'd ever wanted? No, not that, either. It still bothered her, but she had more pressing concerns just at the moment.

Drake. What was the Frenchman going to do to Drake? That was what troubled her, what had been troubling her every moment for weeks now. If anything were to happen to Drake, why . . .

Tears came, quite suddenly, and most miraculously. Payton was so startled she almost stopped crying in her shock. Then she remembered she was *trying* to cry, so she let herself go, and let out a really good, gut-wrenching sob. Lord, but it almost felt . . . well . . . *nice*.

A sly peek at Drake—blurry through her tears, but still quite visible—showed that he was staring down at her with a stunned expression on his face. Good. She hid her face back in her arms. Really, this crying thing was quite effective. She ought to have thought of it sooner.

"Payton." She heard the chains rattle, and then there were twin thumps. Glancing up, she saw that Drake had dropped to his knees. She was still huddled out of his reach, but even from that distance, she could see that he had calmed down, his anger at her forgotten—at least for now—in his concern over her tears.

"Payton, are you all right?" All the suspicion was gone

from Drake's voice. Instead, she heard only the tenderest concern. "Did something happen, honey? Did somebody hurt you?"

*Honey*. He'd called her honey. He'd called her that before. And sweetheart once, too. How nice those words sounded on his lips! She let out another sob, but this one was for joy.

"Payton."

Lord, how the sound of his voice saying her name thrilled her! She'd never noticed before how those two syllables, uttered from those two lips, in that deep, deep voice, could send little chills up and down her spine. It was all she could do not to start laughing through her tears.

And then the extraordinary happened. Something warm and gentle touched her bare ankle.

Payton lifted her head sharply, thinking rats might have invaded the hold. But then she saw that it wasn't rats at all, but Drake, who'd reached his hand out as far as his shackles would allow—as far as her right foot, wedged into the slightly too-small buckle shoe she'd borrowed so long ago from the *Virago*'s cabin boy.

Payton blinked down at that hand, so large and dark against the skin of her slim ankle. If that hand—so intimidatingly masculine, with the gold hairs springing so thickly from the deeply tanned skin; so predatory in its size and strength—had belonged to anyone else, she'd have whipped out the knife she'd stolen from the galley and embedded the blade deep into the middle of it.

But it didn't belong to anyone else. It belonged to Drake.

Lifting her gaze, Payton saw that Drake's was already boring into her.

A second later, she'd launched herself at him. Though she was slight of figure, the force of her catapulting body was enough to knock him flat onto his back. Before he could react—she was fairly certain he was going to do his best to push her away—Payton straddled him, as she had the day before, and promptly stretched out so that her heart lay over his, their faces just inches apart.

"Can we," Payton said a little breathlessly, "try that again? What we did yesterday? Only this time, with our pants off?"

Drake's jaw was set. She saw it, even in the dim moonlight, and knew it boded ill.

"*No,*" he ground out. "Not *here,* Payton . . ."

Doubtless he had some more romantic scheme in mind for her defloration. She was very flattered. Really, she was. But it was far too late. She could already feel him growing hard beneath her.

It may not have been romantic, but it was all they had. All they might *ever* have.

She lowered her head, and brushed her lips against his. Just once. His arms flung out on either side of them, weighted down by the chains, he remained motionless, staring up at the ceiling, his expression stony. She brushed his lips with her mouth again.

"Payton," he said warningly. And this time when he spoke, his voice was little more than a growl. She could feel it reverberating, deep within him.

She ignored him. If he really wanted to stop her, she knew, he could have, despite the chains. He was twice her size. Even with his wrists shackled, he could have thrown her off. But he didn't.

She lowered her mouth to his once more.

And this time, he kissed her back. Kissed her back, and then said, almost savagely, "All right. All right, then. If this is what you want . . ."

Then he lifted his arms, seized hold of both her shoulders, and pulled her down against him, crushing her mouth to his.

# Chapter Nineteen

$\mathcal{J}$t didn't hurt, his kiss. He might have meant it to, but he was too much of a gentleman ever purposely to hurt a woman. Indeed, when she protested—at the suddenness of the gesture, not its violence—he loosened his grip at once. But he didn't let go of her entirely. It was too late for that.

He'd never let her go. Not now.

Not that Payton wanted him to. No, what she wanted—what she'd always wanted—was only to curl as closely to this man's heart as possible. And already, she'd succeeded. She could feel that heart thundering beneath the firm wall of his chest, and thought to herself, with some amazement, I *caused that. His heart is beating so hard because of* me. This thought reasserted itself a second or two later when she felt the stiff urgency of his erection prodding her through the material of both their trousers. I caused *that,* too, she thought.

A giddy sense of power came over her, even as he was kissing her. His tongue swept the insides of her mouth. He obviously intended to be thorough about this. Encouraged by the sound that escaped from Drake's throat—halfway between a groan and a sigh—when Payton tentatively met the thrust of his tongue into her mouth with her own, she was surprised when he abruptly tore his mouth away, and began to burn a trail down her throat . . . though she wasn't surprised enough not to lower her neck toward him, to better receive each fiery lick. Distracted as she was by this sweet torture, Payton was only dimly aware that his hands were moving across her body, caressing her through the material of her borrowed clothes. At least, she wasn't aware of it until she felt his fingers skim bare flesh, and realized that he'd skillfully untied her shirt again.

She gasped as his large, knowing hands closed over her breasts. She had seen what those hands were capable of, knew the strength that lay coiled just beneath those callused fingertips. It amazed her anew that his touch could be so infinitely gentle . . . especially when she was equally aware, from the fire in his kiss, of how long he must have been waiting for this moment. Wasn't that obvious in his uneven breathing, the heavy drumming of his heart? That he could keep his lust in check and proceed with such slow patience, mindful that this was her first time, only strengthened her conviction that this man was the only one for her.

When his palms grazed her sensitive nipples, however, she forgot all about her admiration of his restraint. Instead, her body took over. Her breasts seemed to swell beneath his fingers, filling his palms. At the same time, her legs, still astride him, parted even further, until she felt the hard length of his erection prodding against her very core. The sensation, she knew, should have alarmed her, as it would have any properly brought-up British girl. But as yesterday had proved, despite Georgiana's best efforts, Payton was far from proper. As soon as she felt him pressing so insistently against her, her hips began to move in a manner that was as shameless as it was instinctive.

Below her, Drake let out a wordless sound that seemed to Payton to be a groan of pain. Thinking she'd injured him, somehow, she froze . . . then gasped when, far from hurting, Drake showed his appreciation for her enthusiasm by lifting his head to seize one of her straining nipples in his hot, wet mouth. Now Payton knew what that groan had been about. Not pain. Pleasure. Ripples of it coursed through her body as he suckled on first one, then the other firm, tip-tilted breast.

But while his mouth was raising her to dizzying new heights of arousal above her waist, his fingers were launching a new offensive below it. Without Payton being aware that he'd done so, Drake had unbuttoned the front of her trousers. She was completely exposed to him, though she didn't realize it until his fingers brushed against the silky hair between her thighs. At that light, almost inquisitive touch, Payton's eyelids, which had become heavy with desire, flew open. She was shocked by the sight the moonlight threw into startling clarity, that of his large, tanned fingers parting the soft brown tuft at her center. Never mind that those fingers were doing things to her that she'd never imagined in a million years she'd enjoy— stroking her, petting her, *filling* her. It was wrong, it *had* to be wrong, what he was doing . . .

Which would explain why she liked it so much.

No sooner had Payton opened her eyes than she closed them again, lost in the pleasurable sensations he was evoking with his clever, dexterous fingers. She could stop him now, she knew, before it was too late. Seize his wrist and pull his hand away. It was what Georgiana would want her to do.

But instead of closing her fingers around his arm, she brought them against the iron-hard bulge she could feel straining against her, at the front of his trousers. Would he, she couldn't help wondering, let her touch him this time, the way he was touching her? Did he yearn for her touch, the way she, for so very, very long, had yearned for his?

Payton's question was answered at once. Even though she only brushed the tip of his penis with the lightest of touches, Drake reacted as swiftly as if that touch had branded him. Wrenching his lips from her nipple, he brought his mouth to hers in a kiss that was fiercely possessive. Then, before she was really aware of what was happening, he shifted, and suddenly, what had been covered just seconds before in material was free, singeing the smooth skin of her inner thighs.

Free, and somewhat alarming in size.

Drake looked up at her. He was breathing as heavily as if he'd just run a mile, his golden chest rising and falling beneath her, and yet the words he managed to rasp out made it clear that his only concern, at that moment, was for her: "I don't want to hurt you," he whispered.

She didn't know that the moonlight, which had cast him in complete shadow, had revealed to him a sudden panic in her eyes. She didn't know that the coarseness of his new beard had stained her chin and neck with a permanent blush. She didn't know, as he did, that she was slick with wanting him, wetter than any woman he'd ever been with. All she knew was that, in spite of his own obvious need, his only thoughts had been for her welfare. That, as much as the gentle restraint he'd shown in his handling of her, caused a wave of love for him to wash over her, as powerful as any lust she might have felt for him in the past.

"I know," she told him, suddenly shy. She could tell by his expression that she hadn't reassured him, and she was casting about in her mind for some way to do so when, once again, her body took over—and answered him for her. Before she was even really aware she was doing so, she'd moved her hips slightly, just enough so that the tip of his hard shaft nudged the moist opening of her core. Below her, Drake looked momentarily startled, and instinctively, he froze, his eyes so hidden in shadow that they no longer looked silver, but—she noticed in some distant part of her brain—black, like the sea before a storm.

And then Payton moved again, taking in a little more of him, curious to see how much of him she could hold. Not much, she imagined. He was a very large man, and she was an abnormally small woman . . .

His control broke. All of that restraint she'd so admired was gone in less time that it took for her heart to beat once. Suddenly, he plunged into her, burying himself into that tight, wet heat, where he'd longed to be for what seemed like an eternity . . .

Payton's choice of expletives was graphic as well as colorful, but unfortunately its originality was lost on Drake, who was so concerned for her well-being that, after delivering that first thrust, he immediately came back to himself, and asked, not very coherently, "Are you all right?"

But Payton had found that, after the initial burst of very sharp pain, what followed, while still not exactly comfortable, could not necessarily be construed as painful. Having braced her hands defensively against Drake's chest and locked her hips to prohibit him from moving any further, she began to suspect that this sensation was equivalent to the one she'd felt the day before . . . only better.

"Payton?" Drake asked, sounding more coherent, and a good deal less patient. His chains rattled as he seized her by the arms, to shake her a little. "Payton? *Are you all right?*"

She shushed him and gave a small, experimental undulation with her hips. Drake, dropping his head back down against the floor, moaned. But that wasn't what interested her just then. What *was* interesting, she found, was that she didn't feel any pain anymore. All she felt was an urgent pull, a longing to press herself as closely to him as she possibly could.

And soon that longing turned into an all-out necessity. Moving her hips again, she clung to him, aware, but only dimly, that he was saying things to her. She had no idea what they were. At one point, as she moved against him, she was quite certain he'd said he loved her.

Then he was moving with her, his big hands gripping her bottom, not so much guiding her as attempting to stay with her . . .

And then, as if by a riptide, she was caught, sucked under, a violent and lovely wave of delight breaking over her, shaking her from the scalp of her head to the soles of her feet. For a few moments, she wasn't at sea at all, wasn't anywhere near it. She was between the sea and the sky, shimmering there, like late afternoon sunlight. She cried out his name, because it seemed to her that she oughtn't go flying off like this without him . . .

And then, suddenly, she was back within herself, exhausted and panting, clinging to Drake's naked chest. Only he hadn't noticed, because he was still out there, where she had just been. She could tell by the expression on his face, his eyes tightly closed, his mouth clenched as if in pain. And she could tell by the violence with which he was plunging himself into her, harder and harder, until she was quite certain he was going to split her in half . . . and she didn't even care.

Then, with a final savage thrust, he teetered over the edge, and all the lines left his face, making him look years younger, handsomer than she'd ever seen him, causing her to fall in love with him all over again.

Then he was still, as limp as she'd gone seconds before, spent. They lay like that in the gloom of his cell, still joined together, panting and damp.

Then Drake lifted his head from where he'd dropped it against the floor, and, smoothing her tumbled curls away from her face, asked, a little diffidently, "Are you all right? Did I . . . I didn't hurt you, did I?"

Payton considered the question. She was just the tiniest bit dismayed to find that she *was* all right. She was better than all right, as a matter of fact. She'd never felt quite so good in all her life.

But she knew that wasn't how she was supposed to feel. She was supposed to be in horrible pain, bleeding profusely from the loss of her maidenhead. Only Payton suspected she'd never had a maidenhead, because she'd certainly felt only the slightest pain when Drake entered her—startling, yes, but very brief in duration. She ought to have felt more discomfort, aside from her initial fear that he wouldn't fit. What kind of lady lost her virginity and didn't experience tremendous amounts of pain?

Well, the Honorable Miss Payton Dixon, apparently. More proof that as a lady, she was a miserable failure. She'd no doubt broken her maidenhead a thousand times over, inserting the sea sponges Mei-Ling had taught her to use during her menses. How very anticlimactic.

"I'm fine," she sighed sadly.

He stared up at her, concerned. "You don't sound it."

"I just thought . . . well, I thought there'd be more blood."

"Oh," he said, looking immensely relieved—but whether because there hadn't been any blood at all, or because he knew now that he'd succeeded in making her climax, she wasn't certain. "You needn't sound so disappointed. I didn't want to hurt you, you know."

"I know," Payton said. "But if we lived in less civilized times, you'd be required to produce a sheet with my virgin blood spilled upon it, to prove to your family that I was pure before I came to your bed."

"I hardly think," Drake said, a bit dryly, "that in the unlikely event we live through this, anyone in my family—particularly my grandmother—is going to require any proof of your virginity, Payton."

"Nevertheless, it's a bit of a letdown. A girl only loses her virginity once, and—"

"And she'd like it to be as dramatic as possible?"

"Well, a *little* blood would have been nice."

Drake could not help but feel a cad. He had robbed her of something he hadn't any right to whatsoever. What's more, he had done it knowing full well it was wrong. He had sworn to himself that should he ever be fortunate enough to make love to Payton Dixon, it would be in a bed—preferably their marriage bed. And, failing that, at the very least he'd hoped to be in control enough of himself not to frighten her.

And while he believed that she had derived some pleasure from their lovemaking, he could not help but berate himself for having, essentially, rutted upon her, just as he'd sworn to himself he would not do. Even if she *had* been on top . . .

But how was he supposed to have stopped himself? Never had he been with a woman who took every bit as readily as she gave. And that moment when the trepidation in her hazel eyes had turned to wonder—that had been his undoing. He hadn't been able to stop himself after that—especially after he'd plunged into her, and found that between Payton Dixon's legs lay paradise, the tightest, warmest place imaginable.

He ought to have been able to control himself. It wasn't as if he was some callow youth, completely without experience in the bedroom. But he'd taken her like a wild thing, without a hint of gentleness—and her a *virgin,* no less.

Never mind that she seemed to have thoroughly enjoyed herself, that her only regret—or the only one she'd admit to—was that she'd had no maidenhead to burst. He'd used her abominably. Somehow, he had to make it up to her.

He reached up to cup her cheeks with his hands. "Would it help," he asked, "if I said that I loved you?"

Her heart skipped a beat. "*Do* you?"

One of those tawny eyebrows rose. "Why do you sound surprised?"

"Well, only because I've been loving you for years and years, and I never thought you'd noticed."

"I noticed," he assured her. "It took me a while, but I noticed."

She smiled beatifically, and moved to slip her arms around his neck. But whatever she had been about to say was forever lost when a key scraped in the lock behind them.

In a flash, it seemed, Payton was away from him and on her feet, simultaneously buttoning up her vest and trousers and urging him to do up his, an order he lost no time obeying.

The door swung open, and Drake's jailer raised a candle and peered in at them. " 'Ill," he said, and hiccupped.

"Right here." Payton sauntered nonchalantly into the puddle of light cast by the guttering candle. "What, Tito?"

"Cook wants ye." Tito was not standing very steadily on his feet. The man was only half-conscious, clearly three sheets to the wind. The nearly empty bottle clutched in one of his massive fists revealed why. " 'E's lockin' up the galley fer the night."

"Right." Payton gave her trousers a hitch. Drake, watching from the floor, realized with a start that the gesture was an imitation of her brother Ross, who frequently tugged at his breeches in such a fashion. "Let's go, then."

Tito turned his porcine gaze on Drake. " 'E give you any trouble, then?" he asked, without much genuine interest.

"That one? Naw. Not 'im."

Tito nodded. "Good."

Then without so much as another glance in Drake's direction, Tito turned to go. From the darkness of the giant's shadow, Payton gave Drake one last, fleeting glance. Then the heavy door slammed shut behind them both, leaving him alone once again. The only evidence, he realized, that Payton had ever been there at all was the food on the floor and a slightly damp spot on the front of his breeches.

And a hole, which he was convinced was burning through his heart.

# Chapter Twenty

*P*ayton wasn't particularly surprised when she heard that the ship that appeared on the horizon the morning after her and Drake's—well, *tryst* was really the only way to describe it—was a Tyler and Tyler ship. Having spotted it well before the man in the crow's nest, she'd spent most of the morning harboring hopes that it might be a Dixon clipper, her brothers finally coming to rescue her.

But subsequent reports down to the galley revealed she'd have no such luck. Quite the opposite, in fact. It was a Tyler ship. What's more, it was expected. Sir Marcus Tyler had been scheduled to meet up with the *Rebecca* as soon as it entered Bahamian waters. While disappointed on one front—it would have made things considerably simpler if it had been a Dixon ship—Payton was pleased to learn that at least they were near land. Now she could start making preparations for her escape with Drake.

In the after cabin, she'd noticed while delivering the captain and his lady their breakfast that morning, preparations of a different kind were under way.

"I can't stand it," she had overheard Becky complain to the captain. "I've got to go back to bed."

"Now, darling," Lucien La Fond had replied. He had neglected to close the door to the sitting room all the way, and so their conversation was easily overheard by anyone in the outer room. "You know Jenkins said the fresh air would do you some good."

"Oh, what does Jenkins know? The man's useless. I can't believe you're making me get up to meet him. You know he's only going to shout at you, when he learns Drake and I aren't wed."

"Shout at *me*, dearest?" The Frenchman still spoke tenderly. "But you know *I'm* not the one who spoiled everything."

"No, but you're the one who sent those stupid men to attack the *Constant* before the vows were spoken."

"Well, how was *I* to know the wedding hadn't taken place? You were supposed to be leaving for your honeymoon. Nobody leaves for their honeymoon without getting married first. It's a rather important part of the process."

"I've told you a million times: It wasn't my fault. It was that damned Dixon bitch."

Payton nearly burst out with an indignant exclamation at that point. She only managed to restrain herself by reflecting that she'd referred to Miss Whitby in much harsher terms, upon occasion.

"Yes, yes, I know." La Fond spoke as if the subject had been discussed so many times, it now bored him. "The truth of the matter is, darling, it's *his* fault."

Becky's sigh was audible even as far away as Payton stood. "I suppose you're right. He oughtn't to have risked coming to Daring Park himself. I don't care if he didn't trust anyone else to do it. That was pure idiocy on his part."

"I don't mean that. I mean if he would just learn to keep you out of his bloody schemes, I wouldn't have cause to worry so about you. It was only because I couldn't bear to think what might be happening on that damned ship that I sent the *Mary B* too soon."

"But darling, you *know* me." Becky's tone was distinctly flirtatious, especially for a woman who'd so recently been complaining of illness. "You know I wouldn't have allowed that man to touch me."

"Do I?" The Frenchman sounded a bit aloof. "The same certainly couldn't be said of his brother, now, could it?"

"But I *had* to with Richard, silly."

"That's just it. I don't want you to have to with any man but me."

"Well, you certainly made that perfectly clear."

The Frenchman sounded indignant. "I made it look accidental, didn't I? The way he asked."

"Papa asked that it look accidental. He didn't mention that it needed to be so bloody."

Papa? Payton paused while filling a dish with jam. Who's *Papa*?

"Now that," La Fond said, "wasn't my fault, either. He was already dead by the time those horses dragged him through that briar patch. The surgeon said so."

Becky laughed. "Was that the same surgeon who said Sir Richard died from a blow to the head from a low-hanging bough while out riding? Oh, I certainly have a lot of faith in *his* medical abilities."

"All I'm saying, Rebecca, is that if you didn't let him use you the way he does—"

"But darling, you know Papa's ideas always turn out all right in the end."

"Well, this one certainly didn't."

"All the more reason for *you* to be the one to tell him—"

This bickering went on until the very moment Sir Marcus's ship, the *Nassau Queen,* pulled up alongside the *Rebecca,* and a plank was placed between the two boats. Payton wasn't certain who the *he* in their conversation connoted. Was it Sir Marcus? Or was it Miss Whitby's father? And who was the Richard she'd referred to? Surely it couldn't be anyone but Drake's brother, whom Miss Whitby had fingered as the father of her unborn child. How had the Frenchman known so much about Richard Drake's fatal riding accident?

It was all very confusing. Payton longed to slip below and ask Drake if he could make anything out of it. Unfortunately, she was kept far too busy to find any opportunity to escape her duties. The mood on the *Rebecca* was one of revelry: the arrival of the *Nassau Queen* meant the arrival of fresh supplies, of food and bedding and most importantly of all, *rum*. The crew never obeyed their orders with more alacrity than on that day, when the *Nassau Queen*'s flag was first spotted. Payton was going to have to wait, perhaps until darkness fell, and the rum was flowing freely, before she'd be able to slip away to see Drake.

It wasn't until she and Jonesy, with whom she'd established the shakiest of alliances, had been banished below, with orders to mop up a spill from a cask of molasses that had been brought over from the *Nassau Queen*, that Payton got her first look at Sir Marcus. Payton was nearly ankle-deep in the sticky stuff when, suddenly, the hatch over their heads lifted. Thinking it was some sort of surprise inspection by Clarence, both Payton and Jonesy sprang to attention only to see that it was Sir Marcus, and not the cook at all.

But Sir Marcus as Payton had never seen him before. There was a murderous glint in his eye as he strode past them and headed straight for the place where Tito stood, guarding the door to Drake's cell.

"Open it!" Sir Marcus bellowed at the hapless Tito, who, along with the rest of the crew, had been innocently gnawing on a chunk of salt pork, which had been handed out immediately in an attempt to placate the men's rumbling bellies until Clarence could assemble a proper meal from the *Nassau Queen*'s donations.

Tito rose hastily, and fumbled at his keys. He was clearly hungover from last night's carouse, and had been feeling quite sorry for himself all day. What he needed, Payton had decided, was a little hair of the dog, and she'd already resolved to secure him another bottle, if only because tonight, she fully intended to liberate him of all his keys, and make her getaway with Drake.

As Tito hastened to unlock the door to the brig, more footsteps sounded above their heads, and soon Becky Whitby was tripping down the steps, her high heels clacking.

"Papa," she was saying, in a wheedling sort of voice. "It wasn't Lucien's fault. You know how jealous he gets. Really, if anyone is to blame, it's you. How could you have been so stupid as to show up at Daring Park that morning? Of course you were recognized!"

Payton, watching from the shadows, thought, *Papa? But Sir Marcus doesn't have any children.* Sir Marcus, to her certain knowledge, had never even been married. She imagined he was going to have something to say about Becky Whitby claiming him as her kin. She'd once seen Sir Marcus wave a pistol in the face of a man simply because he refused to move out of his way. How was he going to react to this lunatic woman calling him papa?

Sir Marcus Tyler was not an old man, like Payton's father. He was probably only in his late forties, and was still quite handsome, tall and well-built, with only the slightest bit of gray at his temples. The rest of his hair was very dark and thick, and curled over the edge of his high shirt collar with deceptively casual elegance. In his own way, he appeared to be as fashion-conscious as Lucien La Fond.

What he was not, however, was a very even-tempered man. He turned to bellow at Miss Whitby, "Don't you dare accuse *me* of bungling this! If anyone here is a bungler, it's that thick-headed fool you keep defending. 'It's not his fault.' " Sir Marcus imitated Miss Whitby cruelly. " 'It's not his fault.' Of course it's his fault! If he'd only bided his time, and not attacked so soon, you'd be Lady Drake now!"

Good Lord! He hadn't denied it! Becky Whitby was Marcus Tyler's daughter!

No wonder Marcus Tyler had Lucien La Fond, the fiercest pirate in the South Seas, in his pocket: he was his daughter's paramour!

"No, I wouldn't." Becky trotted down the steep steps, rather nimbly, Payton thought, for a woman in her condition. Her father's rage, while it clearly frightened her, was not going to sway her from her purpose. "I was *never* going to be Lady Drake, Papa. I'm telling you, he sussed it out. I don't know how, but he'd figured it out, even before the Dixon bitch said anything about seeing you—"

Sir Marcus was ignoring his daughter. "Open that door," he bellowed at the unfortunate Tito.

"I'm tryin', sir," Tito whimpered, in a surprisingly small voice for so large a man. "I'm tryin'!"

"I was *never* going to be Lady Drake," Miss Whitby insisted, striding up to her father. Payton, used to the meek, easily frightened Miss Whitby who'd once come to her bedroom and begged her to kill a spider she'd found in her chamber pot, could hardly believe the two were one and the same. *This* Miss Whitby seemed quite fearless. "Do you hear? Drake *knew*, I don't know how, but he *knew* there was something . . . not right about me and Richard. Don't blame Lucien. It was *your* fault, not his."

To Payton's great astonishment, Sir Marcus wheeled around and backhanded his daughter across the face. Becky let out a cry and fell to the floor, her thick red curls tumbling over her face. Without thinking, Payton stepped forward, intending to come to the older girl's aid. A hand on her arm stopped her. Looking back, she saw Jonesy's quick head shake. Apparently, he'd witnessed these father–daughter scuffles before. Even a blockhead like Jonesy knew enough to know it was a bad idea to get involved.

A second later, Becky was on her feet again. Except for the bright red spot on her cheek, one would never have known she'd just been struck with enough force to set her teeth rattling. Could this blazing-eyed beauty be the same girl whom Payton's brothers had stumbled over themselves in an effort to rescue a few months earlier? She looked as if she needed rescuing about as much as . . . well, as Payton did.

"I tell you," Becky shouted, "it isn't Lucien's fault!"

Tito had Drake's cell door open by that time. Sir Marcus, with one last disgusted look at his daughter, turned and disappeared into the brig. Becky, after glaring at his back for a few seconds, whirled around and stormed up the steep steps to the deck, shouting "Lucien!" at the top of her lungs. As she passed over their heads, Payton noticed Jonesy had craned his neck to look up at the furious girl. Following his gaze, she saw that it was possible to see straight up the woman's skirts through the open spaces between the steps. Jonesy was staring, open-mouthed, at the tantalizing glimpses of thigh Becky revealed with each angry footfall.

A second later, the boy was hopping up and down, clutching his arm in pain from Payton's pinch. "Ow!" he cried. "What'ud ye go an' do *that* fer?"

Payton narrowed her eyes at him. "It isn't polite to stare," she said.

Jonesy glared at her. "I swear, 'Ill," he declared. "Sometimes I fink you're nofink but a bloody *girl*."

She glared right back. "Really? Then I don't suppose you'll mind cleaning up this lot by yourself, and let me enjoy my leisure, like a lady."

She thrust her mop at him and stalked away, leaving Jonesy to mutter darkly behind her. She didn't pay him any mind. All of her concentration was centered on what was going on inside the brig, beyond that half-open door.

And she wasn't the only one interested, either. Tito, who in spite of his hangover was still grateful to her for the bottle she'd given him the day before, moved some of his bulk in order to allow her nearer the crack in the door, through which he was peering with almost as much interest as she was.

Only she rather doubted that, as he peered, Tito was uttering the same silent prayer that she was.

*Please, God,* she prayed. *Don't let Drake die today. Please. I'm begging you. If you have to take someone, take me, instead.*

Then she had a better idea.

*Or better yet, take Miss Whitby!*

# Chapter Twenty-one

When Sir Marcus Tyler, ducking his head in order to avoid striking it on the low door frame, came striding into Drake's cell, the prisoner greeted him with a laconic, "Ah, Sir Marcus, at last. How nice. I've been expecting you, you know."

If Sir Marcus was taken aback by this genial greeting, he was further astounded by the prisoner's casual comment. "I'd offer you a chair, sir, but as you can see, there isn't one. I have found that this floor, however, is not as uncomfortable as it looks. Feel free to join me upon it, if you like."

Sir Marcus had been grinning when he'd entered the cell. That grin had faded somewhat upon Drake's nonchalant greeting. How a man chained to a wall—particularly a man like Connor Drake, who had spent so much of his life in the open air—could be so calm, Sir Marcus couldn't fathom. It angered him, Drake's calm, as much as his daughter and her lover's foolishness had angered him. He brought back a foot and kicked one of the legs sprawled out before him, and none too gently, either.

"Get up," Sir Marcus hissed. "Stand up, Drake. You might think this nothing but a great joke, but I assure you, it is serious. Deadly serious."

Drake did not, at first, look inclined to stand. But then, after a moment's consideration, he climbed to his bare feet. And it was then that Sir Marcus realized his error. He ought to have let the prisoner lounge upon the floor. Because that was the only position in which he would have the advantage. Connor Drake, even without his boots, stood taller than the older man by a good inch or two.

Sir Marcus chose to ignore this, however, and concentrate on being pleased that his command had been obeyed.

"Captain Drake," he said, rolling the syllables over his tongue with obvious relish. "The great Captain Drake. Oh, I *am* sorry. That isn't your proper title anymore, is it? No, not since the unfortunate death of your brother. Do you prefer to be called Sir Connor?"

"You can call me whatever you like," Drake said with a shrug. "I'm at a slight disadvantage to stop you." He lifted his chains pointedly.

"Yes, unfortunate, that." Sir Marcus made a tut-tutting noise with his tongue. "But necessary, I'm afraid. We couldn't run the risk, you see, of the great Captain Drake choosing to abandon our hospitality before we'd had a chance to get to know him properly. You've acquired quite the reputation for narrow escapes, you know. Why, you even managed to slip through the marriage knot. I must say I'm all astonishment to find you a bachelor still. I thought your wedding quite a certain thing."

Drake nodded. "You were not alone in thinking so. But in the end, I'm afraid, there were some objections against the lady."

"I can't tell you how sorry I am to hear that." Tyler actually sounded sorry, too. "Might I ask what it was about the young lady that so offended you?"

"The fact that she seemed to have ties to you was part of it," Drake replied, affably enough.

"Ah." Sir Marcus looked a little glum. "Do you despise me so, then, Captain, that the thought of aligning yourself with one of my kin—even one as lovely as my Rebecca—is repugnant?"

If Drake had not known before that moment that Rebecca

Whitby was Marcus Tyler's daughter, he dissembled nicely. "Certainly, sir," he said politely. "Considering that any off-spring of yours must necessarily be devil's spawn."

Sir Marcus laughed as if delighted by the insult. "If you can claim to have spotted a resemblance of any sort between Rebecca and me, then I congratulate you. You're a shrewder man than I. I swear, it took me a while before *I* saw any hint of Tyler in her. You see, it was only a few years ago that a woman of somewhat . . . er, *questionable* virtue with whom I'd dallied in my youth presented me with a scrawny redheaded thing that she insisted—rather stridently—was my daughter. I wouldn't have even considered the fact that this girl—whom the woman rather vulgarly called Becky—might have sprung from my loins if it weren't for the fact that, well, as you so baldly put it, Drake, our minds seemed to be of quite a similar turn. Frighteningly so, at times. You see, it was Rebecca who put together the fact that her mother had once dallied with *the* Marcus Tyler of Tyler and Tyler Shipping. It was Rebecca who thought that I might be applied to for a bit of conscience money. I paid, rather skeptically at first. After all, I'm a busi-nessman. I don't need any negative publicity, especially with that bastion of all that is upstanding, Sir Henry Dixon, as my primary competitor. But eventually, Rebecca and I became friendly, and I began to see the advantages in having a beau-tiful young woman about to help with my more . . . *delicate* plots. She had no objections, of course. Rebecca, like most women, is extremely fond of money. There's little she won't do for it."

"And you wonder," Drake said slowly, "at my objections against marrying the lady?"

"Oh, yes, I see." Sir Marcus, laughing, shook his head. "Yes. A blackmailer, and even worse, one related to me. Weighty offenses, indeed. Ah, Drake. I shall almost be sorry when you are gone. I do so enjoy your company. You are one of the few men in my acquaintance who will tell me exactly what he thinks of me. Most other men are much too frightened, you know. I wield a certain power, particularly around these parts."

"It's not you they're afraid of," Drake growled. "It's La Fond."

Tyler looked perplexed. "La Fond? Oh, well, yes, I suppose I could see it. He can be a fearful fellow—if you don't know him too well, that is. I, unfortunately, have a more than passing acquaintance with him, so I am not quite so impressed." He sighed. "I ought to have known, of course, that a man as resourceful and shrewd as the intrepid Captain Drake would see through my humble little scheme. Not one of my better ones, perhaps." Then he added, as if as an afterthought, "But your brother fell for it so readily, you know. You could see how, after that, I might be led to hope—"

"Hope?"

"Well, certainly. That the new baronet would be just as . . . oh, how should I put it? Besotted by the lady?"

"I've rather begun to suspect," Drake replied stiffly, "that my brother's attraction to your daughter was what ended up getting him killed."

"In a manner of speaking, yes, of course, that's correct. It grieves me to say it, but it is the truth. Your brother's death was ultimately necessary, you see, in my effort to secure your interests in my competitors' business."

Drake nodded. "Of course," he said tonelessly. "You needed me to marry Rebecca so that, upon my death, she would inherit my share in Dixon and Sons Shipping."

But Sir Marcus only laughed. "Not at all. Good Lord, Drake, I may be many things, but clairvoyant is not one of them. I hadn't any way of knowing that my old friend Henry—that soft-hearted fool—would be idiot enough to offer you a share in the family business, let alone a share equal to that of his own sons."

Drake, considering, said thoughtfully, "That's right. They only made that offer the night before the wedding. So what *did* you hope to gain from my marrying Becky? Not Daring Park, surely. You must have been after more than that, or you wouldn't have killed Richard before the two of them had had a chance to wed."

"I never had much interest in Daring Park," Sir Marcus replied. "Though I'll admit, Becky grew quite fond of it. I understand you put it up for sale just before you set sail. Unfortunate, that. She had such plans for settling there, with the child."

"Ah, yes," Drake said. "Whom she'd doubtlessly raise to be the next baronet. I could see how a woman of her pecuniary nature would find such a plan appealing. But that wasn't *your* plan. You wanted something else. What was it? The map?"

Sir Marcus grinned. "I must say, I've always admired you your acuity, Drake. It's a shame, really, that you *aren't* my son-in-law. I might almost be proud to call someone with your perspicacity son, instead of that great foppish Frenchman with whom my daughter had the ill judgment to align herself. Yes, my lord, it was all about that map of yours. Who'd have thought a map you made as a lark would cause so much grief and sorrow? But there it is. As your widow, Rebecca would, of course, inherit all the rights to it, as well as whatever copies you've had made. She would be free to do with them whatever she chose. And she would, naturally, choose to give them to her papa for safekeeping."

"Of course," Drake said. "The existence of that map must be making a number of your employees uneasy. If a copy of it fell into the wrong hands—the hands of the authorities, say—there'd be no more safe harbors, no place to hide, for those felons and thieves you keep on your payroll . . ."

"Ah." Sir Marcus smiled. "That's what I've always liked about you, Drake. You don't hedge. You head straight to the heart of a matter, without flinching—"

"It still doesn't explain," Drake interrupted, in a hard voice, "why you felt it necessary to murder my brother. Wouldn't it have been easier for you simply to send her to my bed, rather than his?"

"Of course. I suppose Becky could have lured you into some Cuban brothel or another, and claimed to have gotten with child by you then. But were you going to marry a girl you'd bedded in a Cuban brothel? Not likely. You'd have thrown some money at her, and gone about your way. But a good girl . . . a chaste girl . . . now *that* kind of girl you'd have felt honor-bound to wed. But when were you ever in port long enough to meet a girl like that? Never. You were always at sea. We hadn't any choice, you see, but to use your brother in your stead, knowing that a man like Connor Drake would feel honor-bound to do right by his brother's intended."

*You were always at sea.* Drake had gone to sea to escape his family. He had hoped to lose them—and his painful memories of them—in the great blue deep. But it now appeared that because of his decision, at least one member of that family was dead. Because he'd always been at sea.

"Who did it?" Drake asked, his voice deadly calm.

"Who did what, pray, young man?"

"Who killed Richard? Not you, I would imagine."

"Lord, no. I don't like killing. Far too messy. No, La Fond did that. Enjoyed it, too, I'm sorry to say. Well, he would, of course. He wasn't at all pleased with the fact that poor Becky had to—well, you know—with your brother, in order for our little scheme to work."

"When I get out of here," Drake said woodenly, "I'm going to kill him."

Sir Marcus threw back his head and laughed. It was a hearty laugh, and it filled the small cell, where laughter had previously been a stranger. "Are you, now?" he asked, when he'd regained his composure. "Pardon me, Sir Connor, but I think not. In fact, I feel obligated to warn you that the complete opposite is going to happen. *I* am going to kill *you*."

Drake laughed at that. "You won't. You're too much of a coward."

"Well, not me personally, of course, but believe me, you *will* die. The only reason you've been kept alive this long is that La Fond is a complete fool. His cronies weren't supposed to attack the *Constant* until *after* you and Rebecca had signed the appropriate documents, making her your legal wife. Since the ceremony was, I understand, interrupted before that could happen, La Fond panicked, and stowed you down here. I don't know why he simply didn't kill you straightaway. He doesn't like you, you know. I don't know which offended him more: your cutting off his mustache, or your heading off for a honeymoon with his woman. I suppose he kept you alive because he thought that there was some chance that when I arrived, I might be able to force you to go along with our plan, and marry Rebecca, after all. He wants that map, you know, almost as much as I do."

Drake shrugged. "We all want things we can't have."

"Ah, but you see, in this one matter, my daughter's feeble-minded beau was correct. You see, I'm glad he didn't kill you. I'm convinced you and I can still work something out. You aren't an intractable man, I know. That's what makes you so admired as a leader. You've a reputation for being quite willing to compromise, and to acknowledge when you've been wrong. While I admit it will look a bit odd if the ceremony is performed at sea—and by a skipper in Tyler employ—it will still be legal. The Dixons will no doubt question it, but, after all, you did leave England saying you'd wed the girl when you reached the Bahamas, and since we're here—"

Drake burst out laughing. "You think I'll agree to marry that girl, after all? You've a better chance of marrying her off to the Prince of Wales than to me, at this point."

"Oh, you'll marry her. It will all be within the letter of the law. At least, that's how it will look to your grieving friends, when your widow returns to England and presents them with the facts of the matter. Your signature on the wedding certificate, your ring on her finger, and a touching tale of love and loss on the high seas to go with them. Good God, it will no doubt make the papers."

"And just how," Drake asked dryly, "do you propose to induce me to sign anything?"

"Oh, it's quite simple, really. If you don't agree to marry Rebecca"—Tyler stepped smoothly from the cell, and then returned a second later, dragging a very alarmed-looking Payton Dixon behind him by the wrist—"then I'll kill the Honorable Miss Dixon."

# Chapter Twenty-two

Payton pressed her ear to the brig's outside wall, straining to hear what was happening on deck above her. She could hear the sound of water lapping—the ships had dropped anchor for the night—and, more distantly, the wheeze of an accordion, and a few snatches, here and there, of a drunkenly slurred sea chantey. Occasionally, footsteps sounded overhead. Apparently, some of the crew were still awake, though it had to be past midnight by now. Still, even with the comparative silence, she could not hear the one thing she'd been listening for above all others—the sound of Drake's voice.

Was he still alive? She didn't know. He'd definitely been alive a few hours ago, before the rum had started to flow so freely. She'd heard the deep rumble of his voice, as he'd uttered his vows. Had they killed him directly after? If only she'd been there! If only she'd been allowed out of this dreadful hole! She could have stopped it. She didn't know how, but she was certain she could have. She'd stopped it once before, after all.

That time, however, she hadn't had Sir Marcus to deal with. Lord, how shocked she'd been, when he'd stepped out of Drake's cell and seized hold of her. How had he recognized her? She'd never even noticed him looking in her direction. How had *he* noticed, in a matter of minutes, that she wasn't who she was pretending to be, when a whole pirate crew had lived and breathed with her for a month, and never known she was a girl?

Well, no one had ever said pirates were clever. Diabolical, maybe, and certainly merciless, but not clever.

How the color had drained out of Drake's face when Sir Marcus had produced her! Why, if it hadn't been for his chains holding him up, Payton was certain he'd have collapsed of shock right then and there. But he'd remained upright and, looking Tyler quite calmly in the eye, said, "If she's harmed, you'll die."

Which had only made Sir Marcus laugh. Because of course what could Drake do to him? He was all chained up, after all, and very much at the disadvantage. Still, Payton had gotten a chill when he'd said it. Because she knew he meant it. Even if he had to come back from the grave to do it, Drake was going to kill Marcus Tyler. There wasn't any doubt about that.

But he wasn't given an opportunity to do so then. Instead, they unchained him, tied his hands behind his back, and dragged him away. Payton they left behind, locked in the very cell where Drake had languished for so long. They tried to chain her up, too, but the manacles that had kept Drake imprisoned were far too big for her slender wrists, and kept slipping off. She didn't suppose they considered her much of a threat, since they just shut the door and locked it behind them—though she did think Tito looked a little sad about it. He had liked Hill, after all.

The wedding had taken place almost immediately afterward. Payton had heard the crew gather to witness it. They made any number of rude remarks during the ceremony, at which the captain of the *Nassau Queen* officiated. And when it was over, there was a general cry of hurrah—though Payton wasn't sure whether that was because they'd killed Drake, or tapped the rum casks. Surely if Drake was dead, she'd know it. She'd have felt it, she was certain, if his life was suddenly snuffed out. She'd loved him for so long, she'd *have* to know it. She'd known everything else about him, for God's sake.

Taking her ear away from the wall, she looked blearily about the cell in which she was locked. If he was dead, there was very little point in going on herself. Could she, she wondered, strangle herself with those thick chains, now lying on the floor? She doubted it. There wasn't even a beam over which to throw them, to make a proper noose. Besides, she wasn't going to leave this life without taking those responsible for removing Drake from it with her. She had killed men before—at least, she thought she had. She had certainly aimed pistols at them, and pulled the trigger, and seen her target go down. It was incredibly easy to take a life, really, if you didn't think about what you were doing. She'd be able to take Sir Marcus's life without a qualm. The anticipation of doing that, at least, was something to live for.

Glancing at her surroundings, Payton couldn't restrain a sigh. How had Drake endured it, these past few weeks? She'd only been here a few hours, and already she was convinced she was going mad. It wasn't the closeness that bothered her, or even the rats. She welcomed the rats, in fact. They were good company, and wanted nothing from her but what crumbs of food she could spare. No, it was the darkness she minded. Only the stingiest amount of light filtered down into the hold, through the cracks in the deck floor. How had Drake lasted as long as he had, without any light?

She leaned her back against the wall, then slid down it until she was sitting with her elbows on her knees. She couldn't stop thinking that the whole thing was her fault. If she hadn't stowed away, like she had, Drake would never have been coerced into marrying Miss Whitby. He'd have died first, she knew. Now she'd put her whole family in a horrible spot. Once they killed Drake, Miss Whitby—or Lady Drake, Payton supposed she was called now—would go back to England and claim Drake's share in Dixon and Sons. The business would be run aground—to coin a phrase—in no time. And it would all be Payton's fault.

Unless, of course, she could escape. She hadn't much doubt

she could manage it. She just had to get someone to open that door.

Of course, she knew what Marcus Tyler intended to do with her. Hold her for ransom. Oh, the ransom note wouldn't come from him. Her family would never guess Marcus Tyler was behind the whole thing. And they would pay, of course. But Marcus Tyler would never let her return to them. He couldn't. She'd tell them the truth about Drake.

So she had the honor of serving a double purpose on board the *Rebecca*. Her presence would insure that Drake did what was asked of him, and she'd earn her captors a pretty penny or two, after which she'd be killed.

How nice, Payton thought bitterly, to be of service to so many.

Above her, the accordion came to a wheezing halt, then clattered, with a thump, to the deck floor. A silence fell upon the deck. The last of the revelers had fallen asleep . . . or passed out from too much rum. She was probably the only creature on board who was awake—the only living creature, that is. Surely Drake, if he wasn't dead, was awake, too. If only she knew! If only she knew whether or not—

A key scraped in the lock of her cell's door.

So she was *not* the only creature on board who was awake.

Scrambling to her feet, Payton darted to stand on the far side of the door, so that whoever was entering would not see her until he'd come round the jamb. If it's anyone but Drake, Payton told herself, I shall cause him a good deal of discomfort. Raleigh had once told her that if she clapped her cupped hands on either side of a person's head very hard indeed, it would break his eardrums. Now seemed like a good opportunity to try his theory out.

Only just as she'd raised her hands, she saw through the gloom that her visitor was about her own size, though considerably wider. He was peering about the cell quite intently, one arm held at an awkward angle. " 'Ill?" he whispered.

Good God, Payton thought, lowering her arms. It's Jonesy.

"Jonesy," she said, from behind the door.

He spun around, and faced her with eyes wide and startled. "That you, 'Ill?" he asked.

"Yes, of course it's me, you bleeding sod. Who did you expect? What are you doing here? You're going to get yourself into trouble." She couldn't help it, this feeling of protectiveness she felt for this idiot boy. Yes, she'd broken his nose. But she'd been quite sorry for it ever since.

"I 'ad to come," he whispered.

Touched, Payton reached out to him. "Oh, Jonesy," she said. "That's so sweet of you. Can you tell me . . . Do you know . . . Is Drake still alive?"

Jonesy squinted at her. Moonlight, very dim indeed, shifted in through cracks in the ceiling, just enough so that she could make out the boy's features. "That bloke what was locked in 'ere? Yeah, I reckon 'e ain't dead yet. They've got 'im tied to the mainmast. 'E's s'posed to stay there, with no water or food or nofink, till 'e's dead."

"Good God." Anguish gripped Payton's heart. She'd heard, of course, that this was a popular way of punishing sailors. Without food and water, tied all day in the mercilessly hot sun, they soon became dehydrated, and were subject to fits and hallucinations before death—excruciatingly slow—came. She supposed Tyler had chosen this mode of murder since it took a long time. Simply keelhauling him, while entertaining to the rest of the crew, would be too quick. This way, they could enjoy torturing him for days, even weeks, before he finally perished.

"Well," Payton said. "I suppose, if you let me have your knife—they took mine, you know—I can cut him down. We'll make for a longboat—"

Jonesy stared at her. "What're you talkin' about?" he asked.

She blinked at him. "Well, isn't that why you've come? To help me get away?"

His upper lip, upon which she'd noticed lately a hint of brown fuzz beginning to grow, curled. "No," he said scoffingly. "I come because I 'eard 'em sayin' you was a girl. Is that true?"

She glared at him, annoyed now. "Well, of course it's true, you great buffoon. It took you bloody long enough to realize it. Now stand aside. I'm getting out, with or without your help."

He shook his great moon head, although she wasn't at all certain he'd heard her. "I want to see," he said.

"You want to *what*?" She didn't think she'd heard him right.

"To see." His voice had gone curiously thick. The fuzz on his lip, she noticed, was glistening a little with perspiration. And then he was actually reaching for the front of her vest. "I want to see," he said, in a much deeper voice than she'd ever heard him use before.

Payton couldn't back up, because there was a wall at her back. She couldn't go right, because the back of the door was there, and she couldn't go left, because there was another wall. He had her quite effectively trapped. Jonesy, for whom she'd been feeling sorry a moment before, had her trapped, and appeared to be intent upon feasting his eyes on her breasts.

"Listen, Jonesy," she said quickly. "I thought we were mates, you and I. Remember the molasses? What fun we had cleaning that up? I don't think this is any way to treat a mate—"

But Jonesy wasn't listening. His gaze was glued to her chest. She felt his thick fingers on the buttons of her vest. She closed her eyes, and uttered a quick prayer, asking for forgiveness for that which she was about to do.

Then she lifted both her hands and, cupping her fingers, clapped them as hard as she could over Jonesy's ears.

To his credit, he didn't bellow. He didn't even utter a sound, at first. He only looked considerably surprised. Then a low sort of keening noise slipped out of his mouth. His hands left the front of her vest and went to his ears, from which she could see twin rivulets of blood trickling. He fell to his knees before her, like a man who'd been smitten from above.

Payton wasted no time. She darted around him and ran to the door. Peering out into the hold, she found it in total darkness, save for the dim light that drifted down from the open hatch above her head. Tito lay slumped on the floor outside her cell, snoring fitfully. One of his hands was clutched around the rim of an empty cup. The other held the keys to her cell.

Quickly, Payton stepped over him and lifted the keys. She eased the door to her cell closed and made quick work of locking the moaning Jonesy inside. Then, pocketing the keys, she reached for the knife she knew Tito kept hidden in his boot. It was a long, cruel-looking dagger, but it would serve her purposes adequately. As soon as she'd tucked it into her belt, she hurried up the ladder to the deck.

Lord, what a mess. She was glad *she* wasn't going to be expected to clean it up. Everywhere she looked she saw unconscious pirates. There were men passed out against the mizzenmast, men draped across the pumps, men curled up in piles of rope against the topgallant. Where there wasn't a snoring body there was an overturned bottle or a puddle of vomit. It reminded her of their London town house after her brothers, recently returned to port, had been out on a carouse.

Men, she thought, in disgust. Revolting creatures, be they pirates or peers' sons.

It took her just a minute or so to reach Drake. As Jonesy had assured her, he'd been tied to the mainmast. But she could not, at first, believe his assurance that the man was not dead. Never had she seen a more awful sight than that of Drake tied to the *Rebecca*'s mainmast, with the possible exception of the sight of Drake marrying Rebecca herself. Both had nearly caused her to suffer an apoplexy of fright.

Stripped naked to the chest, he'd been tied with his back to the thick mast. Only the heavy ropes around him, cutting into the thick fur of his chest, kept him upright. His head hung between his broad shoulders, the taut skin over which still glowed from where the hot sun had beat down on it all afternoon. His arms were nearly hyperextended, they'd been stretched so far around the mast. Even in the light from the half-moon, she could see veins bulging from the undersides of his powerful biceps.

And that wasn't all. It looked as if the crew had been entertaining themselves at the prisoner's expense. Tangled in his thick mane of blond hair was a wreath of flowers—the same flowers she'd seen brought over earlier that morning, from the *Nassau Queen,* as a gift for the nauseous Becky Whitby. And at his feet lay a placard, upon which was scrawled, in crude lettering, "Came there a certain lord, neat, and trimly dress'd, Fresh as a bridegroom." Payton supposed that was Sir Marcus's contribution, since she'd spent a goodly amount of time with the crew of the *Rebecca,* and had never known any of them to quote Shakespeare. She had never liked Marcus Tyler, and now her dislike for him flared to all-out hatred.

It wasn't until she saw that painfully scorched chest move that she realized he was still breathing. She'd taken him for dead, and had been wondering whether Sir Marcus slept here or in the after house of the *Nassau Queen,* and if so, how was she going to sneak on board and slit his throat, if the plank between the two boats had been drawn?

Then Drake breathed, and all thought of murdering Sir Marcus fled. She knew what she had to do. She sprang to action at once.

Tito's knife was a sharp one, and kept in good condition by its proud owner. It was the work of but a moment to slice through the thick knots that held Drake against the mast. She had to support him to keep his unconscious body from falling forward once the ropes were removed, and that was when she realized she had a problem: he weighed a ton, far more than she could lift. Grunting, she heaved a shoulder beneath one of his armpits, and turned her mouth to his ear, hissing at him to wake up. If she was going to get them out of there, she needed a little help from him.

He seemed to hear her. His eyes opened, anyway—no more than mere slits, but the lids parted, and she thought he recognized her. Or maybe his legs straightened on their own accord. In any case, he was standing—at least somewhat. That helped, a little. Slowly, she managed to steer him in the direction of the only longboat that didn't hold fitfully dozing sailors.

There were longboats hanging on both the starboard and the port sides of the *Rebecca*. Reserved for use when the captain decided to go ashore, they hung suspended by ropes, and could be lowered into the water with the help of a system of pulleys. Payton had made sure that her long list of duties aboard the *Rebecca* included oiling those pulleys regularly, so she knew that when she began to lower the boat, there would be no tell-tale creaking to give her away.

She wasn't wrong. Still, it wasn't easy, lowering the heavy boat by herself—and since it bore only a single passenger, the unconscious Drake, the weight wasn't distributed evenly, which made things even worse. But finally, she heard a splash. Peering over the side, she saw that the boat was bobbing gently alongside the *Rebecca*'s hull, Drake resting comfortably in the bottom of it as a baby in a cradle. Well, not really a baby, she corrected herself, since babies did not generally weigh so much, nor were they covered in quite as much thick, tawny hair.

But she hadn't time to ponder that. In a flash, she cut the ropes that tethered the craft. Then she clenched Tito's knife between her teeth, kicked off her shoes, and, trying hard not to think about sharks and jellyfish, swung her legs over the side of the *Rebecca* and dove into the sea.

The dark water was warm. It accepted her as welcomingly as a mother's embrace. Payton's heart felt as if it were bursting by the time she kicked her way back to the surface, but not from lack of oxygen—with joy. It had been a long time since she'd had a bath, and even longer since she'd last been swimming. She felt as comfortable in the water as she did on land, having learned to swim almost as soon as she could walk.

The swells, she saw with relief, as she bobbed along with the waves, were nothing. The sea was gentle and still. Land, in the form of one of the many islands Drake had mapped, was not far. Only that morning, she had seen some far-off humps on the horizon.

They were home.

Well, almost.

Swimming to the side of the longboat, Payton pulled herself up into it, dripping like a mermaid. Drake, who'd regained partial consciousness only briefly, lay dead to the world at the bottom of the boat. Won't he be surprised, Payton thought, with pleasure, when he wakes up, and finds himself far, far away from Sir Marcus, and the Frenchman, and the odious Miss Whitby?

She did not remind herself that the odious Miss Whitby was now his wife. She kept that thought firmly out of mind, in the same place she kept her fear that the midwatchman on the *Nassau Queen* might notice their departure. There was no point in worrying about it. There wasn't a blessed thing she could do about either thing.

Except, of course, pray.

Which, after she laid down the knife and picked up an oar, she began to do with fervor.

# Chapter Twenty-three

$\mathcal{D}$rake's mouth and throat were parched. He could never remember having been so thirsty.

He'd been tied to the mast before. It had been long ago, of course, back in his youth, when he'd set sail under a young captain Sir Henry had only recently hired. The man hadn't been fit to command, but, to his credit, Sir Henry had had no way of knowing that. There wasn't really much of a way to judge how a man whom one had only met before in a comfortable parlor would act once he was out on the high seas. This one had gone fairly mad, punishing his men for the slightest offenses. Drake's had been that he'd dropped the captain's shaving water. For that, he'd been tied to the mainmast for a day, and most of an evening, until the captain had gone to bed and the first officer had cut Drake loose. He'd suffered such severe sunstroke that he hadn't been able to move for an entire day. His skin had blistered, everywhere except where the ropes had held him. Even his lips, chapped from the sun and surf, had swelled to twice their normal size, making it excruciatingly painful for him to sip the water that was eventually offered to him.

Still, Drake didn't remember that he'd been quite this thirsty, all those years ago. Of course, back then, he'd been considerably younger, and able to tolerate hardship better. He was in no condition to do so now.

There would be no sympathetic mate to cut him down this time. He was going to die upon this mast.

That might have been all right—he wasn't afraid to die. It might have been all right, if he hadn't had Payton with him. He couldn't die and leave Payton alone. Someone had to look after her. He didn't know what Tyler intended to do with her. On the whole, he suspected he planned to kill her. He couldn't, after all, let her live. She'd only return to England and tell everyone that Connor Drake had been coerced into his marriage with Becky Whitby—that his father-in-law had been the one who'd murdered him. No, Tyler couldn't afford to let that happen.

But he wouldn't necessarily have to kill her to keep her from talking. There were worse ways to keep people silent than killing them. Particularly women, white women like Payton, who fetched high prices at the sort of markets men like Tyler frequented—markets that specialized in the peddling of human flesh. England had enacted her antislavery laws some time ago, but not every country had followed suit—nor had every shipping company pledged, as Dixon and Sons had, not to transport human chattel.

He couldn't let that happen. Not to Payton.

But what could he do? He was tied here, weak as a kitten already from the burning sun. What was happening down below? What were they doing to Payton now? He'd kill them, kill them all if they harmed her. He'd meant it when he'd said it, though Marcus had laughed. He'd done a lot of laughing that afternoon, as his daughter and Drake had been declared man and wife. It was a mockery of a marriage, Drake knew, but what else could he do? He knew Tyler had no honor. He knew he'd kill Payton—or worse—whether Drake agreed to marry Becky or not. But he had, at least, to hope that if he gave them what they wanted, they'd go easy on the girl. It was all he could do.

And now he was dying. He knew he was dying, because

he was beginning to hallucinate. That was what happened on the mast. First came the hallucinations, then the convulsions, and then, finally, death. His hallucinations, at least, were not unpleasant. He was dreaming that he was lying on cool, soft sand, in sweet, delicious shade. It was really quite a powerful image. He wished he'd begun hallucinating sooner. He could hear birdsong overhead, and smell the sweet scent of lemon blossom. Lemons! They grew plentifully in the Bahamas. When he brought a cargo of lemons back to the British Isles, he was guaranteed an enthusiastic welcome by almost every hostess in London. They were a most sought-after delicacy. The gift of a lemon was a precious one. And oranges, given to children at Christmastime, were a treat treasured above chocolate. How nice it would be, if he could lose himself completely in this hallucination before the fits started. If only he really *were* lying in the shade on a Bahamian island, inhaling the sweet fragrance of fruit trees, listening to the trills of parakeets . . .

The hallucination was so strong that when he flexed his fingers, he could actually feel the cool sand shift beneath them. This was not, he decided, the worst way to die. His lips, when he finally summoned up the strength to lick them, even tasted moist, as if water had been wrung into them recently. Fresh water, too. Water taken from a stream, not from a barrel full of the brackish stuff.

This, he realized suddenly, was no hallucination. This was *real.*

It was difficult—the hardest thing he'd ever had to do—but he managed to peel his eyes open. For a moment, he could only blink confusedly. He couldn't understand what he was looking at. It ought to have been the deck of the *Rebecca,* or, in the event that his head had fallen back, as it appeared to, the mainsail. But what he saw was neither. It was a tangle of tree branches. Tree branches in full leaf. Beyond them yawned a cloudless azure sky. The branches were heavy with fruit. Round, yellow fruit. Lemons.

He was lying beneath a lemon tree. It appeared to be mid-afternoon. And he wasn't hallucinating at all.

Nor was he dead.

Good God. He was alive.

He was alive, and he was no longer on board the *Rebecca*. Rising up to his elbows—he was stretched out on his back beneath the shade—he looked around. To his left appeared to be jungle. He saw a tangle of vines and fruit trees, banana, mango, and lime. To the right, much of the same. Not far off sat a longboat, apparently pulled from the surf, although not far enough to keep high tide from snatching it back again. Looking down the length of his body, he saw the sea, the aquamarine waves curling in a froth of white upon a cream-colored, palm-tree-dotted beach.

Looking down the length of his *naked* body.

That's right. *Naked*. He wasn't wearing a stitch of clothing.

That realization sat him up fast enough. His clothes were gone. His shirt, he realized, had pretty much disintegrated on board the *Rebecca*. But his trousers had been intact, not to mention the fact that he had, last time he'd checked, been wearing underclothes.

Now both were gone.

He couldn't hear much above the rumble of the surf and the twitter of the birds overhead. But it seemed as if from somewhere behind him was the faint but unmistakable sound of running water. That, at least, would explain the presence of a hollowed-out gourd a foot or two from him, filled to the brim with what appeared to be fresh water. Whether this was a gift from the gods or something left by a passing native girl, Drake didn't pause to think. Instead, he reached for the gourd and, raising it to his lips, drained it of its contents.

It was the best water he'd ever tasted. Cool and sweet, it immediately soothed the dryness in his aching throat, and quenched his powerful thirst. When he lowered the gourd from his face, he felt like a different man entirely.

Enough of a different man to wonder just where in the hell he was, and how in the hell he'd gotten there.

He wasn't alone. That was certain. Besides the gourd, he noticed now that there were the remains of a fire a few feet away. A small fire, but a fire nonetheless, and one that he certainly hadn't set. An ivory-handled dagger lay in the sand beside the charred hole. The dagger threw him. He didn't know anyone who owned a lethal-looking weapon like that.

But the fire. The fire looked a bit like the kind Payton constructed, when she was of a mind to build a fire. He'd watched her argue with her brothers in the past over the kindling tower versus the kindling plus wood tower, Payton insisting fires burned better if the kindling wasn't immediately smothered underneath pounds of driftwood, her brothers swearing the opposite held true. The fire before him had an odd appearance, as if someone had built it, spent a few hours trying to light it, then, exhausted, promptly fell asleep before adding the wood.

That someone, he thought, with a suddenly unsteady heartbeat, could only be the Honorable Miss Payton Dixon.

That thought was enough to send him staggering to his feet. His nakedness forgotten, he turned around in a circle, beginning to recognize the terrain around him. Of course. They were on San Rafael Island. He'd pointed it out to Payton himself once, on his map. One of the smaller islets in the Bahamian archipelago, it was not only the most secluded, but also one of the few that boasted its own fresh water source, instead of depending on the storms that regularly battered the tropics to fill its lakes. Because San Rafael was surrounded on all four sides by coral reefs, it was approachable only by longboat. Any larger craft would have their hull torn out instantly by the shoals. In fact, one could see the masts of ships whose captains had had the ill judgment to try to approach the island sticking up out of the sea, a perch for gulls and cormorants, while the rest of the vessel sat, fathoms below, on the reef.

She'd done it. He didn't know how. But she had done it, just like she'd said she would.

And then his feet began to move. He ducked to avoid low-hanging branches and vines as he made his way toward the center of the island, from which he'd heard the sound of running water. His feet were bare, but he didn't notice the sharp rocks and twisted roots that cut into him as he hurried over them. All of his concentration was on what lay ahead.

And then he burst through the last of the palm fronds and lemon-tree branches and vines.

The native Bahamians—those who had not yet been converted to Christianity—considered San Rafael Island a holy place. Their name for it was unpronounceable, but translated, it meant, more or less, Island of the Gods. It was for that reason—and, of course, the dangerous reefs surrounding it— that the island was unpopulated. Once a year, the natives gathered to leave sacrifices there—mostly fruits and vegetables, and the occasional goat—but the rest of the year, San Rafael was empty.

Which was a shame. Because once one got past the reefs, and the thick jungle that grew over most of the island, it really was the most beautiful place imaginable. A spring bubbled up in the center of it; fresh, clean water from deep beneath the earth. It came bursting out through the top of what might once have been a small volcano, but was now a small flower-covered mountain, all of twenty feet above sea level, the highest point on the island. The water burbled up through the crest of this zenith, then flowed down its side until it splashed into a deep spring. The banks surrounding the spring were rocky, and mercilessly without shade, but with water that cool and clear, what did lack of shade matter? It was possible to stand on the rocks beneath the precipice and allow the full force of the waterfall to shower over one, a sensation that was, Drake happened to know, one of the most enjoyable on earth—which was probably the reason why the native gods had forbidden their worshipers from experiencing it: in his worldwide travels, Drake had noticed that gods often forbade that which was most pleasurable.

But the Honorable Miss Payton Dixon was clearly ignorant of Bahamian religious law. Either that, or she was purposely and flagrantly defying it. Because as Drake cleared the thick jungle of growth he'd been fighting his way through, his gaze was drawn at once to the waterfall.

The force of the water wasn't very strong; it really was more of a steady trickle than a cascade. Which was how he was able to see, quite clearly, the young woman standing beneath it, stark naked, and apparently not a whit self-conscious about it.

Well, Drake supposed that if he didn't know he was being observed, he'd be unself-conscious, too. But he'd encountered a lot of naked women in his day, and he had never seen any who'd been quite as . . . well, *happy* to be nude was the only way he could think to put it. Payton Dixon was quite obviously extremely pleased to be without her clothes.

Taking into account that this was undoubtedly the first opportunity she'd had to bathe fully undressed in over a month, he could understand her enthusiasm. Still, there was no denying the fact that before him stood a young woman who was supremely pleased with—and confident in—her own body. Payton had always been more comfortable in men's clothes than in women's, and in that moment, Drake saw why: she was perfectly contented with the way she looked. Why would someone who felt so comfortable in her own skin feel the need to stuff it into a pinching, restrictive corset, and hide it under layer upon layer of petticoat?

Then again, he had to admit he was glad she'd done it. He never would have noticed her bewitching figure if she hadn't shown it off in that ballgown and corset.

But there was no need for her ever to don a corset again, as far as he was concerned. In fact, he was going to do everything in his power to convince her to wear men's clothing from now on. There wasn't any need to let anyone else know that Payton Dixon's body was perfection, the very essence of all that was womanly. Let the rest of the world exist in blessed ignorance of those small but perfectly shaped breasts; that narrow waist; those long, lean thighs; the enticing patch of brown curls between those thighs. He knew it, and she knew it, and that was enough. He anticipated that he was going to have enough problems winning her—let alone keeping her—without inviting competition.

Perfectly ignorant of his presence—he'd seen whores who were a good deal more modest, even when thinking they were unobserved—Payton raised her arms to massage the cool water into her scalp, throwing her head back to reveal the long column of her throat. She was slender as a reed, built on a much smaller scale than most women, yet there was no denying that her curves, though subtle, were very much there. She turned toward the spray, presenting him with an unimpeded view of her bare backside, and he found that he had to sit down, of a sudden, on a nearby stone. Those buttocks, which he'd noted through her trousers were pleasingly round, came together in a perfect heart shape below her small waist. He was going to have to rethink his plan of making her wear men's clothing from this day forward. It would not do for that backside to be revealed to anyone but him, and trousers would certainly show it off disgracefully.

Flour sacks. He was going to have to see that from now on, she wore only flour sacks. That was the only possible answer. Anything else would be too revealing.

As he sat there, unable to take his eyes off her, he became conscious of an unpleasant dampness beneath him. He looked down and saw that he was sitting on his drawers. They had been, near as he could tell, thoroughly washed, then laid out to dry upon the rocks surrounding the spring. Glancing around, he recognized his trousers, then Payton's shirt and vest, similarly strewn in the sun to dry. Well, that explained the mystery of his disappearing breeches. Then he raised an eyebrow, and turned his gaze back toward the bather on the rocks. So the little minx had undressed him. Saved his life; undressed him; then done his laundry. Here was a woman worth far more than her weight in jewels.

He was ruminating on this fact when the woman in question turned around and spotted him. Pushing some wet hair from her eyes, she peered at him as if she couldn't quite believe what she was seeing.

Then she let out a bloodcurdling scream, and jumped into the spring.

Drake sat where he was, the scream echoing in his ears. The shrill sound had frightened a flock of parrots from the treetops. Squawking indignantly, they took flight, their wings flapping noisily. Payton, who'd disappeared beneath the water's surface, reemerged suddenly. Wiping water from her eyes, she blinked up at him.

"Drake?" she asked breathlessly. "Is that really you?"

He looked down at himself. "I believe so."

"Oh, my God." She was treading water. The pool was only six or seven feet deep, but Payton hardly stood higher than five. Her feet could not find purchase on the rocky bottom. And if she thought the water opaque enough to hide her nakedness, she was sadly mistaken. He could see far more, as a matter of fact, than before, since she had to kick her legs open to stay afloat.

"When I turned," she said panting, "and saw you there, I had water in my eyes, and I didn't recognize you, and I thought . . . Are you *all right*?"

He looked down at himself again. "I conscientiously believe so."

"Because you didn't stir." She was paddling around the pool, looking for a place where she could climb out without hurting her bare feet on the rocks. She was talking every bit as fast as she was paddling. "I was so worried. You never stirred all night. Are you *sure* you're all right?"

He grinned. He simply couldn't help it. Never in his life had he felt such an immense attraction to a woman. It was absurd, because she wasn't making the slightest effort to entice him. But that only served to remind him—as if he needed reminding—of how very different she was from all the simpering, flirtatious females he'd known before. Payton Dixon wouldn't have known how to flirt if her life depended on it. And simper? Forget about it.

Drake, feeling suddenly, ridiculously happy, happier than he could ever remember being, stood up and strode purposefully to the edge of the spring. Below him, Payton's eyes went round as saucers.

"W—what do you think you're doing?" she asked.

"Joining you." Drake dipped a toe into the crystal-clear water.

Payton seemed unable to tear her gaze from the region of his body located directly below his navel. Looking down, Drake noted that his state of arousal was blatantly apparent. Too late, he remembered how dark it had been that night in his cell, when they'd first made love. Albeit unknowingly, he'd just supplied Payton with her first daylit glimpse of the nude male form.

And she did not appear the least bit enthusiastic about what she'd seen.

"Um, that's all right," Payton stammered, paddling away from him with alacrity. "I was just getting out—"

Drake realized rapid action was necessary. Always one to keep a cool head in a crisis, he stepped off the rocks, and plunged into the cool water.

# Chapter Twenty-four

Payton, enveloped in the wave created by Drake's enormous body entering the pool, came out of it sputtering. It wasn't so much the water she was choking on, but the knowledge of what that water hid, now that Drake was in it. It appeared that there was a great deal more to that part of Connor Drake that she'd only felt before, but never really seen, than she'd previously thought. So much more, in fact, that it seemed retreat was probably the best strategy at this point. Before he'd even surfaced, she was heading for shore.

But she didn't get very far. Some sort of underwater tentacle reached out and wrapped around one of her ankles, firmly stopping her in her flight.

Drake finally broke the surface, his tawny hair plastered to his head, but he didn't let go of her ankle. In fact, he seemed to be reeling her in by it, the way a fisherman reeled in his catch. First his free hand, the one not wrapped around her ankle, encircled her knee, and then a thigh, and then, inexorably, her waist, until he was drawing her close to him with both arms. And all the while, he was smiling at her in a gentle manner that really wasn't doing her heartstrings the least bit of good.

Payton, her pulse thundering in her ears, still had the presence of mind to stammer, "I think m-maybe you ought to rest a little longer—"

"No, thank you," was his polite reply. "I've had quite enough of resting."

And then he was kissing her. But it was not, to her surprise, a hard, possessive kiss. No, it was gentle . . . like his smile.

At least, it started out gently. It wasn't until she made the mistake—and she realized it was a mistake the moment she did it—of meeting his probing tongue with a darting, inquisitive thrust of her own, that the kiss went from gentle to wild—and in just half a heartbeat, too. One second, he'd been kissing her tenderly, and the next, his month's growth of beard was razing the tender skin around her mouth as his lips seemed to engulf hers.

She had told herself when she'd removed his pants that morning that under no circumstance was she going to repeat what had happened on the *Rebecca*. That, she knew now, hadn't been fair of her. Connor Drake was an extremely virile man, and that had been why he'd reacted the way he had when she'd thrown herself at him. True, he'd said he loved her . . . but he'd felt he had to say something like that, because she'd been a virgin, and she supposed he'd felt guilty . . .

Though it had been all her doing. She had been in love with him for most of her life, and had been actively pursuing him for the last several months. Lord, he had probably only given in to her lustful demands out of pity, or boredom, or the conviction that he was going to be put to death any minute, so why not enjoy the time he had left? He certainly couldn't have been telling the truth when he'd said he loved her.

Or could he?

Because now . . . now there was no reason for him to be kissing her like this, no reason at all. He could have ignored her. He could have walked away, when he found her bathing there, and she'd never have been the wiser, not having noticed him until he'd been standing there some little while, judging from the evidence of his arousal.

Oh, bloody hell. *Of course* he was attracted to her. He was *obviously* attracted to her. And she had not thrown herself at him this time—quite the opposite, in fact. What did it matter, whether or not he'd been telling the truth when he'd said he loved her? Wasn't his kiss convincing enough that he was . . . well, fond of her, anyway?

Her firm decision never to make love with him again crumbled into dust the second his lips touched hers. For one thing, she couldn't very well push him away: his strong arms around her were all that kept her afloat. And for another thing, the feel of his naked body as he pressed it against hers was unlike anything she had ever known: the way his chest hair teased her nipples as it brushed up against them; the cool hardness of the thigh he insinuated between hers, brushing once—as if by accident, and then again, proving it was no accident at all—the soft, pulsing mound between her legs. Her hands were on his broad shoulders, shoulders that just the night before had glowed hotly red, but which had already turned to a deep bronze. She could feel the muscles beneath that tanned skin contract as his arms tightened around her. It seemed as if he couldn't kiss her deeply enough, or press his body close enough to hers.

Why hadn't anyone told her how good it felt, having a man's skin against one's own? Mei-Ling had never mentioned it. Georgiana had never said a word. Why hadn't she ever tried this before? She ought to have ripped Drake's clothes off that night, back on the *Rebecca*. But she'd been too overwhelmed by other sensations to think of it . . .

Then Drake's lips left hers. Gripping her naked bottom—almost the way he had that night in the garden, so long ago—he lifted her from the water, holding her slick and dripping high above him, until his mouth was level with her breasts. And then he pressed those lips that had so firmly entrapped her to one hardened nipple.

She groaned. She couldn't help it, the contrast between the cool water and the heat of his tongue was so delicious. And her groan seemed to do something to him. He tore his lips from her breast and lowered her in his arms until he could smother her mouth in quick, greedy kisses. Suddenly, the hard male thigh that had been brushing against her, lightly as a silverfish, pressed quite emphatically between her legs. And like the wanton thing she knew she was, Payton responded by moving against it in an imitation of the love act.

The next thing she knew, he'd lifted her out of the water again. Only this time, instead of his hands, she felt something cool and hard beneath her buttocks. Looking down, she saw that he'd placed her on a natural shelf formed by one of the flat boulders that surrounded the pool. Payton couldn't think what he meant by it until she realized he was standing between her thighs, in water shallow enough that she was given an unimpeded view of the part of him she'd touched without the least temerity when it had been safely clothed; that organ which, because she lacked it, she'd blamed for any number of disappointments in her life, most recently the loss of the *Constant*.

Only now she had to say a little prayer of thanks that she had been born a female. Because otherwise, there would have been no reason for Drake to open her gently, as he did then, with his fingers, while at the same time invading her mouth with lips and tongue, an assault on so many fronts that Payton was helpless to put up any resistance whatsoever. She could only let out a little murmur of appreciation, and spread her legs even farther apart . . .

That seemed to be invitation enough for Drake to replace those fingers with something a good deal larger.

And then she couldn't talk, she couldn't even think, because his lips were on her neck again, his hands on her hips, and he was moving, slowly, out of her, when he'd only just gotten in, and it felt so good, having him there, so where was he going?

She moved her hips, pulling him greedily back inside. She felt him suck in his breath.

And then he said her name, in a voice that was halfway between a growl and a groan, and his mouth was crushing hers, his hands clenching her buttocks, while his hips moved with frantic urgency between her legs. She could understand the urgency, because she felt it, too. Her entire being was focused upon Drake, on his ragged breathing, the coarseness of the stubble on his chin as it raked her mouth and throat, and above all, on the force behind each thrust, as he plunged so deeply within her.

Her climax, when it came, was nothing like the ones that she'd experienced before, back in Drake's cell. It seemed to her as if one moment, every nerve ending within her was taut with frustration, and the next, she was drowning in a lava flow—yes, a lava flow, even though the volcano on San Rafael was long dead. She was burning up in a sea of fire and light, wave after wave of liquid gold pouring over her. Though she didn't know it, the cry she let out was as much a sob as a scream, and hearing it, Drake lost all semblance of self-control. He gave one final thrust, driving himself as deeply into her as he could, no longer conscious of whether or not he hurt her, seeking only release.

It came, washing over him in torrents, powerful spasms of relief, and he roared his pleasure with such force that he startled the same flock of parrots she'd alarmed earlier, with her scream. He collapsed against her, and for a moment all Payton was conscious of was the pounding rhythm of his racing heart, the heavy weight of his body against hers, and the soft breeze that had begun to blow in from the sea, cooling her fevered skin.

And then she realized, with something akin to awe, that this—*this*, right now, right this moment—was what she had always wanted, what she'd been waiting for her entire life, it seemed. To have Connor Drake in her arms, his heart beating against her own . . . she had never asked for anything more than that, not once.

She felt it appropriate to utter a quick prayer of thanks. She hoped it wasn't sacrilegious to pray naked. But since the Lord had made her that way she didn't suppose He'd mind too much.

# Chapter Twenty-five

*Y*ou can't just wade up to one and heave the knife through it," he said, as they lay on their stomachs, looking down into the pool. "You've got to wait until it comes to you." Drake was trying to impress upon her the subtleties of spearing fish.

Payton took a bite out of the banana she held. "Drake," she said. "Why do I have to know this?"

"In case something should happen to me." He turned his head to look at her. Since she was lying so close to him that their hips touched, he didn't have to turn his head far, and when he did, their noses nearly collided. He leaned back a little. It was important that he made her understand.

"They're going to look for us, Payton. If I know the Frenchman, he'll spend his every waking moment combing the area, until he finds us. That's why it's important for you to know how to take care of yourself."

She turned those eyes upon him, those eyes that were sometimes green and sometimes gold, and sometimes, like now, the deepest, most impenetrable mahogany.

"I know how to take care of myself," she informed him—mildly enough, for her. "Besides, you make it sound as if you think that if they found us, they'd only take you, and let me alone."

"If we plan this out right, that's exactly what will happen.

I've hidden the longboat, so there's no chance of them spotting it from the shoals. And if we stick to making fires at night, and deep enough inland, we've got a good chance. But just in case they stumble upon us anyway, I'll distract them, and you hide."

She laughed, a happy, burbling sound. It sounded familiar, and he realized that the spring, bubbling up from the earth, made much the same sort of sound. *"Where?"* Payton wanted to know. "Where am I going to hide, for heaven's sake? We're on an *island,* Drake, in case you didn't notice."

He pointed to the top of the rocks, where the water arced out, sounding like her laughter. "You could climb up there," he said. "And lie down flat. They wouldn't think to look there."

Payton followed his gaze. "Well," she said. "I could. But I won't."

"Why not?"

"Because I'm not going to sit up there and watch them kill you." She turned her attention back to the pool beneath them. "Oh, there's one, Drake."

She meant to distract him, he knew. She was good at that, at changing the subject when it happened to displease her. But then he looked, and saw that she hadn't been lying. A great gray fish of some sort was peering up at them from the mossy depths. It looked plump and defenseless and eminently edible.

"Right," he said, hefting the spear. "Now pay attention, Payton. The point is not to let the fish know you're there. Then . . . wham! Straight through the eyes." He demonstrated the technique, using the ivory-handled dagger, which he'd tied to the end of a long stick. "You see? You want to throw from the shoulder, not the elbow. Now you try. See if you can get him."

"Drake," Payton said, still looking at the fish, and not at him, "what was it that you did that got the Frenchman so angry at you?"

He lowered his spear. "You don't know?"

She shrugged. "No. Every time I ask, Ross just says it's a long story."

He cleared his throat. "Well, he's right. It's a very long, very boring story."

And he couldn't believe his luck that none of her brothers had told it to her. It was a bit demoralizing, he was discovering, being with a woman who knew absolutely everything there was to know about him . . . or at least thought she did. He did not need her to know that he'd frequented brothels. That had been a long time ago. He was a changed man. She had seen to that.

"And you really think he'll try to come after us?" she asked. "The Frenchman, I mean."

"Probably. That's why the next time you build a fire, it'd be best not to do it on the beach."

She looked up at him sourly. "I only built a fire there because I thought you were cold, and you were too heavy for me to move, you bloody oaf."

It occurred to Drake that most women who claimed to be in love did not refer to the object of their affections as a bloody oaf. But their relationship was still very new, so he thought he'd let it pass.

"I'm not criticizing you," Drake said. "What you did was very brave." He reached down and swept a curl of russet hair from her eyes. "And very foolish."

"I know," she said happily. "Look what it got me. I'm ruined."

She could not have said it in more delighted tones, but still, it bothered him to hear her say it at all. Oh, there was no doubting she was contented as could be. Dressed in nothing more than her newly laundered shirt, her bare feet swinging loosely behind her, she was the very picture of a well-loved, well-fed woman. Still, he could not help feeling that he had failed her, and in more than one way. He could remember nothing of her daring rescue of him. She had told him that he'd been semiconscious for part of it. He could not recall even a single moment of it. That was unforgivable. He ought to have been at least lucid enough to urge her to leave him behind. He ought to have ordered her to make her break for freedom without being burdened by a large and only partially conscious beast who, to pay her back for her unselfishness, was only going to ravage her like some kind of animal every time she turned around.

How could he help it, though? He hadn't wanted it to be like this—he'd wanted to do things properly, to court her, to woo her . . .

Instead, it seemed as if he couldn't even look at her without having to control an overpowering urge to throw himself on top of her.

"Drake," she said, dropping a hand down to the water to stir it a little, frightening away the fish he'd been hoping to spear for supper. For someone who'd been so bloodthirsty a few nights before, she seemed strangely pacifistic now. She wouldn't let him kill any of the parrots, depriving them of the possibility of roasted poultry. She even protested when he offered to slit the throat of a turtle that had crawled by, declaring she hadn't any taste at all for eggs. If she thought that after a month on mash and water, he was going to be content to live on bananas and love . . .

Well, maybe she was right.

"What?" he asked, beginning to feel as lazy as she did. It had been no small feat, moving that longboat into the undergrowth. The thing had to have weighed several hundred pounds, at least.

"Do you suppose Becky Whitby will go back to England and claim to be your widow anyway? Even though they don't know for certain you're dead?"

Becky Whitby? Who cared about Becky Whitby! There were so many more important things they needed to discuss! Like what they were going to name their children, for instance.

"I don't know. She's welcome to try. I imagine that by now, your family must have every ship in His Majesty's navy out looking for you. If they get to the *Rebecca* before the *Rebecca* gets to England, all bets are off."

She glanced at him. "Do you think they'd know to look for us here?" she asked, and there was just the tiniest trace of worry in her tone. "My brothers, I mean."

Drake nodded. "If they have any reason at all to believe we're still alive, they'll find us, Payton. Don't worry."

She smiled at him reassuringly. "Oh, I'm not worried," she said.

It was odd, but he had a feeling that she really wasn't—not about being found, anyway. Could it be that she was as delighted as he was by the way the fates had thrown them together? Or was she simply so confident—so blindly, so childishly confident—in his abilities that she could not imagine anything but that they would be rescued? The thought staggered him a little. He was used to commanding, used to issuing orders and having them followed. But he had never, to his knowledge, inspired that kind of confidence in any of his men. It made even less sense that Payton would feel that way about him, when *she* had been the one who'd rescued them, *she* had been the one who'd brought them here, to safety.

He didn't feel as if he could go on basking in the adoring light in her eyes much longer. It wasn't her fault. He wasn't blaming her. But he couldn't help half-wishing that the Frenchman *would* find them, and that he could take out some of his frustrations on the pirate's handsome face.

"Look, Payton," he said, climbing to his feet. Unlike her, he'd pulled on his trousers. He wasn't quite as comfortable with his own nudity as she was. Well, he had more that needed covering. "I'm going to go and try to find some dry wood, so we can build a fire. You stay here, and if that great gray fellow swims over here again, jab him. All right?"

She took the spear from him obediently enough, but then she rolled over onto her back, away from the rocks, and onto the more comfortable sand, and stared at the sky. "Oh, look," she said, not sounding the least bit troubled by anything. "A pink sunset. It ought to be nice weather tomorrow."

Her shirt, he couldn't help noticing, did not reach much below her waist. Beneath it, she was completely naked. He wasn't too surprised to find that the triangular patch of curls between her legs, which had so attracted him a few hours ago, still held every bit as much fascination for him. It was shameful, his insatiable lust for her body. He had to drag his gaze away, fastening it instead on some less evocative part of her body.

"Here," he said, nodding at her ankle. "What's that?"

She was still blinking up at the evening sky. "What's what?" she asked.

"That ribbon, round your ankle."

That got her up, and fast. In a single, fluid motion, she'd snatched the ribbon away—breaking it, not untying it—and tossed it over her shoulder, into the spring.

"It's nothing," she said quickly. "Just a reminder. I don't need it anymore."

He went to the side of the pool and peered down into it. The ribbon was floating on the water's surface, the gray fish eyeing it from below, mistaking it for something edible. "What was it?"

"It's a very long," Payton said, "very boring story."

He glanced at her sharply, uncertain as to whether or not she was teasing him, since that was the same answer he'd made to her question about the Frenchman. But she only grinned up at him, and asked, "Do you remember that night on the *Virago*—it must have been two or three years ago, at least—when I said I wanted to lie on the deck and watch for falling stars, and you brought me your pillow and blanket?"

He blinked at her. She was trying to change the subject again. "Yes."

"Do you?" She looked mightily surprised. "Ross told me you were too drunk at the time to remember it, or even to know what you were doing."

He felt a sudden and unreasonable dislike for all of her brothers, particularly Ross. "Of course I knew what I was doing," he snapped. "I didn't want you to catch cold. God forbid any one of them should have paid so much as a moment's attention to you. They let you grow up half-wild, you know,

Payton. When I think of some of the things you were subjected to, and on a daily basis—things no woman should know anything about—it makes my blood run cold. They deserve a thorough thrashing, each and every one of them, but Ross most of all, for letting it go on."

She looked up at him, not at all perturbed. "But I turned out all right, in the end," she reminded him, with a shrug.

"No thanks to your brothers! You turned out all right because—well, I don't know. I suppose because you've got sense—more sense, I might add, than the three of your brothers put together."

The smile she gave him was every bit as dazzling as the sunset. "Thank you," was all she said, and she said that simply enough.

But the words caused something inside of him to break, something he'd been struggling to keep in check. And the next thing he knew, he was down on his knees before her, one of his big brown hands on either of her smooth thighs, pushing them apart.

Looking at him down the length of her body, Payton, who hadn't moved, said curiously, "Drake?"

He lifted his head, his jaw clenched. "Could you, for God's sake, call me Connor?"

"Connor, then. What are you doing?"

He showed her, instead of telling her. He showed her by lowering his head until his lips were on that soft patch of down between her thighs. He startled her—he knew he startled her, because she tried to buck away from him. Her fingers flew to his head, and grasped handfuls of his overlong hair.

"*Drake,*" she said, the word nothing more than a gasp.

But he wrapped his arms around her hips, not letting her pull away. He tasted her with his tongue, and found without much surprise that she tasted of the sea, salty and brisk. Well, of course. That was how Payton Dixon *would* taste.

"*Drake,*" she said again, with a little more urgency.

She wasn't wet. When he'd slid into her every other time, it had been startlingly easy, impossibly tight fit aside. If he hadn't known for certain that she was a virgin that night on board the *Rebecca*, he might never have guessed he was the first man she'd ever known, because she'd always been so wet, so ready for him, each time. But now she was dry, spent, her brown curls springing back every time he swept them away in his effort to trace each exquisite curve of her with his tongue. He laid a long and ardent kiss upon that velvet mound. He felt her fingers in his hair curl into helpless fists in response. She bucked again, but she had to know by now he would never let her go. He kept his lips where they were, delving, exploring with his tongue.

And then he was flooded, literally drenched with her essence. He lifted his face to look down at her, and saw that she was lying so that her hardened nipples, straining for the sky, had formed tents of the material of her shirt. Through the thin linen he could see the sweet rose-colored curves of her areoles. With her fingers still in his hair, and her head thrown back, her dark curls spread out like a fan against the sand, she looked the epitome of all that was feminine, more so, strangely enough, than when she'd been fully naked.

Wanting to watch her, wanting to burn the image of her just then into his mind's eye, he put a hand where his mouth had been, and felt her buck again. Now she pressed her pelvic bone against his palm, a helpless murmur, a prayer of longing—or supplication—coming from between her moistly parted lips. Not taking his gaze off her, he moved his callused fingers over her hot, wet mound until they were centered over her very core. She rubbed herself against him as instinctively as a cat, mindless in her pleasure.

And then he could stand it no longer. Jerking his head free from her hands, he reared back and, reaching with trembling fingers for the front of his breeches, tore at the buttons until his erection sprang free. Not bothering to lower his pants any further than that, he centered himself over her, hanging there for just a second, wanting to make sure that this time, he'd be able to control himself, that this time, he'd see to her pleasure first—watch her take it—and then take his own.

But then, just like last time, she moved against him, lifting her hips so that just the tip of his hard staff entered her soft warmth—just the smallest fraction of an inch she moved, taking just the tiniest piece of him into her. But that was enough. Next thing he knew, he'd let out a sort of shuddering groan, and he'd thrust himself deeply into her, so deeply that he was afraid he might have lanced her to the ground. And maybe he'd meant to. Because if he could spend the rest of his life right there, exactly where he was, embedded between her legs, her long, smooth legs, wrapped so tightly around his thighs, he'd die a happy man, indeed.

And then, just as he was marveling at the feel of her, the immense heat that radiated from her core, the incredibly tight grip in which she held him, all without even being aware—he was certain she couldn't be aware of it—of the power she had over him, he felt her arms tighten around his neck, and her back arch. The hot skin that held his erection so firmly prisoner began to spasm, and he realized that, incredibly, she was climaxing, without his ever having moved. Muscles he doubted she even knew she had caressed him, teased him, tried to pull him more deeply into her. He groaned, and dropped his head down so that he could press his mouth, still drenched in her dew, on hers.

This time, when he climaxed, he was no more controlled than before. Only now she had soft sand beneath her, instead of hard rock, so as he pounded her body with his own, he knew he wasn't hurting her. And when he'd finished, and was able to lift himself up to look at her, to make sure she was still whole, she smiled up at him with an expression that could only be called smug.

"I thought," she said huskily, "that you were going to go look for firewood."

He lifted a strand of her hair and brought it to his lips. "I changed my mind," he said.

"You're welcome," she said, "to change it any time you like."

# Chapter Twenty-six

$\mathcal{P}$ayton could not remember ever having been quite so happy. Oh, she supposed that back when she'd been younger, roaming the decks of her father's boats in her bare feet and pigtails, she'd been happy enough. And in the days before Miss Whitby, when it had been enough for her simply to sit next to Connor Drake, now and again, at mealtimes, she'd been happy, too.

But not since she'd become a woman—and she considered that this momentous occasion occurred sometime after her seventeenth birthday, when Mei-Ling had announced that she was returning to her own family, her job being done—had she ever felt this content, this calm, this . . . well, happy.

She probably hadn't any right to feel so self-satisfied. After all, they were still in mortal danger. The *Rebecca* or the *Nassau Queen* could come into view on the horizon any minute. They still had to hide their evening campfires, and stay off the beach as much as possible. But what did that matter? She was marooned on an island with the man she'd been in love with since she was fourteen years old. What was more, he loved her. She was solidly convinced of his love. Besides the fact that he freely admitted it—and at the oddest moments, too, like when she'd just washed her face and was stumbling around, looking for something to dry it with—he proved it a thousand different ways, every single day. She had only to utter the slightest wish—a fancy for lobster for supper, for instance—and he granted it. She was the luckiest girl alive, and she knew it. She had even made a truce with God, and forgiven Him, at long last, for robbing her of her mother. She felt that, in making Drake love her, God had more than made up for any injuries done to her in the past.

And yet, happy as she was, she had to admit to a certain wariness, where Drake was concerned. Not that she felt she had anything to fear—for instance, that should they ever be rescued, he'd leave her for someone else, someone who wouldn't so easily be mistaken for a boy, or who actually knew what in the hell had happened to her maidenhead—but because of something Georgiana had said once, when Payton had asked her why she'd married Ross. She had naïvely supposed that Georgiana was marrying her brother because she loved him, and now, of course, she knew that her sister-in-law really did love Ross . . . at least, in her own way, which wasn't in the least the way Payton loved Drake.

Anyway, Georgiana, who was several years older than Payton, had taken the opportunity to offer her husband's sister a little advice: "It's always better," she'd said, "for a woman to marry a man who loves her just a little more than she loves him. That way, she can always be certain of having the upper hand."

Payton had never forgotten this piece of advice. She had no idea whether or not it was accurate, though she did rather suspect that in Ross and Georgiana's case, it might be. And she had to admit it was causing her some worry, since she knew good and well that she loved Drake with every fiber of her being, with all the fervor and fierceness of a first love. She was not at all convinced that he loved her more than she did. In fact, she couldn't see how he could: he was, after all, a man of the world. He'd surely met dozens of women who were far more worldly and exotic than Payton. If, after they were rescued—and she was quite certain they would be, some day—he stayed with her, how was Payton to know whether he was staying with her because he really loved her, or staying with her because, after everything they'd done together, her brothers would kill him if he didn't?

It was a dilemma. Not one that bothered her hourly, or even daily, but one that occurred to her sometimes late at night, when she lay in his arms, looking up at the stars. Drake was hardly one of those poetic types of lovers—he rarely told her that he loved her without employing an expletive in the sentence (he loved her like hell, or like the devil) and he had certainly never sung the praises of her beauty (except to observe, once, that her feet were shockingly small, compared to his own). But still, she felt that he really was attached to her, in his way. She gathered this not so much through the way he made love to her—which was often, and generally quite emphatic—but from the subtle clues he dropped here and there, most likely not even realizing he'd revealed them.

Take, for instance, the fact that they were trapped together on this island. They could hardly get away from one another. In fact, when she wanted to be alone, she had to wait until he was asleep, or was fully occupied stalking some small beast for supper. The rest of the time, he was talking to her, or making love to her, or simply staring at her, something he did with irritating regularity, to the point that now, when she caught him at it, she heaved a coconut in his direction, if one was handy.

But despite the fact that they were hardly ever out of one another's sight, it seemed as if Drake could not stand to be without her company. Even when she was sleeping, he did his level best to wake her. Head-over-heels in love with him as she was, Payton was still firmly aware of the fact that Drake had faults, and one of the most irritating was his tendency to wake very early in the morning. Since there wasn't a great deal to do on San Rafael, Drake occupied these early morning hours devising ways to wake her. He didn't dare, after their first few mornings together, simply shake her awake. He'd tried that, and nearly had his head bitten off for his trouble. Nor could he try more erotic methods of rousing her—she had wakened, plenty of mornings, to find his face buried between her thighs, and had generally responded by placing a foot on his shoulder and shoving him away.

So Drake had taken to "accidentally" waking her. Some of these "accidents" had included the very loud blaring of a conch shell (he'd had to blow on it, he claimed, to make sure there wasn't a conch inside; she liked conch for breakfast, didn't she?); a shower of spring water from an overturned gourd (he claimed to have tripped); and, Payton's favorite, a butterfly that just happened to perch on her nose as she slept (he stridently denied having sprinkled pollen anywhere near her face, though when she'd rubbed it, telltale yellow had come off on her hand).

What was most infuriating of all was that every morning, after waking her with these preposterous excuses, Drake took no more time explaining them away than it took him to unlace her shirt. And then, next thing she knew, he was kissing her, and she forgot all about how furiously angry she was at being roused with the dawn, and actually proceeded to kiss him back! It was extremely hard to stay angry at someone who was capable, with the merest kiss, of rendering you senseless. Payton feared Georgiana wouldn't think very much of her, had she been aware of how she was conducting herself in this, her very first love affair.

And if Georgiana had happened to witness her behavior one particular evening, after a delicious supper of roast parrot—she'd quickly gotten over her soft-heartedness—and mangoes, she'd have probably disowned her. Having tied off the final knot in a hammock she'd spent, quite literally, days creating out of vines, Payton urged Drake to hang it between two palm trees, down on the beach. Since it was evening, and there was no chance of them being spotted from beyond the shoals, he agreed, and they set off, Drake observing dryly that, considering the amount of time she'd put into the creation, she might have woven something more useful than a hammock. A fishnet, he said, was what they wanted, so he wouldn't have to spend all his time trying to will the fish to come to him: he could just spread out his net and wham! Dinner.

Payton, skipping along behind him, ignored him. It was a beautiful evening—like all the evenings they'd experienced on San Rafael—and she was looking forward to enjoying it from the cradle of the hammock she'd made—if it proved strong enough to support her weight. She wasn't at all certain it would. Which was where Drake came in. She fully intended to make him try it first. If it did not break under his superior weight, she knew it would be safe enough for her.

How Drake might have liked it, had he known she'd required his presence merely as a test subject, she never knew, since she wisely kept it from him. But once he'd strung the hammock up, he didn't even ask her if she wanted to try it first. Instead, he lowered himself onto it, gingerly at first, then with growing confidence.

"I say, Payton," he declared, giving the crude netting beneath him an experimental bounce. "This thing's perfect."

Then, lifting his feet from the sand, he stretched out in the hammock, which groaned only a little bit beneath his weight.

"This," he said, to the moonless sky. "This is the way to live. What have we been thinking, sleeping on the ground? We must have been mad. Come here, Payton, and try this."

But Payton, who'd been standing to one side, watching him, had another idea. She never could say how it occurred to her, or what made her think of it. Maybe it was the way Drake had lifted his arms above his head, revealing the pale skin and silken hair of his underarms. In any case, instead of joining him, Payton reached out and, using a bit of vine she'd had left over, she tied Drake's wrists to the sides of the hammock.

"Payton," he said, sounding only mildly curious. "What are you doing?"

Making sure he was well and truly secured—she pulled on each of his arms to be certain of it—Payton started to remove her trousers. "Remember," she said, "when you were chained to the wall in the hold of the *Rebecca*?"

"I'm not likely to forget it."

"Well, this is what I wanted to do you while you were in there." She pulled off her shirt. "Only you would never have let me. Not then."

His eyes, which were normally so light in color that they still occasionally unnerved her, went dark, the pupils wide as pennies, as he gazed at her. "Payton," he said, his deep voice rich with amusement. "What are you up to?"

Standing by the side of the hammock, she leaned down, her bare breasts pressing up against his arm. Ordinarily, he'd have reached for them. He was inordinately fascinated by her breasts—so much so that she no longer considered them abnormally small, but rather the absolute perfect size for Connor Drake's palms. But he couldn't touch them this time, couldn't play with them, as he was fond of doing, bringing first one, then the other of her nipples to his mouth, because his wrists were securely bound.

"Payton," he said, in a different tone of voice. She felt the muscles in his arm leap beneath her breasts. She ignored them, and reached for the buttons on the front of his trousers.

Now he tried to break the bonds that were tying his arms up over his head. "Payton," he said, when he found he couldn't, not without causing the rough fibers to cut into his skin. "This isn't funny."

She leaned over and kissed him on the lips. "I know," she said. "And don't worry. I'll cut you loose." She slid her mouth down the side of his prickly face—his beard was something to see, it was so bushy and wild—placing her lips against the place in his throat where his pulse beat. "I'll cut you loose," she assured him again, in a husky whisper. "When I'm ready."

Then she ran her fingers lightly over his chest, feeling the raised imprints of old scars, the flat nubs of his own nipples, which were brown and for the most part lost in a field of golden hair. She found one, and pinched it gently between a thumb and forefinger. "Does that feel good?" she asked him.

"It does not," he said. "I want you to go and get the knife right now, Payton, and cut me loose."

"Do you?" She raised a leg and slipped it over him, then

raised the other, until she was sitting astride him in the hammock. The vines groaned a little, but held, to her relief. She looked down at him triumphantly. "Do you still?" she asked, leaning down to nip, with her teeth, what she'd pinched between her fingers before.

She knew perfectly well what his answer was going to be. She could feel him growing hard beneath her. She let go of his nipple and licked it gently, instead.

"Well," Drake said, in a different tone of voice. "Maybe . . ."

She moved her head, raining small kisses down his rib cage; past the scar from an old knife wound; toward the place where the tawny hair that covered him all over grew thickest.

"Payton," he gasped out, as she moved aside the front piece of his breeches.

She didn't reply. Instead, she took hold of his penis—which was really quite outrageously hard, for someone who'd claimed not to like her touching his nipples—and, with extreme delicacy, tasted the tip of it with her tongue—the way he rather regularly tasted her.

A frantic thrashing followed as Drake tried once again to break his hands free. Payton had to raise her head and say sharply, "If you don't stop that I'm going to leave you here all night, exactly as you are."

"Payton," he ground out, as angrily as if it were a curse word and not her name. But she noticed he'd grown quite still.

She turned her attention back to the enormous appendage she held. It seemed to her that if he reacted so intensely to the merest touch of her tongue there, he might have an even more interesting reaction should she slip her entire mouth around the engorged head—if it would fit. Well, there was only one way to find out.

This time, he inhaled, so sharply that she thought she might have caused him an injury. But he didn't try to throw her off, which he certainly could have, if what she was doing was in some way painful. In fact, quite the opposite. He grew perfectly still, hardly even seeming to dare to breathe. So she obligingly slid her lips as far around his phallus as she could. Curling her fingers round it, too, she attempted to simulate what she thought it must be like to him when he was inside of her.

Apparently she succeeded, because she noticed that his breathing grew quite irregular, and that his chest had gotten slick with perspiration, despite the cool night air around them. But he was far too big, and her mouth too small, to continue the experiment. Besides, his blatant excitement was contagious. She'd begun to feel a familiar throbbing between her own legs, a longing to be filled. So she positioned herself over him, and, watching him carefully, lowered herself onto that pulsating shaft, still slick with moisture from her mouth.

He groaned. It was quite a loud groan, too. Payton herself had groaned a little—he had never seemed so big as he did that night, despite the fact that she was more than ready for him; apparently, her kissing him there had caused some kind of correlating reaction that swelled his erection to even greater proportions than usual—but his groan drowned hers out. She began to think tying him up had been rather a good idea. Now she had perfect control over their movements, and could time everything exactly how she pleased . . .

Except that, astride him as she was, she felt rather more of a sense of urgency than usual. That throbbing tenderness between her legs was more easily satisfied, what with that hard wall of muscle that made up his abdomen to rub against. She forgot all about the clinical observations she'd been intending to make, and started moving rapidly up and down the length of his shaft, her hands splayed across his chest. He was moving, too—not to break his bonds, this time, but to plunge himself more deeply into her. She wouldn't let him, this time. Halfway in was as much as she'd allow. This seemed to drive him mad, but there was nothing he could do about it. Without the use of his hands, he couldn't force her to stay still. Intoxicated with her sense of power, Payton rode him with giddy energy, until suddenly, a familiar tingling started in the soles of her feet . . .

And then a celestial hurricane erupted. All around her, a magnificent display of fireworks shimmered and twinkled. It was like that night on the deck of the *Virago* that summer he'd offered her his pillow, only this time, she wasn't lying on the hard wood of the forecastle, but flying above it, in her own chariot of flame. She shuddered all over with the pure joy of it, and collapsed, smiling, onto Drake's damply furred chest.

Only he was still twisting beneath her, trying to find the same release she'd already experienced. Opening her eyes, she saw that his face was tightly contorted, as if in pain. Lethargic in the afterglow of her orgasm, she nevertheless took pity on him and reached up to pull lightly on the vine that had anchored his hands above his head.

His wrists came free at once. She'd always been rather good at slip knots.

Shocked, Drake opened his eyes and stared up at her. She smiled smugly down at him—but only for a second. Because an instant later, she was gasping as he drove himself, with unexpected force, deeply into her. Both his hands had gone to her buttocks, keeping her hips motionless as he plundered what lay between them. He ground himself into her, like a man who'd gone without lovemaking for a good deal longer than she knew, for a fact, he had.

My goodness, she thought. I shall certainly tie him up more often.

Then she felt him explode within her. He did it with such violence that she had to hold onto him rather tenaciously to keep from being thrown out of the hammock.

But he was instantly contrite afterward, reaching up to pull her down against him until her cheek rested against his chest. She could hear his heartbeat, fast as a hummingbird's wings at first, then slowing down to a more moderate thud, thud, thud, as his breathing became even again.

"Don't you ever," he said into her hair, "do that again."

She smiled against his chest. "Which part?" She reached out, and laid a finger over one of his nipples. "This part?" Then she dipped her hand lower, to take hold of his now considerably less engorged genitalia. "Or this part?"

He took some time to consider the question. "The tying-up part."

She lifted her head to look at him. "That was the *best* part."

"Oh, ho," he said. "We'll do it to you next time, and see how much you like it."

She sat up eagerly. "Could we? Could we really?"

"Good Lord." He reached out, and pulled her back down against him. "Go to sleep, Payton."

"But next time, could we—"

"*Yes,*" he said. He said it as if he were exasperated, but Payton saw, before she closed her eyes, that he was smiling.

# *Chapter Twenty-seven*

$\mathcal{A}$nd then, the very next morning, her brothers arrived.

It was unfortunate that this particular morning, Drake—perhaps because he was still exhausted from the activities of the night before—did not wake early. He was sleeping very soundly, Payton snug in his arms, when a thunderous bellow woke them both.

Payton, for her part, mistook the bellow for the blare of a conch shell, and she tried to block the sound out by throwing an arm up over her head—only her arm was caught beneath Drake. But how could that be, if he was the one blowing the conch shell?

And then the bellow turned to words, and she opened her eyes, and saw her brother Ross standing there, his face purple with rage.

"What in the bloody hell do you think you're doing?" he screamed. "We spend weeks—*weeks, do you hear?*—combing the seas for you, fearing the two of you are dead—*dead!*—and what do we come to find? That you ain't dead at all, but quite obviously alive. Alive and *fornicatin'*!"

Payton would have run for her life had not her arm been pinned down by Drake's body. He, a quick glance showed her, didn't look the least bit alarmed. In fact, he was studying Ross with interest from the depths of the hammock, one arm thrown across her, more to cover her nakedness, she supposed, than because he thought Ross might strike her.

But it was rather too late for that. Ross had already noticed her nakedness. And Drake's, too, for that matter.

"Don't just lie there, you black-hearted devil!" Ross shouted. "Get out of that hammock and put some clothes on! *And get your hands off my sister!*"

Payton, her mouth dry as sand, nevertheless summoned up the courage to say, "Ross, you are making far too much of this. Drake and I only—"

"Shhh." Drake tightened his arm around her. "Better let me do the talking, love."

*"Love?"* bellowed Ross furiously. "Get out of that hammock. Do you hear me, Drake? Get out of that hammock before I drag you out of it!"

"I say, Ross." Raleigh appeared from another part of the beach. "I think we've come to the right spot. There's a long-boat hidden in the bushes over—Oh, there they are! Hullo, Drake, hullo, Pay. Good to see you. We thought you were dead."

"Don't," Ross commanded his brother, "come any closer. Just stay where you are."

Raleigh looked alarmed. "Why? Is there a snake?"

"Yes. Of a sort." Ross took off his coat—a heavy black affair, lined with white satin; they had evidently been in mourning for a sister they thought lost to the high seas—and flung it over Payton. She pushed it from her head and glared up at her brother.

"Drake didn't do anything wrong," she informed him. "I don't see what you're being so nasty about. *Raleigh's* happy to see me."

"Damned right I am," Raleigh asserted. "You don't know what it's been like back home. Georgiana weepin' all the time, Papa gone right off his musket balls, Hudson always in a temper. You know he's given up liquor since you disappeared? Hasn't touched a drop. I say." He suddenly looked taken aback. "You two are a bit snug in there, aren't you?"

"*Snug?*" Ross spun upon his younger brother. "I'll tell you how *snug* they are! They neither of 'em have a stitch on!"

Raleigh's jaw dropped. "Oh, Drake," he said with a groan. "Tell me you didn't."

"Why is everybody blaming Drake?" Payton wanted to know. "It was all my—"

"Shhh," Drake said again, laying a finger over her lips. He adjusted Ross's coat so that it covered her completely, then said, in a low voice, "Your brother Hudson is probably around here somewhere. Why don't you go and try to find him?"

"Don't be an ass, Drake," Payton advised him. "They're going to kill you."

"Nonsense." He smiled down at her reassuringly. "We're old friends. Would old friends try to kill one another?"

She scissored a glance in Ross's direction. "Under the circumstances—"

"Go on," Drake said cheerfully. Really, but he was in extraordinarily high spirits. He must, she supposed, a little dejectedly, be pleased that they'd finally been rescued. Funny, she hadn't thought he found her company so very tiresome.

"Go find Hudson, sweetheart," he said to her. "And leave the men to talk."

She glared at him. Leave the men to talk. Wasn't that just *like* a man? As if anything her brothers had to say was going to be the slightest bit worthwhile. Didn't he remember how angry he'd been at them, just the other day? Or at least, she supposed it had been the other day. She had lost track of time, a little. Still. He didn't have to send her off, as if she were a child.

Payton decided, right then, that she'd go and find Hudson, all right—but not because Drake had asked her to. She was only doing it because she had a feeling Drake was going to need reinforcements. From the looks of Ross and Raleigh, fists were due to fly at any moment. Really, how stupid men were sometimes.

Graceful as a cat, she swung from the hammock, clutching Ross's coat closed in front of her. Before she left, she turned and leveled both her brothers with an evil stare.

"If you harm so much as one hair on his head," she hissed, "I'll make you sorry for it until the day you die."

Then she tossed her head and walked away.

She found him at once, of course. He was crouched in the sand, as if he thought he was Natty Bumppo or someone, closely examining a set of her footprints, left the evening before.

"Hi," he was shouting. "I think I've got something over here!"

"Hudson," she said, and he straightened, and stared at her as if she were an apparition.

"Pay?" he said. He looked quite terrible. Dressed all in black, he hadn't had his hair cut in a while. He wore it pulled back in a black ribbon, but some of it wouldn't stay, and it floated round his head in a halo. He looked a bit like a mad Quaker, if there was such a thing. "Is that really you, Pay?"

"Yes, of course it is, you bleeding sod. Who were expecting? The Virgin Mary?"

"Pay! It really is you!"

If Raleigh hadn't already informed her that Hudson had given up drink, she might have accused her middle brother of being drunk. He certainly staggered toward her unsteadily enough. And then, to make matters worse, after he'd wrapped her in a smothering hug, she suspected he might be crying— even though she knew perfectly well Hudson would never do something as maudlin as shed tears of joy at the sight of her.

"Are you all right?" he asked, when she'd finally fought her way out of his affectionate, if restrictive, embrace. "Everyone said you were dead. I never believed it, not for a moment, but it did look bad for a bit."

"I'm fine," Payton said. "Hudson, you've got to come at once. Ross and Raleigh are going to kill Drake."

"Drake?" An expression of even more heartfelt delight broke over Hudson's face. "Drake's alive, too? Why, they were quite emphatic about the fact that *he* was dead. What a happy day! The two of you, alive and well!"

"Drake won't be alive for much longer," Payton said, "unless you come at once. Ross has gone right out of his head." She took his hand, and tugged at it. "He thinks Drake's compromised me, or something, and he looks as if he might do something dreadful."

"Nonsense." Hudson followed along after her, obligingly enough. "Everyone knows Drake would never do any such thing."

Payton glanced at him over her shoulder. "Well," she said. "Exactly. I'm glad one of you still has some sense. You all seemed to have gone positively barmy since I went away. Do hurry, Hud. It's two against one, and that's hardly fair."

"You know," Hudson said happily, "I'm going to have to join the church now. I made a bargain with the Lord. I said I'd enter the priesthood, so long as nothing had happened to you. I'm going to look a bit silly in a white collar, don't you think?"

"Don't be an ass, Hudson. No church would take you."

"You think so?" He sounded eminently relieved. "Oh, good. I was a little worried about that vow of celibacy. The rest of it wouldn't be so bad, but that one . . ."

They'd reached the beach by then, and Payton dropped his hand. Drake, she could see, had gotten out of the hammock, as Ross had ordered him to. They had even, she saw, allowed him to put on his trousers. But there was no indication that any of the *talking* Drake had promised had gone on after that. A good deal of hitting, it looked like, but no talking whatsoever.

And all of the hitting seemed to have been directed at one individual only.

Drake.

Payton let out a shriek and darted forward. Drake's chest rose and fell: that was the only indication she had that he was not dead. Blood streamed from a gash in his eyebrow, and his mouth looked lopsided, but not because he was holding it that way, as he often did when he was trying to look as if he disapproved of something she was doing. He wasn't dead—

not yet, anyway—but he was as close to it as she ever cared to see him.

Ross, seeing her approach, straightened up and shouted, "For God's sake, Hudson, don't let 'er near 'im. That's all we need. Feminine hysterics, on top of everything else."

Hudson obediently put out an arm and caught his sister by the waist before she could reach Drake's side, then slung her neatly over one hip and held her there, seemingly oblivious of her flying fists and feet.

"Put me down, you bastard!" Payton screamed. "I'll kill you for this, I swear it. All of you! I'll kill you all!"

"Oh, *stop* that screaming, you stupid girl," Ross said disgustedly. "It's not as if we've *killed* him, or anything like that. Just taught him a little lesson, is all."

Hudson, glancing blandly at the slumped-over form in the sand, observed that Drake must have really gone off his form, if he'd let a fat ass like Ross drop him like that.

Ross, offended, declared his ass not fat, and thanked Hudson not to disparage his skills as a pugilist again, as they were considerable.

Raleigh snorted derisively at this. "Oh, come off it, Ross," he sneered. "Drake *let* you hit him. He never even tried to lift a finger against you in his own defense."

Hudson commented that it wasn't a bit like Drake to allow any man to hit him, let alone a fat ass like Ross.

"Stop calling me that!" Ross thundered. "And it's a jolly good thing for Drake he *didn't* try to defend himself. I'd have thrashed him within an inch of his life."

Looking down at the unconscious man, Hudson remarked, "Well, it looks as if you did that anyway."

"And why shouldn't I? He admitted everything, easy as you please. Didn't look a bit sorry for any of it, either. You'd have done the same thing, Hud, if you'd been here."

"I wouldn't," Hudson declared truculently. "I've always liked Drake. I don't care what he's done."

Ross eyed him, his hazel eyes glittering dangerously. "Oh, you don't, do you? All right, then if you like Drake so bloody much, I suppose if I told you he'd had Payton, you wouldn't blink an eye."

Hudson looked dismayed. "*Drake* did? Bloody hell. Here, Raleigh, you take Payton for a minute. I'm going to get a few kicks in—"

"Don't you dare!" Payton shouted. "Hudson, if you do, I'll never tie your cravats again!"

"And that's not all," Ross went on, as if she hadn't spoken. "Did y' know they've been running about here, naked as savages, for nearly two months?"

Payton shrieked, "That's a lie! It has *not* been that long—"

"Five miles from New Providence. Five bloody miles," Ross went on. "He could have put an end to all our worrying weeks ago—"

"He couldn't," Payton cried. "The Frenchman was looking for us. Marcus Tyler was trying to kill us both! We had no way of knowing whether or not they were still out there—"

"Marcus Tyler?" Ross interrupted testily. "Marcus Tyler? Marcus Tyler is not trying to kill you. Both he and that nasty piece of baggage who claims to be Drake's wife are now sitting in a Nassau jailhouse, awaiting trial for your murder."

Payton gasped. "*What?* But how—"

Ross looked smug. "Oh, yes. It was nothing, really. You see, once we got the *Virago*'s mainsail replaced, it was only a matter of—"

"What about the Frenchman? Did you catch him, too?"

Her brother glowered at her. "If you would allow me to finish, I was just getting to that." He cleared his throat. "Captain La Fond, unfortunately, got away. We did, however—"

"You let him get away?" Payton's voice rose to screaming pitch once more. "He killed Drake's brother!"

"We did not *let* anyone get away, you ungrateful chit. The Frenchman put up quite a struggle. We lost a dozen good men to his cannons before we got close enough to storm his ship. Am I to be blamed if he, cowardly dog that he is, leapt overboard, and took his chances with the sharks, rather than face trial like a man? Not that I'm particularly surprised by his behavior, mind you. What I am surprised by is the fact that we intercepted the Frenchman's vessel seven weeks ago. That's two months, Payton. Since you were not on board the *Rebecca* at the time, I can only assume that you and Drake have been—*whatever* you care to call it—right here on San Rafael ever since!"

*Two months?* Was it possible? Was it possible that that much time had passed since the night she'd dragged Drake's unconscious body from the *Rebecca*'s longboat, and dropped him in the white sand? No. It couldn't possibly be true. A few weeks, certainly. It had taken her that long just to make the hammock. And the shelter Drake had built, to keep them dry during the rains . . . that had taken a while to construct. Maybe a month, at most.

But *two? Two months?* It wasn't possible.

"We—we had no way of knowing," Payton stammered. "We had no way of knowing you'd already caught Sir Marcus and . . . and . . . and what I'd like to know is, if you thought we were dead, what are you doing *here*?"

"Some big black fellow—I don't remember his name; he was the ship cook aboard the *Rebecca*—told the magistrates you weren't neither of you dead at all, that you'd both escaped. Was quite insistent on it, as a matter of fact. So we thought, what the hell? Better take a look . . ."

Clarence! Clarence had come forward! Lovely, sweet Clarence.

What was she thinking? Horrid, nasty Clarence, to have told all, and gotten her into this current mess.

"But I'll tell you something, Payton," Ross went on. "I would to God Tyler *had* murdered the two of you! I'd infinitely prefer a dead best friend to this lecher"—Ross nudged Drake's limp body with a booted toe—"and a dead sister to the sluttish one it turns out I've got instead."

Payton glared at him. "Oh, well, thank you very much, Ross. I assure you that can be arranged. Hudson, give me your pistol. I'd rather blow my head off than have to listen to another word of this drivel—"

"All right," Raleigh said, holding out both his palms. "That is quite enough. No more theatrics, from either of you. Hudson, take Payton back to the boat. Ross and I will be along in a while with the, er, lecher."

"I hate and despise you all," Payton hurled at them, as Hudson tossed her over his shoulder. "I hope you all burn in hell!"

Ross waved at her dismissively. "Don't take on so, Payton. He'll be right enough in a week or so. In time for the wedding, anyway."

"Wedding?" Payton echoed. "What wedding?" When she received no answer, she began to scream again. "What *wedding*?"

"Stop that screamin'," Hudson grumbled, as he waded out into the surf, toward the longboat that waited there. "You're breakin' my eardrums."

*"What wedding?"*

"Yours, I'd guess. To the lecher." He grunted, and took a firmer hold of her hips. "You didn't think Ross'd be satisfied with beatin' 'im to a pulp, did you? He's got to marry you, too, Pay. It's the only way."

# Chapter Twenty-eight

"Payton, darling, *do* try to eat something. You're looking positively peaked underneath your tan."

Payton picked up her fork and stabbed at the eggs on the tray in her lap, breaking the yolks, and sending yellow fluid streaming toward the roasted potatoes on the far side of her plate. She pretended the eggs were volcanoes, the broken yolks lava, and the potatoes Pompeii. She didn't feel much like eating.

"Are you sure you aren't too warm?" Georgiana plucked at the sheet Payton had pulled up to her chin the minute her sister-in-law had entered the room. "You can't possibly be cold, my dear. Why, it's blazing out there."

"I'm perfectly fine," Payton said. "Only I don't feel much like talking right now. It was sweet of you to bring me breakfast, but if you don't mind—"

"Oh, I don't mind a bit," Georgiana said brightly. "And I understand your not wanting to talk. I'll just sit and wait until you're done, and then I'll take the tray back down."

Bloody hell! Payton watched as her sister-in-law began sifting through the correspondence that had arrived that morning, which she'd placed on the tray beside Payton's breakfast. It seemed as if every Englishwoman in Nassau had come calling on the Dixon's Bahamian villa while they awaited Marcus

Tyler and Becky Whitby's trial. They were all, Payton thought bitterly, in competition to see who could be the first actually to see the star witness, the ruined—and very darkly tanned—*Dis*honorable Miss Payton Dixon.

"Look here." Georgiana held up a calling card, conveniently forgetting Payton's wish not to talk. "Lady Bisson. Did you know Sir Connor's grandmother was here on the island, Payton? We brought her down when we first heard the news that you'd disappeared. You and Sir Connor, I mean. She's been quite anxious to see you, you know."

Payton lifted the pepper and carpeted her plate with it. Volcanic ash.

"Shall I tell her to come for tea? Would you like that?"

Payton glared across the bed tray at her sister-in-law. "Considering the fact that I'm not allowed to leave my room, it might be a bit awkward entertaining Drake's grandmother, don't you think, Georgiana? Unless you suppose I can use this bed tray as a tea table."

Georgiana, completely unruffled by this outburst, calmly laid the calling card aside. "You know your brothers will let you out just as soon as you see reason."

"Reason?" Payton lifted the tray from her lap. She thought about hurling it across the room, but she'd tried that before, to no effect, except that one of the maids had been sent to pick up the mess, and Payton, feeling sheepish over her outburst, had felt obligated to help her.

This time, she set the tray aside, but took care not to let the sheet she'd pulled over her slip down. "Georgiana, surely *you* don't think I'm being unreasonable. I mean, you must see that *they're* the ones who are being completely asinine about the whole thing."

"Asinine?" Georgiana regarded her sister-in-law placidly. Her new, ethereal calm was maddening, but even more maddening was the reason behind it. Well, Payton supposed it had been bound to happen, sooner or later. Even an ogre like Ross must have his tender moments, and it appeared that during one of them, he'd managed to get his wife *enceinte*. Though how

Georgiana could feel so calm about the fact that in four or five months, she was going to give birth to an ogre-baby, Payton couldn't imagine.

"They aren't being asinine, Payton. They're only doing what they think is best for you. *You're* the one who's being—"

"*What?*" Payton interrupted, in a hard voice. "I'm the one who's being *what*, Georgiana?"

"Well." Georgiana looked apologetic. "Stubborn?"

"Oh, I see. *I'm* stubborn, just because I don't happen to want to marry someone my brothers insist I must."

"Yes. Because we all know you want to. Payton, everyone knows you love him. So why are you being so difficult about it? Just agree to marry the man, and then we can all be one big happy family again."

"Has everyone forgotten," Payton demanded, "that he happens to be married to someone else?"

Georgiana waved a lace-cuffed hand in the air. "Oh, heavens. Justice O'Reardon annulled that farce of a union as soon as Drake—I mean, Sir Connor—regained conscious—er, got around to explaining matters to him. *That*'s not what's stopping you."

"No," Payton said, tight-lipped.

"Then what is it? Why all this fuss? You should be over the moon, Payton. You've gotten exactly what you always wanted."

"But Georgiana," Payton said, her voice catching. Oh, Lord, she wasn't going to start crying again, was she? She'd cried for three days straight already. She'd rather hoped she was on the mend. Apparently not. "Georgiana, can't you see? I never wanted him *this* way."

"What way, sweetheart?"

"You know. By *trapping* him. By *forcing* him. This is precisely the way Miss Whitby—"

"It isn't," Georgiana interrupted hastily. "Payton, really. This is nothing like what Miss Whitby did. Did you go to bed with Sir Richard, and then tell his brother you were carrying his child? No, of course you didn't. Your case is quite, quite different—"

"But he still doesn't get a choice in the matter," Payton insisted. "Don't you see? He felt *obligated* to marry Becky Whitby—never mind that that obligation turned out not to be true. And now he's marrying me for the same reason: He feels *obligated*."

"How do you know how he feels? Have you asked him?" When Payton's only response was a sniffle, Georgiana answered for her. "No, you haven't. You've refused to see him. You won't even read his letters." Georgiana reached out to the silver tray of mail beside her. "Why, there's three from him already this morning, and it's only just gone noon. The man is obviously desperate to see you."

"Of course he's desperate," Payton muttered. "He's desperate to restore his reputation, and get back in his grandmother's good graces . . . not to mention Ross's. Don't forget, Georgiana, Dixon and Sons employs him. I suppose he'd do just about anything to stay on Papa's good side."

"Pshaw," Georgiana said, with a laugh. "What twaddle, Payton. Connor Drake isn't exactly Matthew Hayford. He doesn't *need* the piddling salary your father pays him. He has quite a tidy fortune in his own right. And as for his reputation, I never met a man who cared less what anybody had to say about him than Connor Drake."

Payton gritted her teeth. "I won't marry a man just because my brothers say I have to. I *won't*!"

"Then don't. Marry him because you love him."

But Payton ignored her. "My whole life, I've done what my brothers told me to. I've lived the way *they* taught me to live. If any one of them had been stuck on that island, they'd have done *exactly* as I did. So why am I being punished for it?"

And then the tears did start up again. Dammit, and she'd thought she'd cried enough, this past week, to dry her tear ducts out. Apparently not. Apparently, there were still a few gallons or so left.

Sighing, Georgiana picked up the breakfast tray and left the room, taking care to lock the door behind her, as her husband—rather unnecessarily, Georgiana thought—had ordered. There was a large balcony off Payton's room, from which the girl could climb down any time she pleased without a bit of trouble, nimble as she was. So why bother locking her bedroom door? If she wanted to escape, she'd have done it already.

But Georgiana hadn't bothered mentioning this to her husband. It would only cause him to board up the French doors to the balcony, which would quite destroy the charm of the house from the outside, and would inspire more gossip than the youngest Dixon had already managed to engender.

"Well?"

Georgiana nearly dropped the tray. But it was only Connor Drake, eagerly awaiting her reappearance in the breakfast room.

"Nothing's changed," Georgiana said, letting him take the tray. "She still won't budge."

"Did you show her my letters?"

"Of course I showed her your letters. She won't touch them. I told you she wouldn't."

Georgiana didn't like to disappoint the man, as he already looked quite wretched enough, with his split lip, and the jagged wound in his right eyebrow where her husband's wedding ring had left a gash. Still, she thought him every bit as much to blame for the problem as Ross. After all, he ought to have been able to have restrained himself on that island. A gentleman always could.

"Why can't I see her?" Drake spun around to face the men who would be his brothers-in-law. "Just let me go up there. I'll be able to talk some sense into her."

"No!" Ross pushed himself up from the chair in which he'd been lounging. "Gad, no. We can't let her know we've forgiven you."

"Speak for yourself," Hudson grumbled, from the confines of his own chair.

Ignoring his brother, Ross went on. "If she thinks we've forgiven you, then she'll *never* marry you." Ross shook his head. "You have to understand the way a woman *thinks,* Drake. That's your problem. You've never understood how they *think.*"

Georgiana had to bite the insides of her cheeks to keep from smiling at the thought of her husband pontificating on the intricacies of the feminine mind.

"What you ought to have done," she said gently, "was forbid her from marrying Sir Connor. Angry with you as she is right now, Ross, she'd have found a way to elope with him at her earliest opportunity. The way you've got things, refusing to marry him is the only way she can think of to punish you."

*"Me?"* Ross bleated. "What did *I* do?"

"Well, you *are* the one who beat her lover into a bloody pulp," Raleigh reminded him, from the thick stone windowsill on which he lounged.

"Pardon me, Ral, but weren't you standing right there alongside me? I saw you get in a good blow or two."

"Right. But I didn't *enjoy* doing it. I heartily dislike bloodshed."

"That's not why she's angry with you," Georgiana said.

"What do you mean, that's not why?" Ross glanced sharply at his wife. "What *else* has she got to punish us for?"

Georgiana sighed. "Everything. The fact that your father's business is called Dixon and Sons, instead of Dixon and Sons and Daughter. The fact that all of you encouraged her to shoot and climb and sail, then denied her the right to do those things. The fact that any of you, on that island, would have acted exactly as she did, and yet you feel the need to lock her in her room for it."

"That's not why she's locked in her room!" Ross bellowed. "She's locked in her room because she won't marry the blighter!"

"She didn't eat." Hudson was examining the tray Georgiana had brought down. "Look at this. She just moved the food around. She didn't eat any of it. Why didn't you make her eat, Georgiana?"

"I can't force her to eat, Hudson."

"She hasn't eaten since she got here." Hudson lifted a hand and dragged it through his disgracefully long hair. Really, as soon as Georgiana got a chance, she was going to go after that fellow with a pair of shears. "What does she plan on doing? Just wastin' away? Is that the plan? To punish us all by starving herself to death?"

"Look," Ross said, leaning forward. "This'll all be over next month, after the trial. Once she's testified—"

Georgiana sucked in her breath. "Must she? With as much publicity as all of this has already garnered, what with us thinking she was dead, and then finding out she wasn't . . . Goodness, this will only make things worse. Wouldn't Sir Connor's testimony alone suffice?"

"No. For God's sake, Georgiana, Marcus Tyler is standing trial for his life. He's been accused of piracy, for which alone he could hang. But there's also charges of abduction, attempted murder, and conspiring to kill Drake's brother. Payton's a key witness. Her testimony is crucial."

"Still." Georgiana shook her head. "I don't like it. Payton isn't at all . . . well, herself."

"What do you mean?" Drake demanded sharply.

"Just that . . . well, I've never seen her like this. I hardly recognize her. You've kept her locked in that room for a week, Ross, and she hasn't once tried to escape. The Payton I know would have broken out in half an hour, and then laughed in your face about it."

Ross looked troubled. "You're right. By God, you're right!"

"I just find it very hard to believe that the girl who lived for a month aboard a pirate ship disguised in boy's clothes and that girl upstairs weeping into her pillow are one and the same," Georgiana said. "Why, she's acting so strangely, I'd almost think—"

She broke off quickly. Good Lord, what was she saying? And in front of men, too! Why, she was turning into Payton, there was no doubt about it, since she felt comfortable enough to say these sort of things in mixed company.

"You'd almost think what, Georgie?" Ross asked curiously.

Georgiana knew she was opening and closing her mouth, rather like a fish with a hook through its jaw. But she couldn't help it. Every time she thought of something to say, she realized she couldn't, absolutely couldn't, say it. She hadn't any proof. And it wasn't as if Payton had been ill. True, she wouldn't eat, and she hadn't tried to escape, but she had been through quite a traumatic experience, so that was only to be expected.

Or at least it would have been expected, in any other girl but Payton. Payton had always seemed to take traumatic experiences in stride, as if, for some reason, she believed they were her due.

"Well," she said finally, aware that everyone in the room was staring at her expectedly. "I was just thinking that one explanation for her rather, er, uncharacteristic behavior—the not eating, and all the weeping, and the fact that she won't see Drake—I mean, Sir Connor—and that she hasn't tried to escape, might be that she's, um . . ."

"She's um what?" Ross shouted. "Out with it, woman! What is she?"

"Well," Georgiana said, with a gulp. "Expecting."

"Expecting what?" Ross had leaned forward in his chair, but now he threw himself back into it again, disgustedly. "An apology? Well, she'll be waitin' a long time for it. I'm not apologizin' till she does. After all, nobody asked her to save Drake. He could have bloody well saved himself. He's done it a thousand times before."

"Um," Georgiana said. "That wasn't what I meant. I meant she might be expecting, um, a baby."

Georgiana felt her cheeks turn crimson. She couldn't believe she'd just said what she'd said. It was quite unheard of, speaking of such things in front of men, even if the men were family—well, for the most part, anyway. Heat was rising into her face, which was uncomfortable considering it was very hot in New Providence anyway, despite the wide-open seven-foot windows, and the thick stones the villa had been built with. If she didn't have to keep discussing these embarrassing topics, she wouldn't be half so hot.

"Expecting a baby?" Ross blurted out, after a moment's silence, during which she'd heard, quite distinctly, the sound of the gardener outdoors, snipping away at the bougainvillea. *"Payton?"*

It irked Georgiana a little, that he should look so incredulous. Why, perhaps Payton had a point. They had treated her like a fourth brother her whole life, and now they expected her to behave like a dutiful sister. And yet whenever any sort of evidence arose that suggested Payton to be a member of the fairer sex, they still balked like donkeys.

"It would," Georgiana said mildly, "be a natural consequence of what you yourself accused her of doing with Drake. I mean, Sir Connor."

"But—" Ross looked about the room. She didn't know what he was looking for, unless it was some sort of assurance that what she'd said couldn't possibly be true. "But then why won't she marry him?"

"Perhaps she doesn't know it herself. I don't know. I only suspected it this morning, when she still wouldn't eat. It would explain her moodiness."

"But not why she won't marry him!" Ross thundered.

"But of course it does. Don't you see? She told me she doesn't want him to think of her as another Miss Whitby, whom he felt obligated to wed."

"Miss Whitby?" Ross exploded. "Miss Whitby? *Still* Miss Whitby? *When* am I ever going to hear the end of Miss Bloody Whitby?"

"When she's hanged?" Raleigh suggested.

"Drake," Ross shouted, spinning around. "This is all your fault. I told you not to—"

But his voice trailed off, because Connor Drake had slipped from the room some time before.

They found him easily enough, however. His cursing could

be heard all the way down the stairs, when, a few seconds later, he opened the door to Payton's bedchamber and found the room empty, the French doors to the balcony swaying lazily in the afternoon breeze.

# *Chapter Twenty-nine*

$\mathcal{A}$s soon as Georgiana was gone, Payton lifted her face from the pillow she'd smashed it against. Really, she thought to herself. She was getting quite good with the theatrics. She was starting to be able to turn the tears on and off with an aplomb any actress would envy. Smiling bitterly, she pushed back the sheet that had been covering her.

She was, of course, fully clothed beneath it. While that in itself probably wouldn't have startled her sister-in-law very much, the fact that the clothes Payton was wearing belonged to Georgiana might have caused her some consternation. Georgiana was generous to a fault when it came to lending personal belongings, but she might have asked why Payton felt compelled to borrow, of all things, her most voluminous pelisse. It fit Payton so ill that it made her look several stone heavier, and the train dragged rather more than was considered fashionable.

But all this was of course necessary, if the plan Payton had hatched during the night was to work.

It was not a particularly good plan. It was certainly not one of her best. It did not offer a single solution to any of the myriad problems Payton had wakened that morning to face— for instance, the fact that her brothers were trying to force her to marry a man who had only just escaped a forced marriage to someone else. It was, however, the only problem Payton knew of that she had the wherewithal to solve. And since she could not solve her own problems, it struck her as advisable at least to try to solve someone else's.

Scrambling from the bed, she went to reach behind a couch for a bonnet that she'd also taken from her sister-in-law's room. Donning it, she tied the wide yellow ribbons very securely beneath her chin, then lowered the white muslin veil that hung from the silk band. It wasn't impossible to see through the muslin, just not very easy, and Payton wondered why in the world any woman would consent to wear such a thing, except to ward off mosquitoes.

Still, she managed to find her way through the French doors to her balcony. It was only the work of a moment to swing her legs over the balustrade, then climb down the bougainvillea that grew so copiously alongside the villa. Her landing was not the most graceful, and gave her a bit of a jolt, but she soon recovered. She was not, she supposed, quite as young as she'd been the last time she'd jumped from this very same balcony. Not as young, nor anywhere near as innocent, either.

But despite her past innocence, Payton had always known her way around the teeming, pirate-infested town of Nassau. As a young girl, her main entertainment while in port in New Providence had been wandering about the docks, poking into crates containing cargoes from the holds of strange, foreign ships, listening to the far-fetched yarns the sailors tossed back and forth like India rubber balls, and generally getting herself into mischief. Which was how she knew, with perfect assuredness, the location of the Nassau jail, and how she ended up in front of it a mere ten minutes after leaving the confines of her brothers' villa.

The jailers were enjoying their midday meal when Payton knocked. Every bit as hard-bitten as their prisoners—they had to be, otherwise, considering the kind of scum of humanity that ended up in the Nassau jail, outbreaks would have been the norm, rather than what they were, the exception—they did not take kindly to having been disturbed. But when they saw their visitor was a lady—and what's more, the most famous lady in Nassau, the one who'd come back from the dead, and brought with her more than a hint of disrepute—they were a good deal more cordial.

And when the famous lady-who-was-no-longer-dead stated the purpose of her visit, they were downright courtly. The lady wished to visit a prisoner? But of course! The head jailer himself personally escorted Payton to the cell. Due to the special circumstances surrounding the prisoner Payton wished to visit, this personage had had to be housed not in the jailhouse proper, but next door, in the town stables. There had, of course, been considerable outcry that even this was not proper, but, as the head jailer explained to Payton, there was nowhere else to put this person . . . not unless the prisoner was housed in the jailer's own home, and, as he joked, his wife had refused to allow it!

The stables did not seem too bad to Payton. They smelled a good deal better than the jailhouse, that was certain. And the faces that pressed against the bars in the windows, while just as hairy, were considerably friendlier. The guard who'd been posted outside the prisoner's cell door was a pleasant fellow with impressive manners, who leapt up when she entered and gave a low bow, all before learning that she was *the* Honorable Miss Payton Dixon ("Yes," her escort assured him, "the one what was thought dead.")

The guard very obligingly agreed to allow her a brief visit with his prisoner, but only after gravely informing her of his charge's extreme dangerousness. Payton was not to be deceived by the prisoner's outward appearance, which was deceptively innocent.

And with that final warning, and the assurance that he would be but on the other side of the door, and that she had only to call and he would come, the guard opened the stall door, and Payton entered the straw-strewn and sunny enclosure.

Miss Rebecca Whitby, who had surely overheard everything that had been said outside the door to the stall in which she was locked, had risen from the pallet someone had thoughtfully provided for her, and stood staring at Payton with no attempt whatsoever to hide the contempt she felt for her.

"Well," she said, in a hard voice that was very unlike the fluty one Payton was used to hearing her use, "if it isn't the Honorable Miss Payton Dixon, back from the dead. You must be very popular. They don't often see resurrections in this part of the world." She tossed her cinnamon-colored hair. "I'm terribly flattered you were able to find the time to pay a social call on a lowly creature like myself, but you'll forgive me if I don't offer you any refreshment. They have a deplorable lack of amenities at this particular establishment."

Payton pushed back the white muslin veil so that she could get a better look at this woman she'd spent such an awfully long time despising. It had been necessary to jail this particular prisoner in a facility that kept her separate from her fellow miscreants, and Payton could easily see why. Eight weeks of incarceration had done nothing to dim the glow of Becky Whitby's beauty. If anything, she was lovelier than ever, with the sun spilling in through the barred window at her back. It set that thick auburn hair aflame, and brought out the creaminess in the prisoner's skin. Her pregnancy was noticeable now, but rather than simply thickening her body, it brought a certain buoyancy to her figure, a ripeness that even the shapeless cotton gown she'd been given by her wardens could not hide.

She was, in every respect, still the most beautiful woman Payton had ever seen. A fact that had nothing to do with Payton removing her bonnet and passing it, expressionlessly, to her.

"Here," she said.

Becky Whitby looked down at the hat. It was a frothy creation, far better suited to Georgiana than to anyone else Payton knew, and had probably been purchased for a handsome sum, and over Ross's strong objections. Becky Whitby, however, did not look all that pleased to be presented with it.

"And what," she demanded, her rose-colored upper lip curling, "am I to do with *this*?"

Payton, busy undoing the mother-of-pearl buttons to her sister-in-law's pelisse, said simply, "Put it on."

Becky Whitby laughed. It was a brittle sound, like glass breaking.

"Are you dense? They're hanging me, Payton. This might serve to disguise my neck from the ax-man, but that is not, I understand, to be the mode of my demise. And while I certainly borrowed a good many of your things back when I stayed with you in London, this particular accessory does not exactly suit my coloring. I'm much obliged to you, but—"

Payton said, "You know, I always thought you were a great many things, Becky. Selfish, vain, manipulative, shallow—"

"Thank you kindly," Becky interrupted sarcastically. "As long as we're being honest, allow me to return the compliment by saying that I found you excessively irritating, with your ridiculous *frankness* and your mannish obsession for all things nautical. Most pathetic of all, however, was your little obsession with Connor Drake, whom, I might add, told me in confidence—I hope you don't mind my saying it—that he always thought you quite unfeminine, to the point of being physically repellent to him."

Payton lifted an eyebrow at this—really, the last time she'd seen Connor Drake, he'd seemed anything but repelled by her, but she certainly wasn't going to stand there and argue the point—and then said calmly, as if Becky hadn't spoken at all, "The one thing I never thought you, Miss Whitby, was stupid. But that's what you're being now. Stupid."

"Oh? Stupid, am I? Because I won't accept this idiotic hat as a gift?" Becky threw the offending bonnet down upon the floor. "I don't *need* a hat, you ignorant girl. I *need* a decent attorney."

Payton looked surprised. "I thought surely your father would provide that for you. Sir Marcus has always had such powerful friends—"

"He did have, until he chose to tangle with you lot. Apparently—don't ask me how—you Dixons have assembled quite a powerful bank of friends back in England. The kinds of friends who do things like exert pressure on public officials, and keep them from stepping forward on the behalf of the innocent men like my father—"

"Oh, please," Payton said. It was her turn to laugh. "You forget. I was there, Becky. I heard it all. I know everything. I'm to testify, you know, at your trial, as well as at your father's." She shook her head. "You're wrong, you know. They won't hang you. They can't hang a pregnant woman. Besides, you never killed anyone . . . that I know of. It's your father they'll hang. And you know where."

Becky flinched. Well, Payton hadn't wanted to remind her of it, but really, there was no call for the girl to be so cocky. Her father was going to endure the same fate as any pirate who'd been found guilty of his crimes: he'd be chained to a post at low tide on the sand bar in the bay. And there he'd be left, to dangle *intra infra fluxum et refluxum maris,* between high and low tides, until his trussed bones, picked clean by gulls and fish, finally crumbled into the sea.

Not a pleasant way to die. Becky might, perhaps, be forgiven her foul temper.

Not, of course, that she was going to suffer a similar fate.

"They'll transport you, you know, Becky," Payton said. "After the baby is born. Probably to Australia. Or possibly to the Americas."

Becky Whitby stared at Payton, hard. "Where I'll certainly be the most stylishly garbed convicted felon in history," she said bitterly. "In your fancy hat."

Payton shrugged, and the silk robe that she'd unbuttoned fell a little down her arms. "And my pelisse," she said.

Becky narrowed her eyes. They were very blue, almost the same blue as the bay her father was going to drown in. "What," Becky demanded suspiciously, "are you talking about?"

Payton let the pelisse fall to the floor. She had only a thin white lawn dress on beneath it, a dress far too young for her, and a little tight, besides. Since her family had thought her dead, they had not brought any clothes for her from England, and so Payton had been forced to wear what she'd left behind during her last stay in Nassau: a good many white dresses far better suited to a fourteen-year-old than a nineteen-year-old who'd just spent two months marooned on a tropical island with a baronet.

"Put on the hat," Payton said, speaking through gritted teeth not so much so that the guard wouldn't hear her, but because she was rapidly losing her patience. "And the pelisse. They should fit. They're Georgiana's and she's about your size. Tuck up your hair and pull down the veil. Then go."

"Go?" Becky shook her head bewilderedly. "What . . . ?"

"Go. Your Frenchman is out there, somewhere. Go and find him."

Becky's ruby lips fell open. "You're mad," she murmured. "Absolutely mad."

Payton shook her head. "Not at all. You love him, don't you?"

*"Who?"*

"The Frenchman." Payton rolled her eyes at the older girl's slowness. "Captain La Fond. Don't you love him?"

Becky could only nod, a good deal more stupidly than Payton might have expected from a young lady so skilled in the art of manipulation.

"Well, there, then. I know he loves you terribly. You two are better off together than apart. I know if I were having a man's baby, I'd want to be with him, if I could." Payton made a shooing gesture. "You'd better hurry, before they suss it out."

Becky looked down at the pelisse, and then at the hat. Then she looked back at Payton. "You're serious," she said. It wasn't a question.

"Yes, I'm serious," Payton said. "You'd better give me that brown thing you've got on. I'll hold them off as long as I can, but—"

In a flash, the dress Becky wore was over her head. Beneath

it, she was clad in a rather surprisingly daring pair of pantaloons, and a hand-embroidered silk camisole. "Here," she said, practically throwing the shift at Payton, as if she feared she might change her mind at any moment.

Payton calmly donned the smock. It was still warm from Becky's body, and hung on Payton's smaller frame like a sack. She knew she did not look either buoyant or radiant in it.

And that, she had decided at long last, was all right.

Becky, of course, was a vision of loveliness in her borrowed clothes—the pelisse fit her to perfection, its high waist hiding her pregnancy, and the turquoise of the silk brought out all the ivory tones in her skin. Skin that was, unfortunately, hidden a moment later by the muslin veil. Looking at her, Payton knew that any woman would have been able to tell the difference between the woman who'd gone into the stall, and the woman who was exiting it, in a second. But none of the people they had to fool were women, so that was all right.

Payton went to the pallet Becky had abandoned upon her entering the stall and lay down upon it, making sure her back faced the door. She was about to call to the guard, "Please let me out now, sir," when Becky held up a hand to stop her.

"I just have to know," she said in a lilting whisper. "Why?"

Payton had known the question would be put to her eventually. The problem was, she was as unprepared to answer it now as she had been in the wee hours of the night, when the scheme had first occurred to her, and she had asked herself the very same question. Why, indeed? Why go to so much trouble for a woman she had despised for so long?

"Really," Becky whispered. "I've got to know. Why are you doing this for me?" Then, before Payton could open her lips to make any sort of answer, Becky went on breathily, "It's because he's in love with me, isn't it?"

On the pallet, Payton leaned up on her elbows and said, "What?"

"He's in love with me." Payton could see only the faintest outline of Becky's head beneath the veil, and couldn't see her face at all, but she saw the hat move, and could only assume the older girl had nodded. "I knew it. He put you up to this, didn't he?"

"Who?"

"Why, Captain Drake, of course." Becky laughed, a sound that had thrilled many a man's veins, but that Payton nevertheless found hard to discern from the neighs of the occupants of the adjoining stalls. "He was always in love with me. I suppose he couldn't stand to think of me locked up in here, and put you up to this. And you're such a stupid little thing, you agreed." The veil swayed from left to right. Becky was shaking her head. "Poor, poor Payton."

Payton smiled. She couldn't help it. It wasn't funny, really, except that . . . except that, well, it *was.*

"That's right," she said to Becky Whitby. "That's exactly right."

The veil jerked. Becky was tossing her head in triumph. "I knew it," she said. And then she was calling for the guard to open the door.

Payton had plenty of time, during that long afternoon she spent imprisoned in Becky Whitby's stead, to reflect on the reasons behind what she'd done. Was it, she asked herself, because of Mei-Ling's assertion that women must be supportive of one another? Or was it because she hadn't liked to see a pregnant woman in jail? Or was it because of the expression the Frenchman had worn that morning she'd brought his breakfast, when he'd been so concerned for the health of his mistress and their unborn child? Payton hadn't known then the identity of that mistress—she had seen only that Lucien La Fond, the self-proclaimed scourge of the South Seas, was a man every bit as violently in love with someone as she herself was in love with Connor Drake. And could a man who loved like that be all bad?

Then she'd shaken herself. But of course he could! He was Lucien La Fond, the man who had killed Drake's brother! What had she done? Oh, what had she done?

By the time she was finally discovered—she feigned unconsciousness when the guard opened the door to bring in the prisoner's supper, and then, when roused, claimed that the wicked Miss Whitby must have struck her from behind, and stolen her clothes—she had a headache that was every bit as painful as if she really *had* been struck from behind. But her headache wasn't from any blow delivered by Miss Whitby, unless one counted the blow to Payton's conscience over what she'd done. What was Drake going to say when he found out? He would despise her—if he didn't hate her already, for refusing to see him all week.

It wasn't until the magistrates finally—and reluctantly—released her, frustrated by her lack of answers to their many questions, that Payton walked out into the evening air, saw her brothers waiting for her, and knew. She knew, right then and there, exactly why she'd done it.

Now her only problem was how—how in the *world*—was she going to explain it to Drake?

It was only Hudson and Raleigh who came to retrieve her from the offices of the magistrates. When she asked where Ross was, they only glanced meaningfully at one another, and then Hudson replied lightly, "Well, when he'd found out you'd gone, and we didn't know where, he started drinking—"

"Because of the shock, you know," Raleigh put in. "He never expected you'd disobey him quite so . . . blatantly."

"Right. And then when the messenger arrived a little while ago, to tell us you were down at the jailhouse—"

"Well, he was a little angry."

Payton, seated between her two brothers in the chaise, glanced from one to another. "How angry?" she asked resignedly.

"Well," Hudson said, after giving the question serious consideration. "Angry enough to try to put his fist through a wall."

"Right," Raleigh said cheerfully. "Only he forgot we aren't in England. The walls here are made of stone, not plaster. He'll be all right in a few weeks, I expect."

Payton nodded. She'd known Ross would have to have been seriously incapacitated to send these two in his stead—and to send them in an open carriage, no less. Payton, still dressed in Miss Whitby's jail smock, was quite an object of interest to passers-by, many of whom pointed and said, quite audibly, "That's her! That's the one what was dead, and came back again!"

Payton had never before realized quite how far the city jail was from her family's villa. But it was far enough for Hudson to comment, as they drove along. "I expect your head must be smartin' a bit, from where she hit you."

Since Payton's head *was* smarting, she didn't think it a lie to reply, "Yes, a bit."

"What'd she hit you with, anyway?" Raleigh wanted to know. "Horseshoe?"

Payton craned her neck to look up at the night sky. "I suppose," she said.

"What balderdash." Raleigh snorted. "Really, Pay, you're goin' to have to come up with something a bit better if you don't want Ross chawin' you to bits. Hit you with a horseshoe. Pshaw!"

Hudson, holding the reins to the matched set of bays that drew them, agreed. "He'll ask to feel the bump on your noggin," he said. "You better come up with a damned good explanation, Pay, and right quick."

Miserable, Payton looked away from the sky. "I suppose I could just tell him the truth."

"The truth?" Raleigh rolled his eyes. "What for? You already told 'im the truth once, and look where it got you: locked in your room for a week."

Payton sighed. "I expect you're right. Was . . . Does Drake know?"

Neither Hudson nor Raleigh answered right away. Payton, sensing something was wrong, looked from one to the other and repeated her question, with a growing sense of unease. Finally, Hudson replied, "If he don't know, then he's the only one. Every man, woman, and child on this island knows that this afternoon, the Honorable Miss Payton Dixon—"

"Otherwise known as the young lady what was dead," Raleigh inserted helpfully.

"—was involved in a jail break that resulted in the escape of a wanted felon."

"Wanted or wanton?" Raleigh quipped.

Ignoring him, Payton asked, "What exactly did Drake say? When he found out, I mean."

"Not much." The chaise had pulled up alongside the front of the villa, and Hudson laid down the reins. "He was the one who found you gone, you know."

"What?" Payton gasped in astonishment. "But how? I thought Ross wouldn't let him anywhere near the house!"

Raleigh clambered down from the vehicle. "Don't be an ass, Pay," he advised. "You know Ross. He can't stay mad longer'n a mosquito can stay in one place. Drake's been here all along, waitin' for you to stop actin' like such a girl. When he found you gone, he went straight back to his house, thinkin' sure that's where you'd gone. When you didn't show up after a bit, he went out lookin' for you. I don't expect it occurred to him to look in the jailhouse, however."

"He was here when the messenger arrived," Hudson put in. "He'd stopped in to see if we'd had any word yet. When he heard what happened—about you havin' gone to visit Miss Whitby in jail, and her boltin' like she did, he . . ."

"He *what*?" Payton gripped the side of the chaise, blinking up at him in the soft lamplight reflected from the villa's windows.

"He left," Hudson finished, with a shrug.

"Left?" Payton cried. "Left for where?"

"Well, how should I know? 'Snot *my* turn to look after 'im." Hudson climbed down from the chaise, then turned to offer Payton a hand.

"But how . . . how did he *look*?"

"Disgusted's the only word I can think of. I got the feelin' he knew."

"Knew what?" Payton was so distracted, she didn't even ask herself why her brother was helping her from the carriage, an act of chivalry he had never before performed for her benefit.

"Well, that poor ol' Miss Whitby didn't exactly get away all on her own." Hudson shot her a meaningful glance. "Now did she?"

Payton swallowed. Good Lord. This was worse than she'd ever expected. Drake, disgusted? Disgusted by *her*? Well, disgusted by what she'd done, anyway. And why shouldn't he be? She'd helped a woman who'd played an integral part in his brother's murder to escape from prison! How had she expected him to feel? Delighted? A man like Drake—a proud man; a man's man—wasn't likely to look upon what she'd done with any sort of understanding. Fury, maybe. But not understanding.

"Oh," she said, under her breath. She tried to think of a swear word appropriately awful enough to describe her feelings just then, but all she could come up with was, "Dear."

She'd made, she realized, yet another bloody mess of things.

# Chapter Thirty

Sleep was a long time in coming that night. Not that Payton wasn't exhausted. Although she hadn't exerted herself physically in any significant way, she went to bed as tired as she'd used to back on the *Rebecca*, when her limbs would fairly ache from the labors she'd performed during the day. She supposed she'd done quite a bit of emotional laboring throughout the day, and that might have counted just as well.

Still, tired as she was, she couldn't sleep. How could she sleep, knowing her life was over? Because it was. She hadn't needed Ross to tell her so, although he had, roundly and savagely, the minute she'd come through the front door. The surgeon had been there, placing a splint over her brother's broken hand, so that might have had something to do with Ross's foul mood. But there was no denying that his accusations were founded in truth, however hurtfully he hurled them at her. She *was* a fool—a double-damned one, just as Ross said. It was no good, Sir Henry's happy greeting of her, and Georgiana's warm embrace. Ross was right. Payton Dixon was a fool. What else could she do, but go to bed?

Maybe, Payton thought to herself. Maybe in the morning, things would be better.

But she didn't see how. Not really. Not unless Drake forgave her. But how could he? From the very beginning, she had done nothing but interfere in his life. From stopping his wedding to getting him practically killed by her brothers, she had made his life a living hell. Granted, she had saved his life, back on the *Rebecca*. And he had seemed to have had a pleasant enough time on San Rafael. But other than that . . .

Other than that, she had pretty much systematically destroyed his life.

Well, it would all stop now. It was true that she still loved him. She would never stop loving him . . . *could* never stop loving him. But she could stop seeing him. She could stop interfering in his life. She could go back to England and have her season out and marry Matthew Hayford and settle down and have babies, the way her brothers wanted her to. Forget about Drake. Forget about the sea.

Forget about her heart.

It was just after Payton had decided that she would sooner jab a whaling hook through her foot than ever be able to forget about Drake that she heard an unfamiliar sound. Or, rather, a familiar sound, but a sound that was out of place. Sitting up, Payton peered through the darkness of her bedchamber, and saw, through the glass panes in the French doors to her balcony, a dark silhouette. Good Lord! Someone was trying to break into the villa!

Then, her heart hammering, she realized it wasn't a thief at all. It could only be Drake. Of course it was Drake. Who else had such a large, imposing shadow? But what would Drake be doing, climbing up onto her balcony and worrying her door like a burglar?

He wanted something. An explanation, most likely. But maybe . . . just maybe . . . he wanted *her*!

That thought alone sent Payton flopping back against the pillows, feigning sleep with as much theatrical energy as she'd feigned unconsciousness, back in Miss Whitby's jail cell. Well, she couldn't let him think she'd been lying awake, worrying about him, could she?

She heard the doors open finally—she hadn't locked them— and then footsteps—cautious, surreptitious—approached her bedside. She had time to ask herself if she should let her eyelids flutter gently open, the way Miss Whitby's had, after she'd fainted in the church on the day of her wedding, or if she should continue to feign sleep for a while. And then a huge hand, its grip one of iron, clapped hard over her mouth, and she forgot all about feigning anything.

Her eyes flew open—there was no fluttering about it—and she saw that the person who'd come in through her balcony doors wasn't Drake at all, but rather, Sir Marcus Tyler.

But not the Sir Marcus Tyler she'd last seen in the hold of the *Rebecca*. That Sir Marcus had been clean-shaven and elegant, coolly sarcastic and dry-witted. This Sir Marcus looked as if he hadn't seen a razor in months—and, in fact, he had not, razors not being provided in the jail in which he'd spent the past eight weeks, for fear the inmates might use them upon one another, or themselves. His hoary face was pressed just inches above her, and there was nothing the least bit elegant about the way he smelled—quite pungently male. In addition, his fine clothes were grimy with dirt and tattered from constant wear. It wasn't a wonder that, following his escape from jail, he'd been able to wander the streets of Nassau without being discovered, since he looked no different from many a weary sailor who, after months out at sea, staggered down the gangplank looking for wine and women.

But it wasn't wine or women Sir Marcus wanted.

It was revenge.

"Well, well, well," he said, in a horrible, rasping whisper. His breath was rather horrible, as well. "If it isn't Miss Payton Dixon, back from the dead. I couldn't believe it when I heard, but then, I should have known. You're rather like a cat, you know, Miss Dixon. You seem to have any number of lives. Only allow me to assure you, this one is quite definitively at an end."

It was impossible for Payton to reply, with his hand pressed so tightly over her mouth. But she didn't need words to answer him, not when she still had use of her extremities.

She swung one of those up with lightning quickness, intending to plunge her fingers in her assailant's right eye, another one of the defensive tactics Raleigh had taught her. She hadn't counted, however, on Sir Marcus's speedy reaction. He seized her hand an inch within reach of his face.

"Tsk-tsk, little cat," he said chidingly. "It's not a bit ladylike to scratch—"

He broke off as Payton sank her teeth, as hard as she could, into the hand that pressed against her mouth. With a grunt of pain, Sir Marcus jerked his fingers away, then brought them back again before Payton could move, this time holding something shiny and sharp against her throat. She grew very still, feeling the prick of a knife-point against the place in her neck where her pulse beat.

"That's right," Sir Marcus said. "It's a knife. You see, Miss Dixon, when you helped my Rebecca to escape, she was so moved by the sweetness and generosity of the gesture that she felt compelled to repeat it. Her methods of setting me at liberty from my prison were a little different from yours, but then, Rebecca's a bit more skilled than you are where men are concerned. There are some very happy guards down at the jailhouse tonight, I must say. How happy they'll be in the morning, when their employers realize I've gone, I can't say, but—"

"It's really very unsportsmanlike of you to kill me, Sir Marcus," Payton couldn't help interrupting, "after I helped your daughter the way I did."

Sir Marcus, she could see, even in the darkness of her bedroom, was grinning, his teeth yellow amidst his beard. "Unsportsmanlike? How charming you are. You know, in a way, I feel I'm almost going to regret killing you."

"Why do you have to kill me at all?" Payton asked. "I give you my word I'll never say anything about how you had Lucien La Fond kill Sir Richard, or how you tried to kill Drake—"

Sir Marcus looked, and sounded, quite regretful when he said, "Ah, but you see, Miss Dixon, the word of a woman doesn't mean so very much to me. I've found that, for the most part, your sex is not to be trusted. So you'll pardon me, but before I can leave the island, I must insure that should I ever again be brought to trial, the key witnesses against me will be regrettably unavailable."

"Does that mean—" Payton's blood went cold in her veins.

"Regrettably no, not yet, my dear. I haven't been at liberty all that long. But I promise my blade will still be wet with the blood from your throat when it pierces his—"

A deep voice cut through the darkness that permeated Payton's bedroom. "I think not, Marcus."

Drake! Her heart, which she suspected had stopped beating, started up again joyfully. It was Drake!

Then her pulse skittered to a halt again. Drake! What was he doing here? He was going to get himself killed!

A second later, the knife was gone. Payton didn't know if Sir Marcus, startled by the sound of that low voice, let it slip, or if he'd turned to hurl it in the direction the voice had come from. She didn't waste time trying to figure it out, though. Instead, she rolled away from Sir Marcus, toward the far side of the bed. And she didn't stop there, either. She kept rolling, until she landed on the floor. Then she crouched behind the bed frame, uncertain what to do next. Light a candle? No, that might reveal both her hiding place and Drake's whereabouts in the room. Run for help? No, she couldn't leave Drake alone with this madman. Scream? Should she scream? She would have, if she could. But no sound whatsoever would issue from her throat.

"Who's there?" Sir Marcus was hissing. Payton saw moonlight, filtering dimly through the windows in the French doors, reflect against the blade her attacker still held, as he searched for the owner of that deep, penetrating voice. "Is that you, Drake?"

"It is." Drake's voice came rumbling from the darkness, low and steady, as if he were greeting Sir Marcus casually in a ballroom, and not in the middle of a murder attempt. "Put the knife down, Tyler."

Marcus Tyler showed no signs of doing as Drake asked.

Instead, he moved in the direction of Drake's voice, the knife poised dangerously. "Show yourself, Captain," he said sneeringly. "Or should I say *Sir* Connor?"

"You should have run when you had the chance," Drake said, amusement in his voice. "You could have made it off the island by now. But now it's too late. You're caught again."

"No," Sir Marcus said. "*You're* the one who's caught. After all, *I've* got a knife."

And he raised that knife. Payton saw it glitter, the whole of Sir Marcus's arm silhouetted against the blue light seeping through the French doors. Then another arm shot out, and a hand seized Sir Marcus by the wrist. The knife trembled for a moment or two in Sir Marcus's fingers ... and then it dropped, with a clatter, to the floor. A second later, Drake had tackled the older man. There was a struggle, during which Payton could see nothing but two dark shadows that suddenly became one ...

And then the shadow crashed into the French doors, splintering them apart, sending glass flying. Moonlight flooded the room.

And Payton, who up until then hadn't been able to find her voice, let out an earsplitting scream.

A second later, she had flung herself at Drake's back. Gripping his shoulders, she cried, "Drake, don't! Don't, you're killing him!"

Because that's what Drake seemed to be doing—fulfilling the promise he'd made back in the hold of the *Rebecca,* that he'd kill Sir Marcus, when he got the chance. Straddling the older man, Drake had wrapped his fingers around Tyler's throat, fingers that had gone bloodless with the amount of pressure they were exerting. In a few seconds, he might snap the older man's neck with the grip of his hands alone. Even in the uncertain light of the moon, Payton could see that Sir Marcus's face was turning blue.

Drake was like a man possessed, however. He didn't seem to hear her, didn't seem even to be aware of her presense. He would not release his hold ...

Until Payton's family, roused by her scream and the sound of breaking glass, came racing into the room. It took all three of her brothers to pull Drake off Marcus Tyler, and when they finally did, everyone—with the possible exception of Drake—waited with bated breath as Ross bent down to check the unconscious man's throat. A collective sigh of relief sounded at Ross's terse assertion, "He'll live."

To Payton, the rest of the night passed in a sort of blur. Someone sent for the magistrates, who eventually came and placed Sir Marcus, who'd regained consciousness a few minutes before their arrival, in chains. He did not struggle at all. He seemed almost grateful to be taken away again. Payton supposed that was because he had finally figured out that while Connor Drake walked the earth, jail was the safest place he could be.

Someone else sent for the surgeon. Payton was surprised when she learned he hadn't been summoned in order to tend to the injured Sir Marcus at all, but for her. She was even more astonished when she looked down and saw that she had bled all over the carpet from the cuts she'd sustained when she'd run across the broken glass to stop Drake from killing Sir Marcus. She hadn't felt these injuries at all, but she certainly felt them very well indeed while the surgeon dressed them.

No one, she discovered later, sent for Lady Bisson, but she came anyway, and in her nightcap, looking extremely put out at having been roused so early in the morning, and for what she called a ridiculous reason. She berated her grandson for taking part in fisticuffs like a common footpad—Payton heard her doing so, out in the hallway—and then announced that she was going back to bed. But before she left, she insisted upon seeing Payton, who'd been put in Hudson's room, with orders not to try walking for several days, to give her feet a chance to heal.

But all Lady Bisson did when she got into the room was glare at Payton, and not a bit kindly. "I *thought* as much," the old woman said obscurely, but with feeling.

And Payton, who hadn't any idea what Lady Bisson could be talking about, but who was certain that all of it, every little bit of it, had been her own fault, quite suddenly—and extremely loudly—burst into tears.

This seemed to satisfy the old lady no end, and she left the house with a contented smile on her face.

But Lady Bisson was the only one who greeted Payton's tears with a smile. Everyone else stared at her in complete incredulity—particularly her brothers, who had rarely, if ever, seen their sister cry. It was Georgiana who finally managed to rouse them all, but not into giving Payton their sympathy. No, Georgiana made them all exit the room, leaving Payton alone . . .

Or so she thought. It wasn't until the door had clicked firmly shut behind her sister-in-law that Payton saw that one person, and one person alone, had remained behind.

Drake.

# Chapter Thirty-one

She'd known he was there. She'd known all along that he was sitting in one of the wicker chairs beside the bed in which she'd been placed. He'd been sitting there for a while, she realized, the whole of the time the surgeon had been mending her feet, not moving even during his grandmother's upbraiding. She could see, through tears she was helpless to control, that he looked a good deal different than the last time she had seen him, which was back on San Rafael Island, when her brothers had knocked him senseless. The bruises were still there, but they were fading. He had incurred no fresh ones during his fight with Sir Marcus.

He had obviously been to a barber since their return to civilization. His beard was gone, his golden hair neatly trimmed so that instead of hanging down to his shoulders, it was now even with the high collar of his shirt. And he had most certainly been to a tailor, as well. She did not recognize the blue morning coat he wore—rather rumpled now, due to his encounter with Tyler—but the fawn-colored breeches were of the same cut as all his others—far too snug for her peace of mind.

To make matters worse, she could see that he was looking at her, his expression very serious, indeed. His silver-blue eyes looked brighter than ever in his deeply tanned face, and since the sun was just coming up in the glass doors that led to Hudson's terrace, he had to squint a little in order to see her, revealing the tiny creases at the sides of his lids that showed whenever he laughed.

It was exceedingly difficult for Payton to keep herself from leaping up and throwing herself into his arms right then and there. She longed to seek comfort in his embrace, to feel his heartbeat beneath her cheek, to smell him, to feel his warmth. Only two things kept her where she was: her pride, and her extremely sore feet.

After a while, she stopped crying and, feeling ashamed of herself, was able to say, in an unsteady voice, "I—I'm sorry."

Drake's expression did not change. "Sorry for what?" he asked.

"For everything." Payton reached up to wipe the tears from her face with the lace cuff of her nightdress. "I'm sorry I let Miss Whitby go. Only I didn't think . . . I didn't think she'd do anything like . . . like . . ."

"Like help her father to escape?"

"Yes. I just . . . I just felt so *sorry* for her."

Now his face showed some emotion: it showed disbelief.

"*Sorry* for her? After what she did?"

"I know," Payton said. "I know. Only I kept remembering that morning on the *Rebecca,* in the hold, when Sir Marcus hit her. You didn't see it, Drake, but he hit her very hard across the face. She fell down, but then she jumped right back up again, as if it had been nothing. Drake, if anybody had ever hit me like that, I probably would have—well, I don't know what I'd have done. But I wouldn't have been able to get up so soon, that's certain. And that's when I realized that the reason Miss Whitby was able to get up like that was because she was *used* to being hit that way. She'd probably been hit like that every single day while she was growing up. And *that's* why she's the way she is, why she did the things she did. She isn't evil, Drake. She's just never known kindness. She's never known decency. She doesn't know what those things are, because no one's ever shown them to her. It's no wonder she's the way she is, really, if you think about it."

"And so you thought it might be wise," Drake said dryly, "to release someone like that back into the general population."

"Well, no, that's not what I was thinking. I was thinking that maybe if someone, just once, showed her some kindness, she might . . ."

He quirked up an eyebrow. "Change?"

"Well." Payton could feel that her cheeks were starting to burn. She was so ashamed! She knew she was a fool. She hadn't needed Lady Bisson to tell her so. "Well, that's what I thought, anyway. I realize now it was stupid. Of course she wasn't going to change. The very first thing she did when she got out was send her father to kill me."

"No," Drake said. There was something thoughtful in his tone, and she looked at him curiously. "No, I don't think Miss Whitby sent her father to kill you. I'm sure she urged him not to, as a matter of fact."

Payton smiled a little. "Really? Do you think so, Drake?"

"Oh, not because she'd learned anything from your example, Payton. But because killing us was risky. It might get him in even more trouble. And Miss Whitby, if she is anything, is practical."

Payton stopped smiling. "Oh," she said. She wasn't certain what she'd been expecting, when she'd realized Drake had stayed behind after the others had left, but she certainly hadn't thought he'd treat her like *this*. So . . . coldly. So indifferently.

But why shouldn't he? She certainly deserved it. She took a deep, trembling breath. "I suppose you hate me now, don't you, Drake?"

"Would you please," he said tiredly, "and for the last time, call me Connor? And no, I don't hate you. I think helping Becky Whitby to escape was one of the stupidest things you've ever done, but I certainly don't *hate* you for it."

"*One* of the stupidest things I've ever done?" she echoed. Her feelings of hopelessness were forgotten as her temper flared. "And just how many stupid things, in your opinion, have I done?"

"Well, following me onto the *Rebecca* was one." He held out his hand, and began to tick points off on his fingers. "Not leaving it when I told you to was another. Running across a carpet of glass in bare feet. Now *that* was impressive. But I would have to say, out of all your idiotic stunts, refusing to marry me was by far the stupidest."

She blinked at him. "But . . . but I didn't want you to have to . . . I mean, you'd already been forced into one marriage, and I didn't want—"

He shook his head. Really, she was the stubbornest, most contrary woman he had ever known.

"First of all, Payton, no one forced me into my decision to marry Miss Whitby—not the first time around, anyway. I was marrying her of my own free will, and you were quite right back on board the *Rebecca,* when you suggested that I was doing so because I needed a wife and she—well, she seemed good enough. I made the decision to marry her, you understand, before I fully understood what you meant to me—"

What he meant, Payton thought to herself, was that he'd made the decision to marry Miss Whitby before he happened to notice how well Payton looked in a corset. But she decided to let the statement pass without comment.

"And secondly," Drake went on, "how could you ever think, after everything we'd been through together, that I would ever consider spending the rest of my life with anyone but you?"

Payton blinked at him some more. "It—it's just," she stammered. "It was just that after I saw you lying there, in the sand, after Ross had hit you, I just—"

"You just wanted to punish him for it," Drake finished for her. "And by refusing to marry me, you succeeded admirably. But don't you think, Payton, that your brothers have suffered enough?"

She wasn't certain she understood. "Do you mean . . . do you mean that you still want to marry me?"

He pushed himself out of his chair suddenly, crossed the room, and dropped down to sit beside her on the bed. Reaching out, he took one of her hands in both his own, and flipping it over, kissed the place where her pulse beat.

"You know," he said to her wrist, "you're a very difficult woman to love, Payton Dixon."

She swallowed. "I don't try to be. Only I . . . well, I like having things my own way."

"I noticed that." He looked down at her, and his eyes were brighter than she'd ever seen them. It made her feel breathless just to look at them.

Her gaze was on his mouth, which was just a few inches from hers, and so she didn't see the mischief in his gaze. "That's not a very good trait," she said, "for a wife."

"No," he said, reaching out to lift one of her russet curls from the pillow beneath her head. "It isn't."

Payton, although she found it was quite difficult to keep her head about her while he was so close, playing with her hair, was nevertheless determined to make him see the error of his ways.

"A wife who could never mend your clothes, or run a household," she said. "Really, Drake, on land I'm pretty well useless."

"Useless?" The fingers Drake had been running through her hair dipped suddenly to close over one of her small breasts. Gasping at the sudden contact, Payton raised startled eyes to meet his.

"You've never struck me as useless, Payton," Drake said, his fingers moving lightly over the soft flesh. "Actually, I can think of any number of things at which you've proved quite useful—"

So saying, he lowered his head and, through the thin batiste of her gown, delicately tasted the nipple his fingers had aroused. Payton nearly bucked from the bed, she was so startled—not so much by the way his hot mouth felt on that extremely sensitive area, but by the boldness of the gesture, which she found brazen in the extreme: he was *licking* her, in broad *daylight,* in her *brother's* bedroom . . .

"Stop it," she said, glancing furtively at the door, to reassure herself that it was shut.

"Stop what?" Drake asked, all too innocently.

"You *know* what." Payton, suddenly overwhelmed with feelings of warmth, pushed back the sheets that covered her, revealing long legs bared from the thighs down, since the hem of her nightdress had become twisted round her hips.

Noticing this, Drake lost no time in sliding his free hand between those slim thighs, before Payton, her cheeks blazing, could adjust the gown. Really, she hadn't meant to provoke him—not at all! But when she made a movement as if to snatch away from him, Drake rose up suddenly. The next thing she knew, he'd lowered his heavy body between her legs, effectively cutting off all escape routes.

"Why, look at this," he said, his blue eyes gleaming down at her. "For the very first time, we've got actual bedding beneath us. Not floorboards, or rocks, or sand, or hammock strings, but actual, honest-to-God *bedding* . . ."

At the reminder of the hammock, and what had occurred in it, Payton's cheeks flamed even hotter. She was struggling hard to keep her wits about her, but the introduction of those hardened thighs between her legs made rational thinking impossible. Drake's body was weighing down upon hers, and it was a weight she welcomed, for her body was instantly reminded of pleasures received in the past. Before she could stop herself, her arms were curling around his neck, her legs spreading to better accommodate him. Good God, but she wanted him. Perhaps it was better that they get married after all . . .

And then Drake's lips came down over hers, and all ability to think left her. She closed her eyes, feeling a familiar rush of warmth between her thighs. Instinctively, she arched her pelvis against him, and had the satisfaction of hearing him moan.

"Not yet, love," he whispered raggedly against her mouth. "Not yet."

His hands moved to the neckline of her gown. Payton's eyes flew open as she heard the fabric rend. Gasping as he tore her nightdress down the middle as effortlessly as if it were made of parchment, Payton cried, "Drake! Have you lost your mind?"

Now that her scandalously tanned skin, tip-tilted breasts, and the silken patch of brown hair between her thighs were completely revealed to him, Drake grinned, eminently satisfied. "No. I simply can't say I think much of your sister-in-law's taste in nightdresses."

Payton eyed him, thinking—not for the first time—that it was likely there was more barbaric pirate in him than courtly peer. She was about to make her feelings on the matter known when the lips that moments before had ravaged her mouth suddenly settled over a pink nipple, bare to his touch this time, teasing it into ready hardness. The sharp words that had been on Payton's lips turned to a moan of pleasure as Drake's mouth, hot on her tender skin, forged a path down her flat belly, until his tongue was laving the curls at the jointure of her thighs.

She gave up after that, all the fight gone from her trembling limbs. It was as if he possessed a magic touch that rendered her compliant to his whims. She didn't care if they got married or not, so long as he kept sending such delicious sensations through her body, eliciting these soft murmurs of pleasure from her. In some distant part of her mind, she might have thought it a little strange to be making love in broad daylight in her older brother's bedroom. But it didn't seem to matter where they were when Drake wanted her, and made her want him, too.

Drake felt her surrender and took full advantage of it. Perhaps it wasn't fair, to seduce her in this way, after the fright she'd had, and the injuries she'd sustained . . .

But he wasn't about to take any more chances, or feel any guilt over it, either. Not while he had her exactly where he'd been wanting her since . . . well, since that evening back in Daring Park, when he'd rescued her from being tossed over Raleigh's shoulder. She was his, and he was going to prove it to her once and for all, and he didn't much care what she had to say about it.

Drake, delighting in her soft cries of pleasure and the uncontrollable writhing his tongue wrought from her slim body, didn't raise his face from between her legs until he was certain she was ready for him. Only then did he rise to his knees, and reach for the buttons of his breeches.

He looked down at her in time to see her half-lidded eyes widen as she took in the immensity of his erection. Her lips parted moistly as if she was summoning breath to protest—undoubtedly that someone might walk in on them—but Drake was too close to the edge to waste time arguing. Kneeling between her tanned thighs, he took hold of her buttocks in shaking hands, and then thrust himself into that velvet furrow, plunging into her tight warmth. He watched her face carefully as he entered her, saw her astonished expression as he pushed deeper . . . and then deeper into her. He heard her cry out in wordless objection as he drew back, and then gasp as he entered her again, harder this time, though he was trying—Lord, he was *trying*—to go gently with her. Not that it seemed to matter to her. The buttons of his waistcoat were pressing into her bare flesh, the soft frills of his cravat brushing her face, but she didn't seem to care. Nor did she seem to mind that he was keeping such a firm grip on her hips that she couldn't move them. He tried to be conscious of her injured feet, but how could he, when he was also conscious of what she craved?

And then he couldn't be conscious of anything. Once again, that animal lust that surfaced every time she was near, that uncontrollable craving that only she could satiate took over, and he was like a wild thing in his need to embed himself within her. He began thrusting more and more quickly, with an urgency Payton understood as she thrashed, helpless in her own desire, beneath him. When release came, it crashed over both of them simultaneously, rocking Drake forward again and again, until he drove Payton deep into the mattress with the force of his thrusts. But she was hardly aware of the battering her body received, so caught up was she in her own passion. Crying out hoarsely as wave after wave of pleasure rolled over her, Payton only dimly heard Drake's triumphant roar as he collapsed against her. Her last conscious thought, before she was swept away, was a distant concern that her brothers might have heard them, and would come running, thinking Drake was murdering her.

It was only when the two of them finally lay still, their hearts pounding against one another's, their breathing ragged, that Drake raised his head from Payton's damp hair and asked, "*Now* will you marry me?"

Payton sighed. "I suppose so. If I must."

"I rather think it advisable, considering the fact that you're carrying my child."

"I'm *what*?"

Drake's voice was casual, though the effect his words had on her was anything but. "Think about it, Payton. We were on that island for two months, and in all that time you never—"

"Wait." Payton counted the weeks swiftly on her fingers. The last time she'd menstruated had been on board the *Rebecca*. She'd been at her wits' end, trying to steal enough sponges from the kitchen to—

"Oh, bloody hell!" No wonder she'd felt so weepy lately. And that jolt she'd felt, leaping down from her balcony. Good Lord! She wasn't getting old. She was pregnant! Payton Dixon, who knew everything there was to know about the family arts, had failed to put a single one of them into practice!

"Well, you needn't look like *that* about it," Drake said, in slightly offended tones.

She blinked up at him. "Like what?" she asked.

"Like the bottom of your world had dropped out."

"But Drake, I'm not going to be any good at motherhood,"

Payton cried. "I'll make no better a mother than I'll make a wife. I'm too bossy by half—"

"Nothing wrong with being bossy," Drake said, with a smile that tore at her heartstrings. "It can be quite a good trait. It's a vital trait, actually," he said, "in a sea captain."

"Right," Payton said, no small amount of bitterness in her voice. "Only I'm not a sea captain, remember?"

He gazed down at her tenderly. "Payton, haven't you wondered what it was I was doing on your balcony at three o'clock in the morning?"

She decided that she liked him better without a beard. It was easier to trace the curve of his lips with her finger, as she did just then. A baby. She was going to have Drake's baby. "Yes," she said, not having really heard him.

He reached out and captured her hand in his. "I wanted to let you know," he said, with sudden seriousness, "that a ship of particular interest to you had just sailed into the bay."

That got her attention, as he'd known it would. Anything to do with boats tended to get her attention. "A ship? What ship?"

"Can't you guess which one?" Seeing her shake her head, he sighed, and rolling off her, climbed to his feet. "I suppose I'll have to show you, then."

"Show me?" Payton looked a little alarmed as she watched him fasten up his trousers. "But my feet—"

"Don't worry about your feet." He bent down and, wrapping her up in the sheets they'd crumpled beneath them in their recent ardor, slipped one arm beneath her knees, and the other behind her back. Then he lifted her easily from the bed, and carried her the few feet across the room to the French doors to the terrace. Unlatching them, he threw them open, then brought her out into the bright morning sunlight. The view was spectacular. They were high enough that they could look out across all of Nassau, and toward the azure bay. But Payton, he noticed, hadn't taken her eyes off him.

*"Look,"* he urged her.

She squinted in the bright hot sunlight. "Look at what?"

"That ship there, in the middle of the bay. Does it look familiar to you?"

He watched her face carefully as she looked. She had excellent eyesight—always had. A moment later, her jaw dropped, and she turned her astonished gaze up toward his face.

"But that's—that's impossible. She sank. I *saw* her—"

"You didn't," he said, smiling down at her. "You watched them blow a hole through her hull. But she's a good ship. It would take a lot more than a hole in the hull to sink her. When I heard Ross had sent her down to Key West for repairs, I had them bring her back. I thought she might make rather a good wedding present."

Payton's eyes widened. "For *me*? You're giving her to *me*?"

"On one condition."

Her gaze narrowed. "What?" she asked suspiciously.

"That you don't take her out without your first officer." He grinned. "Namely me."

Payton, after staring at him for a moment, burst into laughter. She couldn't help it. It seemed to come bubbling out of her. She couldn't remember ever having felt quite so happy. She reached up and placed a hand on either side of his head, then dragged his face down toward hers so she could plant a joyful kiss upon his mouth. Her happiness must have been contagious, because Drake returned the kiss with abandon. In fact, they were still kissing when Ross came stomping out onto the terrace a few minutes later.

"We heard all the shoutin'. Haven't you two made up yet?" He stared at them. "Oh. I see that you have."

"Oh, Ross!" Payton cried, her arms still around Drake's neck. "What do you think? Drake—I mean, Connor—has given me the *Constant*! We're going to spend our honeymoon on her."

Ross glowered at them. "You have to get married before you can have a honeymoon," he informed them testily. "Besides, haven't you two already *had* your honeymoon? I'd say it's bloody well over by now."

Drake looked down at his bride. "Not quite yet," he said with a smile.

## *Survey*

TELL US WHAT YOU THINK AND YOU COULD WIN

# *A YEAR OF ROMANCE!*
### *(That's 12 books!)*

Fill out the survey below, send it back to us, and you'll be eligible to win a year's worth of romance novels. That's one book a month for a year—from St. Martin's Paperbacks.

Name _____

Street Address _____

City, State, Zip Code _____

Email address _____

1. How many romance books have you bought in the last year?
   *(Check one.)*
   __0-3
   __4-7
   __8-12
   __13-20
   __20 or more

2. Where do you MOST often buy books? *(limit to two choices)*
   __Independent bookstore
   __Chain stores *(Please specify)*
       __Barnes and Noble
       __B. Dalton
       __Books-a-Million
       __Borders
       __Crown
       __Lauriat's
       __Media Play
       __Waldenbooks
   __Supermarket
   __Department store *(Please specify)*
       __Caldor
       __Target
       __Kmart
       __Walmart
   __Pharmacy/Drug store
   __Warehouse Club
   __Airport

3. Which of the following promotions would MOST influence your decision to purchase a ROMANCE paperback? *(Check one.)*
       __Discount coupon

      __Free preview of the first chapter
      __Second book at half price
      __Contribution to charity
      __Sweepstakes or contest

4. Which promotions would LEAST influence your decision to purchase a ROMANCE book? (Check one.)
      __Discount coupon
      __Free preview of the first chapter
      __Second book at half price
      __Contribution to charity
      __Sweepstakes or contest

5. When a new ROMANCE paperback is released, what is MOST influential in your finding out about the book and in helping you to decide to buy the book? (Check one.)
      __TV advertisement
      __Radio advertisement
      __Print advertising in newspaper or magazine
      __Book review in newspaper or magazine
      __Author interview in newspaper or magazine
      __Author interview on radio
      __Author appearance on TV
      __Personal appearance by author at bookstore
      __In-store publicity (poster, flyer, floor display, etc.)
      __Online promotion (author feature, banner advertising, giveaway)
      __Word of Mouth
      __Other (please specify)_____

6. Have you ever purchased a book online?
      __Yes
      __No

7. Have you visited our website?
      __Yes
      __No

8. Would you visit our website in the future to find out about new releases or author interviews?
      __Yes
      __No

9. What publication do you read most?
      __Newspapers *(check one)*
        __*USA Today*
        __*New York Times*
        __Your local newspaper
      __Magazines *(check one)*

_People
_Entertainment Weekly_
__Women's magazine _(Please specify:_____)_
_Romantic Times_
__Romance newsletters

10. What type of TV program do you watch most? _(Check one.)_
    __Morning News Programs (ie. "Today Show")
      _(Please specify:_____)_
    __Afternoon Talk Shows (ie. "Oprah")
      _(Please specify:_____)_
    __All news (such as CNN)
    __Soap operas    _(Please specify:_____)_
    __Lifetime cable station
    __E! cable station
    __Evening magazine programs (ie. "Entertainment Tonight")
      _(Please specify:_____)_
    __Your local news

11. What radio stations do you listen to most? _(Check one.)_
    __Talk Radio
    __Easy Listening/Classical
    __Top 40
    __Country
    __Rock
    __Lite rock/Adult contemporary
    __CBS radio network
    __National Public Radio
    __WESTWOOD ONE radio network

12. What time of day do you listen to the radio MOST?
    __6am-10am
    __10am-noon
    __Noon-4pm
    __4pm-7pm
    __7pm-10pm
    __10pm-midnight
    __Midnight-6am

13. Would you like to receive email announcing new releases and special promotions?
    __Yes
    __No

14. Would you like to receive postcards announcing new releases and special promotions?
    __Yes
    __No

15. Who is your favorite romance author? _____

# WIN A YEAR OF ROMANCE FROM SMP
## *(That's 12 Books!)*
### No Purchase Necessary

## OFFICIAL RULES

1. To Enter: Complete the Official Entry Form and Survey and mail it to: Win a Year of Romance from SMP Sweepstakes, c/o St. Martin's Paperbacks, 175 Fifth Avenue, Suite 1615, New York, NY 10010-7848, Attention JP. For a copy of the Official Entry Form and Survey, send a self-addressed, stamped envelope to: Entry Form/Survey, c/o St. Martin's Paperbacks at the address stated above. Entries with the completed surveys must be received by February 1, 2000 (February 22, 2000 for entry forms requested by mail). Limit one entry per person. No mechanically reproduced or illegible entries accepted. Not responsible for lost, misdirected, mutilated or late entries.

2. Random Drawing. Winner will be determined in a random drawing to be held on or about March 1, 2000 from all eligible entries received. Odds of winning depend on the number of eligible entries received. Potential winner will be notified by mail on or about March 22, 2000 and will be asked to execute and return an Affidavit of Eligibility/Release/Prize Acceptance Form within fourteen (14) days of attempted notification. Non-compliance within this time may result in disqualification and the selection of an alternate winner. Return of any prize/prize notification as undeliverable will result in disqualification and an alternate winner will be selected.

3. Prize and approximate Retail Value: Winner will receive a copy of a different romance novel each month from April 2000 through March 2001. Approximate retail value $84.00 (U.S. dollars).

4. Eligibility. Open to U.S. and Canadian residents (excluding residents of the province of Quebec) who are 18 at the time of entry. Employees of St. Martin's and its parent, affiliates and subsidiaries, its and their directors, officers and agents, and their immediate families or those living in the same household, are ineligible to enter. Potential Canadian winners will be required to correctly answer a time-limited arithmetic skill question by mail. Void in Puerto Rico and wherever else prohibited by law.

5. General Conditions: Winner is responsible for all federal, state and local taxes. No substitution or cash redemption of prize permitted by winner. Prize is not transferable. Acceptance of prize constitutes permission to use the winner's name, photograph and likeness for purposes of advertising and promotion without additional compensation or permission, unless prohibited by law.

6. All entries become the property of sponsor, and will not be returned. By participating in this sweepstakes, entrants agree to be bound by these official rules and the decision of the judges, which are final in all respects.

7. For the name of the winner, available after March 22, 2000, send by May 1, 2000 a stamped, self-addressed envelope to Winner's List, Win a Year of Romance from SMP Sweepstakes, St. Martin's Paperbacks, 175 Fifth Avenue, Suite 1615, New York, NY 10010-7848, Attention JP.

# KAT MARTIN

## Award-winning author of *Creole Fires*

GYPSY LORD
_____ 92878-5 $6.50 U.S./$8.50 Can.

SWEET VENGEANCE
_____ 95095-0 $6.50 U.S./$8.50 Can.

BOLD ANGEL
_____ 95303-8 $6.50 U.S./$8.50 Can.

DEVIL'S PRIZE
_____ 95478-6 $6.99 U.S./$8.99 Can.

MIDNIGHT RIDER
_____ 95774-2 $5.99 U.S./$6.99 Can.

INNOCENCE UNDONE
_____ 96089-1 $6.50 U.S./$8.50 Can.

## LOSE YOURSELF IN THE PASSION OF
## PATRICIA CABOT'S FABULOUS FIRST NOVEL

# Where Roses Grow Wild

Only one thing stood between Edward, Lord Rawlings, and his life of rakish debauchery: a spinster—guardian to ten-year-old Jeremy, the true heir to the title Edward did not want. Edward was sure he could charm the old girl into getting his way. But Pegeen MacDougal was not old, nor a girl— she was all woman, with a prickly tongue, infernal green eyes and buried sensuality that drove him mad. And Pegeen knew she could resist Edward's money, his power, his position...his entire world. It was his kiss, however, that promised to be her undoing...

"Passion, wit, warmth – thoroughly charming."
—Stella Cameron, author of *Wait for Me*

WHERE ROSES GROW WILD
Patricia Cabot
0-312-96489-7_____ $5.99_____ $7.99 Can.